QUICKSAND

Quicksand

BRYAN FORBES

HEINEMANN : LONDON

First published in Great Britain 1996
by William Heinemann Ltd
an imprint of Reed International Books Ltd
Michelin House, 81 Fulham Road, London SW3 6RB
and Auckland, Melbourne, Singapore and Toronto

A CIP catalogue record for this title
is available from the British Library
ISBN 0 434 26826 7

Typeset by Miller's Publications
Printed and bound by Clays Ltd, St Ives plc

The author would like to place on record
his indebtedness to
Professor Brian Simpson
for his generosity in making available
the research and scholarship contained in his definitive
work on the wartime 18b detainees,

In The Highest Degree Odious

For
Michael Loxton MD and
Michael Powell FRCS
Without whose skills
this book might never
have been finished

To betray you must first belong
                    - Kim Philby

Hate is the consequence of fear;
we fear something before we hate it
                    - Cyril Connolly

PROLOGUE

In 1909 the then Secretary of State for War came to be concerned about spies and set up a subcommittee to determine the steps to be taken to safeguard national security. The eventual report is said to be one of the more entertaining in the Public Records, rivalling in absurdity the file containing the Home Office Rules for the keeping of pet mice in HM Prisons. The subcommittee duly recommended establishing (in secret naturally) a Secret Service Bureau, the existence of which was not revealed until November 1914. It became what is now known as MI5.

The first head of the Bureau was a professional soldier with the splendid name of Vernon George Waldegrave Kell. In keeping with the British obsession with closed government, from the very outset the new department was structured in such a way that nobody could be held politically responsible for its operations. Kell and his staff immediately set about diligently collecting information about suspected subversives, but they did not act upon it if arrests, searches or interrogations were needed: such tasks, if required, were conducted by Special Branch and the CID, the final say resting with the Director of Public Prosecutions and the Law Officers. Thus the buck could be passed down a long line if there was any mishap, until, eventually, it was swept under a variety of Whitehall carpets.

The senior complement of the Bureau was exclusively recruited from the ranks of officers and gentlemen, the criteria being the right accent rather than any intellectual attainment or natural aptitude for intelligence work. From day one, Kell and his staff set about assembling a central index of every person ever suspected in any part of the world of anti-British activities. This index eventually contained an incredible 4,500,000 names, suggesting a global conspiracy the size of the entire German army.

By 1936, with the chance of a second European war moving inexorably from the possible to the probable, MI5 was instructed to prepare a new code. As a consequence of the immense extension of bureaucratic power during and after World War One, Whitehall assumed that a future conflagration could only be carried on in conditions in which civil liberty had, as a matter of law, been abolished. What the government now demanded was the authority to detain people simply as an instrument of political control,whether they were actively disloyal or not. Nothing was recorded of this decision, but the process of implementing it was commenced.

Thus, prior to 3 September 1939 covert steps had already been taken to widen the powers of MI5 and the Home Office. At 1 p.m. on the day Germany invaded Poland, the Privy Council caused regulation 18b to become law. It meant that anyone at all to whom the Home Secretary took exception could be locked up for an indefinite period. The prime purpose of the new Act was to round up and detain without trial members of the British Union, the neo-Fascist organisation that had Sir Oswald Mosley as its leader. This, despite the fact that the BU had not been proscribed, was a legitimate political party, and was fielding (with some irony it must be said) a candidate in a by-election due to go to the polls that very day.

Kell had supplied Special Branch with an initial list of thirty-six names, headed by Mosley, all of whom were deemed highly dangerous. A fortnight later the list had grown to 350 – a motley collection which in certain instances was more suggestive of a Ben Travers farce than any real threat to the nation, containing as it did such divers characters as a masseuse working for Elizabeth Arden, the wife of the Headmaster of Poole Grammar School, the Revd Montague Yates-Allen (dubbed the 'Nazi Vicar'), a former British heavyweight boxing champion and his wife, Prince Henry of Pless, an ex-Mayor of St. Pancras, and a name from the future – Kim Philby's father. Others, described as 'prominent persons', who were seriously considered for arrest but who escaped immediate *incarceration, included the Duke of Bedford, the eighth Duke of Buccleuch, Major General ('Boney') Fuller, Sir Jocelyn Lucas, Bt, MP, and Air Commodore Sir J. A. Chamier. Admiral Sir Barry Domvile, together with his wife and one of his sons, was detained at a later date.*

The granting of these powers to the executive was later to be described by Churchill as 'in the highest degree odious'.

1

LONDON 1940

Even in wartime it was highly unusual to find tanks in a side street close to Piccadilly, yet early on the morning of May 23rd 1940, a detachment of the Royal Tank Regiment took up their positions to seal off both ends of Albemarle Street, normally a peaceful thoroughfare where various traders flourished in less critical times.

Thus, on that morning of May 23rd, arrest for Carl Hain and his family came, as for others, without warning.

Hain, a specialist dealer in Viennese painters of the L'Apocalypse Joyeuse period, lived above his gallery in a comfortable two-bedroomed apartment. Until the outbreak of war he had made a modest living, some good years, some bad, depending on the always fickle tastes of his clientele, but he had the reputation for being honest and his expertise was widely respected in the trade. His paternal grandparents, originally from Hamburg, had settled in England during the 1860s, establishing a bespoke tailoring workshop in the East End of London. Their only son, Hain's father, had wider ambitions and was drawn to the artistic life. He attempted to make a living as a painter but, after marriage and the birth of Carl, was forced to accept that he had limited talent and turned his hand to the more lucrative pursuit of selling the works of others. Here he succeeded, for he was a natural salesman, and in time could afford to open his own gallery, which, after his death, passed to Carl.

May 23 was a day like any other for the Hain family. As usual, Hain was the first to be up and about. Still in his pyjamas and frayed dressing gown, he switched on the radio for the news. He was grinding fresh coffee beans, as was his habit, when the shop bell called him downstairs. He answered it, expecting to be greeted by the postman with a registered letter, only to be confronted by four large men in lounge suits, big boots and bowler hats – somewhat obviously policemen disguised as gentlemen. Beyond them he was amazed to see a tank with its gun swivelled to face his premises.

Hain had an academic appearance, accentuated by the fact that he wore strong bifocals and was prematurely stooped for his forty-five years. Now, unshaven, his sparse hair uncombed, he presented all the stereotypical characteristics of an alien to his unexpected callers.

He was brusquely asked to confirm his identity. Understandably perplexed, but not unduly alarmed, he gave his name. He was then quoted the authority for his immediate detention and advised of his scant rights, which in any case were later to be ignored. The police spokesman then informed him that his wife would also be detained, that his premises would be searched and any subversive material confiscated and removed.

'But why? What are you saying?' Hain protested, shocked and trembling from the suddenness of it all. 'What subversive material? I have none.'

'I think you know well enough, sir. Don't let's waste time on the obvious.'

Two of the policemen accompanied him upstairs to the living quarters, which, to their way of thinking, seemed to vindicate their visit. The lush trappings betokened foreign decadence: the rooms were furnished in a heavy, un-English style, for they included many pieces that had been handed down from Hain's parents. The walls were hung with his private stock of paintings, mostly examples of turn-of-the-century European works, including several by Klimt, Schiele and – his proudest possession – an exotic nude by Modigliani.

'Not only a traitor, but a pervert too, I see,' the senior policeman observed as he eyed the Modigliani.

'What right do you have to come into my home and call me by such names? That is a great painting. You have no reason to speak of it or me in those terms.'

Disturbed by the unfamiliar voices and likewise still in her dressing gown, Mrs Hain appeared in the doorway. It should have been immediately apparent to the searchers that she was pregnant, but her condition was not commented upon.

'Why are these men here, Carl? Who are they?'

'Policemen, dear.'

'Policemen? In our home? What are they looking for?'

'I don't know, dear, they seem to think I have forbidden material. All I know is I have been told we are to be detained.'

'What does it mean, detained?'

'My dear, I've told you, I have no idea.'

'Carl, you must telephone our solicitor. Get help, there must be some mistake.'

'No mistake, madam, and no calls are allowed,' one of the policemen answered, brushing past her to search the contents of a sideboard.

'Do you have a safe?' his companion asked.

'Yes,' Hain said. 'But there's nothing in it except documents concerning the provenance of the paintings.'

'Show me.'

Hain took him to a small closet where the safe was bolted to the floor.

'Open it.'

He did as he was told and took out a collection of files. The policeman placed these with other documents the search had produced.

'You must be aware that my wife is expecting a child,' Hain remonstrated. 'She has a delicate disposition and her doctor has told us she must not undergo any stress. All this is bound to affect her.'

'You should have thought of that before,' was the unsympathetic reply. 'If I had my way people like you would be put against a wall and shot.'

'What d'you mean, "people like us"? What have we done?'

'There's a war on, in case that escaped your notice. People who aren't for us, are against us.'

'I'm a loyal citizen. So is my wife.'

'Well, that remains to be seen, doesn't it? We're just here to carry out orders. You'll have a chance to state your case in front of the tribunal in due course.'

'Tribunal? What tribunal? This is monstrous. It's like Kafka.'

'And who might Kafka be?'

'A famous writer for your information.'

'But not a *British* writer from his name,' the policeman said, recording the exchange in his notebook. 'And now I must ask you both to dress.'

'What about our small son?' Mrs Hain said. 'We can't leave him alone here.'

'Your son, madam, will be taken into care by the authorities.'

Their further protests were ignored and they stood by helplessly as the apartment was turned over. All Hain's personal files, accounts and stock books were removed, together with a quantity of art brochures, many of them written in German. Particular interest was taken in a spiked, German army helmet, *circa* 1914, a trophy brought home from the trenches by Hain's father. The three members of the family were only allowed to pack one suitcase apiece. While helping to dress his small and frightened son, Hain managed to secrete over a hundred pounds on the child's person, the proceeds of a sale he had made the day before and had not had time to bank. The premises were then locked and the family driven to nearby Bow Street police station where they were again told of the authority for their arrest. Hain and his wife were documented, body-searched and fingerprinted before being separately interrogated by the CID.

Hain's interrogator was a Detective Inspector Mathews, a burly man with a face like a cratered landscape, the aftermath of adolescent acne.

'Don't try and bluff me, Hain,' Mathews began, 'because it won't wash. We know all about your hostile associations.'

Disorientated by the speed with which his entire life had been taken apart, Hain struggled to maintain his composure. A small part of him clung to the belief that he was in the grip of some terrible nightmare from which he would soon awake, yet the pockmarked face across the bare table, and the institutional, distempered walls of the room belied his last hopes. It seemed inconceivable that he and his family could have been plucked from the familiar warmth of their apartment without warning. As he answered his interrogator's barked questions he strove to recall anything in his past that could have had a double meaning, for he refused to accept that British justice could act in this manner. In other countries, yes, but even in wartime, not in Britain.

'What does that expression mean?' he said. '"Hostile associations"? It conveys nothing to me, and I demand to know who has laid these false charges against me and my wife.'

'We didn't need anybody to denounce the likes of you, Hain. We have a file on you. We know all about you, the company you keep, the trips you made to Germany before the war, your political views, you name it. So, you see, it wasn't necessary for anybody to lay charges, you were already in our bag.' Mathews tapped the file that lay between them. 'Let's begin with basics, shall we? We have it on record that you're a member of the British Union.'

'No.'

'Don't lie, Hain. Lying will only prolong matters, and I'm not a patient man. We have a copy of your membership card.'

'I am not lying. It is true that for a period, a short period, less than a year, I was interested in their aims. They represented themselves as a party dedicated to avoiding war.'

'And you became a paid member.'

'Was that illegal?'

'Just answer my question. Were you or were you not a member?'

'I've told you I joined to find out more, then I disassociated myself when Hitler annexed Czechoslovakia. I saw then that war was inevitable.'

'You sure you didn't go under cover so that some of your German friends could contact you later?'

'What German friends?'

Mathews opened the file and took out one of the documents. 'During the years 1929 to 1934 you made eleven visits to Germany.'

'They were not secret visits. Since you know so much about me you must know they are stamped in my passport. I went openly to make purchases in the legitimate pursuit of my business.'

'So you say now. Let's move on to something else. On at least two occasions your so-called "leader", Sir Oswald Mosley, came to your premises.'

'He was interested in my paintings.'

'Your *German* paintings,' Mathews said with heavy emphasis.

'Austrian, but what is odd about that? I specialise in such works.'

'Why not some good British paintings?'

'Art is not concerned with politics. The works I sell were painted long before the Nazi party came into being.'

'You don't deny, though, that you were on intimate terms with Mosley?'

'Certainly I deny it. That is an exaggeration. He was merely a potential customer. As it happens he admired my stock but did not buy anything.'

'At a time when you were a member of his Fascist organisation?'

'I was never a Fascist.'

'At a time when you were a member,' Mathews repeated. 'An active member. Just to refresh your memory, you were seen on Wanstead Flats in June 1936 when Mosley addressed a rally of the faithful.' He took a photograph from the file and passed it to Hain. It showed Mosley speaking from a van that had been adapted to his needs: a square had been cut out of the roof of the van and a raised steel cage installed. The van was flanked by two lines of black-shirted bully-boys facing the crowd; Hain was discernible in the second row of the crowd and his head had been ringed with red crayon.

'You don't deny that is you?'

Hain stared at the incriminating photograph but did not answer.

'I'm waiting.'

'Yes, that is me.'

'Progress at last. So at that time at least you hadn't "disassociated" yourself, correct?'

'I've told you my reason for leaving the party.'

'So you have, yes. Well, let me ask you something else. Your family name is Henke, is it not?'

'That was my grandfather's name, yes.'

'But not yours.'

'My father changed it by Deed Poll in 1915 because of the strong anti-German feelings prevalent at that time.'

'Conveniently, shall we say?'

'So did the Royal family,' Hain replied gamely. 'I take it you must also know that my father volunteered to serve in the British Army and was wounded at Ypres. He subsequently died from his wounds.'

'What have you volunteered for, might I ask?'

'I offered my services to the ARP but was rejected on account of my poor eyesight.'

'Well, we wouldn't want scum like you protecting us anyway. Right,' Mathews concluded, 'in view of the unsatisfactory answers you have given me in response to these questions, I am therefore informing you that you will be detained under Section 18b of the Emergency Powers (Defence) Act. Do you have anything further to add?'

'What about my wife and small son?'

'What about them?'

'I wish to know what is happening to them.'

'That's not my concern. Somebody else is handling your wife's case. Should she also be detained your son will be placed in care.'

Mathews closed the file and stood up.

'There is no case for us to answer,' Hain said. 'We are innocent, loyal people. A terrible mistake has been made.'

'Yes. You could say that. The mistake was to throw your lot in with the wrong side,' was Mathews's parting shot as he left the room.

An hour later, manacled to another detainee, and denied any further contact with his wife, Hain was taken to Brixton prison in a Black Maria. There he and other detainees were submitted to the pseudo-sanitary rituals of degradation: the bath and baring of privy parts; some were merely made to step into and out of an empty bath in order to keep the record straight. Only then, when the cell door closed on Hain, did the full realisation of his plight sink in.

Meanwhile, his wife, wrenched from her eight-year-old son, had given her stuttered and innocent responses to a similar interrogation, at the conclusion of which she had been removed to 'F' wing at Holloway, occupying a darkened cell, the blackout being rigidly enforced. Conditions in Holloway, where the staff were unprepared for the sudden influx of prisoners, were wholly inadequate. Largely unheated, the eleven by seven feet cells were infested with bed bugs and extremely dirty. Washing facilities were minimal and for many there was no toilet paper and no newspapers to use as a substitute. The issue blankets were made of canvas and disgusting.

On the third night after her incarceration, weakened and demoralised, she started to haemorrhage. Her condition was not discovered until the following morning. Taken to hospital too late, both she and her unborn child died later that day.

A week later and still in ignorance of his wife's death, Hain was transferred to Liverpool to be held in the disused women's prison where the decrepit accommodation had previously been the habitat of pigeons. Unlike Brixton, the prison staff in Liverpool were armed when supervising the infrequent exercise periods, for all the 18b detainees endured long bouts of solitary confinement; even during air raids they were not moved to shelters. It was over a month before the ponderous wartime bureaucracy got around to informing Hain of his wife's death. Returned to his cell and convinced that he would never see his son again, he used his last razor blade to commit suicide.

Hain's now-orphaned son spent the remainder of the war with a variety of foster parents, finally ending up with a Quaker family in Swindon who legally adopted him. Not until he was in his teens and a scholarship student at Cambridge did he discover the true facts about his parents' incarceration and their subsequent fates.

2

ATLANTA 1997

It could scarcely have entered Dr Josef Freidler's reckoning that the last woman he would ever speak to would be a naked dancer at the Club Alpha with the improbable name of Starr Faithful. Like her siliconed breasts, which Dr Freidler was able to ogle but not touch, the name was a fake, chosen because an account of the real Starr Faithful – the victim of a salacious and never solved mystery which the dancer had read as a teenager – appealed to her sense of the romantic.

The Club Alpha was one of a growing number of similar establishments that had sprung up to satisfy American male fantasies in the age of safe sex. There was none of the sleaze of the older strip joints where bored showgirls gyrated their cellulite: the girls at Club Alpha were a superior breed, selected for their beauty, youth and an ability to put more than three words together. They were dressed in couturier gowns which, in the course of their duties, they were happy to discard. Their customers then paid to be treated to a tantalising display in the nude, termed 'lapdancing', for which the girls were handsomely rewarded, many of them taking home five figure earnings if they stayed the course, for at the end of their act the average punter placed fifty, even one hundred dollar bills in their garters, the only physical contact allowed. It was *Playboy* magazine brought to life, the voyeur's dream of the girl next door suddenly stepping out of the centrefold, exposing her perfect pneumatic breasts, the smooth stomach devoid of any blemishes, the carefully shaven pubic hair – all displayed at close proximity, the untouchable turn-on.

From the exterior, the club's premises had been designed to reassure – clean lines suggesting an up-market DIY store where all the family would be welcomed, except here they weren't: this was primarily aimed at men stalking sterilised sex, the very antithesis of DIY.

D. Freidler, born in Israel but now a naturalised Swiss citizen, was President of a private Zurich merchant bank but maintained strong connections with his native land. In his early fifties, he was considered to be one of the most influential European financiers, his opinion sought by the Bundesbank, his manipulation of the markets noted on every board from London to Tokyo. It was said that what Freidler did today everybody else should have done yesterday. A multi-millionaire, he kept houses in the Hamptons, Cap Ferrat and his adopted Switzerland. Married over twenty years to the same wife, he had two teenage children and a discreet mistress in Monaco. His personal affairs were managed through a number of shell companies operating from tax havens. When at home, he entertained on the grand scale, his invitations being eagerly sought. An outstanding scholar, he had won a place at the Harvard Business School, and after graduating with honours had been swiftly recruited by the Kreditanstalt Bank in Austria. From there he was poached by Morgan Guaranty in New York, quickly rising to a position of authority, then resigning to form his own bank. Noted for his ruthlessness in dealing with competitors, he had the reputation of a man who brooked no interference with his dictates. He was not liked, but, as with most men in his position, his financial standing ensured that he was courted by those who feared him. Consummately vain, he had a personal hairdresser and a manicurist in daily attendance wherever he travelled, always wore pure silk shirts made for him in Jermyn Street and perfumed himself with Guerlain's *Eau de Cologne du Coq* at $300 a bottle. He moved in a closed international circle where money, and only money, talked and decided world economies. The inner sanctum he inhabited was seldom penetrated by outsiders, and although his legitimate activities were widely reported in the world's financial press, his other, more labyrinthine, deals were seldom traced to their source. He and his kind were the currency determinators who ensured the scales were always tipped in their favour.

Freidler was in Atlanta for his bank's annual convention. Like most similar jamborees, in reality it was merely an excuse for the senior officers to have a free holiday. They met every day to plot future strategy, but the really enjoyable business was conducted at night. On this particular trip Freidler's public relations man had arranged a visit to the Alpha Club on the last evening of the convention, promising a unique experience.

'I think you will be pleasantly surprised, sir,' he told his employer. 'This is like nothing you've seen before.'

'Really? Such as?'

'I'd prefer you to wait and see, sir.'

'I don't care for surprises.'

If there was one thing Freidler liked as much as money, it was the company of beautiful women. On this occasion his initial, venal anticipation was blunted when he became acquainted with the house rules, but once inside it was too late to turn back and lose face.

'What do you mean, we can't touch them?'

'I apologise, but they're very strict, sir. It's a new concept.'

'Only in America,' Freidler sneered. 'Only here could they get away with putting the goods in the shop window and then not let anybody buy them. What a way to do business, no wonder their economy is shot.'

Despite his initial disappointment, he was impressed with the ambience of the club; the decor was luxurious but discreet, the service impeccable. There was no raucous disco music and guests were not pressured. Freidler and his party were conducted to one of the private rooms, furnished with a number of sofas arranged in a semicircle. It was there, somewhat placated by the excellence of the champagne he was immediately served, that he was introduced to the girl who called herself Starr Faithful. She was twenty, blonde, with a full, sensuous mouth and impossibly long legs. Like the other hostesses she wore nothing under her expensive gown except a minute black G-string and garters. After conversing for ten minutes or so she asked him if he would like her to dance for him and taking his acceptance for granted, unzipped and stepped out of her single garment. Although Freidler was astounded by the sight of her body, he was conscious of his watching colleagues and maintained a bland expression while his eyes remained fixed on her impossibly perfect young breasts. (Later, in the shared dressing room, she compared him to earlier clients. 'I knew that fat old Jew was a tit man,' she said. 'I can always tell what melts their butter the moment I strip. Just watch their eyes. They either go straight to your legs, your butt or your boobs, don't they? He locked on to my boobs like somebody tracking Challenger.')

Although she had described it as 'dancing', the routine she performed for Freidler was not anything that would have impressed Bob Fosse. Removing her G-string she went through a series of writhing gyrations, gradually working closer to Freidler until, bending over him, she swept his face with her hair and brought her breasts tantalisingly close to his mouth so that it would have required the minimum effort on his part to lean forward an extra inch and kiss her prominent, rouged nipples. Very aware that his underlings were watching, he controlled his natural urges and maintained an outward composure. At the conclusion of her performance he placed three one hundred dollar bills in her garter, helped zip-up her gown and was rewarded by a chaste kiss on the cheek – the sole act of intimacy permitted under the house rules. Now that he had shown the way, others in his party paired off with their own choices. Starr sat down next to Freidler and sipped her soft drink.

'That was very beautiful. You dance very well. But what are you drinking? Wouldn't you rather have champagne?' Freidler asked.

'No, we're not permitted alcohol, Mr Freidler.'

'Please call me Josef. What else isn't encouraged?'

She had heard it all before, but pretended ignorance.

'How d'you mean, Josef?'

'A girl like you could have a different, easier life than this, surely?'

'I love this life.'

Freidler shrugged. 'I'm sure. But if you met the right person, somebody like me for instance, he could show you more of the world.'

The dialogue these old farts trot out, she thought, keeping her smile in place, it's out of the ark. 'No, I'm very happy here in Atlanta. It's my home town.'

'You wouldn't want to travel?'

'I do travel. Last year I went to Tahiti. You ever been to Tahiti?'

'No,' Freidler said. 'I was thinking more of Europe.'

Bending to place her glass on the coffee table Starr caught the eye of one of the security staff who were always discreetly situated and gave him the signal.

'If you'd allow me,' Freidler was saying, 'I could arrange for you to have a long holiday in Europe, show you my country.'

'That sounds very enticing, but unfortunately I have a contract here,' she said. The security man, who was wearing a well-cut dinner jacket, arrived by her side.

'Please excuse me, sir,' he said to Freidler, 'I'm so sorry to interrupt, but your companion has a regular client who has asked for her. Would you perhaps care for me to send another of our hostesses to keep you company?'

There was a warning note in his voice that did not escape Freidler. Although furious at being outsmarted, he controlled his anger. 'Thank you, no. I'm leaving.'

'So soon? I trust you enjoyed yourself, sir?'

Starr knew better than to linger. 'Thank you so much, Josef,' she said. 'It was my pleasure to meet you.'

'Likewise,' he said tersely.

He watched her cross the room, then beckoned to his public relations man. 'That girl who just left. I want you to bring her to my hotel suite later.'

His PR looked dubious. 'Well, I'll try, sir, but it's my understanding that the club rules strictly forbid these girls dating any of the customers.'

'I'm not talking about their rules, I'm talking about what I want. Just find who you need to bribe and get her for me. I don't care what it costs.'

'Yes, of course, sir.' He moved the coffee table to allow Freidler a free passage. 'You wish your car, sir?'

'Of course I wish my car. You think I'm going to walk?'

Freidler gestured to the others as he went out of the room. 'Stay and enjoy yourselves. I have to work, but don't let that deter you. Good-night.'

He returned to his hotel, stopping in the foyer to purchase a pair of diamond earrings which he took to his suite. There he rang room service and ordered two dozen oysters and a magnum of Cristal champagne. After changing into pyjamas and dressing gown, he sat in front of the oversized television and watched the stock market reports on CNN, confident that his instructions would be carried out. When his room service order arrived, he told the waiter to open the champagne and pour him a glass. Never one to let an opportunity for profit pass, having seen how the market had opened in London, he rang his broker and purchased ten million dollars worth of futures through one of his nominee companies. Later, another news item caught his attention. He made a second phone call, this time instructing his office to set in motion a hostile bid for a company he sensed was vulnerable.

He was still sitting in front of the television set when the door to his bedroom was opened with a pass key. He never heard or saw who entered behind him and the champagne glass was still at his lips when it was shattered by a single bullet from a silenced handgun which passed through his neck and blew away the lower part of his jaw, killing him immediately. Blood spurted on to the oysters, staining them in an imitation of the Tabasco sauce he never lived to enjoy.

3

ST PETERSBURG 1997

Afterwards, Hillsden was hard put to recall why he had given the man a second look, but from habit he had registered the face. One never knew when the blow might fall.

At the time he had been standing in a long line outside a bakery in a side street off Nevskiy Prospekt, resigned to his daily two-hour wait to purchase a loaf of bread. As the queue slowly shuffled forward he played his usual guessing game of trying to estimate how many noughts had been added to the price since the previous day.

The early March temperature hovered just above zero and Hillsden's fur coat, purchased with hard currency in the days when he had enjoyed the rank and salary of a Colonel in the GRU, attracted envious glances from his huddled companions. Even without the coat he stood out, for with his trim beard and tidy, greying hair there was an aloofness about his manner that set him apart. Shunning conversation with his neighbours, he also avoided eye contact as far as possible. He did not look his age, for since his new marriage he made an effort to keep in good shape. Only those few in St Petersburg who chanced to read the London *Times* might have noted a small item in the diary column a few weeks previously which listed *George Arthur (Alec) Hillsden, the ex-MI6 defector,* and even then, it was doubtful whether any would have made the connection. One of the British tabloids had picked up on the item a few days later under a headline

WHERE ARE THEY NOW? with an old, and now unrecognisable, photograph of Hillsden in British Army uniform standing with Margot, his wartime first wife. Rehashing some of his background, the accompanying story gave him the credit for exposing Glanville – the so-called 'Fourth Man' in the Cambridge spy ring made famous by Philby, Burgess and Maclean – but the main thrust of the piece gave greater emphasis to his own subsequent flight to the then Soviet bloc. The article concluded that, because of the new relationship between the two countries, it was possible that he could now be extradited to stand trial for the murder of the diplomat, Sir Charles Belfrage.

None of this was of interest to the bread queue: the past world of the Cold War did not figure hugely in their daily struggle to live with the new freedoms – freedoms which, for the majority, had not brought the promised, less-fearful future. Now, bemused by the constantly changing situation, most lived as best they could, taking life one day at a time. Like spring bulbs, past hatreds lay just beneath the surface ready to bloom.

Although more fortunate than his immediate companions, Hillsden shared their sense that nothing was permanent. Still one of the privileged by current Russian standards, he and his family enjoyed sole use of a four-room flat, gifted to him when finally he had been accepted as a genuine defector from British intelligence seven years previously. His GRU pension, eroded by inflation like everything else, had never been rescinded, somehow overlooked in the chaos left in the wake of the *coups* and counter-*coups*. Luck had played a part: many of the old guard of party bureaucrats had, of necessity, been left in place; Hillsden had no illusions that, without them, the entire edifice would have collapsed. The cumbersome machinery of Stalinist Russia, corrupt and terminally incompetent, had only been partially dismantled; many of the reinstated bureaucrats interpreted the new rules with a well-honed disregard for change. After a period when the novelty of broadcasting the truth after decades of calculated disinformation had proved counter-productive, the official Moscow news agency had reverted to its previous habits. There was a local joke: *only believe what they don't tell you.*

As part of the deal they had struck with him, Hillsden had been granted Russian citizenship and counted himself fortunate that, under the new regime, his position had not been reviewed by the authorities. Now, when he had nothing left to betray except memories, he lived in no man's land: he was no longer British and not truly Russian, just a non-person. He had learned that the recipe for survival was to keep a low profile. Thus far he had managed to provide for his Russian wife and small daughter, although every week saw a perceptible decline in their standard of living. There were luxury foods and Western goods available, but only at black-market prices: the emerging Russian mafia now controlled large sections of the economy; armed gangs of highly organised criminals either hijacked the supplies of food that came into the cities, or else cynically destroyed them in order to keep prices high. Whereas before everyday crimes such as the West had long become inured to had been ruthlessly suppressed, casual murders, muggings and robberies were now commonplace. Along with Western imports like Coca-Cola, Big Macs and the pop culture, the drug barons had become an integral part of the emerging, quasi-capitalist society. The old social order – feared, but at least familiar – had disintegrated, to be replaced by the gangster face of the new privileged.

That particular morning Hillsden was more than usually conscious of being alienated from his surroundings. Assuming he was successful in the bread queue, he faced having to join another line to attempt to buy some cheese – any cheese, for there was seldom a choice. On average he passed three hours every day in these quests. Once a week he used a portion of his sparse funds to try to purchase a small, black-market chicken or piece of meat which Galina, his Russian wife, had become adept at eking out over three or four meals. If he had anything left over he spent it on books, anxious to keep his brain alive, for in the past he had always apprehended the world through literature.

He and Galina had made few new friends since the collapse of the old regime and for obvious reasons Hillsden did not openly advertise his previous connection with the security services. Immediately following the revolution, members of the KGB and GRU had struggled to come to terms with their new status as reformed citizens, but few believed they would not, one day, return to power, called by another name, wearing different uniforms but once again finding their place in a country that, from the days of the Tsars, had tested the limits of fear. And so it had proved. Renamed, regrouped in a different form, they had crept back into the fabric of everyday life; it was as if, Hillsden thought, the Russian soul required an element of terror in order to function.

Now, as the bread line moved forward a few paces, Hillsden saw the same man again on the opposite side of the road. Their eyes met for a second, the man being the first to break contact. He was tall, clean-shaven, wearing an overcoat of obvious Western origin buttoned to the chin. Hillsden watched as the man consulted his wrist-watch and then moved off, his face dipped against the wind-swirled snow.

The only contact from the old days with whom Hillsden still kept in touch from time to time was his erstwhile controller, Victor Abramov. Denuded of his senior GRU rank, Abramov had secured a lucrative job as adviser to an American computer company. Paid in dollars, he now drove a Mercedes coupé and mixed with the foreign jet-set as an equal. He had made an effort to share some of his sudden affluence with Hillsden, often taking him for a meal in one of the starred hotels. Abramov was no longer the trim officer; easy living had given him a slight paunch and his complexion betrayed his conversion to claret.

'I could cut you in, Alec,' he said. 'There are so many openings. Somebody like you could be useful to my business acquaintances. They're always on the look-out for people with your know-how.'

But the offer held no attraction for Hillsden. 'I could never fathom computers. They terrify me.'

'You don't have to fathom them, you only have to sell them, my dear Alec. Today they're user-friendly, children master them in a few hours. Big bucks, Alec. It's the next quantum leap forward. Forget dead-letter drops and all that Cold War crap. Now, if you want to pass on stolen information, you do it instantly by electronic mail. Believe me.'

'I do believe you, but no thanks.'

'You're making a big mistake. Get on the gravy train, everybody else is, why miss out, buddy?'

The odd bits of Americanese slipped easily off his tongue. Victor now travelled widely, wore Armani suits and had already acquired the casual vernacular of the successful entrepreneur. Sitting across from him, carefully saving a portion of his meal to take home to Galina, Hillsden found it difficult to make the association with the time he had first been brought to Moscow; he had long since slaked off memories of the debriefing sessions Abramov had conducted in the Lubianka, when he had been forced to shed the skin of his old existence. Now it was only rarely that he recalled particular incidents. Mercifully, pain was not something one carried forward. Even so, the bond of a past, shared nightmare gave their relationship a special quality; they had been birds of a feather. It's just as well, Hillsden thought, that murder doesn't stay etched into a face. There had been murders along the way, episodes that he strove to forget but which, at intervals, entered both waking and dreaming thoughts. Often, when trimming his beard in the bathroom mirror, he wondered if Galina ever saw traces of the past in his face. He envied Abramov's indifference to those events, though whether it was assumed or genuine he could never be certain.

Save for Abramov's treats, Hillsden's life was uneventful, a backwater existence he had schooled himself to accept. Very occasionally the authorities asked his analysis of new developments in the West, but for the most part his presence in their midst seemed to be ignored. Like the Cold War, he had become history. Because of her past association with the university, Galina was given the odd commission to translate Western textbooks which Hillsden helped her revise. This supplemented their income and allowed them to buy extra clothes for Lara, their daughter. Occasionally they would pool their resources with one of Galina's old tutors and splash out on a dinner party. When the good weather came they picnicked in the Tauride Gardens which boasted an antiquated fair-ground and was a favourite haunt of sunbathers and courting couples. Lara was bilingual and Hillsden's own Russian had become passably colloquial, though he still could not write it fluently.

Now, as he neared the head of the queue, he was able to see inside the bakery: he counted the loaves still remaining on the shelves and matched the total with the number of people still in front of him. There was a good chance his luck was in. It was at moments like this that England seemed as remote as a country he had never visited.

Abramov passed on his copies of *Time* and it was from one issue that Hillsden had been surprised to learn that the Firm had a woman as Director General who openly spoke to the press, a far cry from Lockfield who had studiously courted anonymity – a false entry in *Who's Who*, no photographs on file, his true character only penetrated after death. The existence of the Firm had finally been acknowledged, but only in the usual hedged-about British fashion – throw the public a few titbits, but never invite them to sit at the table and read the full menu. He wondered how the lady had fared in that previously male-dominated Disneyland, with its layer upon layer of intrigue and partisan back-stabbing. He was sure that, whatever the cosmetic changes, the major concern would still be to smother as much information as possible and ensure that the parliamentary estimates were kept high. Gone were the days of moles in royal circles, mavericks like old Peter Wright intent on mayhem, endless speculation about how far the Firm had been penetrated – that lucrative cottage industry of exposure feeding the media's insatiable appetite for scandal and keeping a score of novelists in clover. From a distance, the recent past now seemed like a film run out of sequence. Occasionally, anger (the useless sort that recognised his inability to change anything) made him replay the cycle of events that had condemned him to exile – how cynically he had been stitched-up and manipulated. Sometimes, in the middle of a sleepless night, bitterness welled up like bile. Now, when it was all too late, he could identify every wrong move he had made, allowing himself to be taken in like some guileless, unguarded innocent. 'Go back to where it all began,' Lockfield had urged, as though there was ever a beginning in the endless game they had all played in those days. Espionage was a shared ball of tangled string that was never completely unravelled by either side – the hunters or the hunted, the deceivers and the deceived – for the players' only object was to keep the game going at all costs. So he had gone back into the cold, severing his umbilical cord as he went, ensuring that he could never return home, driven by the need to solve the murder of a girl he had once loved. And, of course, betrayed from day one, since that had always been Lockfield's intention. Now all that lay ahead was a placid bourgeois existence in an alien country that neither claimed his imagination nor aroused any excitement – the flow of adrenalin in his veins was as frozen as the Russian winter landscape. He felt dulled and saw no end to the dullness. He had been a prisoner when he first arrived in Russia and now, despite a sort of freedom, he was a prisoner still.

Finally gaining entrance to the bakery he secured the last loaf but one. As he paid and left the shop, those denied surged forward to remonstrate with the bundled crone behind the counter. Hillsden tucked his prize inside his coat and hurried towards his second port of call. He felt curiously elated by his good fortune; it might be one of those days when he got lucky twice. The cheese shop was a few streets away and as he turned the last corner he was further encouraged to see that the line here was shorter than the last. That could mean that, for once, supplies were plentiful and those waiting were being satisfied quickly. He took his place and fumbled with his free hand to light a Camel cigarette, one from a carton Abramov had given him the last time they had met. The pungent odour of Virginia tobacco made several in the queue turn their heads and sniff appreciatively. Inhaling, the smoke warmed his lungs and for the first time since he had left the apartment he felt reasonably happy.

It was then that a voice behind him said, 'Ya angliskiy muzhchina' – 'I am an Englishman' – using that plummy accent some members of the British upper-class affect when speaking a foreign language, letting the locals know that although they have bothered to learn it, it really is rather inferior and tiresome.

Taken off guard by the sudden intrusion, Hillsden swung round and came face to face with the man he had seen earlier.

'So am I,' Hillsden replied for want of anything better to say.

'Oh, good. Took a chance. Sorry if I startled you. Look, awfully rude of me, but could I possibly cadge a cigarette?'

Hillsden hesitated a moment, then said: 'Yes, of course.' He proffered his packet. 'Do you have a light?'

'Thank you, yes.' The man, whom at close range Hillsden judged to be in his thirties, loosened his top coat to feel in an inside pocket, revealing as he did so an MCC tie.

'Awful thing to admit,' the man said, as he lit his own cigarette with a silver Dunhill lighter, 'I'm trying to give up, but catching a whiff of yours was too much temptation. The local brand are so filthy, aren't they? Bought a packet of Marlboro at the hotel only to find they were counterfeit. Fairly disgusting.'

'Yes,' Hillsden said guardedly, 'they usually are.'

'Reason I approached you was because you didn't look like one of the natives.'

Those immediately in front and behind Hillsden in the queue shifted uneasily. The exchange betokened a vague menace.

'Bit of luck then,' Hillsden said. Something about the man's accent alerted him: it was unmistakably Establishment, the sort that some politicians employ when caught out on a manifesto pledge. He was instantly on his guard. 'Are you here on holiday or business?' he asked, past instincts rather than mere politeness pushing him to find out more.

'Business. Of sorts. Yes. Just trying to get the feel of the place. You know how it is.'

'How what is?'

'The old economy back home. Still dicky, lurching from boom to bust as usual. So, thought I'd give it a whirl here. Emerging market and so forth, get in on the ground floor, nothing ventured et cetera, got to move with the times, don't you agree?'

'Yes, I suppose so.'

'Can't quite get the drift of this place. They haven't thrown off their past, have they?'

'No.'

'Wasn't expecting all the water. Don't know why. Reminds me of Seattle in a curious sort of way. Ever been there?'

'No.'

'Bit warmer than here.'

'Everywhere's warmer than here,' Hillsden said, by now tiring of the conversation. They all moved up a few paces.

'What're you queuing for this time?'

His use of the phrase 'this time' was a giveaway.

'Cheese, hopefully,' Hillsden replied.

'Cheese, eh?' There was a pause, as though the man was searching for a more entertaining comment. Then he said, 'Interested in cricket?'

The non sequitur threw Hillsden for a moment. 'Cricket? Yes, I used to be. Why?'

'I've got the latest Test score if you want it. The Aussies are taking our knickers down as usual. That young spin bowler has gone through the pack. Backs to the wall stuff. Ashes to ashes it looks like. Should have brought Gower back. He now does commentaries or something. Great loss to England, beautiful stroke player.'

'Yes,' Hillsden said as the line edged forward again.

The man stepped on to the road. 'Mustn't take somebody's place,' he said, 'might start a riot.' He smiled at the old woman immediately behind Hillsden, but got nothing but a blank stare in return. 'Look, can I return the favour, buy you a drink?'

Why would you? Hillsden thought, and took his time before answering. 'I have to go straight back with the shopping, I'm afraid. But thanks all the same.'

Something did not add up. In the ordinary course of events he would have welcomed a rare English voice, a chance to relax over a drink and learn the latest gossip about what was happening at home, but an icicle of suspicion had entered his mind from the very first moment the man had approached him.

'Fair do's,' the man said. He hovered on the edge of the kerb, then reached into his inside pocket and produced a wallet. 'Just in case, take my card. I'll be at the Grand for another three or four days. Give me a bell if you feel like it. Doesn't have to be a drink, we could make it a meal. Something better than bread and cheese. Thanks again for the cigarette, hope it hasn't launched me back on the downward path.'

When he left, Hillsden glanced at the business card he had been given. It read: *Gerald Pitchforth-Swanson, Managing Director, Beaver Enterprises Ltd. Enquiries welcomed.* The address was Orchard Mews in Hammersmith. It was printed rather than embossed. Studying it, Hillsden was taken back to the time when he had operated from the Firm's bogus wine business. It was from those fake premises that he had gone to old Hogg's post-mortem to learn how Caroline had been murdered and his journey back through the maze of deceit had begun. He put the card away and went into the cheese shop, still puzzled by the encounter, but more intent on getting his share of whatever was on offer that day.

4

ZURICH – LONDON 1997

Freidler's sudden death had sent shock waves through the financial world. One London paper made an attempt to connect his death to the still unsolved Calvi murder in order to make a splash headline, but the possibility of a link with the Vatican was discounted by most commentators. Bank shares generally were heavily marked down, the insiders hedging their bets against any incestuous fall-out. In times like these everybody looked over their shoulders. One tribute in *The Economist*, signed by Sir Raymond Charters, a prominent British figure, accorded Freidler near-sainthood, describing him as a gifted philanthropist with a social conscience whose loss would be felt throughout the Third World, whereas in truth he was just another successful predator who had exploited every financial loophole for his own gain.

His body was flown home to Switzerland in his private jet after the Atlanta authorities had conducted their post-mortem. It was established that the bullet had been fired from a standard German police automatic, readily obtainable over the counter in the United States. The identity of his assailant remained a mystery and there appeared to be no conventional motive for the murder; the newly acquired diamond earrings had not been stolen, nor were any of Freidler's possessions disturbed. The waiter who brought the champagne to the hotel suite, and Starr Faithful were dismissed from the case after being interviewed: it was established beyond any doubt that the girl had remained in Club Alpha until the early hours of the morning. She gave evidence that she had been approached by a member of Freidler's party and offered the sum of five thousand dollars to render services of a more intimate nature, and had refused, reporting the incident to the club management as she had been schooled to do. After a week or so, the story disappeared from the headlines until it was revived by a tabloid story claiming that the hotel housekeeper had seen a swastika sprayed on to the bathroom mirror. This was denied by the hotel management, anxious not to have the incident affect the tourist trade, and the housekeeper was subsequently dismissed.

The directors of Freidler's bank conducted their own internal investigation and were horrified to find more alarming skeletons in Freidler's cupboard. It appeared that their late president had made a number of unsecured loans to companies he controlled and that documentation concerning these transactions was, to say the least, sketchy. Far more disturbing to the senior officers entrusted with the task of opening and examining the contents of Freidler's private safe were damaging documents relating to undisclosed large sums being passed to parties in Israel, though the ultimate destination was unclear. What was not unclear was that he had used the bank's money and enhanced his own fortune to the tune of eight million dollars without the transaction appearing on any balance sheet. At a specially convened Board meeting, the directors took a decision to destroy the evidence.

. . .

Far from these developments the Rt Hon. Kenith Logan, the Home Secretary in Her Majesty's recently elected Labour government, sat in his huge office looking at the Lowry over the fireplace, pondering whether he had been handed a poisoned chalice.

Life had not dealt him an unbeatable hand, but until now he had always known in what order to play the cards he had been born with. He had studied and learned the rules of the power game from an early age; the first dictum he had taken to heart in the slums of Liverpool was that the poor and the meek, far from inheriting the earth, were lucky if they obtained anything more than beer money and a council flat. He was an observer as well as a doer, seldom wasting his time on envy, and had spent his formative years noting what made others tick and deciding that few actions taken were either objective or fair, but based on self-interest and advancement. A Geordie MP for fifteen of his fifty-two years, prior to entering the House he had played an active role in local politics, while at the same time amassing a modest fortune from a chain of DIY warehouses operating on a cash-only basis. ('I don't like the credit card companies milking my cows,' was one of his favourite expressions.) These efforts had enabled him to claw his way out of his working-class background and had given him a veneer of sophistication to complement his street-wise business acumen. He had long been able to suit his accent and manner to whatever company he kept, for he was an adept political chameleon who had carefully steered a path between both factions of the Party – a Jack-the-Lad when dealing with the unions, well equipped to hold his own at shop-floor level when required, while presenting a potentially ministerial face to the Whips and the Front Bench. He was popular with the faithful at Conference times, skilfully judging which motions openly to support and which to duck. Four years before Labour swept back to power he had been voted on to the National Executive Council and had first been rewarded with the post of Shadow Minister for Sport (as a schoolboy he had had a trial for Everton), before being promoted to Transport, acquitting himself well at the Dispatch Box against a lack-lustre Tory counterpart. Gaining in confidence, he had slowly honed the rough zircon of his basic personality until it shone in such a way that many took it to be the genuine article. He was always willing to talk off the record to the parliamentary lobbyists, but with a wink and a nod, knowing that there was a good chance his indiscretions would find their way into print. Nobody really knew him, but he was generally reckoned to be a coming man. He lived modestly, dressed conservatively and, covering his options, courted two Aids charities, was a life-member of the RSPCA, opposed blood sports, was pro-abortion and anti the House of Lords. In the last reshuffle before the General Election he had been moved up to Health and Welfare and had expected to retain that position in the Cabinet if Labour swept back into power. The sudden death of the incumbent Home Secretary a matter of days after the outcome of the election had meant a further panic reshuffle, and to everybody's surprise, including his own, Logan had found himself elevated to that well-known political graveyard, the Home Office.

In his first weeks as a senior Cabinet Minister, thrust into an office he had never expected to occupy, he frequently felt like a certified lunatic, completely cut off from ordinary life, protected by male and female trained nurses who, although behaving with every outward show of deference, had quickly hinted that sweeping changes were not on their agenda. He found the comparison with hospital routine apposite, for he was given a mental blanket-bath by his Private Secretary, his own ideas of what he might or might not do gently washed away, and his hesitant protests talcum-powdered with soothing Whitehall-speak. It seemed that the most important function he could perform for his servants was to allow their established routines to proceed without hindrance. The early pulse of his adrenalin soon slowed under their ministrations, for Logan was smart enough to acknowledge that in many cases he knew next to nothing of the brief he held.

He was still staring at the Lowry, at the myriad matchstick figures in a northern landscape so familiar from his own childhood, when Sir Charles Slade, his Permanent Private Secretary, knocked and entered the room. Slade would have been rejected by any film casting director as too obvious for the role he played, for he epitomised the urbane courtier who was aware that, whatever human flotsam the political tides deposited on his private beach, he would always secure the best deckchair. Beneath his impeccably tailored dark suit he wore a corset to help support a back injured in a hunting accident and flatten the old tummy. To those not in the know it gave him a ramrod appearance in keeping with his Guards background. In his middle fifties, with a moustache more like an upper lip smudge, he bore a passing resemblance to the late Ronald Colman.

'Good morning, Minister.'

'Morning, Charles. Is it going to be a good one?' The use of Slade's Christian name came out hesitantly. How to address Slade had given Logan problems at first. He still retained enough of his working-class background to be impressed by titles.

'Oh, I'm sure, Minister. The deputation is here, by the way,' Slade added, 'but it never hurts to keep them waiting a few minutes.'

He placed some cuttings he had extracted from that day's newspapers in Logan's in-tray, together with some letters prepared for signature. 'The deputation from Greenwich, Minister,' he added, noting that Logan's expression had gone blank. 'You've read the briefing, I'm sure.'

'Oh, that, yes. Yes. How many are they?'

'Three, Minister.' Slade discreetly edged a piece of notepaper in front of Logan.

'Tricky?'

'Not at all, Minister. I'm sure you've taken on board the department's ongoing view of these matters. Any multi-racial society is bound to throw up these incidents from time to time. Sadly, they are the unwelcome manifestations of the slow process of integration.'

Logan allowed himself to disagree. 'I hardly think murder is an acceptable part of the process and if you ask me progress has been minimal. I'm going to change all that,' he added allowing himself a rare statement of intent, 'so pass the good news down the line.'

'I'll certainly make sure it reaches the right ears, Minister. Of course,' he added with just a smidgeon of caution in his voice, 'it's always best to take the House along slowly. And where these ethnic issues are concerned, history has shown us that no change is achieved without a measure of discontent.'

Logan frowned before looking down at his papers. It was never easy to decipher Sir Charles. From a study of his boxes the previous night Logan had discovered that Greenwich enjoyed the dubious accolade of being top of the league in racial murders. There had been three in the past month alone, attributed to the fact that First Legion, a breakaway section of the National Front, had recently set up its headquarters in a quiet residential area of Greenwich, provoking strong protests from the ethnic community. Popular feeling was strongly critical of the police, since so far no arrests had been made.

'Well, you'd better show them in, then.'

'Your next engagement is at eleven, Minister, so might I suggest giving them half an hour at the most? I shall have your speech to the Law Society ready when you return.'

'You saw the amendments I made?'

'Yes, indeed. If I may say so, pertinent though they were, they were at variance with the major policy decisions you'll be presenting in your White Paper in due course.'

He withdrew before Logan could respond. A few moments later three men were ushered into the office. One of them Logan immediately recognised as Luther Smith, a prominent black activist, who was frequently to be seen taking part in television debates. Articulate and with well-marshalled opinions, he belied his burly appearance. According to Slade's briefing notes, he was a graduate of the London School of Economics, had twice been arrested during protest marches, and was considered still to hanker for a return to old-fashioned Marxism. The second man was also black and introduced himself as the lawyer acting for the family of one of the murder victims. The last member of the party was an official of a local racial surveillance organisation named Streetwatch.

'Please sit down,' Logan said. 'And smoke if you wish. I do.'

They took the proffered seats.

Addressing Smith, whom he rightly assumed would be the principal spokesman, Logan began with, 'Let me say, Mr Smith, I'm fully aware of the purpose of your visit, and I share your concerns.'

'Perhaps what you're not aware of, Minister,' Smith broke in, 'is that another man was torched last night.'

'Torched?'

'Beaten up, doused in petrol and set on fire,' Smith said. He opened his briefcase and took out some photographs which he tossed on to Logan's desk. 'Take a look, Minister. They torched his crotch. And why? Because he dated a white girl. He was abducted by a group of fascist thugs whom your government has allowed to set up shop in my neighbourhood and terrorise the coloured population. Three murders, over sixty assaults, shit put through letter boxes, arson, ram-raiders, you name it, and I'd like to know what you intend to do about it.' He had not raised his voice, but there was no mistaking his hostility. 'I'm not just concerned with this latest outrage, hideous though it is, I'm asking you to take immediate action and proscribe First Legion. Shut them down before you have a full scale riot on your hands. You have the powers, use them.'

Taken off guard by the vehemence of Smith's opening attack, Logan stared at the graphic photographs while he searched for the right response. 'I'm not sure that you're correct on your last point. In the first instance, these are properly matters for the police and I have no doubt that they are already being dealt with by them.'

'Then let me disabuse you, Minister. So far no convictions have resulted from any of the murders.'

'Convictions depend on hard evidence.'

It was now that the lawyer interrupted. 'With great courage, my clients are prepared positively to identify two of the assailants if given the chance, but so far the police have done little or nothing. A fuse has been lit, Minister, and unless the authorities act quickly, I fear the consequences.'

Logan studied the photographs again. 'Is this man going to live?'

'He's in the intensive burns unit. They give him a fifty-fifty chance.'

Logan nodded. 'Quite hideous. Can you leave these with me? I shall personally take up the incident with the Commissioner at the earliest opportunity.'

'What about First Legion?' Smith asked.

'Do you have any direct evidence to link these atrocities with their members?'

'Isn't it obvious?' the lawyer said. 'The moment they set up shop in the area the number of racial attacks increased by some three hundred per cent. That can't be pure coincidence.'

'But proof? I have every sympathy with your situation, but for me or the police to take action, proof is required. Come to me with proof and I promise that I will act immediately.'

The three men on the opposite side of the desk exchanged glances. Smith said: 'What further proof do you need? Another three murders? Read your own manifesto again. You were voted in on a promise of justice for all.'

'I can assure you these issues are high on my agenda,' Logan replied stuffily. 'You have to remember we inherited a great number of problems, crimes of this nature being one of them, but they can't be dealt with in isolation. They're all part and parcel of a much wider social sickness. As you must know, we shall be publishing a number of White Papers designed to tackle the root causes.'

Smith got to his feet. 'Yeah, we've heard all that before. First from the Tories, now from your lot, but nothing ever happens.' He gathered up the photographs. 'I'll take these back, in case they gather dust, and before you publish your White Papers I'm going to spread them all over the tabloids.'

He made for the door. The other two followed him, only the lawyer making a lame attempt to exit on a placatory note. The last thing Logan heard was Smith's muttered, 'Another useless prick.'

Fifteen minutes later, still smarting from the exchange,

Logan got into his armoured Jaguar and, accompanied by his personal detective and a police back-up car, set off for his next appointment. What rankled most was the awareness that in dealing with the three men, all too soon, all too glibly, he had found himself using the bleak language of power and saying nothing.

5

ST PETERSBURG 1997

Galina said: 'Why, what makes you suspicious?'

Before answering Hillsden glanced at their small daughter who was concentrating on a jigsaw. 'Haven't I always been?' he said softly, 'ever since you've been unlucky enough to know me.'

'Don't say that. I hate it when you say things like that.'

'Well, if it wasn't for me, you could have a more interesting life now that the barriers have been lifted. You'd be free to travel, something you say you've always wanted to do. It isn't exactly an advantage being married to me. Because of who I am, you're trapped here.'

Now it was Galina's turn to shoot a look at their daughter. 'I know who you are and what you were, and I'm not trapped, I'm content.'

'Are you? Well, I'm not. It's a slow death here, and you and Lara deserve better.'

'What else happened this morning, something happened, didn't it? I want to know why you came back in such a funny mood. Was there something else you haven't told me?'

'No.'

'Then what was it about that man that made you suspicious?'

'I just don't believe it was a chance encounter. How did he pick me out as British in that queue?'

'You look British.'

'I don't think so. Not any longer. I certainly don't feel British. He was too pat.'

'Pat?'

'Yes. Meaning his dialogue came out as rehearsed.'

They sat opposite each other on either side of the stove. Through the thin walls of the apartment they could hear their drunken neighbour singing an old McCartney standard – 'Yesterday'. It seemed to be the only item in his repertoire and he repeated it endlessly, his sodden voice cracking whenever he reached for a high note. Hillsden had a sudden yearning for home, for different comforts, familiar landmarks. He was happy with Galina; not content, as she put it, but on the whole happy. At least he did not have to deceive her as he had been forced to deceive Margot, his first wife. Now, when he put his head on the pillow beside Galina, he no longer had to think twice before answering her night questions. Sometimes, denied sleep, he could see his past life so clearly; the suburban house where he had once lived, crammed with the kitsch trimmings that Margot had collected – all those special offers she had religiously answered, his marriage compiled from mail order catalogues, the outward signs, he now recognised, of her consuming loneliness. He had been forced to shut her out and the wonder of it was how he had managed to sustain the deception all those years, bound not by the vows exchanged in church, but the more monstrous ties of the Official Secrets Act.

Galina interrupted his memories. 'What else could he have wanted you for?'

'No idea.'

'Then why give him a second thought?'

'I explained why. I'm always expecting the past to catch up with me.'

'In a cheese queue?' Galina said, trying to make him see the humour of it.

'You didn't live the way I had to all those wasted years, never knowing what was round the corner.' He broke off as he became aware that his daughter had stopped doing the jigsaw and was listening to their conversation. 'Have you finished it, sweetheart?'

The child shook her head. 'Why are you and Mummy sad?' she said, her wide eyes boring through him.

'We're not sad. Let me see.' He picked up one of the spare pieces. 'The sky is always the difficult part. I could never do skies.'

He tried the piece in several places without success. 'What d'you know? I'm no better than you. Anyway, it's past your bedtime, young lady. We'll finish it in the morning. Off you go. Give me a kiss.'

She climbed on his knee and put her arms around his neck, planting multiple kisses on his cheek in quick succession.

'My word, how many is that?'

'A hundred, because I love you a hundred.'

'And I love you too.'

'How many?'

'Oh, three hundred at least.'

'Will we go to the park tomorrow?'

'If it's fine.'

'Promise.'

'I promise.'

She gave him one last kiss and then went to her room with her mother. Watching her go, Hillsden thought, by the time she's seventeen I'll be an old man, and the prospect chilled him. He put some more wood on the stove and poured himself a small measure of Scotch – another gift from Abramov and one that he rationed. Savouring the drink, he remembered the good gone times that he, Jock and Caroline had spent together in the old Austrian station. The preferred tipple then had been Hunter's Tea – local, home-made schnapps topped up with hot water – one of those lethal potions, like too many Pimm's downed on a hot summer's day, that floored you without warning. It all came flooding back, that past, foreign country where certainly we did things differently, he thought. Even his adultery with Caroline had had a sort of innocence about it, unjustified but nevertheless real, neither of them counting the true cost until it was too late. Was that the same with all lovers or just peculiar to them? He remembered the night walks by the dark, still lake at Anif, reliving those last days when, despite all his efforts, he had failed to dissuade Caroline from going back to East Berlin that final time. Within a few years, but all too late to save her, the Wall came down, the old futilities rubbled, Honecker's machinery of terror dismantled. Now, remembering the span of the Cold War, it was like looking at history through the wrong end of a telescope: the major players reduced to dwarfs. Were the deaths, the sacrifices worth it? he wondered. Did we make any difference to the inevitable outcome? In the end it wasn't our efforts but an act of spontaneous human combustion that overturned a whole continent. After Caroline's death he had attempted to build his own wall, to keep past and present separated, forgetting that memories had a way of jumping any barrier. Now, as he waited for Galina to return from putting the child to bed, those same, recurring memories touched the sciatic nerve of disloyalty. I should be happy, he thought. I have a good wife and child I love, I'm alive, be thankful for those mercies.

'D'you want a drink?' he asked when Galina came back.

'No, it's nearly finished and I know how much it means to you.'

'Have some, come on, I hate drinking alone.'

'I'm not that keen, really.'

'Vodka, then? Have a vodka.'

He got up to pour her one. 'Has she gone to sleep?'

'Yes, for once. Why is it that children never want to go to bed?'

'It's primeval,' Hillsden said. 'Fear of the dark, the unknown. Weren't you like that as a child? I know I was. I still am, sometimes.'

He paused as he went to hand her the drink, bending and kissing her on the lips.

'What's that for?'

'Can't a man kiss his wife when he feels like it?'

42

'I'm not complaining, I just asked why.'

'Because I fancy you.'

'Suddenly?'

'No, not suddenly.'

'Well, you're out of luck tonight, because my period just started.'

'Ah!' He handed her the drink. 'Then I'll have to settle for a cuddle. Come here. Sit on my lap.'

'Like daughter, like wife,' Galina said as she nuzzled him. 'You have two women who love you.'

'Yes, I'm a lucky sod, don't think I don't know it.'

They kissed.

'You're not really worried about that man, are you?' Galina said.

'No. You're probably right, maybe he did only want to cadge a cigarette. Did you read that in America there's a lobby gathering momentum to ban cigarettes altogether.'

'Pity they don't try the same here. I do so wish you'd give up.'

'Aren't I unbearable enough as it is? It's easy for you, you've never smoked.' Denied the ultimate intimacy, he stroked her hair, then dropped his hand to let it rest on her breast. 'Are you *really* content?' he asked as the same tuneless singing began again in the next apartment.

'Yes, I've told you.'

'But don't you long to get out of this city, escape the daily drudgery of it all? Maybe I should go and work for Victor, he keeps asking me to.'

'You'd hate that.'

'With the money he says I'd earn we could perhaps buy a *dacha*. It'd be good for Lara to be in the country when summer comes. I thought she looked pale tonight. You too, for that matter. We live like caged birds.' As he said it he was reminded of the canary Jock had once given him and nicknamed Gromyko, the only company he had had in that first cold-comfort Moscow apartment. Why did so many things from those days come back to haunt him? Although he had now made light of the chance encounter in the cheese queue, some unease remained. No matter how many changes had taken place, he believed that good old-fashioned evil still stalked the streets. There were past scores that remained to be settled. For all he knew, somebody in the Firm wanted to balance the books for personal reasons. He had never ceased to be on his guard.

. . .

As it happened he did not have long to wait.

Although the following morning it was still bitterly cold, the skies were clear and Hillsden gave in to Lara's repeated pleas for him to honour his promise. Swathed in extra layers of clothing they set out hand in hand to walk to the Tauride Gardens.

It had always seemed odd to Hillsden that, despite their love of the open air, Russians displayed little or no interest in gardening. He supposed this could partly be explained by the fact that few city dwellers had plots of their own, but even the communal gardens usually presented a pathetic sight. There would be spring flowers, of course, planted haphazardly, not in the meticulous patterns of London parks, and swiftly neglected except by weeds. Even the *dacha* plots were not given the slavish devotion the British lavished on their gardens; grass grew wild, trees were untamed, the idea of mowing a lawn anathema.

The Tauride Gardens looked particularly forlorn in winter, though Hillsden could appreciate why little or no maintenance was attempted: the frozen earth would have needed pneumatic drills to penetrate it. The only thing that could be said for the excursions he and Lara made was that they got him out of the apartment for a few hours. Lara had brought her skipping rope with her and he tied one end to a tree and patiently swung the other while she displayed her prowess. Hillsden went through the motions automatically, his thoughts elsewhere, and it wasn't until the man who called himself Pitchforth-Swanson was upon them that he was even aware of his presence.

'You play the good father, I see.'

Involuntarily, Hillsden stopped swinging the rope and Lara tripped over it. He rushed to pick her up before facing Swanson.

'Oh, dear, that was my fault,' Swanson said.

'No harm done.' Lara stayed close to her father's side.

'Well, we meet again.'

'Yes,' Hillsden said. 'But not by coincidence, I take it?'

'Well, I had rather hoped you'd take me up on my offer of a meal,' Swanson replied. He smiled as he said it, revealing bright, but uneven, teeth. 'You didn't call me, did you?'

'No.'

'I only ask because the hotel's not very good with messages.'

Irritation welled up in Hillsden. Why am I being so polite with this bullshit artist? he thought. He knew the Swansons of this world: lifted from a mould that had been in use since the days of the Empire, they looked down on anybody who hadn't been to the right school, condescending time-servers treading water until they received their mandatory K. Swanson had the sort of face that frequently adorned the social pages of *The Field*. 'What d'you really want?' he asked. 'I'm not so green as to think you turned up here on the off chance you might bum another cigarette.'

'I just want a chat, Alec.'

The use of his Christian name checked Hillsden momentarily.

'Just a friendly chat. To put a proposition to you.'

'Who sent you?'

'We'll get to that. Let's just say that it would be worth your time to have that chat.'

'I'm not going to talk in front of my daughter.'

Sensing a different note in her father's voice, Lara's grip tightened on his hand.

'No, I quite understand. Why not come to my hotel? It has

some of the best food around. My treat, of course.'

His smile, which Hillsden did not return, gave his mouth a lop-sided look.

'When?'

'Tonight?' Swanson said. 'Shall we say seven, in the foyer?'

Hillsden nodded.

'That's splendid, I look forward to it.'

Hillsden and Lara watched as he walked away towards the old fair-ground and was lost amongst the empty booths. Then Hillsden untied the skipping rope.

'Aren't we going to play some more?' Lara asked, her face puckered against a wind that had suddenly gusted.

'Not today, darling.'

'Is it because of that man?'

'No, nothing to do with him. It's getting too cold.'

'I didn't like that man,' the child said. 'You didn't like him either, did you?'

'Not over much,' Hillsden said.

'Then why are you having dinner with him?'

'That's enough questions.' He took her gloved hand. They walked slowly home while Hillsden tried to guess Swanson's real purpose in seeking him out.

. . .

Swanson was occupying a comfortable two-room suite. A table had been laid with drinks and a crystal bowl of imperial caviar on cracked ice, enough for half a dozen people.

'Are you expecting others to join us?' Hillsden asked. He shook the snow off his coat, folded it and placed it over the back of a chair.

'No, there's just you and me,' Swanson said. 'What's your tipple?'

'I prefer Scotch, but it doesn't sit well with the caviar, so I'll take the local poison.'

Swanson began: 'Well, you may be pleasantly surprised to

know that London are prepared to entertain a deal, all things being equal.'

'They never are, are they?'

Swanson paused from pouring the vodka and gave him a look. 'Sorry?'

'All things are never equal. In any deal one of the parties always comes out top.'

'Oh, I see, yes.' Swanson gave a short, mirthless laugh, but his face betrayed a trace of uncertainty. 'You want to help yourself to the feast?'

Hillsden moved to the table and spread caviar on the coarse brown bread rather than the blinis. 'I see the Firm can still push out the boat. I thought things were tight in dear old England.'

'For some. I'm sure the axe is poised to fall one day, given our new masters, but for the moment they need us. It's remarkable how power changes attitudes. Give a Minister an armour-plated Jaguar and a police escort and many of his liberal beliefs evaporate.'

Hillsden took the offered glass of vodka and waited until Swanson had poured for himself and heaped a dollop of caviar on to a blini. A few of the eggs dribbled out of Swanson's mouth on to his chin as he took a large bite.

'Who would have thought it?' Swanson said.

'Thought what?'

'Us being here together like this. Not so long ago it would have been unthinkable. I mean, being able to talk freely.'

'Are we talking freely?'

Swanson smiled. 'What a guarded character you are, Alec.' He spread another blini. 'Do have some more.'

'I don't have a large appetite these days,' Hillsden answered. He resisted the temptation to lean forward and wipe the caviar from Swanson's slack mouth with a napkin. 'You said you had a proposition to put to me, wasn't that the object of this meeting? Let's forgo the philosophic tiny talk and get down to that.'

'If you wish. I rather thought we could enjoy the meal first.'

At long last Swanson became aware of the state of his mouth and tidied it with a forefinger. 'Let's start by stating the obvious. You're quite right, I didn't come across you by chance.'

If he expected Hillsden to react he was disappointed. Taking another mouthful of caviar he continued, 'As you can imagine, this isn't somewhere I prefer to Henley, any more than you.'

'I've never been to Henley,' Hillsden said.

'Really? One of the few things that hasn't changed in England. Most everything else has. Changed for all of us. Different horses for different courses, different jockeys riding them.'

'Do me a favour,' Hillsden interrupted. 'I've had my fill of men of mystery. Just get to the point.' The belligerence in his voice was all too obviously not to Swanson's liking.

'Well, now, chummy, I don't think you're in a position to dictate.' The use of the word 'chummy' was deliberately offensive, but Hillsden remained impassive. 'If you want me to put my false teeth on the table, I'd suggest your situation is not so secure that you can afford to be cocky. As I said, times have changed, and that's true, but not in every respect. I hate to bring up the subject, but there's still a warrant out for your arrest and the long arm of the law can now reach this far . . . That isn't a threat, just a statement of fact. Equally, there are always ways and means of disposing of such inconveniences. Take the case . . . well, just suppose I was to tell you that in return for your co-operation you and your new family could kiss goodbye to cheese queues and go back to shopping at Tesco.'

If Hillsden felt any surprise he did not show it.

'You'd be buying a new life. The record wiped clean, a new identity, a home back in your own country, your daughter educated in a good private school, financial security for your wife. It's a good package, Alec.'

'And what's the price tag?' Hillsden asked after a slight pause. He reached to pour himself another vodka.

'Well, let's not call it a price, nothing so vulgar, just a return consideration.'

'Well, whatever you'd call it.'

'I happen to think your talents should not be allowed to rust. Somebody like you still has a lot of mileage in him. Alec Hillsden may be a burnt-out case, but give him an oil change, a totally new personality, and it's a different ball game as the Yanks say,' Swanson said in a flurry of mixed metaphors.

Hillsden downed his ice-cold vodka in one go, then shook his head. 'No, forget it. Not interested. I'm too old to go back in the game, and maybe too wise. You must have dozens of eager beavers to choose from. Why would you come all this way to head-hunt a burnt-out case like me?'

'But you don't know the game I have in mind, Alec. As it happens, your age, the fact that you're charred at the edges, fits the scenario I have in mind. I'm not looking for youthful brawn, I'm looking for guile born of long experience.'

'Well, there's plenty of that in this room.' Despite his antipathy towards Swanson, he found himself drawn into the cat and mouse tactics. 'Okay, tell me this "scenario" as you call it.'

'Oh, come on, Alec, you can't have forgotten how these things work? We don't accept post-dated cheques.'

'What I haven't forgotten is how I was stitched-up last time. What makes you think I should trust you or anybody else this time around? You want to trade, trade. You don't catch old fish with dead bait. How do I know you're not just the errand boy sent to snare me? Don't read the fine print, Alec, just sign on the dotted line and trust me. Bullshit! I've been there before.'

Swanson's face flushed but he did not reply in kind. 'That's where you're wrong, Alec. You haven't been there before. Nobody has. I can understand your caution, but it's misplaced, believe me. The deal I'm authorised to offer is a good one, but it won't come again.' His body language and tone softened – a Harrods salesman now urging a customer to take the suit he has suggested. 'I can't believe you want to spend your remaining years living on Russian charity, a forgotten dinosaur from a bygone age. Not a man of your abilities. So before you make a hasty judgement, why not hear me out? You see, I've studied your file very thoroughly, and you fit my role model. I want somebody with a burning need to get even. I've always thought nothing spurs one on like the prospect of revenge, don't you agree? You did your duty, Alec, served your country well, and in return got short shrift. I'm offering you a chance – a last chance – to go back and rehabilitate yourself.'

Hillsden listened without any change of expression, hearing an echo of Lockfield in Swanson's dialogue.

'I'll go this far with you,' Swanson continued in the same plummy tone. 'Because of the past I can well appreciate your caution . . . Let me tell you what's been happening in the real world. Labour swept in at the last general election on a manifesto they patently couldn't deliver, but the public bought it and the Tories were decimated, reduced to a rump. The "natural party of power", as they liked to think of themselves, now has to face a long stay in the wilderness. A small caucus of hard case right-wingers didn't take kindly to that. They split from the party and formed their own secret agenda with the aim of exploiting the race card and fomenting widespread social unrest. A motley crowd, Alec, with a hang-'em-and-flog-'em mentality, but not to be under-estimated. They have a lot going for them despite Labour's attempt to paper over the cracks. The England of today is a tinder box waiting to be ignited. Many of the inner-cities have no-go ghetto areas, but as far as the new government is concerned it's politically unacceptable to admit the problem exists. Continuing high unemployment mostly amongst the ethnic minorities which, like the Tories, they can't solve without draconian measures, allied to a horrendous, drug-related crime rate, has stymied them. That gives the ultra-rights a lot of ammunition to play with. We believe they're biding their time until they can mount a *coup.*'

'It'll never happen.'

'You say that, but you've been away a long time, Alec. The England you knew no longer exists. We're edging closer to 1933 than drawing away from Orwell's '84.'

'Where does your role model fit into that?'

'Whether the enemy comes from the Left or the Right, Alec, some of us have to do what's required. Uncle Joe and company depart, enter the Fascists stage right. We know some of it, but not enough. We need to get closer, to infiltrate, stay ahead of them. There's the added factor, which you couldn't possibly be aware of, that, post Lockfield, certain elements within the Firm itself moved too far to the Right. Thatcher's long reign made sure of that.'

'Identified?'

'We sorted out two of them, but I suspect they were only the tip of the iceberg. The DG and I are convinced that some of the new intake are in contact with the Tory breakaway group and constitute a threat from within. Hence our need for somebody untainted to smoke them out . . . and who better than you, somebody from the old school who has such special qualities? You'd be working with a very small, hand-picked team, with me running the show. In return, your file would be wiped clean, deleted without trace. Doesn't that tempt you?'

'This team, do I know any of them?'

'One, I think.'

'Who?'

'Come home and find out,' Swanson said. He looked long and hard at Hillsden before helping himself to another drink. 'I can make it an attractive package, Alec.'

'What special qualities do I have? I'd like to know.'

'You're the man who never was, Alec. Part of the plan would be to arrange for you to die. By the time you arrive in England your obituaries will be wrapping fish and chips. We've thought of all the loose ends. I don't know why you're hesitating. Most people would jump at a chance of starting again with a clean sheet.'

'Except, I'm not alone, I have a wife and a daughter. And the fact that, in some ways, despite everything, familiarity has certain compensations,' Hillsden replied after a pause. 'Are you saying the murder charge would be dropped?'

'Absolutely. And eventually a pardon. That would have to be held over for obvious reasons.'

'I'd want a copper-bottomed guarantee before I leave here.'

'That can be arranged. What else?' Confident that, finally, he was winning the argument, Swanson returned to the caviar.

'A lump sum equivalent to back-dated salary for the past seven years, placed in my wife's name, in a Swiss numbered account.'

'I don't see any problem there. Officially you won't be listed in any of the Firm's accounts. You'll be paid from a secret slush fund not even the Select Committee know about.'

'I'll think about it,' Hillsden said after a long pause. He put his topcoat on, then picked up a bottle of Scotch and the half-finished bottle of vodka, together with the bowl of caviar. 'You don't mind, do you? Treat for the wife.'

He made for the door. 'I'll give you my answer two days from now. Let's meet in the park again and if there's anything still to talk about I'll take you back to our apartment. Eleven o'clock, by the fair-ground.'

'Why not give me your answer now?'

'Two days,' Hillsden repeated. 'I'm being generous. The Firm kept me waiting seven years.'

He left.

. . .

'Did you convince him?' the London voice asked.

'I don't know,' Swanson replied. 'He's not an easy customer.'

'What's the snag?'

'It's difficult to read him. He wants forty-eight hours to think it over. I still believe he's our best bet, for all the reasons we discussed.'

'How much did you tell him?'

'Just the bare essentials. Plus the offer, of course.'

'And that didn't sway him?'

'I think it interested him.'

'Well, if he finally says no, move to the contingency plan. Let's not leave anything to chance.'

'Understood.'

The line to London went dead.

. . .

'You know it means you becoming me, changing places,' Hillsden said. 'Relearning a life.'

'You did it,' Galina said.

'I had no choice.'

'Do I?'

'Yes. The choice is yours.'

'But you want to go home.'

'I haven't said that.'

'I know you do. It's in your face. If I spoilt it for you you'd always hold it against me.'

'You're wrong. Either way I'd only be doing it for you and Lara. You decide. It's your life I care about.'

6

ARKANSAS, USA

Marvin Schmidt had never witnessed an execution before, let alone a triple execution, but as the leading member of the FBI team that had brought the three murderers to justice, he felt a morbid compulsion to see it through to the end. God knows he had waited long enough: all three convicted men had been on Death Row for several years, their lawyers lodging appeal after appeal, but every legal loophole having been explored and rejected, the verdict of the court was finally going to be carried out.

Executions in the State of Arkansas being by lethal injection, the Governor of the prison had decreed that the three men would be terminated, in alphabetical order, during a two hour period commencing at midnight. At a press conference he stated his reasons: the procedure would be a cost efficient exercise, reducing overtime and stress on his staff. 'Executions ain't no picnic for those who have to carry them out and I have to think of that.'

It was out of character for Schmidt to become so emotionally involved in the aftermath of any case: some you lost and some you won, it more often than not depended on whether the defendant could afford a top lawyer; justice in the US of A was now just another adjunct of show business, he felt – trial by television in many cases. Normally, whatever the verdict, he tried to wipe it from memory, but this particular crime had never left him. A Jew himself, twelve years previously, being made aware of the anti-Semitic undertones in the case, he had put in a special request to be assigned to the Federal team handling the investigation. The crime in question was the brutal murder of a small town businessman killed, together with his wife and daughter, in what at first appeared to be a break-in that went horribly wrong. Then the Arkansas State police unearthed more sinister clues. The murdered man, Gerard Heinz, a Polish Jew, the only surviving member of a prominent Warsaw family, had been admitted to America as a refugee immediately after the war. He had married a Jewish girl, also a refugee, and after a period living in the Queens district of New York where they both worked long hours at menial tasks in order to amass some capital, they had moved to Arkansas and established a flourishing haberdashery store. The murderers had first tortured Heinz in front of his wife and daughter, then both women had been brutally raped before all three members of the family were shot at point blank range. The house and shop had been totally trashed, the murderers urinating in the beds, though, curiously, very little had been stolen. A respected, well-integrated member of the local community, Heinz had no known enemies and the initial investigation produced no leads. It wasn't until three weeks later that the State Prosecutor's office received an anonymous and crudely written communication.

Three of the scum eliminated. This is just the beginning.
Soon the gas chambers will be back and the Jews
will be made into soap which is all there (sic) fit for.
By order of The SS Action Committee

Curiously, the note had been posted in Chicago. Although it produced no fingerprints, forensic experts determined that the watermarked paper it was written on was manufactured by a small company in the Evanston district and only distributed and sold in Illinois. They checked all outlets but the trail went cold. Then an apparently unrelated incident attracted Schmidt's interest – a gun-dealer with known underworld connections was arrested on a charge of failing to keep proper records and an alert member of the Chicago police noticed that his invoices were printed on the same, suspect, notepaper. This in itself was not sufficient to tie in with the Arkansas murder, but in addition a quantity of anti-Semitic literature was found amongst the dealer's sequestered files, together with evidence of membership of a quasi-Fascist organisation calling itself Partisans of the New Front. Under interrogation Schmidt trapped the gun-dealer into revealing the name of a fellow member, a man called Mitchell who proved to have some form: he had once been arrested for attempted rape, but had been found not guilty for lack of corroborating evidence. He was currently on parole for a lesser offence.

Mitchell, a hardhat, was working on a construction site when tracked down. He was a thick-set man in his forties and carried a pronounced beer gut with a swaggering gait. His torso was extensively tattooed, including a small swastika on his right upper-arm. Schmidt went undercover, calling himself Joe Spader. After gaining a job on the same building site, he made it his business to get friendly with Mitchell during the lunch breaks, deliberately encouraging Mitchell's coarse sense of humour. They went bowling together and after a few weeks, the relationship cemented. Mitchell, who lived alone in a trailer park, invited 'Spader' back for a barbecue meal.

Schmidt was wired that evening. He sat in a plastic lounger, drinking beer out of a can watching Mitchell fuss over the charcoal.

'Take a look at these mothers,' Mitchell said. 'You ever seen T-bones like these? You can't buy these from a fucken market, you have to wait for them to fall off the back of a lorry.' He squeezed his empty beer can and reached for a second. 'I'll put you in touch with my supplier. Best fucken meat you ever tasted. Cheap, no questions asked.'

'Can't beat it,' Schmidt said.

'I don't pay those fancy Jew prices. No way. The kikes have got this country over a fucken barrel, know that?'

'You think so?'

'I know so,' Mitchell said as he basted the steaks with sauce and forked them on to the grill. 'Those Jew pricks control everything. You name it, they run it. The banks, movies, garment trade, supermarkets. Forget the Mafia, they ain't the threat.'

'Guess you're right. I never thought of it that way.'

'A few of us have got wise. How d'you like yours, rare or ruined?'

'Rare.'

'I like to see blood.' Mitchell flipped the steaks over. 'Couple more minutes and these beauties will melt in your mouth.'

Schmidt had to admit that the meat was exceptional, which gratified Mitchell. 'Listen, nothing but the best for a buddy. You married?'

'No. Was. No longer.'

'Me neither. Who needs it? Like they say, why keep a cow when you can buy milk at the K Mart? Ain't that the truth?'

'Ain't it just,' Schmidt agreed.

'I up and go wherever I please. Been all over. See, I got friends everywhere in the fraternity.'

'What fraternity's that? You mean the Elks?'

'Fuck, no! Fucken Elks are a bunch of nothings. I'm talkin' of real buddies, know what I mean? Guys who think alike, who see where this country's headed. Nothing but bleeding-heart liberals, fucken gays, blacks and rich Jew boys running our lives. But we're doing something about it. You wait.'

Schmidt nodded.

'Take Nixon, he was a prince and they fucken shafted him. Know who was behind Watergate? A whole bunch of Washington kikes.'

'Really? I didn't read that.'

'Course you didn't read it,' Mitchell said. He picked his teeth and hawked. 'Never got in the papers. But that's the bottom line, you'd better believe it. Some of us know and are doing something about it. Only a matter of time. Let me show you something.' He went inside his mobile home and emerged carrying a book. 'Take this back and read it. It'll open your eyes to what's really going on. But keep it to yourself, don't leave it lying around, that fucken book's a hand grenade.'

Schmidt studied the title, *The Only Solution*, before flicking through the pages. The chapter heading he stopped at read: 'The Purification of The Nation'.

'Looks interesting,' he said.

'Bet your fucken life it's interesting. That there's our bible.'

They had some more beers, though Schmidt was careful not to match Mitchell's consumption. When the mosquitoes began to bite they moved inside. The interior of the mobile home mirrored Mitchell's personality. Copies of *Hustler* lay on the unmade single bed, the pillow stained with the greasy hair preparation Mitchell used. The driver's swivel armchair and a matching companion were on a raised portion and behind them was a small dining table with bench seats either side, the table strewn with dirty crockery and a brimming ashtray. Schmidt noted a skeleton mascot dangling from under the rear-view mirror.

'Bet these are great pyjama wagons,' he commented.

'The best. Great for short-arm practice.' By now Mitchell's speech was getting slurred. 'You ever want to borrow it for a little goona-goona, just pass the word. No charge and you don't have to smuggle them past the landlord.'

Schmidt swivelled into the driving seat and fingered the steering wheel. There was a metal decal fixed to the centre of the wheel which he recognised as a Nazi SS insignia. 'And I bet this baby moves when you put your foot down.'

'Straight V-eight,' Mitchell answered through a belch. 'Taken her all over – Carolina, Texas, Arkansas, Arizona, just up and go.'

'I ain't never travelled far,' Schmidt said. 'Been to Texas once, Dallas, and I went to a funeral in Philly, but that's about it. What's Arkansas like? Ain't that where Clinton come from?'

'Clinton. What a dummy. You know who bankrolled him into the White House don'cha? Fucken Jew commies again. But we're getting around to him.' He belched again and went to use the small toilet, repeating 'fucken commies' several times as he urinated noisily. Schmidt used the moment quickly to rifle through some papers and road maps on the dashboard. Scrawled on a map of Arkansas were the words *Heinz tomato catsup* and a date. He pocketed this and was finishing his beer when Mitchell returned with his flies gaping. 'Say, listen, I've got to get some shut-eye. Thanks for the steak and beer.'

'Any time.'

'And you must tell me more about this fraternity.'

'Read the book. If you're hooked we'll get together on it.' Mitchell flopped on to the bunk. As Schmidt stepped outside he caught the rancid smell of burnt meat from the barbecue.

The date on the map was the date the Heinz family were murdered. Armed with this and his tape, Schmidt convinced his superiors that there was now sufficient circumstantial evidence to take it further. In the first instance, Mitchell was arrested on a charge of receiving stolen goods. While he was in custody the mobile home was taken apart. The search revealed two handguns, neither of which was registered, but little else, until a vigilant member of the search team noticed an irregularity in the ceiling over the shower. The removal of one of the tiles revealed a hidden compartment concealing an SS ceremonial dagger, which was subsequently proved to have been one of the murder weapons, a membership list of the Action Committee along with a quantity of violently anti-Semitic pamphlets and pornographic photographs.

Broken after prolonged interrogation, Mitchell finally confessed to being present at the murders, but blamed the actual killings on his two confederates. In preparing the State's case, the prosecution pieced together the journey to and from Arkansas through credit card vouchers from petrol stations along the murderers' route. Mitchell's attempt to plea-bargain was refused and all three men ensured the verdicts of guilty by turning on each other.

Just before midnight on the night of the executions, Schmidt took his place with ten other witnesses in the observation booth. A panel of one-way glass allowed them to watch the proceedings in the execution chamber. The observers had been informed that the three men would be terminated at forty-five minute intervals, giving the officials time to carry the body out in a bag, clean the hospital trolley and change the needle before the next man was brought in. Since doctors were forbidden to administer the killing injection there were often difficulties in locating a vein for the catheter through which the sedative, paralytic agent and lethal chemical must flow. Since calculation of the dosage was not an exact science, especially when dealing with condemned men who had drug histories, mishaps were not uncommon.

Unsettled by these revelations, Schmidt braced himself amongst the other witnesses, but immediately after the first man was brought in and strapped to the trolley, he regretted his decision to attend. He had anticipated being present at the carrying out of a calm, judicial sentence that the law and society sanctioned as befitting the crime. Instead, he found himself a voyeur sickened by a tableau which brought to mind experiments on human bodies that, with disturbing irony for this particular case, had been a feature of Nazi Germany. The second man to die needed a venous cutdown before a clean opening could be made and by Schmidt's watch it took twelve minutes before the vein was pierced. The entire procedures overran the estimate by some thirty-seven minutes before Mitchell, the last of the three to die, was pronounced dead at 2.17 a.m.

Afterwards, the shaken witnesses assembled in the Governor's office for a drink. The Governor raised his glass of Jack Daniels. 'To Henry Ford,' he said.

'Henry Ford?' Schmidt queried.

'He invented the production line, didn't he?'

Schmidt downed his drink and left. Outside there was still a small batch of demonstrators kneeling in prayer. As he drove off, he said his own prayer in Hebrew for all the Jews who had taken longer than twelve minutes to die at the hands of their oppressors.

7

ST PETERSBURG AGAIN

'Robert Bartlett,' Hillsden said, reading the name in his new passport. 'Who chose that?'

'Who knows?'

Swanson had a slightly peeved expression and was in a more subdued mood than on their previous meetings.

'Does it really matter what you're called in future?' Swanson asked. 'I would have thought that was the least of your worries.'

'No, probably not, except there used to be a Bartlett in the Firm years ago, that's all. One of the men that fancy old queen Glanville betrayed. Of course they sent a different breed into the field in those days,' he added pointedly.

'We have to have a new photograph taken. They want you to dye your hair a different colour. Shave your beard but leave the moustache. I shall take it with a Polaroid camera.'

'They think age will take care of the rest, do they? I've had a facial before, you know, courtesy of the GRU. Maybe you'll end up employing Dorian Gray,' Hillsden said with glacial humour. 'I hope you take flattering pictures, since it'll probably be my last likeness.' He put his own passport to one side and examined the ones for Galina and his daughter. 'I see they've changed the format while I've been away.'

'Yes, as I warned before a lot of things have changed,' Swanson snapped. 'Most of them at the behest of those overpaid bureaucrats in Brussels.'

'These look a very cheap job compared to the old type, more like driving licences. No longer does Her Britannic Majesty request and require all those whom it may concern to allow me to pass freely. Still, I dare say nobody touches the forelock these days when you present them.' He noted that Galina was now to be known as Georgina Bartlett and their daughter had been renamed Laura.

'They'll have to be rehearsed,' Hillsden said.

'Who will?'

'My wife and daughter. It won't be that easy for them to get used to new names.'

'Have they been told?'

'I've discussed it with my wife, yes. There was no sense in worrying my daughter until everything was agreed. So let's check the rest of my shopping list, shall we? The money. Let's begin with that.'

Swanson laid a document in front of him. 'As requested, a numbered account in Credit Suisse, Geneva, in your wife's new name, so they'll require a specimen signature.'

Hillsden nodded. 'Yes, we'll both have to practise those.' He studied the document closely.

'You'll see that the numbered code they chose is her birthday – seven, three, fifty six – day, month and year – as being the easiest to remember without it being written anywhere.'

'Good idea.' Hillsden looked at the amount and tried to work out if it was correct. Seven years back pay meant over two hundred and forty thousand pounds expressed in Swiss Francs – enough, he calculated, to take care of Galina and Lara if and when he fell or was pushed off the perch.

'Yes, that seems in order. Next thing. Has it been decided where we're to be relocated in England?'

'We chose a small village in Suffolk, near to Bury St Edmunds, and reasonably out of the way.'

'Isolated?'

'Yes, I suppose so, but isn't that a good thing?'

'In one way, but I have to think of my wife.' Now that the

plan was no longer conjecture but becoming reality, a splinter of doubt crept back.

'Assuming we're in business,' Swanson said, searching Hillsden's face, 'the procedure is that once the passports are complete our man at the Embassy here will take care of the exit. You'll fly to Paris, spend a week or so there, during which time all three of you will be provided with pocket money, kitted out with new clothes and various other day-to-day essentials, all British, naturally. Then enter the UK via Heathrow normally, as though a family returning from a holiday in France. What is vital is that, apart from what you stand up in, everything else has to be left here. You must divest yourselves of anything that could be traced back to Russia. Burn all personal papers. The Embassy will dispose of the rest once you've left and our Paris man will get rid of the stuff you arrive in.'

Hillsden took this in. 'Understood. Fine. Except for one thing.'

Swanson frowned. 'What?'

'The small question of my pardon.'

'Oh, that, yes.'

'That, yes. Where is it?'

'I can confirm it's in hand,' Swanson said, looking away. 'These things take time.'

Hillsden shook his head. 'Not good enough. I spelled it out for you. No pardon, no deal.'

'They're waiting for the Home Secretary to approve the wording. The latest information I have is it will be signed and given to you in Paris.'

Again Hillsden shook his head. 'No way. I want it here before we leave. Get back to them and tell them they're wasting their time.'

'I'll do what I can,' Swanson said.

'No, do better than that. Get it here or forget the whole deal. Another question, has anybody given any thought to how our disappearance from here will be explained? Although I only have one contact worth bothering about, Galina has a number of friends at the university who'll notice she's gone.'

'I don't see that as a problem. You've moved to France leaving no forwarding address. Who is this contact of yours?'

'Oh, come on, Swanson, you know my file. His name's Abramov, ex-high-ranking GRU, the man who handled me when I first arrived. I guess you might say he's been my only friend. We shared a lot.'

'So? He can be told the same story,' Swanson said.

'He might not believe it.'

'Then don't tell him, just disappear.'

'That would be a mistake. You don't know my man as well as I do. A disappearance would make him suspicious, he'd follow it through. Not for any sinister motive either, just habit. You'll find this difficult to believe, Swanson, but he cares about me. We drank from the same cup, you see. Since the *coup* he's become a high-flyer, moves around a lot, dresses rather smarter than you as a matter of fact. And he was never a man you could fool for long.'

'Except that at one time you did.'

'Ah, yes,' Hillsden said, 'but then, it was life and death in those days. I didn't arrive here with a Business Class return ticket like you. It wouldn't do to disappear without saying goodbye. But leave my friend Victor to me, I'll deal with it.'

Swanson looked dubious. 'I'll have to get clearance on that. There can be no question of telling him the truth.'

Hillsden said, 'Do either of us know what that is any more? And for your information, how I tell him and what I tell him is my business.'

'This is a delicate operation. If there was any leak, the whole thing would be called off. You can't want to risk that.'

'You think risk vanishes because one shaves off a beard and moves house? You've got a lot to learn. Take-offs and landings are the moments of maximum danger, any experienced traveller knows that. Don't try and get clearance, Swanson, just stay on the ground. As you say, a delicate operation. Ask London for clearance and if anything goes wrong, your card will be marked, you'll take the can back. A promising career blighted.'

Swanson stared at him, his cheeks suddenly mottled, like a schoolboy reprimanded by the head. 'Well, I realise I lack your superior experience, but don't ever forget who's running this show.'

'My superior experience wasn't much use when the Firm decided to shaft me. I want sight of that pardon so that Galina can lodge it in her Swiss bank. Otherwise your journey was wasted.'

Swanson looked as though he was searching for a suitable, face-saving rejoinder, then thought better of it.

When Swanson left and while he waited for Galina and Lara to return from a shopping expedition, Hillsden took stock. Looking around the apartment he saw, as though for the first time, how dingy it was. At the same time it had the comfortable dinginess of familiarity and he acknowledged that part of him would miss it. One stupendous error, one blind act of belief, a belief that he needed to repay a debt of love, had altered the course of his life and brought him to this alien city, and now he was about to leave it to journey back to a place he had once counted as home. He wondered how Galina would react to their changed circumstances. Suffolk, he thought, trying to picture what it would be like. Was it flat like Norfolk and the black fen country where once he had cornered Glanville? Had they selected a picturesque cottage of a sort photographed from the best angle for *Country Life,* or one of those hideous, nondescript post-war red brick horrors with their cramped metal windows and poky rooms? He wasn't so concerned about Lara (*Laura,* I must start getting used to that) – children adapted more easily and he could picture her in the playground of some village school amongst new friends. As for Galina – correction, *Georgina* – undoubtedly she would find it more difficult, especially if I'm not around all the time, he thought. The British were curious about foreigners, never really tolerant towards anything that was outside their immediate comprehension, condescending, addressing them in louder-than-normal voices as though in addition to being foreign they were also deaf. On the credit side he would now be able to give *Georgina* (God! that would never have been his choice) some of the luxuries she had always been denied: she would get a kick out of the promised week in Paris – hotel rooms, abundant hot water – and he would enjoy showing them both around, introducing them to the uniqueness of Paris, a relief from the grimness of Russian streets. He suddenly felt light-headed, and the mood stayed with him as he went through the apartment and for the second time in his life began the task of destroying traces of his old self.

8

WUNSIEDEL, GERMANY – LONDON

A few days after Swanson returned to London, a procession of young far-Right skinheads, estimated by the police to number three hundred, and distinguished from the Red skinheads by the white laces in their Doc Marten boots, marched through the narrow streets of Wunsiedel, a small town not far from Bayreuth.

The burial place of Rudolf Hess, Wunsiedel now attracted a flow of pilgrims from the radical Right. This day, the procession, headed by standard bearers carrying banners honouring Hess as a martyr for Germany, was the object of a counter-demonstration by elements of the anti-Fascist organisation, Antifa. White-helmeted police walked alongside, keeping the two groups apart, while a police helicopter hovered overhead. Most of the Hitler disciples wore a quasi-uniform – black or brown shirts, heavy, studded belts. From time to time some of them left the procession to attack the Antifa supporters. The ensuing scuffles were quickly broken up by the police, although, surprisingly, no arrests were made. Groups of elderly local inhabitants watched with mixed feelings, as the evocative chants of 'Fatherland, we are coming' were repeated over and over again. Press photographers ran alongside; one, a British freelance journalist named O'Neill, had his Nikon knocked to the ground and, as he bent to retrieve it, he was kicked in the head, but again his assailant was not arrested, but merely pushed back into the procession. The marchers finally halted and assembled in the town square, where they were addressed by a man later identified as Gottfried Sonntag, a one-time native of East Berlin, author of *Das Zweites Deutschland (The Second Germany)* and a spokesman for the *Hilfsorganisation für Nationale Politische Gefangene und deren Angehörige e. V. (Relief Agency for National Political Prisoners and their Dependants).* Unlike his audience, Sonntag was dressed in a smart suit and had a conventional haircut. Using a megaphone to drown out the noise of the helicopter, he launched into a denunciation of the authorities, his voice often shrill and incoherent with hatred.

'The rabble who have come to mock this homage to a great patriot and peace-lover, who once stood side by side with the Führer, have renounced their German consciousness. This collection of two-legged rats shelters under the protection of the police, since, like rats, they are scared to meet us one on one. We, who are proud to display our pure Aryan blood and affirm our German stock, will one day sweep these vermin from our streets. We think of them as devils from the deepest hell conjured by Dürer. They will be left behind when we are the only rulers, marching into the future under the flag which will lead us to the end of time . . . '

His speech was punctuated by frequent outbursts of cheering and the waving of banners, while the counter-demonstrators kept up a constant barrage of taunts. The police maintained a passive role, positioned at the rear of the assembly keeping the opposing factions apart.

After the meeting ended, small groups of skinheads separated themselves from the main body, acting on a pre-arranged plan designed to put the police at full stretch, and roamed the streets looking for trouble, openly declaring their intention of 'fucking up some niggers'.

Coming across a lone foreign worker, a nineteen-year-old Kurd, they attacked him with baseball bats, stabbed him and jumped on his head. He was left lying in a pool of blood in the street a few yards from the immigrant hostel where he lodged. It was only when the skinheads had disappeared from the scene that the victim's friends, who had witnessed the beating, ventured from the hostel to recover his body. When the police and ambulance finally arrived the young Kurd was pronounced dead. Later the witnesses could only positively identify one of the attackers. Brought before the courts, the accused skinhead, the same age as the dead man, was arraigned on the lesser charge of 'second-degree murder with qualified criminal intent', his lawyer successfully pleading, as grounds for the qualification, the extraordinary defence that 'the victim's skin colour significantly contributed to the crime'.

The court accepted this and the accused youth was given a cursory sentence of five years detention in a reformatory.

Although the incident aroused little comment beyond a few regional newspapers, a monitoring unit in Copenhagen staffed by members of Amnesty logged a report broadcast on a German radio station. Sonntag's name was included in the report. In due course, along with details of other atrocities perpetrated on ethnic minorities, this was circulated in one of Amnesty's regular bulletins and, via Interpol, reached Special Branch in London, since Sonntag's movements and activities were already of interest to police forces in several European countries. The British Home Office had twice refused him entry to the United Kingdom, though on at least one occasion, using a false passport, he had managed to slip in to address a meeting of The British Movement in Wolverhampton. It was one of a number of similar incidents brought to the Home Secretary's notice in a lengthy study commissioned by the European Parliament on the plight of ethnic minorities and the growing resurgence of Fascist organisations.

Having been briefed on this and other matters, Logan chaired the regular monthly meeting of the Combined Security Committee, a homogenous collection which took in elements of MI5 and MI6, including Swanson and a Commander Pearson, together with the RUC, the SAS, the GPO Letter and Telephone Interception units, as well as the

Commissioner of the Metropolitan Police. Sir Charles Slade was also in attendance.

Logan entered the committee room without a greeting to those present, sat in the centre of the long table and poured himself some coffee from one of the Thermos flasks placed at intervals along the table. His bad mood stemmed from a hangover and his wife's revelation at breakfast that she believed their teenage son was on drugs.

'Right,' he said. 'I take it the minutes of the last meeting have been circulated? May I sign them as correct?'

There was a murmur of assent.

'Matters arising?'

'Item seven,' the Secretary prompted. Everybody turned to the page. 'The question of protection for the minor Royals.'

Logan looked up at the Commissioner. 'Hasn't that been dealt with yet?'

'Not entirely, Minister.'

'Well, either it has or it hasn't. Which is it?'

'We have a meeting at the Palace scheduled for next Tuesday. It's a question of striking a delicate balance between available manpower and cost. As you're aware, Minister, there's continuing hysteria in the tabloids on this subject.'

'Well, you know my views. In the present climate I consider there are better ways of spending public money. I doubt if any of them are in any danger, unless they act true to form and shoot themselves in the foot.' Logan sipped his coffee and grimaced. 'Who buys this stuff?'

'Central Requisitions, sir.'

'Well, it's filthy. In future we'll buy our own. I'll tell you where to go. There's a wonderful little place in Soho.' He pushed his cup to one side. 'Right, let's take the rest of the agenda. Ignore the first item for the moment and go to item two. Which department requested we should put a phone tap on this man Attenborough? Why would we tap a distinguished actor?'

'No, it isn't him, sir. Not Lord Attenborough. Our man is a northern industrialist, owns a machine tool factory.'

'I see. Well, I'll repeat the question, who requested it?'

'We did, Minister,' Commander Pearson answered.

Logan looked down the table to the speaker. 'Why?'

'We were approached by the Yanks to aid them in an investigation.'

'You mean the CIA?'

'Yes, Minister'

'Well, say so. What were the grounds?'

'They suspect he could have a connection with the supply of detonators of a type used in the Oklahoma bombing.'

Logan stared around the table. 'So we jump, do we, every time the Yanks want us to fish in our waters?'

'I don't think that's quite the position in this case, Minister,' Slade murmured when Pearson looked across the table to him.

'No? What is the position then?'

'They think they have reasonable cause to make the request.' Slade produced documentation. 'As you will note, he was previously questioned during the investigation into the Iraqi super-gun case.'

Logan scanned the document. 'Questioned, but not charged, I see.'

'No, sir. At the time, you recall, there were certain irregularities in the procedures.'

'A cock-up, you mean? Well, let's be clear about one thing, shall we? You won't find me as easy to persuade as my predecessor. While I'm sitting in this chair phone taps will only be authorised on grounds of proven national security. And I'm certainly not going to be dictated to by the Americans. I don't consider this application falls within that category. Refused. Item three.'

A few looks were exchanged before they moved on. Logan prided himself in demolishing an agenda quicker than some of his Cabinet colleagues. He was constantly sending his department reminders to keep the paperwork down and their memoranda as concise and brief as possible. This didn't apply to his own verbose papers, which were often collectors' items. He worked through the rest of the agenda and set the date of the next month's meeting.

Swanson gave a discreet cough. 'We still haven't dealt with item one, Minister.'

'I'm aware of that. I wish to take that in a more closed session. If you and Commander Pearson and the Commissioner would care to remain. Thank you, gentlemen,' he nodded to the others, who gathered up their papers and left. Sir Charles remained where he was.

'Now,' Logan began once the door had closed, 'this other business. What's the man's name?'

'Hillsden,' Swanson answered.

'Yes, well I've studied the papers very thoroughly and I have grave misgivings. You'll have to make out a very strong case to convince me. The man is a defector and wanted for murder.'

'I think if it ever came to trial, Minister, we'd all be very embarrassed.'

'In what way?'

'Evidence which came to light subsequently would lead us to believe that he was innocent of both charges.' Swanson produced a document from his briefcase and passed it across. 'Because of the nature of the material I thought this should be for your eyes only.'

Logan took the document and began to read. The other three men waited. Finally Logan looked up. 'This reference to Hillsden's memoirs. Were they ever authenticated?'

'They were instrumental in exposing Lockfield,' Swanson answered.

'Remind me. Was he the ex-Director General of MI6 who topped himself?'

'Yes.'

'Your section has always had a murky past,' Logan said testily, 'let's hope we're not subjected to any repeat performances. From this sordid little history, which reflects no credit on anybody, your lot seem to have been penetrated more times than a whore. I'm amazed you don't have a permanent plumber on the staff to plug the leaks. What makes you think this man Hillsden is now reliable? If he was wrongly accused all those years ago, he must be harbouring a considerable resentment.'

'I think that was true, Minister.'

'Why "was"?'

'I interviewed him on a number of occasions in St Petersburg and gained the firm impression that he could be appeased by the offer we're making him.'

'Money doesn't buy loyalty. I would have thought your outfit would have learned that by now.'

'Agreed, Minister. But the terms reflect a legitimate entitlement. If he chose to fight it in court a jury might well treble the damages in view of what he has suffered.'

'We could block anything like that under the Official Secrets Act,' Logan snapped.

'Not if he stayed beyond our jurisdiction.'

'Well, I don't like it. I'm being asked to give him a *carte blanche* pardon. What if it all blows up in our faces? The last thing I want is another security scandal. Let's be quite clear, this government is not going to be made to look incompetent like the Tories were. Let me ask you this, why risk somebody like Hillsden? Why take such a chance?'

It was Pearson who now took over. 'It was felt that if we are to infiltrate this organisation, Hillsden is one of the few, if not the only operative with the necessary field experience to undertake something as delicate as this. You will have noted that we intend to give him a new identity, but, more importantly, because he has been out of circulation over a long period he will have the added advantage of being an unknown quantity. I might add that prior to his incarceration in Russia he was considered one of our top operatives.'

Logan opened the document file again and stared at it afresh before turning to the Commissioner. 'What's your view?'

'Well, I agree, sir. I've studied the papers, as has the DPP and we're both convinced the murder prosecution wouldn't stand up in court. The case was based almost entirely on Lockfield's evidence. The word of a dead traitor would be demolished by any competent defence lawyer. Plus it would inevitably mean washing a lot of dirty linen.'

'Who took over from Lockfield?'

'Keating, Minister.'

'Did you get his views?'

Swanson coughed again. 'That would be somewhat difficult, Minister. He died of a heart attack some years ago.'

Logan tapped on the table, then got up and walked to the window, his back to them, 'So, what you're actually saying is that your department, despite its inflated budget, can't put its hands on any other suitable candidate? I'm still waiting for you to advance a compelling reason why I should rubber stamp this man.'

Swanson looked at the other two before answering. 'If I might say so, I think you've already answered the question yourself, Minister. It would be a disaster for the government to risk a security scandal so early in its term. We know Hillsden is an angry man – this way we buy his silence and at the same time avail ourselves of his considerable expertise. Obviously, we *could* use somebody else, but this kills two birds with one stone.'

There was a long pause before Logan spoke again. 'Has he accepted all the terms and conditions?'

'Subject to your final word, yes.'

'It'll have to come under the fifty-year rule, of course,' Logan said as he returned to the table. He felt inside his jacket pocket but before he could produce his own pen, Sir Charles handed him his.

'I'd like you to minute my misgivings, Charles. I won't say I'm signing under duress, but I remain dubious about the whole operation. There's a lot that could go wrong. *Should* it go wrong quite a few people will be staring at early retirement. Perhaps you'll bear that in mind, gentlemen.' He unscrewed the top of the pen and signed the document that Swanson now slid in front of him.

'Thank you, Minister.'

'I expect to be kept fully informed.' He emphasised the

word 'fully' and laid down the pen. With Sir Charles following, he left the room without another word, leaving behind an air of disapproval as pungent as stale cigar smoke.

'Finally,' the Commissioner said. 'I must say there are times when early retirement doesn't sound all that unattractive.'

Swanson gathered his papers together. 'Join the club.'

'Now all we have to do is get him home,' Pearson said.

9

CLOSE ENCOUNTERS – ST PETERSBURG

'Why tell me?' Abramov asked. His face was half in shadow, making it difficult for Hillsden to judge his expression.

'Because I trust you, Victor, and because I need an insurance policy. I thought if you kept a copy of the pardon and they ever reneged on the deal, you could make it public. For all I know it's just a trick to get me back within their jurisdiction, and then spring the trap. It's happened before, as you have good cause to know.'

They were sitting in Abramov's new Mercedes coupé, parked in a side street on the outskirts of the city. Abramov switched on the interior light to study the piece of paper he had been given. 'What an Alice-in-Disneyland world we live in, Alec. Such a generous favour they're granting you – forgiveness for a murder they committed and blamed you for. That's more Russian than British! You're right to be suspicious.'

Sitting there beside him as Abramov extinguished the light, Hillsden had a sudden feeling of *déjà vu*. 'Doesn't this remind you of something?' he said.

'Remind me? What of?'

'Moscow, that time in Gorky Park? We sat together in a car then, admittedly an inferior model, and you asked something of me. You can't have forgotten, surely?'

'Alec, my friend, we don't talk of those days any more, or the things we had to do.'

'You might not talk of them, but I don't forget them.'

Abramov shrugged and adjusted the heater fan to clear the windscreen. Hillsden leaned forward and before the efficient demister had time to work he wrote the word 'Jock' on the steamed glass. 'Does that bring it back? You used that ploy when you revealed the last piece in the puzzle, remember? That's how you finally told me who was responsible for Caroline's death.'

'Did I? What a memory you've got, Alec.'

'Should I forget that I killed a man who had once been my friend? That was what you demanded of me in return, the quid pro quo, a murder I *could* have swung for.'

'Ah, Alec, my friend, at that time we were both condemned to play out the same cynical game.' He added something in Russian – an oath, a curse? – that was unfamiliar to Hillsden. 'We had no choice. What had to be done, had to be done.'

'Meaning, you had got used to it?'

'Used to what?'

'Murder.'

Abramov brushed some ash from the lapel of his jacket. 'I obeyed orders.'

'That's what they said at Nuremberg.'

'Semantics, Alec. You have no real idea what it was like to live under our old regime. You saw only the tip of the iceberg in the dying years. But I was born under it, grew up under it and never for one moment could I ignore it. The only way to survive was to accept everything without question.'

'Everything?'

'You want a confession from me? Let me tell you something that I've never told anybody before.' He paused to light a cigarette, staring straight ahead as he exhaled the first intake of smoke. 'I turned in my brother, my younger brother.'

'How d'you mean?'

'What I say. I reported him to the authorities for distributing subversive literature. Why? Because it was him or me. I could have been tarred with his crime if I hadn't. That's how they operated. Collective guilt. One member of a family was guilty, all of the family was guilty. You're a well-read man, Alec, so you know the way people disappeared without trace into the Gulags. Millions. Labour camps for homosexuals, the old, the mentally sick, the dissidents. My brother was homosexual, very pretty – he could have passed for a girl. Pretty and arrogant like so many of the people he kept company with. No, perhaps "arrogant" is the wrong word, unfair to his memory. He thought he was smart enough to beat the system, and he wasn't, nobody was, not even Beria himself.' He stubbed out the rest of the cigarette, as though the acrid taste accentuated these memories. 'I loved him, but I suppose I did not love him enough. I loved myself more. So don't think you're the only one with something to haunt you. What did you do? You disposed of a useless individual – your friend Jock was a drunken, burnt-out case, somebody who had killed many times, not only your Caroline, but others, half a dozen others – he isn't worth losing sleep over. You did everybody a service.'

'Except myself,' Hillsden said. He did not speak for a few moments, then asked: 'What happened to your brother?'

'I don't know. I never saw him again.'

'But you were safe?'

'Safe? No, it didn't work like that. I was still tainted by association, under suspicion, watched all the time. I had to work extra hard to establish my reliability. You helped my rehabilitation. Turning you was a feather in my cap.'

He took out his gold cigarette case again, this time offering Hillsden one and lighting it for him. 'Go home by all means, Alec, but forget the past. Of course I'll take care of this for you, you know that. I'm offended you ever doubted me.'

He smiled and patted Hillsden on the thigh, but Hillsden was still digesting what he had just been told. As he jolted his lungs with a shot of nicotine he felt bile at the back of his throat. It was a long trail they had both travelled to a dead end. Future generations would study the KGB's and the Firm's Dead Sea Scrolls of betrayals and be stupefied, not only at the horrors revealed, but the sheer futility of it all. The meek never inherited the earth – that was just a sop hawked by the Jesus salesmen – the real world was run by men who looked like janitors in a tenement block: no casting director would have given Stalin a leading role other than as a small-time thug; the hideous Ceausescu and his wife were bit players in a Hammer movie; Lenin, only fit for playing the town schoolmaster who molested children; Honecker, perfect for a grubby little pimp. The list was endless – Dzerzhinsky, Himmler, Beria, Idi Amin, Papa Doc – how did they achieve and hang on to power for so long, all these squalid nonentities who kept whole countries in chains, the rest of the world on edge? It was as if some mad scientist had produced a race of mutants and programmed them to be leaders, having first removed the compassion factor and substituted a quartz-driven mechanism of terror.

'Wasn't there ever a moment when you questioned what you were doing?' he asked. 'In the still, small hours of the night, when you weren't wearing the uniform, what thoughts did you have?'

'One had night thoughts, yes. Bad dreams, very bad dreams. But, you see, when you woke up there was no door you could open which led out. You in the West have never known that. There was always an escape route for you. Isn't that true?'

Hillsden nodded. 'You're right. We always took the high moral ground. Officially, we were incapable of acting in the same way as you. Crap, of course. All prisons have to have warders. Had the Nazis conquered us in '40, we'd have produced our own crop of gauleiters, depend on it. It was just that we were never put to the test. Look at the French, it's only now that they are acknowledging some of their skeletons. And we weren't as white as the driven snow. We arrested and interned without trial.'

'I didn't know that.'

'Oh, yes. We had something called regulation 18b . . . Isn't it funny how all such laws hide behind numbers?'

'But you didn't have a deliberate policy of killing your own people.'

Hillsden said, 'Oh, we didn't shoot them and bury them in mass graves, we just shortened their lives in other ways.'

While he talked he fiddled with the glove compartment. It sprang open to reveal a revolver clipped to the shelf. He took it out to examine it.

'I see you don't leave anything to chance, Victor.'

'Not the way things are here.'

'Perhaps you should leave as well?'

'In time, in time maybe, when I've made enough.'

He took the gun from Hillsden and checked the magazine. 'People like us, Alec, who led double lives . . . what d'you think now? You have regrets? I sense you do.'

'More a feeling of waste. There must have been a moment – maybe it was, I don't know, Yalta perhaps – when three old men, one near death in a wheelchair, one exhausted and the third a certified monster – and between them they fucked up. All the effort, all the millions of dead, the bombed cities, for what? There was that moment when they could have changed it all, but instead they condemned us to another forty years of horror. You were fooled, I was fooled, the madness went on in a different form. The wealth that could have transformed the world spent on the ultimate weapon.'

'Which kept the peace,' Abramov interrupted.

'What peace? The killing didn't stop.'

'All the same, Alec, we're still here.'

'And a new monster waiting in the wings.'

'Of course, what else do you expect?' Abramov said, placing the gun on the top of the dashboard. 'Remember that story we all told? If the bomb wiped out the world and there were only a hundred people left alive, within twenty-four hours somebody would have appointed himself leader and claimed privileges.' He stroked the soft leather upholstery. 'Of course, if you're still undecided, then stay here, join forces with me and you could be driving one of these babies. It's all here for the taking. Make clay while the sun shines.'

'Hay,' Hillsden corrected. 'Make hay. You always did get those things wrong.' There was a fug of cigarette smoke in the car and he pressed the switch to let down the window on his side.

'Whatever. Listen, have you any idea of the opportunities out there? Give you an example. Yesterday, I did a deal with an ex-nuclear physicist for a truckload of Levis. A year ago he was running a whole plant in the Ukraine, now he's happy to take ten per cent on black-market jeans, no questions asked. I'll have off-loaded the entire lot by the end of the week and made myself another Mercedes. That's the only game in town, Alec.'

'What about protection?'

'What about it?'

'Do you have to pay?'

Abramov smiled. 'Put it this way. I didn't sever all contacts with my past. Memories are long here, Alec, and nobody's quite sure that the old order is completely dead and buried. I have my own protection – files I smuggled out ahead of the mob, safely hidden, as will be the insurance policy you've just given me.'

He turned the ignition key. 'Don't you just love the noise of that engine? I used to dream of owning one of these.'

'I've never cared much for cars,' Hillsden said. 'Except as a means of getting from one place to another.'

'That's because you've always had a choice.'

'Probably.'

'You said yourself you're not sure of London's true motive. So what is yours?'

'That's a good question. Maybe I don't have one beyond a homing instinct.'

'How about your wife, how does she feel?'

'Perhaps she's the reverse of what you told me. Maybe, like your brother, she loves me more than she loves herself . . . And that's ironic in a way. It was love that brought me here in the first place. Love's always a risk, isn't it?'

'So they tell me. I wouldn't know. Emotional involvements get in the way, I've found.'

He was just about to put the Mercedes into gear when two shadowy figures appeared on either side of the car. Abramov

Yorkshire, travelled everywhere in the company's private jet (which included a Maxwellian device he had purloined from the late Captain Bob, namely a switch above his seat that enabled him to bypass his pilot and speak directly to air traffic controllers, berating them if he was kept in a holding pattern for too long). But so far his wealth had not bought him the total social acceptance he craved.

Ignoring the hotel commissionaire who stepped forward, he was saluted by the doorman at the adjacent Ritz Casino. As a frequent visitor to the tables he was a welcome high-roller and treated with the staff's customary courtesy. Signing in downstairs he first looked to see whether the gambling salon was busy before going to the cloakroom. He had a fetish about cleanliness, often showering three times a day, and now he scrubbed his hands after relieving himself and applied some Dunhill cologne to his face. The cloakroom attendant brushed his jacket and was rewarded with a five-pound tip.

Charters entered the salon and was annoyed to find that the table he normally played was occupied by a group of foreign gamblers. One of the assistant managers came forward to greet him and offered to open another table for him. Charters accepted with ill grace and asked to be given twenty thousand pounds. He changed one of the five-thousand pound lozenges into hundred pound chips, and began playing, using a system that allegedly had been Winston Churchill's – betting on alternate spins of the wheel and then placing a maximum neighbour bet on the last but one winning number. Like most systems it was fallible, but Charters used it religiously and he won sufficiently often not to lose faith in it.

This was not to be one of his successful nights. After one win early in the session, he lost steadily, going through his first twenty thousand and calling for a further twenty, signing the cheque brought to him with a scrawl. A senior manager appeared to keep a watching brief and when other less affluent players drifted in from the dining room, they were tactfully diverted to other tables. When Charters was down to a few thousand, he switched from his favoured system and began to back single numbers *en plein* with maximum bets. He struck lucky once, then went cold again. He got up abruptly, scattering his remaining chips. 'Cash me in.' He flung the words at the cashier.

While waiting for his money, he wandered to the next table and there, like many an unsuccessful gambler, he could not resist a final bet, placing a hundred pounds cash bet on his favourite number, twenty three. It lost. The manager appeared by his side and Charters pocketed the six sealed packets of brand-new notes for his cashed chips and walked out without a word. Win or lose he was always the same, showing neither pleasure nor annoyance, for he prided himself on never letting anybody know his true feelings.

His taxi was waiting outside and Harry, his driver, was the recipient of his ill-humour. 'D'you know a club called Tudor's?' Charters snapped.

'Yes, sir. Greek Street.'

'Your style, no doubt. Well, take me there.'

They set off in the direction of Hyde Park Corner.

'Not that way, you stupid oaf. Make a U-turn. I haven't got all night.'

Harry complied. He had been on call without a break since ten o'clock that morning, but Charters's staff were expected to suffer such inconveniences without complaint.

The amplified sound hit Charters like a wall. There were three couples clinging to each other on Tudor's small dance floor. When his eyes had become accustomed to the darkness he made his way to a table in a corner where a man called Carstairs, middle-aged, of nondescript appearance, rose to greet him as he approached.

'Good evening, Sir Raymond.'

There was something more than servility in his voice, something approaching fear.

The owner of the club came up. 'This is a great pleasure, Sir Raymond. Are we eating tonight, sir? Can I send a waitress?'

'Yes, do that.'

'Something to drink meantime?'

'A bottle of Chablis, if it's really chilled.'

'Of course, Sir Raymond. Right away.'

Charters eyed the couples on the floor, picking out an American actress who had once achieved a certain notoriety in a long-running sit-com. She was dancing with a long-haired youth half her age who looked more feminine than she did.

'I used to follow her series,' Carstairs said, seeing Charters studying the couple.

'Mutton dressed as lamb.'

'Oh, do you think so? I'd say she's worn rather well.'

'In this light, maybe. I wouldn't fancy waking up and finding it on my pillow.'

A waitress arrived with the drinks at this point. She was wearing a scanty Tudor-style dress which revealed a lot of cleavage. When she had opened the wine and Charters had sampled it without comment, just a nod of the head, she waited for the meal order.

'Bring me a plate of smoked salmon and scrambled eggs. I want the salmon cut wafer thin and the eggs runny.'

'And for you, sir?'

'Nothing, thank you,' Carstairs said. He was drinking whisky. When the waitress left he raised his glass to Charters, but the toast was ignored. There was a certain sad seediness about Carstairs – flecks of dandruff on the shoulders of his blue suit, a creased shirt collar.

'So, what did you want to see me about so urgently?'

Carstairs framed his reply carefully. 'Well, we've run into a slight problem, sir.' His hand clutching the whisky glass had nails bitten to the quick.

'What sort of problem?'

Although there was no need, given the loud music, Carstairs lowered his voice. 'Nothing that can't be speedily rectified, sir, but I thought it best to bring it to your personal attention.'

'What sort of problem?' Charters repeated.

'Well, unfortunately the consignment of Sonntag's book

was seized at Harwich.'

'You call that slight? Why was it ever sent to Harwich? I gave orders for it to be flown in at night to the usual drop.'

'Yes, I agree, sir. Somehow, your instructions were not relayed to the right person. An unfortunate misunderstanding. By the time I discovered what had happened the shipment was already *en route*.' Carstairs took a large gulp of Scotch.

'Who made the mistake?'

'Van Elst. Usually so reliable.'

'Can they be traced to us?'

'Oh, no, sir. They were documented as fax rolls and the shipper's name was false. I ordered another print-run immediately.'

'Well, cancel it. Have them put the text on disc and brought over by courier. Better still, bring it yourself.'

Some of the Scotch dribbled down Carstairs's chin. 'Me?'

'Yes. And get it here by Monday.'

'I don't think that's possible.'

'Make it possible. And find out who leaked it.'

The hapless Carstairs made an attempt to defend himself. 'I'd be amazed if it was a leak, sir. More Customs being unusually vigilant in my opinion.'

'I'm not interested in your opinion. Somebody must have tipped them off. Who? I want to know.'

'I have the utmost trust in everybody.'

'That's where you're a fool,' Charters said. He broke off as his food was served, waiting until it was placed in front of him before continuing. 'You think I trust you? I trust you until a mistake like this, then I start to ask whether that trust is misplaced.'

'You've no reason to doubt me,' Carstairs said. He looked around the dance floor as though expecting someone to challenge the statement. The actress and her young boyfriend drifted close, kissing each other and trailing a heady perfume.

'Don't depend on it,' Charters said. 'There's no room for mistakes in our operation.' He forked some scrambled eggs

88

into his mouth, grimaced and pushed the plate to one side. 'Put this right or your days are numbered. And another time, don't drag me to a place like this even for good news. Just deal with the problem and deal with it fast. I want that disc here Monday first thing.' He got up abruptly and pushed his way across the dance floor, bumping into a couple. Concerned at seeing him leave so abruptly, the club owner stopped him on the way out.

'Leaving so soon? Nothing wrong I hope, Sir Raymond?'

'No, everything's fine,' Charters said without stopping. The owner went over to Carstairs.

'Was there a problem with Sir Raymond's food?'

'No, nothing like that, it was just that he was late for another meeting,' Carstairs answered, but there was no conviction in his voice.

'Can we bring you another drink?'

'No, thank you. I have to be going myself.' He waited for the bill and settled it with cash, and was halfway to the door when he went back and picked up the receipt.

Outside in the street he looked both ways before walking to Soho Square where he had parked his car. He sat behind the steering wheel for several minutes, trying to stifle a rising nausea. Then he opened the door and vomited into the gutter.

11

HOMECOMING

Swanson met them in Heathrow's Terminal 4 arrivals hall, wearing his peeved expression – presumably, Hillsden thought, to signify that such a menial assignment was beneath him.

They had passed through passport control without incident, although, approaching the desk, Hillsden had felt suddenly naked without his beard.

Greeting them abruptly with, 'Heathrow is a nightmare,' Swanson shepherded them across the road to the car park. 'It's about time they scrapped the lot and began again.' He led them to a black Ford Mondeo. A much younger man who was seated behind the wheel got out as they arrived and opened the boot to take their hand luggage. He nodded at Hillsden, but said nothing by way of greeting.

'This is Hadley,' Swanson said. 'One of the team. He's driving you part of the way. I'll contact you once you've settled in. No snags, I hope?'

'No,' Hillsden said. 'I'm just getting used to the smell again.'

'What smell?'

'England.'

After helping Galina and Lara into the rear seats, Hillsden climbed in the front. As Hadley reversed out he saw Swanson walk to a Jaguar saloon.

'We don't rate a Jag, I see,' Hillsden said, breaking the ice with the silent Hadley.

'No. There's only one in the car pool and Swanson claims it as his own. Anyway, this is less conspicuous.'

'It's odd for me, sitting on this side.'

'How's that?'

'Driving on the left again.'

'Oh, I see. Yes, of course.'

Once clear of the airport they crawled towards London, negotiating the snaking avenues of cones that transformed the M4 into an assault course for formula one drivers.

The new clothes Hillsden had been provided with in Paris still felt stiff, reminding him of the one time, aeons ago, when he had taken part in some amateur theatricals (a now almost-forgotten play, *The Passing of the Third Floor Back*). On that occasion, forced to wear a hired suit reeking of cleaning fluid, he had experienced the same feeling of being detached from his normal self. Sitting in the front passenger seat, he fingered his now soft, beardless chin as though that, too, belonged to a stranger. It was curious, he thought, but when you shaved off a beard the revealed skin looked as though you had lived for a period under a stone.

'Where are we heading for?' he asked.

'Ultimately, Suffolk.'

'Yes, I know that, but where in Suffolk?'

'A place called Walsham le Willows.'

Hillsden repeated the name. 'Never heard of it, but it sounds romantic.' He swivelled to look at his wife. 'Hear that, sweetheart?'

'It's just a small village,' Hadley said.

'Swanson didn't really introduce us, did he?'

'No, he's not given to politeness.'

'But it's Hadley, is it?'

'Yes.'

'How long have you been with the Firm?'

'Seven years.'

'As long as I've been away,' Hillsden said. He felt suddenly elated, like somebody waking after a long illness to find himself recovered, taking in every passing scene, anxious not to miss anything. At intervals they passed signs informing road users that 'Construction Operatives Are At Work'.

'What do they signify?'

'Oh, that's the new, politically correct term for what used to be called "navvies"' Hadley replied.

'Where are they? Can't see any.'

'No, that's another innovation, you'll find. Nearly every road in the country is under repair, but nobody actually mends them, they just put out lots of cones.'

Hillsden turned to see if Galina and Lara were sharing his excitement. His daughter was wide-eyed, taking in her first glimpses of a landscape that had hitherto only been a name in a school textbook, but Galina seemed withdrawn.

'Okay, darling?' he asked.

Galina nodded. During the week they had spent in Paris, Hillsden had urged her to spoil herself with hair and beauty treatments, a luxury she had been denied for years. Looking at her he thought how much he loved her, suddenly conscious of the sacrifice she had made for his sake. I'm home, he thought, but she's homeless.

When they finally reached the Hammersmith flyover Hillsden looked for known landmarks, but he recognised little except the old Victorian church standing in the Broadway island. Now it was surrounded and dwarfed by new office blocks, on one side a gaunt pink monolith and on the other an extraordinary bulbous, glass structure.

'What the hell's that?'

'It's called the Ark, it apparently slipped through without Prince Charles noticing.' The comment went over Hillsden's head.

'Like the Bible?' Lara chirped, head poking between the two front seats. 'Are there animals in it?' But Hadley had to brake sharply and did not respond.

More roadworks slowed their progress again. Examples of graffiti were everywhere: faded exhortations to *Ban Trident* which recalled memories of the once annual march from Aldermaston – how remote that moral gesture now seemed,

Hillsden thought. Further along a humorist had been at work, modifying *God so loved the world He gave His only Son* to *He gave His only Sony.* A group of winos sprawled on a thin patch of grass by the roadside, passing each other a shared bottle, mirroring the derelicts Hillsden had left behind in St Petersburg, while above them revolving hoardings advertised aspects of a life style they would never know. At the traffic lights Hadley waved away a youth with a Mohican haircut who attempted to wash the windscreen. The youth thumped his annoyance on a side panel as he went to the next car.

Progressing towards Knightsbridge, they entered the world of anonymous hotels: once elegant town houses now displayed torn signs on their flaking porticoes: *Room for the Night £25, Vacancies, Open 24 Hours.* Further down the Brompton Road, outside the modern hospital, elderly Arab men wearing slippers shuffled along the pavement, their veiled wives a few, dutiful paces behind. Watching the flow of pedestrians as they passed Harrods, it seemed to Hillsden that the majority of young girls had opted to dress as medieval troubadours, wearing abbreviated tunics over thick black tights that accentuated their arses, their tights ending in heavy boots that had once been the hallmark of Teddy Boys, as though they were determined to obliterate all traces of their sex.

Compared to the French capital, it seemed to Hillsden that London was cramped, pushed in on all sides and he felt cheated. His initial elation – like that of a lover keeping a long-delayed reunion – began to slip away.

'Wouldn't it have been quicker to miss the centre of London?' he asked.

'Like Swanson said, I'm only taking you part of the way,' Hadley answered.

'So where are we going now?'

'East End. Forest Gate. There's a safe house there. Then Rotherby's taking you the rest of the way.'

Hillsden could not keep the surprise out of his voice. 'You mean *Colonel* Rotherby? Is he still with us? I imagined he'd have fallen off the perch by now.'

'No. The Firm still enjoys his presence.'

'God! Dear old Rotherby, eh? We used to call him Lawrence of Wapping because he owned up to a turgid admiration of T.E.'

'T.E.?'

'Aircraftman Shaw, if you prefer.' Then, when Hadley still did not get it, he elaborated. 'Lawrence of Arabia.'

'Oh. Why him?'

'Never quite figured it out. We used to put it down to a romantic streak. I think he served in the desert during the war. Well, it'll be great to see old Rothers again. That's cheered me up no end.'

Hadley had to stop at traffic lights. 'And why Lawrence of *Wapping*? What's the connection?'

'Ah, well, the time I'm talking about we operated from a bogus wine importers in that part of the world. Rather a good cover in that we could help ourselves to some of the stock. Just plonk of course – there was an economy drive on even then.'

Passing under Admiralty Arch from the Mall, Hadley edged between cars coming from all directions as he manoeuvred the Ford around Trafalgar Square and headed for the Strand. It was getting dark by now and grey clouds of pigeons rose and headed for their night roosts. This sight brought a cry of excitement from Lara.

'Look, Papa!' she exclaimed in Russian.

'In English, sweetheart. From now onwards, always in English, remember?'

'Sorry, sorry, I forgot. But look how many there are!'

'Bloody sky rats,' Hadley muttered. 'They're diseased, you know, foul everything with their droppings. Breed as fast as rabbits. Completely ruined the window boxes outside my office. I want the Firm to recruit some hawks.'

Hillsden noticed that the drifters still gathered on the steps of St Martin's, and, in the Strand, where yet more roadworks again slowed their progress, the homeless were already taking up their positions in shop doorways, arranging their cardboard bedding as the commuters passed with heads averted, hurrying towards Charing Cross Station and the comforts of suburbia.

They picked up speed again as they reached the Aldwych and passed Bush House, where once a foreign journalist had been murdered by the tip of a poisoned umbrella, like an expendable featured player in a James Bond movie. They eventually gained the Mile End Road, making the transition from the anonymous office blocks and modern architectural glitz to the shabby wasteland of the East End with its boarded-up shops and general air of decay. The Luftwaffe had done its best to obliterate the old, tight-knit Cockney communities, and for fifty years bureaucracy and the speculators' greed had combined to squander the opportunity for a renaissance. There was little glitz here, just crumbling squalor punctuated by fenced vacant lots. Even the parked cars revealed the class divisions that England had never been able to renounce; gone were the Mercedes and BMWs that choked the West End, here there were only battered relics, their sides blotched with amateur repairs like vivid birthmarks. The pavements were strewn with junk-food cartons and plastic bags of refuse that awaited collection. Aimless groups of youths slouched on street corners, impatient for the night's violence.

As they reached the outskirts of Forest Gate in the gloom, Hadley asked him to check a street map. 'Ridley Road is what we're looking for. Close to Wanstead Flats.'

The parallel, tree-lined streets of Forest Gate had once boasted rows of genteel terraced houses but, thinned out early in the Blitz, their scars had long since been built over with a variety of nondescript post-war dwellings, some of which had already begun to self-destruct. Here and there, the lower windows were crudely shuttered against squatters; in many, the front gardens had been concreted over to provide off-street parking for rusting hulks. Turbaned Sikhs trod the uneven pavements with an air of sadness; bands of children still played a makeshift game of football in the gloom, using rolled-up coats for goals, their amusement constantly interrupted by passing traffic.

With Hillsden acting as navigator, they finally arrived at their destination. The safe house in Ridley Road backed on to an old cemetery and once might well have been a vicarage, for it stood alone and was larger than its neighbours, though it shared their look of neglect. A pollarded plane tree stood in the front garden behind a moth-eaten privet hedge. The railings had been shorn off close to the ground; only the iron gate remained, hanging at an angle from the one remaining hinge.

Hadley parked the Ford a short distance away and, having made sure no bystanders were paying any attention, motioned for Hillsden and his family to get out. They traced an uneven path to the rear of the house. Light from a street lamp glistened on the broken glass of a derelict greenhouse and an emaciated black cat scurried away at their approach. Hadley led the way and knocked four times on the frosted glass of the kitchen door, giving what Hillsden took to be a prearranged signal. There was a pause and then a light went on inside and the outline of a figure was projected on to the glass. Hadley repeated the same knock. The light was extinguished before the door was opened.

'Welcome back,' a voice said, and they stepped forward into darkness.

A torchlight came on and Hillsden turned to confront a familiar face.

'Well, who would have thought it, Colonel?'

'Who indeed!' Rotherby embraced him, kissing him on both cheeks, in a rare show of emotion. 'Go on through, all of you.' Using the torch, he ushered them through the kitchen and a small hallway into the living room. The inside of the house belied the exterior, for it was comfortably, though not luxuriously furnished, like the home of some white-collar worker forced by reason of his job to live in a location not of his choosing.

'I thought,' Rotherby said, going straight to the drinks

table, 'that the occasion demanded something a little special, Alec . . . My God! Listen to me, a bloomer straight off . . . Robert, Robert, Robert! Get your act together Rotherby, you stupid twit.' He turned to Galina. 'Forgive me, Mrs Bartlett, completely forgetting my manners, but seeing your husband again after such a long time . . . Welcome to England. And you, my dear,' bending to pat Lara on the head, 'I've got something you might like.' He produced a box containing a doll. Lara looked to her father to get his approval before taking the gift. 'Such a beautiful little face,' Rotherby said. 'You must be proud of her, Robert. God damn it! It's ridiculous calling you Robert, you're Alec to me and you always will be. Don't worry,' he added, as he caught Hadley's warning glance, 'I won't forget when we're outside, but this place is safe enough, swept once a week. Now then.' He produced a bottle. 'Johnnie Walker. Not Red label, not Black label, but *Blue* label, old son. I told housekeeping to lay in the best. Don't suppose you've seen one of these for a while.'

'Not ever,' Hillsden said. 'Didn't know it existed, Colonel.'

'You haven't changed.'

'That's not what I wanted to hear,' Hillsden said. 'I thought I'd returned a master of disguise.'

'I meant about calling me Colonel. You always did take the micky. No, the appearance is very good. Wouldn't exactly fool me, but it'd pass muster to strangers. However,' he said, unscrewing the bottle, 'let's baptise this. How about you, Georgina . . . There! Got that one right . . . Would you care for whisky?'

'Not really,' Galina said, 'but thank you all the same.'

'A glass of wine perhaps?'

'That would be nice.'

'Red or white, we've got both.'

'Red, please.'

'And what about the young lady?'

'Have you got a Coke?' Hillsden asked.

'Ah! That could be beyond us. Lime juice perhaps?'

'Try her.'

'Could I use the bathroom?' Galina asked.

'Of course, yes, sorry. Hadley show them where, will you? Second on the left.'

The moment Hadley left the room with Galina and Lara, Rotherby dropped his voice. 'Can't get used to them being so young. And what did you make of our friend Swanson?' Before Hillsden could answer, he added, 'Too tight-arsed for me. Not my style. Not like the old team, not like Jock and old Wadders.'

'No,' Hillsden said, accepting the glass of whisky.

'Let's drink to them. And Caroline. Three of the best.'

'Yes,' Hillsden said.

'While you were over there, did you ever find out what happened to Jock in the end? I know he was meant to be dead, but then somebody reported a sighting.'

Hillsden hesitated before answering. Was Rotherby ferreting? Had the truth ever filtered back? 'No, he was dead. I got that at first hand,' he said flatly.

'Betrayed, like Caroline, by that bastard Lockfield. And for what? Now that it's all over, for what? Cat and mouse, Alec, old son, but did the cat get the mouse or vice versa?'

'Who knows?'

'And mind you, Keating wasn't exactly another Rebecca of Sunnybrook Farm, he was another devious bastard. It's made me very cynical in my old age. Now I'm just treading water until pension time. Roll on the bus pass.'

'You never took a bus in your life, Colonel.'

'True, true. How well you know me. God! It's good to have you back. What was it like over there?'

'Not too hot.

'I can imagine. I never believed you were a scrimshanker, needless to say. I always figured that Lockfield had it in for you. Events proved me right. But at least you came home in one piece, and with a wife.'

'Yes.'

'And a daughter.'

'Yes.'

'Well, that's more than I've got. Cecily died.' He downed his whisky and looked past Hillsden. 'And we never had any children. Well, that's a lie. I had a child once. Not by Cecily and not in the sight of God. Happened when I was stationed out in Malaysia. Took up with a girl there. Rotherby's gone native was the word. Sweet girl, much younger than me. Never told Cecily, of course. No point, didn't want to rock the boat. I sent money for ten years or more when I got home. Then, one day, word got back she and the child had been murdered by guerrillas. I often think about it.' He went to pour himself another drink, then stopped. 'Better not. I'm driving and the Old Bill's very hot on that these days. Course the pubs stay open longer now and you can shop on Sundays. Progress, old son.'

'I never thought of you as an adulterer,' Hillsden said, then immediately regretted the remark. He tried to retrieve his embarrassment by adding. 'Me, yes, but not you.'

'Well, you can't go by appearances.'

Now that he had a chance to study Rotherby more intently, Hillsden saw remains of the man he had once worked alongside: thinner now, the cheeks hollowed, the sparse hair swept straight across to hide the balding crown and the hand gripping the whisky glass mottled with age spots. It was like being at a school reunion, where you come face to face with your contemporaries after a long separation and are amazed how much they have aged. It never occurs to you that undoubtedly they are thinking the same thing about you.

The others returned at that point and as soon as everybody had finished their drinks Hadley looked at his wrist-watch. 'Don't leave it too late,' he cautioned. 'You've still got a long journey, and I expect the child's tired.'

Lara looked up from playing with her new doll. 'No, I'm not,' she said.

'Yes, you're right,' Rotherby agreed. 'Just a couple more things I have to discuss with Alec, and then we'll get on our way.'

Hillsden followed him out of the room and was led into a

small study off the hallway. Rotherby went to a desk and took out a wallet. 'Lovely money, chum. Five hundred in used notes as a float. Have to sign for them, I'm afraid. Driving licence. There'll be a car registered in your name waiting in Suffolk. Credit cards. I had one done for the wife, too. Is she familiar with how they work?'

'I'll show her.'

'Never found Cecily had any problem grasping their use. And don't worry about how the accounts get paid, they'll be automatically debited to the Firm's closed account.'

'Oh, good.'

'Then deducted from your pay,' Rotherby added as he opened another drawer in the desk and removed a handgun and a leather shoulder holster. 'And lastly . . .'

'I need that, do I? I've never carried one before.'

'The rules have changed, old son. Quite a few of the police forces go around armed now. When you get settled in they'll give you some practice on the range.'

Hillsden took the gun from him and examined it.

'Magazine releases from the bottom. Safety catch here. Two trigger pressures. German. Very reliable, stop anything.' He watched as Hillsden detached the magazine and put it in a pocket.

'What am I?' Hillsden asked. 'Has that been decided? I notice the new style passports don't give occupations like the old ones.'

'No. Well, I don't have the answer to that. That hasn't come down from on high yet. I think that's the lot. Put everything in this holdall. Oh, and sign the receipt. Our new masters are sticklers for bloody paperwork. Gone are the days when we used to get paid in golden sovs, no questions asked.'

'Are you filing reports nowadays? What happened to your philosophy?'

'Did I ever have one?'

'Yes, don't you remember? You used to say, "If you don't write it, they can't read it. If they can't read it, they can't copy it. If they can't copy it, they can't steal it, and if they can't steal it, they can never hang you for it. " Or words to that effect.'

'Did I say that?'

'Frequently . . . How different are things at the Firm?'

'Well, the wind of change blew through the corridors for a while. They appointed a headmistress.'

'Yes, so I read. How was that?'

'Interesting. I was all for her. A big improvement on that other old woman, Lockfield. Didn't last though. I think she frightened the Establishment. The biggest change is we're no longer looking for Reds under the beds.'

'So what occupies the Firm these days?'

'Well, we've got the Islamic fundamentalists, the anti-Turks, followed by the anti-Cypriots, nuclear smugglers, and the neo-Nazis to keep us in business. Trade is still quite brisk.'

'And you've no idea what they've got in mind for me, why they brought me back?'

Rotherby looked him straight in the eye. 'Truthfully, no, and I wouldn't hesitate to tell you if I had. Hey, we'd better get going! Don't want to make Hadley late for his Horlicks.'

They rejoined the others and after telling Hadley to lock up the house when he left, Rotherby took them through the unkempt garden and through a gate in the wall. This led to an alleyway where another car, this time a Volvo, was parked. 'We're lucky,' he said.

'Why lucky?'

'Lucky it's still got four wheels. They say a car is stolen every thirteen seconds in the Greater London area.'

He de-activated the alarm and they transferred the luggage from the Ford. Lara was asleep as soon as they were under way.

'How long will it take?' Hillsden asked.

'Shouldn't be too bad at this time of night, and I know a few short cuts. Lived in that neck of the woods myself once. Cecily kept dogs then. Bred them. Setters. Lethal halitosis, farted a lot as they got older, bed always covered in hairs. Substitute children. Prefer cats myself.'

They drove on in silence for a while. When Hillsden

glanced over his shoulder he saw that Galina, too, was asleep.

'Thanks for buying Laura that doll. Thoughtful of you.'

'My pleasure. How d'you feel?' Rotherby asked.

'D'you mean, am I tired?'

'No, how d'you feel about being home?'

'Strange. Rather like *The Passing of the Third Floor Back*.'

Rotherby gave him a look.

'It's a play I once acted in, for my sins,' Hillsden explained. 'That was the title.'

'You always were a literary man, Alec. Never saw it myself. What was it about?'

'The second coming,' Hillsden said, staring beyond the headlight beams into the darkness.

12

COUNTRY FOLK

It was the silence that woke Hillsden the first morning in the new house. For a few moments he had no idea where he was. Thin sunlight slanted across the uneven bare walls and a moth fluttered against a window pane. There were age-blackened beams above his head and a scent he could not place immediately – heady and sweet, unlike the smells of the St. Petersburg apartment – but as he sat up in the bed he saw that somebody (had Rotherby mentioned a housekeeper?) had placed a bunch of freesias in a vase on the chest of drawers. Galina was still asleep and he eased back the duvet carefully and swung his bare feet on to the peg-boarded floor, padding his way to the window. It had been too dark for him to get any clear idea of the countryside when they arrived, but now he saw scattered cottages, smoke from their chimneys drifting straight upwards. The vista reminded him of the posters that used to adorn pre-war railway stations. This is the England I've missed, he thought, and emotions he had hidden surfaced, so that, for a moment, he could easily have given way to tears. He remained by the window a long time, noting that it was double-glazed and had security locks fitted.

Leaving the bedroom, he used the bathroom, with its old-fashioned taps and deep cast-iron bath, stained with lime scale where the tap had leaked. Then he looked inside Lara's room; like her mother she was still fast asleep, one arm thrown across the new doll that Rotherby had given her. Have

I done the right thing for them both, bringing them here? he thought, the innocence of his sleeping daughter reviving doubts.

He went downstairs to the kitchen which was warm and well stocked with all the basics and made himself a cup of coffee, boiling the water on a gas-fired Aga which, thoughtfully, had been left ignited. The rest of the kitchen was fairly rustic and he went around opening cupboards and trying sink taps, finding the water had a silky, country softness to it when he splashed his face. Leading off the kitchen was a utility room equipped with a deep-freeze, a washing machine and dryer, which he knew would please Galina. Taking his coffee mug with him, he went on a tour of the rest of the downstairs. There were two adjoining living rooms, both with low ceilings, the larger of the two having an inglenook fireplace. What pleased him most were bookshelves on either side of the fireplace housing a small library. He lingered in front of them and was somewhat surprised to find a section devoted to the global resurgence of neo-Nazi movements, with titles such as *The Fourth Reich* and *The Coming Racial War*. Surveying the rest of the room, he took in the nondescript, but comfortable furniture, the matching sofa and chairs covered in flowered chintz. Whoever had been responsible for the freesias in the bedroom had placed another bunch on the windowsill. Ducking his head under a slanting doorway he went into the hallway. There was a double porch to a front door fitted with two Chubb, double-mortice locks, the frame reinforced with a steel surround. He was still inspecting this when he heard a sound from the kitchen and a voice behind him said: 'Mr Bartlett?'

Hillsden turned, conscious that he was only wearing pyjamas and instinctively looked to see if his flies were gaping. He found himself facing a well-built, middle-aged woman with smart, greying, cropped hair and wearing a green tartan skirt and Norfolk tweed jacket. Her stocky legs were covered with knee-high woollen stockings and on her feet she had chunky, rubber-soled mountain boots. She looked, if anything, like a jolly hockey mistress and his immediate reaction was to take her for a lesbian of the old school.

'Sorry if I startled you,' she said. 'Came in the back way and didn't expect you up this early. I'm Audrey, though some people call me Major. I answer to both,' she added with a short, smoker's laugh that ended in a cough, 'although I think clinging to rank is a bit orff unless you're still at it. Don't you agree?'

'Doesn't bother me one way or the other,' Hillsden said, taken aback.

'Well, it's a bit la-di-fucking-da. Sorry about that, just slipped out, won't do it in front of the wife. I was a convent girl and we all swore like troopers so we had something to confess. Slept well, I hope? I tried to get the house warm. Didn't show my face last night, know what it's like after a long journey, last thing you want is to be social. You've got coffee, I see, what about breakfast? I've brought some fresh bread, bloody good local bakery, not that packaged muck. I'm not much of a cook, but I can do passable bacon and eggs.'

'Sounds good,' Hillsden said. 'My wife and daughter are still asleep, but you've sold me.'

He followed her back into the kitchen. 'Was it you who put the flowers in the rooms?'

'Yes. The place was like a bloody morgue when I took up residence. I doss down in the annexe, by the way. Converted stables.' She busied herself preparing his breakfast. 'They got me out of semi-retirement for this. Not that I mind, it was becoming a bloody drag babysitting other people's pets, which seemed to be my main function in life since I was put on the reserve list, and quite frankly Audrey can do with the extra dosh, so I was more than happy when this came up. The house has been swept, in case you were going to ask, and I've been round it myself, just to make sure.'

'What's the form going to be here?' Hillsden asked.

'With me? Well, officially, I'm your housekeeper. Been with you for years. Story is, which I've put about in the village shops, you decided to move the family here because you didn't think London was safe any more, and I came on ahead to get the house straight.'

'Sounds plausible. Are the natives friendly?'

'On the whole, yes, those I've met. Usual mixture for these days. Majority born and bred hereabouts, I suspect, with a touch of the Archers here and there.'

'They're not still going, are they?' Hillsden asked.

'Good God, yes. Part of our heritage, like Coronation Street. Then we have a sprinkling of outsiders with second homes – you know the type, vote Lib-Dem, recycle everything including their wives, have this dream of living under a thatched roof with tits nesting over the front door until the patter of rats' feet in the eaves sends them scurrying back to Chelsea.'

Hillsden nodded. 'How much were you told about me?'

'All they thought necessary. The fact that you've been out of circulation for some time, and that your missus and child will find everything a bit strange to begin with. You can tell Audrey more if you want to, or not as you think fit, suit yourself. Old Rotherby likes you and that's good enough for me. He's a card. One egg or two?'

'Yes, isn't he?' Hillsden said. 'Er, two, please.'

'Oh, shit, Audrey, you've broken that one, you silly mare. Still, all goes down the same way, doesn't it? Yes, Rotherby and I go back a while too. I got to know him on a couple of other jobs, not as well as he would have liked I might add.' She looked up from the frying pan and winked. 'Got a roving hand. Bit of a taxi tiger.'

'Really? That's a side of him I haven't come across.'

'Well no, you wouldn't, would you? Lonely, that's his problem. Wife died about four years back. Easy to handle though. Slap his wrists and he's quite harmless. Told him if his old wink stirred to put a hat over it and smuggle it up West. He rather went for that, though I think it was a touch of down-memory-lane. How about some fried bread?'

'Fried bread! God, I haven't had that for ages.'

'Well, you look as though you could do with putting on a

bit of weight. Unlike some. I've tried every bloody diet, but our Audrey's given up now and lets it all hang out.'

Hillsden had forgotten how delicious the pungent aroma of bacon was and he stood mesmerised, watching the sizzling pan.

'Doesn't seem to be a dining room, so d'you mind it on the kitchen table?'

'Anywhere's fine,' he said. Audrey placed the heaped plate in front of him. 'Mustard?'

'Mustard! Yes, please.'

She watched as he studied the small yellow bottle, turning it round and round in his hand. It was as if she had given him a jewel. 'Colman's,' he said. 'I haven't seen that in nearly eight years.' He cut a piece of fried bread and dipped it in the egg yolk, then took the first bite.

'How is it?'

'Unbelievably delicious.'

'Now, look,' Audrey said. 'You and I must establish a working arrangement.' She took a tin of small cheroots from one of the kitchen shelves and sat opposite him. 'This won't make you gag, will it?'

'No, go ahead.'

'Tried everything to kick the habit – acupuncture, the patch, hypnotism, but then I decided that life was such a crock anyway one might as well stick to vice. Do you smoke?'

Hillsden nodded.

'That's two things we have in common then.'

'Two? What's the other one?'

'Well, we're both birds of a feather. I did a stint in Belfast, working undercover as the manageress in a restaurant, then my cover got blown and they had to get me out fast. Nothing as exotic as you, I'm sure.'

'Oh, my past wasn't exotic,' Hillsden said. 'Not even dangerous for long periods, just dull.' He savoured his meal while Audrey got up to make a fresh pot of coffee. 'Any idea what they've got in mind for me?'

Audrey rested her cigar on the lip of a saucer and poured

the coffee. 'Haven't they told you? That's so bloody typical of the Firm. Well, they told me, so it can't be a state secret. My brief was you're an insurance broker.'

Hillsden grimaced. 'What genius thought that up? The only thing I know about insurance is that the premiums used to go up every year and that they questioned every claim. What about Galina, my wife, how is she explained?'

'Georgina, you mean, don't you?'

'Yes, sorry.'

'We should start using the new names. Make them second nature. If we get used to it in private there's less likelihood of a slip up in front of strangers.'

'Yes, quite right, remiss of me.'

'What's your wife's English like?'

'Pretty good. A trace of an accent still.'

'And Laura?'

'The same.'

'What do their passports say?'

'Born in Belgium.'

'Fair enough. As for schooling, I made discreet enquiries and there is a local church school, but I'd be happy to tutor if you think that's safer until she's really settled in. I can manage the basics.'

'Wouldn't that arouse comment?'

'I don't see why.'

'I mean, is that allowed?'

'Wait until anybody enquires. By then she'll have found her feet.' Audrey lit a second cheroot. 'Two with coffee,' she explained. 'Two after lunch and two with a nightcap. That's my ration.' She offered the tin to Hillsden. 'Want to try one?'

'No, I'll stick to cigarettes.'

'What's your usual brand?'

'I don't have one. I used to smoke Red Dunhills. Where I came from I smoked anything I could lay my hands on.'

'I'll get you a carton next time I'm out.' She got up suddenly and took down a biscuit tin from one of the shelves. 'Nearly forgot.' Opening the tin she produced a sealed envelope and a pair of spectacles. 'I had to give you these.'

Hillsden examined the spectacles. 'What am I supposed to do with these?' He held them up to the light, then put them on. 'Non-prescription.' Next he opened the envelope. Inside was a plain piece of paper with a London address typed on it – *Flat 6, 440, Bickenhall Street, W1* – a date two days hence and a time.

'Bickenhall Street,' he said, showing the note to Audrey. 'That's a new one. What goes on there?'

'No idea, new one on me. Can you remember the details?'

'Yes,' Hillsden said after studying the note again.

Audrey took the paper from him and tore it into small pieces, then put them in her ashtray and burned them. 'I remember when I was first recruited I had to report to a shop off the Marylebone Road. Had some very odd stuff in the window – breast supporters and artificial limbs. Very kinky, Audrey, I thought, what have you got yourself in for here? I take it they supplied you with a pea-shooter?' she added, letting the sentences slide into each other.

'Yes. I hate the bloody things.'

'Likewise, but all too necessary these days. They gave me a refresher course, and although I'll never be chosen for Bisley I can handle myself, so when you're not here don't worry, I've got no moral objection to using one if necessary. Funny old game we're in,' she added. 'Never quite believe it myself, but at least it's less boring than doing needlepoints, which is what my mother did. Every bloody room was crammed with them. Never got on with my parents. Mostly my fault, but they were paralysingly dull.'

Hillsden wiped his plate with his last piece of bread. 'God, that was good.'

'Now, what else have I got to tell you?' Audrey asked, pouring him a second cup of coffee. 'Transport. With what I can only believe was a sudden rush of blood to the head, they've given us two cars, a Rover for you and something called a Clio for me. Your keys are on the mantelpiece. Don't forget to drive on the left and watch out for the boys in blue, they're very keen these days. I bought you a road atlas, since I thought you'd need one.'

'I expect it'll all come back to me, given time.'

'Oh, and most important, you don't have to give me any housekeeping, that's taken care of, paid into a bank in Bury St Edmunds. But what I'll need to know from the wife is what she and your daughter like to eat, what they're used to.'

'No, don't give them what they're used to,' Hillsden said, with a smile.

'Your wife cooks, I take it?'

'Yes, she became a dab hand at producing miracles from nothing.'

'I got her this,' Audrey said, picking up a copy of Delia Smith's latest. 'Thought it might come in handy. No recipes for caviar, though,' she added, letting slip she knew more than she had professed. 'Anything else I should mention?'

'Your surname, I ought to know that.'

'I was hoping you wouldn't ask. Daddy was double-barrelled and possibly double-gated as well, always had my suspicions. The family name was Warrington-Smythe, can you believe? I never use the last bit, too fucking la-de-bloody-da – there you go again, Audrey, now watch it, don't go blotting your copybook the first day. Daddy was a manic snob, kept his one invitation to the Buck House garden party framed on the Bechstein. Can you imagine?'

'What did Daddy do?'

'Oh, Foreign Office, how else d'you think I got involved?'

'It's just Warrington then? You never married, Audrey?'

'No,' she said, taking his dirty plate and putting it in the sink. 'Plenty of hot water you'll be glad to hear,' she continued in the same breath in an obvious change of subject.

Hillsden got up from the table. 'I'll check whether my two are awake yet and have a bath. Then take a stroll, get acquainted with what's outside. Thanks for breakfast, Audrey. I think we'll all get along famously.'

He mounted the bare, creaking stairs, thinking, so it all begins again – the deceits, the nightmare of love, trusting my life to strangers – nothing's different, just a new set of characters in a changed landscape. He lingered in the doorway of Lara's room, staring at her unmarked, sleeping face, wondering how long it would be before the age of innocence ended for her.

13

WHITEHALL DOUBLE-SPEAK

'You'd better come up with some answers fast, Kenith,' the Prime Minister said pointedly across the Cabinet table. 'Put some firecrackers up the Commissioner's arse, and tell him to get his men out of their bloody Panda cars and on the streets. Those are our people getting hurt out there.'

Logan's fellow ministers shuffled their papers, not displeased that he was taking most of the flak that morning.

'Well, not entirely *ours*,' Logan said with a whisper of emphasis, for once letting his prejudices show. 'Half of them don't vote for anybody.'

'It can't have escaped your notice, Kenith, that we've got a by-election coming up which I don't want to lose,' the PM snapped. 'Imagine what play the Tory press would make of that so soon after we got in. We promised a new era of law and order and we've got to start delivering.' Much younger than his colleagues, he was at some pains to assert his authority.

Instinctively, Logan reached for his cigar case, then, just in time, remembered that smoking was off limits in the Cabinet room. During the election campaign the image-makers and spin doctors had been brought in – gone was the pipe-smoking informality of the Wilson days, now everybody wore suits and sober ties when appearing on the goggle-box, reliable respectability was the order of the day in an attempt to lull the electorate into believing that the Party was safe, forward looking and squeaky clean.

Logan cleared his throat. 'In my view, we should not dismiss the option of proscribing this First Legion outfit,' he said, employing his ministerial voice.

The PM shook his head. 'No, forget that, smacks of panic measures. Looks as though we've lost our nerve overnight. The existing laws are quite sufficient to handle it providing they're enforced, but all I ever get from the Commissioner are bleatings about lack of manpower and resources. If you ask me he's not quite sixteen annas to the rupee,' he said, expecting and getting a smile from most of the faces around the table. It was an expression he had purloined from the Permanent Secretary to the Treasury. 'Find out when he's due for retirement.'

Logan took this reproach and diligently made a note. 'I think one of the difficulties we face is that a lot of people out there don't give a toss whether Salman Rushdie and his kind get their comeuppance. Regrettable, but true.'

There was a moment's silence around the table before the PM said: 'Don't minute that,' to the Cabinet secretary and flashed a warning look at Logan. 'Yes, well, let's not open that can of worms.' He switched topics abruptly. 'Have we selected a candidate for the by-election?'

'Yes, after some heart-searching,' replied his Deputy.

'Is he any good?'

'Well, he's black. Or rather, West Indian. A solicitor. Very active in civil liberties.'

'I'd better see him. Fix it with my diary.' He returned to Logan. 'So, Kenith, I think you should do a little PR, visit the worst areas, get yourself photographed in hospitals wearing your compassionate face.'

'You mean the one I wear all the time?' Logan said, using his charm in an attempt to defuse the charged atmosphere.

Logan refused to dwell upon the PM's veiled sarcasm when the Cabinet meeting finished. Given time, and given the fact that nobody else wanted the job, he was confident he could produce results. He cancelled the rest of the day's appointments and that afternoon travelled to Slough, where the previous day a mosque had been burnt to the ground and the leader of the Muslim community savagely beaten up. In retaliation, well-organised groups of Asians had smashed and looted a dozen shops in the high street before the situation had been brought under control.

Ignoring the more pressing documents in his red box, he relaxed by reading an article in *The Economist* about the fall-out following Freidler's murder. High-flyers in the financial world had always intrigued Logan, for like most socialists in power he did not want to spend the rest of his days practising what he preached to others.

'Bet your life there's more to come out yet,' he muttered.

Andrews, his armed, Special Branch detective, turned round from the front passenger seat of the Jaguar. 'Sorry, sir?'

'Nothing. Just talking to myself,' Logan said. 'There's more to the murder of this banker, Freidler, than has come out yet, you mark my words. Have you been following it?'

'No, can't say I have, sir.'

'Bound to have had his hands in the till and salted away millions. The whole banking system is corrupt. They're all morally bankrupt.' Logan put the magazine to one side as he noticed something ahead. 'What's this we're driving into?'

'Looks like some sort of demonstration, sir.'

Logan's driver slowed down and allowed the police back-up car to overtake them.

'Can we turn off anywhere and avoid it?'

'Not off this road, sir,' the driver said. He checked that the door locks were on.

'Well, go on, don't stop.'

The driver exchanged a glance with Andrews. Fat chance, he thought.

Despite the fact that the back-up car had activated its lights and siren, the crowd refused to give ground. Very soon both cars were surrounded and although half a dozen local policemen tried to clear a path they were overwhelmed by the sheer numbers and the small convoy was forced to a standstill. Angry faces pressed close up against the windows of Logan's car, shouting slogans; one of the demonstrators wielding a wooden stave threw himself on to the bonnet and attempted to smash the windscreen before being thrown off.

'Drive on,' Logan shouted, 'get us out of here.'

'Can't, sir,' the driver said. 'There are kids lying down in the road.'

Andrews put out an alarm call on his radio as the Jaguar was violently rocked. 'Try reversing out,' he ordered. The driver did as he was told, but it was soon obvious that this would not work.

'Bloody people, don't they know I'm here to try and help?' Logan said. He sat in the centre of the rear seat, hardly able to make himself heard over the noise on all sides. 'This is ridiculous! The police are supposed to have this sorted out.'

'Not always that easy, sir,' Andrews said, defending his own.

'Well, I shall want a full explanation from the Chief Constable and the ringleaders prosecuted.'

Three more police cars arrived on the scene, together with a van-load of officers in riot gear. Those demonstrators lying in the roadway were forcibly dragged to one side and eventually the convoy was able to proceed. The incident was filmed by a newsreel camera team who had appeared from nowhere.

'How do those bastards always turn up when they're least wanted?' Logan muttered. 'Who tips them off?'

'You're news, sir,' Andrews said with just a touch of irony.

On arrival at the hospital, a still ruffled Logan was relieved to find that word had preceded him and there was a large police presence holding back another crowd of demonstrators. As he got out of the Jaguar the obligatory smile was wiped off his face as an egg just missed him, splattering the roof of the car. He was quickly hustled inside.

After being introduced to the senior hospital staff, he was conducted to the ward where two victims of racial attacks were recovering. Visiting the first bed, he arranged his face and spoke words of comfort to an elderly Sikh who had extensive head wounds.

'I'm afraid he speaks very little English,' one of the hospital officials said when Logan got no response from the old man. 'We believe there's also some brain damage.'

'Ah, yes. Tragic,' Logan said. He smiled at the old man and moved to the next bed where a young West Indian had both arms in plaster.

'What's your name?' Logan asked.

'Montgomery.'

'After General Montgomery, eh?'

'Who's he?' the young man asked.

Logan ploughed through this. 'Comfortable, are you?'

'Not very. Got a bleeding headache.'

'Well, I'm sure these good people are looking after you and you'll soon be back at work.'

'Haven't got any work to go back to.'

'Well, we must do something about that.'

'Yeah, well don't leave it too long, willya?'

Logan managed to keep his compassionate expression in place, conscious that the cameras were turning again. Nothing, that day, was turning out as he had hoped. In order to avoid a second clash with the demonstration he slipped out of a side entrance and was taken to the town hall where a reception committee hosted by the mayor and including senior police officers from the Thames Valley force had been assembled.

The mayor was a woman and Logan was unsure how to address her – the gender vocabulary had become an issue which always confused and irritated him – should she be addressed as the Lady Mayor, or, ludicrously, as Mayor Person? A somewhat dumpy little woman, weighed down by her chain of office, he drew some comfort from the fact that in this case she was also the leader of a Labour Council. Some tea, cakes and a variety of desultory sandwiches had been prepared for his visit, and Logan made a short speech to the assembled great and good, stressing the need for calm and assuring them that all those responsible for the racial attacks

back to Whitehall, conscious that not only had he lost the argument, but that once again he had no compelling answers.

14

EYE CONTACT

Carstairs knew they would kill him; it was only a matter of time. He told himself, I mustn't give way, there has to be a way out, but fear was batting to and fro in his mind, like a shuttlecock. His future was etched with the acid of the inevitable.

He lay, fully clothed, on the single bed in the anonymous Bayswater hotel he had chosen as a last refuge, registering under a false name. There was an illustrated tourist guide on the bedside table, alongside a soiled handkerchief, the bottle of Valium and his car keys. The photograph on the cover of the guide showed a big-breasted girl in a bikini lying on an inflated Lilo in impossibly blue water. *Affordable Luxury Holidays*, the legend said, *Your unique made-to-measure experience. Discount fares if you book early.* Just another lie, Carstairs thought. There were no bargains to be had in the world he had chosen to inhabit, no return tickets, only a last painful journey. 'You'll be set up for life,' Charters had said, and he had believed it. 'Just a few telephone calls to this number at the right times, that's all you have to do, there's no risk, nothing can go wrong.'

I didn't do it for myself, I did it for her, so I could give her the good life, the life she craves, he said to himself, and thinking of the love he was about to lose for ever brought a stab of pain to his chest. If only God could take the final step for me, he thought, but it was too late to rely on God. He shook a handful of Valium capsules into his palm and went into the small bathroom. A notice pasted on to the mirror reminded him that the management took no responsibility for articles of value left in the rooms. He filled the toothpaste glass with tap water and after a moment's hesitation, swallowed the capsules, staring at a stranger's face in the mirror. Then he went back into the bedroom and lay down once more. He tried to remember a childhood prayer, one last insurance policy, but his mind wandered as an unaccustomed calm began to sweep over him. Before he slipped further into the abyss, he reached under the pillow and took out a .25 calibre automatic pistol. Turning on his side, he rested the cold metal against his left temple. 'Forgive me, darling,' he murmured. He stared one last time at the holiday brochure before he gave himself the unique made-to-measure experience of blowing his head apart.

· · ·

The Bickenhall Street address Hillsden had been given proved to be an ornate mansion block close to the area in London, bordering Harley and Wimpole streets, that had long been the province of the medical profession. He was wearing the plain-glass spectacles he had been given and made a show of peering at the panel listing the residents, most of whom appeared to be foreign with medical credentials after their names. Pressing the requisite bell on the panel and waiting for a response on the entry-phone, he recalled an A.J. Cronin novel he had read long ago – *The Citadel* – that in its time had aroused a certain amount of controversy, pulling aside, as it did, some of the veils doctors hid behind. It seemed to him appropriate that the Firm would choose to operate cheek by jowl with another profession that thrived on secrecy.

A muffled male voice said 'Yes?'

Hillsden answered close to the microphone. 'Mr Bartlett,' he said, 'I have an appointment.'

'Third floor,' the voice responded.

There was a pause and then the automatic lock clicked open and he pushed the heavy door inward. The carpeted entrance hall was spotless, bare of furniture except for a console table with some uncollected mail on it. He walked up a short flight of stairs to the lift: there was a distant clunk from above as the pulley mechanism engaged, then he heard it stop again. When eventually it reached the ground floor, the doors slid open to reveal a middle-aged couple. Confronted by Hillsden, both ignored him, but before the woman averted her head he saw she was crying.

The third floor was as characterless as the entrance, the same patterned carpet and absence of furniture. There were brass panels on all the doors. The one on number six was engraved *Mr C. Smith FRCS, Ophthalmologist*. Hillsden knocked and again the lock was opened automatically. He entered an empty waiting room. This was decorated in a different style from the rest of the building: stipple-painted walls hung with a few posters for contact lenses, a cabinet containing a variety of spectacle frames, a modern sofa and desk. There was a closed door to one side of the desk. After a slight pause this door opened and Swanson appeared.

'You found it all right, then,' Swanson said.

'No Mr Smith?'

'Ah! No, out to lunch I'm afraid,' with a flickered smile. 'Permanently.'

'Can I dispense with these?' Hillsden asked, removing the fake spectacles. 'I take it I'm not here to have my eyes tested?'

'God no! Had somebody press our bell by mistake last week. Threw me for a loop. Had to pretend Mr Smith was away sick and I was the secretary. Anyway, let's go into my den.' He pressed a switch on the desk and Hillsden heard the door lock behind him as he entered the second room where there was another desk with an Anglepoise lamp on it, together with three telephones, two comfortable leather chairs and a filing cabinet. On the far wall was a test chart with diminishing lines of letters and, opposite, the elaborate testing equipment eye-specialists use.

Swanson took the chair behind the desk. 'Necessary window dressing. Sit you down. Too early for a drop of Vera Lynn?' He swivelled to open the top drawer of the filing cabinet and took out a bottle of gin and two glasses.

'Why not?' Hillsden said. This was a more relaxed, altogether more pleasant Swanson, less guarded now that he was on home ground. 'Haven't heard it called that in a long time.'

'Got some tonic somewhere.' Swanson searched the back of the filing drawer. 'Here we are. No ice, I'm afraid. Say when.'

'When.'

Swanson slid a glass across the desk. 'Well, here's to your new life. How did you find our Audrey?'

'Fine.'

'Formidable creature. The word is, don't mess with Audrey. She's part of the team, together with Rotherby – I included him to make you comfortable – Hadley, Commander Pearson and his side-kick.'

'Who's Pearson?'

'You never came across the good Commander?'

'I don't think so.'

'George Medal, and two Queen's commendations, all earned in Belfast. And that's it. I kept the numbers down for obvious reasons, as I'm sure you would agree.'

Hillsden nodded.

'Everything else tickety-boo in darkest Suffolk?'

'The house seems very comfortable.'

'What about the wife? Happy?'

'Well, everything's bound to be strange for her at first, but I'm sure she'll soon adapt. It's strange for me, too, come to that.'

'Bound to be.' Swanson took out a gold fob-watch from his waistcoat, consulted it and then polished the face with a silk handkerchief before putting it back. 'I suppose we should get down to the nitty-gritty. We'd better start with you signing this.' He took a sheet of paper from a file.

'I thought the Official Secrets Act stayed in force for the rest of my natural life?'

'This is something else, preventing you from ever publishing your second volume of memoirs.' Swanson handed him a pen and waited for Hillsden to read what was before him. 'Okay?'

'Well, I don't have any choice, do I?'

'Not if the pay cheques are to come in regularly,' Swanson said evenly.

Hillsden took the pen and signed.

'Right,' Swanson said, 'onwards and upwards. Well, now, new name, new game'. He savoured a sip of gin, looking at Hillsden over the rim of the glass. 'Recently it was deemed expedient to ginger up the anti-Fascist section of F Division. The sound of jackboots is being heard again in the land. There's always been a latent Fascist element – apologists, Hitler-worshippers, Holocaust sceptics, unrepentant Jew-haters, all tumbled together with your Paki-bashers – but until recently they didn't pose any real threat. Too scattered, all doing their own thing. But what we're now facing is something much more organised and well funded – an international fraternity with various groups colluding to exploit mutual hatreds.'

Swanson took another sip of his gin. 'My old physics master used to say that once you create a vacuum, something always fills it. Politically, that certainly holds true.'

Hillsden nodded agreement, then said: 'In St Petersburg you talked about an undercover operation.'

'Yes, after a great deal of thought, I've devised a fairly elaborate scheme.'

'I gather I've got a new career as an insurance broker.'

Swanson looked miffed. 'Who told you that?'

'Audrey.'

'I wish people wouldn't jump the gun,' Swanson said. 'None of her bloody business. Your age presented a problem – I had to come up with something that was as watertight as I could make it. I hit upon insurance, then decided to narrow it down to car insurance. Premiums are at an all-time high, but recently a number of new firms have come on the market offering cut-price rates, so one more shouldn't arouse any suspicion. Your operation has been designed as the genuine article, able to issue policies at attractive rates and, if necessary, pay claims – there's a separate slush fund set up.'

'How am I meant to operate?'

'This is where I think your age is an advantage.'

'Ah, I wondered when you'd explain that,' Hillsden said.

'As I told you, I wasn't looking for brawn. The scenario is, you were unable to make ends meet on your pension, so you took up part-time work as an independent insurance agent. I've prepared a fake CV for you to study and learn, which gives Robert Bartlett's family history.' He passed another document across the desk. 'You'll note you're a widower.'

'Yes, I saw that.'

'Sensible precaution, I thought. We don't want the little woman put in the line of fire.'

'Nor my daughter. How much should my wife know?'

'The minimum you can get away with. And from time to time it may be necessary for you to spend time in the safe house in Forest Gate. Does that worry you?'

'It'll need explaining to my wife.'

'I'm sure you're good at that sort of thing,' Swanson said blandly. 'The way I see it is you start with a mail shot which will include half a dozen names of known players. Hopefully, one or more will take the bait and contact you to hear more. Then it's up to you to secure their business and establish an ongoing relationship. You'll be interested in their lives, sympathetic towards their political views because, as you will discover in your CV, you were made redundant in your previous job for voicing racial slurs against a fellow worker. Are you with me so far?'

'More or less. What if we don't get any of the right takers?'

Swanson flashed his annoyance at this quibble. 'I've put a lot of thought into this and I'm assuming you will come up with at least one positive response.'

'But, assuming you're wrong, obviously the operation's not repeatable. What happens to me then?'

'Let's not look on the black side. No pun intended,' Swanson said with his thin smile, but he could not keep the annoyance out of his voice.

'From where I'm sitting, I have to.'

'Well, yes, should the operation prove negative, you couldn't be used again. We'd have to have a rethink. Let's cross that bridge when we come to it, shall we?'

'These "known players", who are they?'

'Mostly small fry Special Branch have been keeping an eye on. Until recently they've been operating solo without any discernible pattern, doing their own thing locally, but then we noted a change in their activities. Suddenly they seemed to become organised. They had access to funds, they could afford premises, produce literature, field political candidates – echoes of Mosley and his blackshirts. But beyond that, we started to notice a new trend which suggests the nature of terrorism itself has changed.'

'In what way?'

'In your field days, terrorists mostly had nation-states as patrons: Libya, Iran, Palestine and, of course, Russia itself. The Yanks, too, for that matter, with their covert operations which frequently backfired. The targets were usually heads of state, or symbols of state power. Now the focus has shifted. There seems to be a common political end that crosses frontiers closer to home, the threat coming from extreme right-wing groups and always racially motivated. Jewish cemeteries desecrated here, foreign immigrants attacked and murdered in Germany and France, a Fascist revival in Italy, not forgetting the growing armies of militiamen in the States prepared to take the law into their own hands. Study the press now you're home, you'll find examples any day of the week. Have a look at this thing. Acting on a tip-off from our man in Copenhagen, Customs at Harwich confiscated several hundreds.'

Taking a booklet from the desk drawer he swivelled it

across the desk. 'Written by a certain Gottfried Sonntag, a prominent German Jew-baiter, although he uses a pseudonym for the English translation. It's the usual filth, on the same lines as that *Protocols of the Elders of Zion* thing old Henry Ford treated as the gospel. The title tells it all – *Sin of the Blood.*' Taking back the book, Swanson flicked through the pages. 'Open it anywhere, the message is the same.' He read aloud: *"'With satanic joy in his face, the black-haired Jewish youth lurks in wait for the unsuspecting girl whom he defiles with his blood."'* Turning to another page, 'And listen to this, *"The Jew virus constitutes a far greater threat than Aids. We shall regain our political and social health only by eliminating the Jew."* We're dealing with animals. Animals,' he repeated. 'You aren't going to find this a pleasant assignment because to be accepted you're going to have to speak their language. Are you up to that?'

'I guess I'll have to be,' Hillsden said. He looked straight at Swanson. 'But you seem to have paid a high price for my temporary services. Should I be flattered?'

'From what I know of you, Hillsden, you've always known your way around the maze. I depend on you to deliver and lead us to whoever's at the top. That's the objective.'

'Where do I run the operation from?'

'You'll operate out of an office we've set up for you in Docklands, with an assistant to handle enquiries and mail. I should have mentioned her before.'

'Her?'

'Yes, girl called Sarah, ex WPC in the Met. It's all equal opportunities now. Official Labour policy. When you've studied all the material, I'll have Hadley take you down to Docklands and get you acclimatised there. After that you work to your own timetable. If you need to contact me or Pearson, use this number and it'll be automatically patched through to one or the other of us on a scrambler. Just ask for another eye appointment.'

He finished his gin. 'I won't pretend it isn't a dangerous assignment. What's out there is not a game of ring-a-roses.

What has changed is England itself. Make the wrong move
and A-tishoo, A-tishoo, we all fall down.'

15

COUNTRY FOLK CONTINUED

'Is it dangerous, what they've asked you to do?' Galina asked.

Lying beside her in bed, Hillsden looked up from reading the fake CV. 'To do what?' he said, his brain momentarily refusing to work.

'Don't keep it from me if it is.'

'Why d'you say that? I told you, they've given me an office job.'

'And you expect me to believe that's all there is to it?'

'I promise you.'

'You've changed,' she said. 'Don't you know you've changed?'

'I'm home,' Hillsden said. 'Home after a long time away. I'm sure I seem different, but then who wouldn't be? You're different too. We've got to get acclimatised. I don't say it's as difficult for me as it is for you and Lara, but all the same I'm not finding it easy.'

'Except to lie to me.'

'Who's lying?'

'You don't have to shield me. I'd rather know. Just tell me, so I'm prepared: is it dangerous, this work you're involved in?'

'No. I'm more likely to be run over crossing the road. I'm still having to think twice about which side we drive on.' He closed his book and put his arm under her, drawing her closer so that her head nestled on his shoulder and he caught the scent of the shampoo she had used.

'When I first met you,' Galina murmured, 'you told me it was all over, what you did, and I didn't mind the past, there was nothing to be afraid of in the past. Now it's all started again, I know it has, and I need to prepare myself.'

'You are a silly creature. Prepare yourself for what?'

'Losing you.'

'You're not going to lose me. Whatever put that in your head? This is a better life than the one we left, isn't it? We have a home, your first real home, no money worries, you can go out and buy things you never dreamed of, anything you want.'

'All except one thing,' she said.

'What's that?'

'Peace of mind.'

To give himself time to frame his next answers, Hillsden leaned across to the bedside table to take a cigarette.

'Don't smoke in the bedroom,' Galina said.

'Sorry.' He left the packet where it was.

'That's an indication. You always reach for a cigarette when you're worried.'

'No, I'm a lifelong addict. Tell you what, tomorrow, why don't we drive into Bury St Edmunds, have lunch in some posh hotel, and then I'll take you and Lara to buy some new clothes? How does that sound?'

'That you don't want to tell me the truth.'

'There's nothing to tell.'

'Then why are you studying all those books about Nazis? You left one in the bathroom. And why don't you tell me what you do when you go to London?'

'I sit behind a desk and read files.'

He attempted to stifle her concern with a kiss, but she avoided his mouth. With despair he could see their life ahead. Galina was right, he had been trapped once more. What a fool I was, he thought, what a fool to believe that the Firm ever give you the best of a bargain. The only winners were those who acted from conviction, idealism, the certainty, however mistaken, that theirs was the only true faith. I never had that,

I was driven by the one emotion we all betray sooner or later.

He kept his arm under Galina until the rhythm of her breathing told him she was asleep, then slowly eased it free. 'I love you,' he said softly, hoping it would penetrate her dream. It came to him then, as he turned over and closed his eyes, that nobody deceived as well as lovers.

. . .

The Chinese chambermaid was puzzled. For over thirty-six hours a 'Do Not Disturb' notice had swung from the door of Room 18. In such cases there was normally a tray of used coffee cups and empty wine bottles left outside, for the hotel catered mostly for clandestine one-nighters and their girlfriends.

Putting her ear to the door she listened for any sounds from within, but all was silent. Next she knocked, and said 'Room service', but there was no response. After knocking again, she decided to risk it and used her master key. She pushed the door open a fraction and said, 'Maid, please.' Nothing. She allowed the door to open fully and looked inside. Then she screamed.

. . .

'You'll have to excuse me,' Hillsden said, 'if I sometimes appear to be a fossil from a bygone age, but I've been out of circulation for a while. Did they tell you that?'

The young woman looked at him from across her desk. 'The story I had was you'd been brought out of retirement for a special job.'

'That's about it. Well, I'd like to get off on the right foot, so how d'you like to be addressed? Is it Mrs Carter, Miss or Ms? I'm told it's important these days.'

'Well, certainly not Mrs because I've never walked up the

aisle,' his new assistant said. 'Not for want of trying, I might add. Why don't you just call me Sarah, Mr Bartlett? I don't give a toss about all that feminist lark, so don't worry, you'll never be greeted by the smell of burning bras.'

There was just a hint of a long-buried Cockney accent in Sarah's voice. Hillsden guessed she was in her late twenties, possibly a year or two older, smartly dressed, her short blonde hair neatly arranged. A waft of perfume reached him as she handed him a cup of freshly brewed coffee.

'Oh, thanks. You already figured out one of my weaknesses.'

'Have you got many?'

'More than is good for me.'

'It hasn't got sugar.'

'I don't take it.'

'Well, that's one on the plus side, Mr Bartlett.'

'Look, Sarah, when there's nobody here, for God's sake call me Robert.' The assumed name still came uneasily to him. 'As far as I'm concerned, you and I are working for each other. What's that perfume you're wearing?'

'Poison.'

'Poison? There's a perfume called Poison?'

'Oh, sure. There's also a cigarette called Death.'

'Do you smoke those?'

'I don't smoke,' Sarah said.

'Oh, dear, is that going to be a problem, because I do?'

'No sweat. My boyfriend smokes.'

'I'll try and cut it down while I'm here. What does your boyfriend do?'

'He's in the Met. Diplomatic protection. He gets to wear a suit, but I guess you could say that the relationship isn't exactly tailored for romance. They work him all hours.'

Hillsden was studying the layout of the office as they conversed. It was impersonal but functional: two desks, two PCs, laser printer, filing cabinets, fax and copying machines, three telephones ('The red one's the scrambler,' Sarah told him). A small kitchen and a bathroom led off the main room.

'And you, what brought you into the Firm?'

'I was in the Met, too, did eight years with them, ended up working for the anti-terrorist squad, personal assistant to the boss man.'

'Who was that?'

'Commander Pearson. He's been seconded to our team.'

'Yes, Swanson told me.'

'When this came up, he was the one who thought my face might fit in here.'

'Mine too, apparently.' Hillsden sat at his desk and rifled through a stack of the insurance brochures. 'He thought you might make an insurance agent, did he?'

'Always willing to learn. It's a pretty neat scam if we can work it.'

'Well, we're going to try. At least it's original,' Hillsden said. He brandished one of the insurance brochures. 'Have you had a chance to study these?'

'Yes, I was impressed. They've done a professional job. If that came through my letter box I'd give it a second look. Matter of fact, the rates are so good I wondered whether I could write a policy for my own car. D'you think they'd wear it?'

'Maybe not. Is there a list of the first mailing shot?'

'Top left-hand drawer, but I've already put everything on both computers while I was waiting for you to arrive.'

'That was very efficient. Don't expect me to use one of these things, I haven't got a clue. You're a whiz, no doubt?'

'Not bad. Well, very good actually, no point in being modest. You needn't worry, I programmed it to be really easy, but you have to key in the code word to get started . . . I thought "Hitler" was appropriate. Okay?'

'Yes, I think I can manage to remember that. It's what comes after the code.'

'It's simple. When the menu comes up, you type the first letter of whichever heading you want. Let me show you.' She came behind him and put in the code. 'They're really fast these machines,' she said as the menu came on screen. '486s with a Pentium chip and turbo drive.'

'That's good, is it?'

'State-of-the-art. Now then, you see how I've categorised it. Names: so supposing you typed "N", you'd get a complete list in alphabetical order. Date when contacted. Reply. Action taken, et cetera. If you get your knickers in a twist, don't worry. Both machines are linked and I'll be doing all the spade work. When we're bored we can play games.'

'We can?'

'Sure. Go to Windows in the menu. Watch.' She used the mouse and clicked twice on an icon. 'Have to use the mouse though.'

'Mouse, windows, it's all a foreign language.'

'Click twice for Solitaire. That's the one I like best.'

Hillsden stared in amazement as a deck of coloured playing cards appeared and Sarah began to manipulate the mouse with great dexterity. 'Here,' she said, 'you try. But I warn you, once you get hooked, it's a great time waster. Move the red six over to the black seven. That's it. Now go to the pack for the next card.'

'This might prove my undoing, you should never have shown me.' He relinquished the mouse. 'Shouldn't we make a start?'

'I already did.' Sarah went to her own desk and picked up a stack of stamped and addressed envelopes. 'The priority twenty names on the list are ready to go.'

Hillsden examined the envelopes.

'Okay to post them?'

'Why not? Let's cast our bread upon the waters and see if any of the fish bite.'

As she passed him, he got another whiff of her heady perfume.

'Poison, you say? I must remember that and get some for my wife.'

'Not mad about it myself, but it turns my boyfriend on. Every little helps. Gives him all sorts of ideas,' she said. 'All except wedding bells.'

When she left to catch the post, Hillsden could not resist

resuming the computer game. Engrossed, it was some moments before he became aware of the reflection of a red dot blinking on the monitor screen. He swivelled round to see the call-light signalling on his scrambler phone. He picked up.

'Bartlett?' a voice said.

'Yes. Swanson?'

'No, Hadley. You took your time.'

'I was in the loo.'

'Isn't Sarah there?'

'She's gone out to the post.'

'Oh, right. You're up and running then?'

'Yes, all stations go.'

'Good. Just checking. Any problems?'

'Not so far.'

'Good. Keep me in the picture, won't you? If I'm left in the dark I can't be much help,' Hadley said.

'I'll make it my life's work,' Hillsden said.

He put the phone down and sat looking at it for a time, wondering why he had reacted in such a prickly manner. Hadley probably meant well, it was just that he was young and gung-ho, anxious to prove his worth. It was funny how old suspicions still lurked just below the surface, immediately activated by a chance remark. Resuming the game of Solitaire, he came close to getting it out, but was denied success by one card – the ace of spades.

16

A MURDER INVESTIGATION

'Why do we have to be involved?' Commander George Pearson said to Lloyd, his number two. 'Can't the bloody CID sort out their own problems?'

He searched in the glove compartment of their unmarked car for his bottle of antacid tablets. They had been stalled in the heavy traffic around Hyde Park Corner for the past five minutes.

'Who asked for us?'

'Gilbert.'

'Oh, that useless sod.' Pearson shook two tablets into his palm and mouthed them. 'He couldn't solve the *Standard* crossword. Traffic warden, that's all he's good for.'

'I've always got on well with him.'

'Yes, well you're going to end up in the *Guinness Book of Records* for kissing the most number of arses.'

Lloyd tapped a drumbeat on the steering wheel rather than respond, an action which seemed to fuel Pearson's irritation. He was frequently on a short fuse these days. The vehicle in front of them jerked forward a few feet.

'Got kangaroo petrol in his tank,' Lloyd observed.

'What's that mean?'

'Just an expression. Haven't you heard that before?'

'No. Put the siren on,' Pearson said, 'otherwise we'll be here all day.'

'Well, what good will that do? I can't drive over the top of them.'

'Never any police here when you need them,' Pearson said with conscious irony. He crunched the tablets noisily. 'God, I can't wait for retirement. Only six more months and I'm out of it. Out of it,' he repeated, reaching under the dashboard to activate the siren. 'Roll on the Costa bloody Brava. You meet a better class of criminal there.'

'Told you,' Lloyd said. 'Siren doesn't make any difference. We're in a gridlock.' But, even as he spoke, miraculously, the traffic began to move again, though he couldn't decide whether it was the shock of their siren or one of those unfathomable occurrences that every day managed, at the last moment, to unclog London's jammed streets. With the siren still blaring, they shot round the war memorial and cut across into the park.

'Where're we making for?' Pearson asked.

'Hereford Road. Hotel Methos.'

'What is it, Greek?'

'Who knows?'

They weaved in and out of another jam on the Bayswater Road, sometimes using the right lane, as Lloyd put his foot down.

'Don't go mad!' Pearson said.

'Thought you were in a hurry.'

'I'm not in a hurry to be dead. We're going to a homicide, remember, not a premature birth.'

They came to a stop in front of the hotel where already two squad cars and an ambulance were parked. A small crowd of onlookers was grouped round the entrance.

'Where's the incident?' Pearson said to the officer standing at the door.

'Second floor, sir.'

They went inside. The dilapidated foyer was typical of the hotels in the area. Mostly owned and run by Asians, many of them charged exorbitant rates to foreign students during term time, and relied on prostitutes for the rest of the year.

'Don't imagine Egon Ronay gave this any stars,' Pearson observed as they mounted the stairway. They wound their way up to the next landing, passing through the obligatory fire door into a dimly-lit corridor. Room 18 was the last they came to. Pearson and Lloyd entered and took in the scene. The fingerprint and forensic teams were still busy around the single bed where the body of a fully clothed male lay on top of the tired floral bedspread. One side of his face had been shot away; the lower jaw lay on his chest, the stiffened left arm outstretched at an angle as though its last act had been to ward off a blow. Cobwebs of blood and hair, mixed with dried brains, had spattered the faded striped paper of the wall behind the bedhead.

'So what's all this about, Archie?' Pearson said.

Detective Superintendent Gilbert, kneeling by the side of the bed, turned at Pearson's voice.

'You took your time, George,' he said.

'I hope it wasn't a waste of time. What've you got?'

'On the face of it suicide, but time will tell.'

'So, why would I be interested?'

'Couple of things. Come outside.' He ushered them out into the corridor. 'I'm reasonably certain he was a suicide, but chummy in there doesn't conform to type. He left too many clues behind. My theory is that a lot of them choose dumps like this for it because they want to do an ostrich act. Know what I mean?'

'Not really, no, but tell me,' Pearson said, and Lloyd recognised the boredom in his voice.

'Well, like they feel they're anonymous, that's the way I'd put it. Head in the sand stuff.'

Pearson lit a cigarette. 'Oh, that. Yes. Not too many documented cases of ostriches being able to use a handgun, though.'

'George, I'm doing you a favour bringing you here, don't give me a hard time. In my experience, the majority think they've covered their tracks. Usually there's nothing on them to identity them. But chummy was the exception. If you ask me, he wanted us to know exactly who he was.'

'And who was he?'

'One of yours, George, one of yours, on the face of it.'He opened his hand and revealed a plastic security pass for Century House.

It was Gilbert's big moment and he enjoyed the brief look of surprise on Pearson's face. Pearson took the pass from him and examined it.

'Know him?'

Pearson shook his head. 'No, but that doesn't mean anything.'

'Can I see?' Lloyd asked.

'I'm not saying it belonged to him,' Gilbert continued. 'Have to rely on fingerprints for a positive identification, given what he did to his face, but it was found on him.'

Lloyd also examined the pass but, taking his cue from Pearson, was also non-committal. 'Looks genuine enough, but you never know. They can fake anything these days. I got passed a dud twenty-pound note yesterday.'

'Could he be one of your mob?'

'I'll certainly check,' Pearson said.

'Well, I thought it was worth putting you in the picture,' Gilbert said, waiting for a pat on the back.

'Yes, thanks,' Pearson replied. 'I'll owe you one. Can we keep this?'

'If you sign for it.'

'What did he use?'

'Not regulation issue. Point twenty-five. But they're easy to come by.'

'Who found him?'

'Chinese chambermaid. She went in because she thought he'd done a runner without paying his bill.'

'How long had he been dead?'

'The doc made it a day and a half.'

'Sometime on Wednesday then,' Pearson said. 'Any note?'

'Haven't found one. The only other thing in his pockets was a bill from Tudor's. That's a night club, as you probably know.'

'Why would I know that?' Pearson said. 'I don't have your

exotic lifestyle, Archie. That's one of your regular haunts, I'm sure.'

'Ha ha. Chance would be a good thing.'

'So, nothing else?'

'Not so far, but we're still working on it. D'you want to take another look?'

'I don't think so. I'll let you have all the fun stuff. Well, thanks again, Archie, glad to see somebody's on the ball. You're not just a pretty face, after all. I'll get back to you when I've made my own enquiries. Let me know if the forensic boys come up with anything else of interest.'

The repeated use of his first name appeared to gratify Gilbert.

'Will do,' he said. 'Thought it was worth bringing you in.'

Once they were back in their car Lloyd and Pearson looked at each other.

'Carstairs,' Pearson mused. 'Glad you played dumb as well. Doesn't do to let the Yard know all our secrets. Question is, why? Why would he top himself, *if* he topped himself?' He crunched on another antacid tablet.

'Maybe he was getting a bit on the side. The night club receipt might be a pointer. I know he was married, but maybe he put it around.'

'Did you ever meet him? Not exactly Richard Gere.'

'I thought he was working out of Copenhagen.'

'He was.'

'So how come he ends up stiff in a Greek hotel here?'

'Perhaps he had some air miles he wanted to use. Don't keep asking me bloody silly questions. I'm not taking part in *Mastermind*.'

'God, you've got the hump today. Everything I say, you jump down my throat. Entitled to voice my thoughts.'

Pearson didn't answer, but continued to study Carstairs's security pass. 'How to play this,' he said.

'Well, one thing, we could do the decent thing and be the ones to break it to his wife,' Lloyd ventured, still smarting from the last exchange. He got no response from Pearson.

'Yes? Good idea? Have I said something right for once?'

'Let me get his address.' Pearson picked up the car phone and dialled.

'Messy way of doing it,' Lloyd said as he executed a U-turn and headed for the Bayswater Road.

'Messy, but usually conclusive.' Pearson spoke into the mouthpiece. 'Commander Pearson here. Give me records.' He waited. 'I mean, if you've made up your mind to do it, don't take chances it won't work and end up a vegetable. That seems to me the worst of all possible worlds.' He took out Carstairs's security pass again. 'Oh, records. This is Commander Pearson. Can you give me a home address for somebody. Serial number seven two four zero eight seven.'

He clicked his fingers at Lloyd. 'Pen.'

Lloyd handed him one and he scribbled the information. 'Thanks.'

'Where is it?' Lloyd asked.

'Putney. Deodar Road.'

'God, that takes me back. I used to date somebody who lived there. Stunning little number, a dancer in that show . . . what was it called?' He hummed a few bars of a well-known tune. '*A Chorus Line*, that was it. She was very keen.'

'Keen on you?'

'Keen on *it*. And keen on me, too, I have to admit. For a time, anyway. The gardens lead down to the river. Nice in summer. Those houses are pricey these days.'

'How pricey?'

'You wouldn't get much change out of four hundred thousand.'

'Sounds a bit rich for Carstairs. Unless he was on the take. So what happened?'

'What happened to what?'

'Your dancer?'

'Well, you know me, the jealous type. She was too career-minded.'

'You should have taken up ballet and joined her. Broke your heart, I expect?'

'Did, as a matter of fact. Funnily enough, I dreamed about her the other night. It's the ones who get away we remember, isn't it?'

'True,' Pearson said. He burped.

'D'you remember your first?' Lloyd asked after a pause.

'Yes and I remember the venue too. I booked us for a dirty weekend in some hotel in Midhurst. Ghastly place as I remember. Flock wallpaper everywhere and full of County types drinking double gins before breakfast. I checked us in under separate names and gave the night porter a hefty tip. Crept along to her room at midnight.'

'Very Agatha Christie.'

'You're not far wrong. It was the sort of hotel where you expected the vicar to have done it. Unfortunately my lady friend got the curse the moment she stepped over the threshold. Nerves, I expect. Anyway, it was a complete disaster. Rained the entire time and she cried her eyes out.'

'Well, it wasn't your first then.'

'It was the first *attempt*,' Pearson said with a tinge of nostalgia in his voice. 'You're heading in the wrong direction, by the way.'

'How come?'

'Putney.'

'We're going there, are we? You didn't say.'

'Yes, I did. Or if I didn't I meant to, start reading my mind.'

'Jesus!' Lloyd activated the siren again and swung across the oncoming traffic to go in the opposite direction. 'D'you ever wonder what happened to her?'

'Who?' Pearson asked.

'The bird you took down to Midhurst.'

'No.'

'That's not normal.'

'I'm not normal. Haven't been normal for years. How can you be normal in our job? Stands to reason.'

They both pondered these and other inescapable truths for the rest of the journey to Deodar Road.

Carstairs's house had a somewhat gloomy aspect; the front

garden had a mixed holly and laurel hedge instead of the smartly painted iron railings of its immediate neighbours.

'Well, if he was taking the dropsy,' Lloyd said, 'he certainly didn't spend it on the paintwork.'

They walked to the front door and pressed the bell. There was a *Vote Lib-Dem* sticker fixed to the inside of the downstairs bay window. A dog started to yap, one of those croaky barks peculiar to very small dogs. Then a woman's voice said, 'Now go back, Monty, go in your basket. Go on, do as you're told and shut up.'

The door was not opened immediately. Instead the woman spoke from behind the frosted glass panel. 'Yes? Who is it?'

'Colleagues of your husband, Mrs Carstairs.'

'He's not at home,' the woman answered guardedly.

'No, it's you we wanted to see, Mrs Carstairs.'

Mrs Carstairs opened the door a fraction, but it was still held on a security chain.

'D'you have any identification?'

'Of course.' Pearson handed her his wallet through the crack in the door, the wallet opened to reveal his plastic security pass.

After a slight pause, Carstairs's wife closed the door again and released the chain. When she opened it, she wasn't what either of them had expected. Not in the least. Had they been asked, they'd have guessed she'd be middle-aged and mousy, a gender clone of her late husband, but Pearson and Lloyd were confronted by somebody who looked as though she might have been cast as a barmaid in some sit-com. Of indeterminate age, probably late thirties, blonde, heavily made-up, painted fingernails, numerous gold bracelets, wearing a tight sweater and smart slacks. An Aids bow was pinned to the sweater. Her breasts, whether true or false, pointed at them like twin shell cones.

'Sorry to put you through the rigmarole,' she said, 'but you can't be too careful these days, can you?'

'Absolutely right,' Pearson said as she stood to one side and allowed them both to enter.

'You read such dreadful things in the papers. Seems as though serial killers are on the increase. I was reading about that American chap who kept the bodies in his fridge . . . And that film! I didn't think that nice Tony Hopkins should have played that part. I like it best when he's a butler. I walked out, couldn't take it after a while. Come on through into the lounge.' She spoke in a strange, little girl's voice, with an accent that suggested she had taken a correspondence course in posh, but had failed to complete the curriculum. 'Wasn't expecting company, so you'll have to excuse the mess. My daily had one of her turns and didn't show up.'

The dog started to bark again as she led them into an over-heated room that had been extended by a conservatory and looked out on to the garden and the river beyond. The main suite of furniture was in leather, arranged in front of a fake log fire. Various women's magazines and dirty coffee cups were strewn around and there was an open box of chocolates on the hearth.

'Can I offer you a drink?' Mrs Carstairs asked.

'A bit early for me,' Pearson said.

'And, no, thank you, I'm driving,' Lloyd replied.

'Quite sure? Well, do you mind if I do? I could just kill for a crème de menthe. My weakness,' she said with a flirty smile, adding 'one of them anyway.' She helped herself from a garish drinks trolley that held a formidable array of bottles. At that moment, the small dog – a minute Yorkshire terrier – crept into the room, took in Pearson and Lloyd, and gave a solitary yap before scurrying to a distant corner of the conservatory.

'Oh, don't be so silly, Monty, come and make friends, come on. Proper little poof, you are.' But the dog stayed put, quivering. 'Funny, dogs, aren't they? Some people they take to straightaway and others make them go all peculiar. As if they sense something, bad vibes or something. You'll have to excuse him. Well, now, what can I do for you? Do sit down. Sling those magazines off the chairs.'

They all sat in an uneasy semicircle. Pearson cleared his

throat. The dog finally crept to its mistress and she picked him up on to her lap.

'Well, I don't know whether your little dog picked up bad vibes from us, Mrs Carstairs,' Pearson began. 'They do say animals have premonitions . . . I'm afraid the reason for our visit is we don't have good news concerning your husband.'

About to take a sip of her drink, Mrs Carstairs paused. Her eyes, heavily outlined in mascara, opened wider.

'I'm sorry I have to tell you this, but he's met with an accident,' Pearson continued in an attempt to cushion the blow.

'What sort of accident?'

'A bad one, I'm afraid.'

'How bad?'

'I'm sure this will come as a terrible shock to you, but it was a fatal accident, Mrs Carstairs.'

'Fatal? Oh, my God! Don't say that. Not my darling, not my Freddie?' She put her drink down clumsily on the coffee table, spilling it across a magazine cover showing Princess Diana. 'How? What sort of accident?'

'He was found dead in a Bayswater hotel.'

'What d'you mean, a hotel? How could he be in a hotel? He couldn't be in Bayswater. He telephoned me on Wednesday from Copenhagen.'

'You're sure of that?' Pearson asked gently.

'Course I'm sure. He'd been delayed over there, said he'd be back today.' She hugged the dog to her bosom. Although obviously distressed, no tears came, but her voice got huskier.

'Well, it appears he changed his plans, Mrs Carstairs, and we were wondering whether you could tell us why.'

She ignored the question. 'Was it . . . Did he have a heart attack? I mean, how did it happen?'

Pearson exchanged a look with Lloyd before answering. 'No, it wasn't a heart attack . . . at the moment, and it's by no means confirmed, it looks as though he took his own life.'

She stared at him without comprehension, then buried her face against the dog. 'He couldn't, why would he do that?' she said in a muffled voice.

Pearson waited, then said: 'I know how distressing this is for you, but anything you can tell us about your husband's state of mind the last time you saw him would help us. Was he depressed about anything?'

She shook her head, her mouth pressed against the dog. 'Not more than usual.'

'What does that mean?'

'Well, he was never what you'd call, how shall I put it? . . . You know, chirpy.'

Lloyd and Pearson avoided each other's eyes. 'Can I ask you if you were aware of the sort of job he was engaged in?' Pearson continued. 'Or, put it this way, did he discuss things with you?'

'All he ever told me was it was sort of police work. Not murders, mostly investigating financial people and that.'

'Nothing else?'

'No. Not anything that comes to mind.' She downed the crème de menthe and poured herself another.

'Well, of course, any police work carries an element of risk these days. And . . . Some of the jobs put us in danger because we're fishing in murky waters. I'm sorry to press you at a time like this, but he never mentioned names, did he? Names of people he was investigating. If you could think back.'

She shook her head. 'Oh, no. My Freddie was very conscientious like that. Not that I ever probed. We kept that part of our lives very separate.'

'Was it money?' Lloyd put in. 'Did he have money worries?'

'Not that I know of. We always had enough. He never kept me short. I could have anything I wanted, I only had to ask.'

'So you can't think why he would do a thing like that?'

'I don't believe he did. Not my Freddie.' She reached for her drink and spilt it again.

'Let me,' Lloyd said, going to the rescue. 'The same, or would you like something stronger?'

'Yes, I'll have a snifter of brandy.' It was only now that her face began to fall apart. A trickle of mascara started to edge down both cheeks.

Lloyd got up and poured the drink for her. As he came back from the trolley he noticed stray black hairs on the nape of her neck protruding from under what he now realised was a blonde wig. Handing her the brandy he shot a quizzical look at Pearson, but Pearson failed to pick up on it.

'What're you saying? I mean, tell me, I can take it now I've got over the first shock. Did he take pills or what?'

'Not pills,' Pearson said gently. 'He used a gun.'

'Oh, my God!' Brandy seeped from the corners of her red mouth, and she choked back a sob.

'D'you have any relatives or friends who could stay with you tonight?' Lloyd asked.

'No relatives, but I've got a friend.'

'Would you like us to contact her for you?'

'Him. No, I'll do it when I've pulled myself together. Where's my Freddie now?'

'I imagine he's been taken to the mortuary.'

'Will I have to go there to identify him?'

Pearson and Lloyd looked at each other before Pearson answered. 'Well, I'm sure somebody else from the department could spare you that. Leave that with me, we wouldn't want you to be more distressed than you obviously are. I'm sorry we had to be the bearers of such sad tidings.'

'No, I'm grateful. Excuse me a minute.'

She put the dog down and left the room. It started to quiver again, then jumped off the sofa and scurried after her.

'Clock the hair when she gets back,' Lloyd whispered.

'What?'

'The hair. It's an Irish.'

'What're you talking about, Irish?'

'Irish jig . . . wig. Doesn't matter, I'll explain later. Let's go, shall we? We're not going to get anything more out of her in the state she's in.'

They stood as Mrs Carstairs returned, having partially repaired her face.

'Look, Mrs Carstairs, if you assure us you won't be on your

own tonight, we won't bother you any more. If you need to contact me or Mr Lloyd here, I'll leave a number where we can both be reached at any time.' He scribbled it on a notepad and left it on the coffee table.

'Thank you. You've both been very kind.'

'We'll see ourselves out. Don't you bother.' As they went into the hallway they heard the chink of a bottle against glass.

Once back inside their car Pearson said, 'What were you trying to tell me in there?'

'Her hair. It's a wig.'

'So? A lot of women wear wigs.'

'Know what I think? I don't think she's a bird. She's a bloke.'

'Come off it!'

'I'm telling you. That's a bloke. I studied her very closely. From the moment she opened her mouth I thought there was something odd about the voice. Didn't you notice it got deeper?'

'Well, she was upset.'

'And she crossed her legs.'

'What does that prove?'

'Okay, then, what about the Aids bow?'

'What about it?'

'Another pointer. It's mostly men who wear those.'

'Mostly, but women aren't excluded, are they?'

'All right, you have it your way,' Lloyd said as he turned the ignition key. 'But I'll take a bet I'm right.'

'You've always had a thing about poofters. Bloody homophobia.'

'Okay, okay, time will tell.'

'You seriously telling me that Carstairs was gay and shacked up with a cross-dresser?'

'Well, it's not exactly unknown,' Lloyd said, increasingly irritated that his judgement was being questioned at every turn. 'Given the moral climate of this country, I'm amazed you're so naive about certain matters.'

'Who said I'm naive? I just don't happen to buy it, that's all.'

They both remained silent until Lloyd said: 'Never really fathomed it.'

'What?'

'The gay scene.'

'What's there to fathom? Some are, some aren't. Some are born like it, some are converted. Some are butch, some are camp, some are screaming. Same building we all inhabit, some just enter by the back door is how I think about it.'

Lloyd took his eyes off the road and glanced at Pearson.

'I've never heard it described like that before.'

'Well, stay around me and you learn something every day.'

17

DOWNING STREET

'I can't say that I'm happy about bringing this Hillsden fellow back,' the Prime Minister said as the sound of Big Ben striking midnight penetrated No. 10's living quarters. 'I made my views clear to the DG yesterday.'

Swanson sat somewhat awkwardly on the edge of a sofa, nursing a gin and tonic. It was the first time he had been received in the inner-sanctum and he felt uncharacteristically nervous. He cleared his throat and started to respond but the Prime Minister cut him short.

'What has to be emphasized . . . excuse me . . . is that we can't afford for there to be any slip-ups. It seems to me that the previous lot were constantly dropping the government of the day in the shit. In the past the word "security" was usually a contradiction in terms.'

'Following the Home Secretary's guide lines, procedures have been considerably tightened, Prime Minister.'

'Well, long may it continue. This whole racist business is as explosive as Semtex. The tabloids – in fact the media in general – give it too much bloody prominence, helped along by some monumental police fuck-ups.' He looked to see how Swanson reacted to the expletives. Relaxed, sure of himself, conscious that he enjoyed the reputation of being somebody who had finally tamed the loony Left wing of the Party, he had a tendency to use shock tactics with anybody he could push around.

'I'm sure that some of the legislation you introduced in the Queen's speech will go a long way to damp down the situation,' Swanson said at his most unctuous.

'Let's hope so. Getting back to this man Hillsden. I've now had a chance to study the papers. I should have got to them before, but for some reason I was kept in the dark about his past. If he was turned once – isn't that the expression you lot use? – what's to say he can't be turned again?'

'Well, since you've now studied the papers, you will have seen that he was deliberately framed by Lockfield.'

'Yes, well, we can't disinter Lockfield, can we? So his side of the story will never be told. In any event, that whole sorry era is best left buried. What I'm saying is, why should we take Hillsden's version as gospel? Philby's autobiography was exposed as a tissue of lies. Spies live by concealing the truth.' Before Swanson could reply, the PM continued: 'I might add that the Home Secretary also had considerable reservations about signing the pardon.'

'I'm aware of that, sir.'

'But you forced it through, right?'

'It was our view, sir, that we needed a highly experienced officer with a low profile – in Hillsden's case, no profile at all, having been out of circulation for seven years. I'm sure you've been told we've also given him a totally new identity as an added safeguard. I believe we've covered all the bases.'

The PM topped-up his own brandy glass. 'So what is the overall aim of this exercise?' he asked. 'Give it to me in a few words, I've got my boxes to do.'

'The plan is for Hillsden to infiltrate – in the same way that undercover intelligence agents infiltrated the IRA with notable results.'

'I wouldn't call them notable,' the PM snapped. 'We had twenty-five years of it and three thousand dead. Let's not equate the Irish situation with something that hasn't even happened.'

'Well, I think we have to,' Swanson said with a flash of spirit, but then immediately used a more placatory tone. 'In many ways it could be even more threatening to mainland Britain than the Irish situation was. There are shades of the 1930s here. My father always used to say that had we had the will then we could have stopped Hitler with one brigade of Guards. Sadly, we didn't have the will. I hope we don't make the same mistake again. The compulsive purifier is the most dangerous extremist.'

'"Compulsive purifier"? What does that mean?'

'You haven't heard that expression, Prime Minister?'

'No, I haven't.'

'Somebody who divides the human race into the ideally good and the intrinsically evil. The more generally used expression is "ethnic cleansing".'

'You're not saying that we face that?'

'It's a logical extension of what these people in our midst believe.'

'I refuse to countenance that. Unthinkable.'

'I'm sure you're right, Prime Minister. But I'm sure you agree we should maintain vigilance. The last thing we would wish would be to lay your government open to the charge of complacency in security matters.'

'Um. Well, provided we don't have any loose cannons as in the past, I'm prepared to give you a limited amount of rope, but I'm not too keen on any American involvement. I don't trust them. Their "special relationship" with us usually means whatever is in their best interests, rather than ours. That's off the record, of course.'

'Of course. I have to say that their co-operation is useful. They recently supplied us with a hit list of prominent Jews as a result of their investigation into the Freidler murder.'

'Freidler?'

'The banker who was murdered in Atlanta.'

'I'm not *au fait* with that.'

'There was a *Panorama* programme about it a few weeks back.'

'I don't watch television if I can help it. More important things to do.'

'According to the FBI, he was murdered by the National Socialist Action Front, a neo-Nazi group banned by the West Germans in '83, but who have since been operating out of Chile.'

'When you say "hit list", you mean it included names on this side of the water?'

Swanson nodded, delighted at being able to score a point. 'Including a member of your Cabinet.'

For the first time the Prime Minister was visibly disconcerted. 'Who?'

'Montague,' Swanson answered, giving the name of the Minister for Social Services.

'Does he know?'

'We thought it best not to alarm him, but the police are providing extra protection.'

'Well, I insist he's told. That's exactly what I mean. You people are a law unto yourselves, and I'm not prepared to be surprised at Question Time in the House. I shall raise it with the DG.' He got up and made a note in his diary.

'We believed we were acting in the Minister's best interests.'

'God forbid you have to say that to his widow. I insist that the Home Secretary and myself are kept fully informed at all times. Is that understood?'

'Of course, Prime Minister.' Swanson got up and placed his empty glass on the coffee-table. 'I'll take personal responsibility for keeping you up-to-date, and I'm most grateful to you for finding time to see me.'

Winding his way down the staircase, he glanced at the framed photographs of past holders of the highest office, most of them looking like average bank managers staring fixedly into camera, their expressions as blank as their achievements. He thought how much he despised the entire political arena. Politicians came and went, relishing their moments of power, but never solving the eternal problems, merely handing down the ragged legacy of their mistakes to those who replaced them.

18

DOCKLANDS

Hillsden had spent the morning on the police firing range testing his rusty skills.

'Either aim at the head or the balls,' his instructor advised. 'If you ever have to use that thing make sure they go down and stay down. You don't get a second chance these days and you're not exactly in line for taking home a coconut at the moment. Here, try another magazine.'

At the third attempt, Hillsden landed a few shots on target. 'That's more like it, but you're still jerking the trigger. Squeeze it gently. And it's got to be instinctive, like this.' The instructor took the gun from him and fired an entire magazine in rapid succession, scoring every time. 'See what I mean?'

'I see what you mean, but I doubt whether I shall ever be a top gun.'

'You don't have to be that good. Just be accurate.'

Hillsden went back to his office in Docklands in chastened mood.

'Any takers, Sarah?' he asked.

'Well, maybe our first customer.' She held up a letter.

'Who is it?'

'Would you believe, a Mr Hyde?'

'I won't make the obvious comment. Is he one of our specimens?'

'Yes, as luck would have it. Lives in Wolverhampton, drives a 1992 Honda Legend, three years no claims bonus and wants us to give him a quote.'

'What other details?'

'Gives his age as thirty, unmarried, and says he has a clean licence and no previous convictions. Which is a lie because he has some form. I ran him through the central computer and came up with two entries. He was bound over for uttering threats against a neighbour in 1988, and then got two weeks for assault in 1990.'

Hillsden took the man's reply from her and studied it. 'Wouldn't win any awards for calligraphy. What was the assault charge?'

'Arrested during a cup tie. In possession of a dangerous weapon, to wit a bowie knife.'

'Just your average football fan out for a quiet afternoon's fun. What are we quoting on a 1992 Honda Legend? Have you looked up the scales they gave us?'

Sarah gave him another sheet of paper. 'Yes, but I'd like you to check it. Does that seem right to you?'

'Very reasonable. Over a hundred pounds less than he's paying on his existing policy.'

'So, shall I write back and give him a quote?'

'No, better still, phone him. I need to get face to face. Thank him for his reply and say you're sure we can quote a substantially reduced rate. Say that, as it happens, one of our representatives, a Mr Bartlett, covers his area and would be pleased to call on him. Ask when it would be convenient and fix it. Use your charm. We're a friendly company, don't forget. That's our image.'

'Is it?'

'Absolutely. Ring him now. And if you get him and he agrees, try and fix an appointment for tomorrow. Oh, and look up the trains to Wolverhampton and see if I can make a connection from Suffolk.'

'Won't you drive up?'

'No. According to the news every bloody motorway to the North is under repair for months, probably years. I'll pick up a hire car when I get there. Oh, and I'll need a street map of the area.'

. . .

The next day as he was preparing to leave, Galina said, 'It's not like I thought.'

'In what way?'

'I thought we'd be together more, but you're always away in London.'

'Isn't Audrey good company?'

'She's all right, but I don't understand half the things she says to me. Her accent.'

'Well, early days yet. But you're happy, aren't you? You like this house?'

'I'm not unhappy. Just lonely. How long will you be away in this place you're going to?'

'Only a day. I'll be back tomorrow. Why don't you ask Audrey to drive you into Bury St Edmunds?'

She shrugged.

'D'you have enough money?'

'Yes, I have money. It's not money.'

'What then?' Hillsden said, keeping his voice even, though he was anxious to get away. 'I thought, later on, you should have lessons and take a driving test. Then you could drive yourself around, explore the countryside. No?' when she shook her head. 'Isn't that a good idea?'

'Perhaps. I don't know.' Then she added, 'Lara has nightmares, too. And every day she asks why we've all got different names. She doesn't like her new name. She's only tiny, she doesn't understand, and I don't know how to explain it to her. Can you think of something?'

'I'll try. What did you mean, you have nightmares, too?' He kept the question casual.

'Well, I do.'

'Why didn't you tell me?'

'You've always said you hated hearing about other people's dreams, that they bore you.'

'Well, maybe as a general thing, yes, but nightmares are different,' Hillsden said with a quick glance to the mantelpiece clock. 'If you're troubled you should tell me, that's what I'm here for,' then, as her expression changed, he immediately wished he had put it another way, softened the obvious.

'It's always the same nightmare,' Galina said. 'I'm being questioned by you in a bare room and you're in uniform, like the KGB. You're very angry and you keep shouting at me, but I can't hear the questions so I can't answer you. And then you take out a gun and Lara's there . . . and you shoot her in front of me. That's when it ends.'

Hillsden put his arms around her. 'Oh, sweetheart, that's horrible and I'm sure it's upsetting, but it is just a dream. I wouldn't harm Lara, I love her, I love you and this is a bad time we've got to get through. I wish you could make some friends in the village. Somebody with children of Lara's age. There seem to be plenty about.'

But, even as he spoke the words, he thought, what have I condemned her to? There were fault-lines running through any advice he gave her, since he knew the immediate future held nothing but further loneliness for her. Village life, he thought, why should she get a thrill out of that? I know I wouldn't. The minutia of over-the-hedge gossip, the everlasting British obsession with the weather, local politics that were even more boring than the national variety, elderly women exercising equally elderly dogs, the vicar chatting up church-going spinsters after communion – why am I trying to pretend any of it holds the slightest interest to a Russian girl dumped down in the back of beyond? He remembered a line of Larkin's – *Life is first boredom, then fear.*

'The reason I haven't made friends is because I'm scared.'

'Scared of making friends?'

'No, I'm worried that Lara might say something . . . See, even I use the wrong name . . . Not that she'd mean to, but because she doesn't understand the situation, she might put us in danger.'

'You're not scared living here, are you?'

She shook her head. 'But I only feel safe when you're here.'

'Nobody'll get past Audrey, she's better than a Rottweiler.' He looked at the clock again. 'Darling, I have to go now, otherwise I'll miss the train, but I'll be back tomorrow evening at the latest, and I'll ring you as soon as I get there. When I get back we'll have a proper talk about it and work something out. I can't bear to leave you like this.'

'I'm probably just being silly. Forget it. You get off.'

'No, I can't forget it, and I'll make it right somehow.'

They kissed and he made his escape. Audrey was in the kitchen, swearing to herself, as he appeared downstairs.

'What's wrong?' Hillsden asked.

'Audrey's made a cock-up of these waffles. Thought they'd be a treat for Laura's breakfast. I read somewhere kids like them, but you could re-tile the kitchen with these.' She indicated a stack of rejects on the kitchen table.

'Never mind. The thought's the thing. Do me a favour, try and think of something to amuse them both while I'm away. Georgina seems very depressed this morning. See if there's a good film on. But nothing scary.'

'I'll look in the local paper. Good luck with your trip.'

As he reversed the car out, he realised how swiftly he had once again been absorbed into a world he had thought he had renounced for ever, a world where ordinary emotions were pushed into second place – no time for endearments, no time to make love, just the necessity of the treadmill. On the surface everything was normal: to a casual onlooker in the village he would appear to be a man leaving to go to work, another breadwinner with all the usual worries the struggle for survival imposed. How easily I lie, he thought with a sense of revulsion. To myself, to her. Half of my life has always been hidden. The only person I was ever able to speak to without prudence was Caroline. 'You poor sod,' he said aloud to himself as he adjusted the rear mirror and hit the de-mister button, 'you're back in the game with a vengeance.'

. . .

When he arrived at the station he was greeted with a notice crudely chalked on a blackboard announcing a number of train cancellations due to lack of staff, including the one he had intended to catch. His enquiry at the ticket office produced only a surly and non-committal answer from a fat, unshaven youth wearing what looked like a cast-off uniform several sizes too small for him. The station itself seemed, to his unaccustomed eyes to have been assembled from building blocks. In his memory, he had always retained an image of simple, well-proportioned country stations such as Betjeman had spent a lifetime extolling. Now there was only a plastic uniformity copied from the Siberian model and announcements made in an unintelligible language so that one might as well be an alien visiting earth for the first time. He waited, pacing the platform with fellow disgruntled travellers, until finally the loudspeakers crackled another announcement.

'What did that say?' he asked the man next to him.

'Where are you trying to get to?'

'Wolverhampton.'

'We have to change at the next stop. That is if we ever make the next stop,' the man added with that cheerful fatalism programmed into those who daily entrusted their lives to the British rail system. 'This one terminates there.'

When the train arrived, he and the man got into the same dusty carriage. Discarded beer cans rolled backwards and forwards with the jerky motion and although there were prominent 'No Smoking' notices, Hillsden saw that the floor was littered with butts. He made an effort to put Galina's anxieties out of his mind and to concentrate on what lay ahead. His companion opened his newspaper and Hillsden stared at the headline: *Revealed: the secret thoughts of Harold Macmillan*. As if, he pondered, secret or otherwise, they have any relevance now, except to fill a few column inches, but then he remembered that, when put out to pasture, politicians were always brimming with hindsight. It was a British failing always to hark back to a halcyon past that never existed – to a time when, allegedly, we exerted a benign moral influence, whereas in truth we had always been the bad schoolboys of Europe, breaking the rules with a chilling superiority, Harry Wharton and Co. with an X-rating.

It was mid-morning before he finally arrived at Wolverhampton. He organised a hire car, then checked into the motel that Sarah had booked, paying for it with his credit card and managing to write a decent cópy of his well-practised new signature. Like many of its kind, the motel had been designed like the lower decks of a cruise ship – endless narrow corridors, intersected every twenty yards with fire doors, giving access to the identical cubicles. Hillsden opened the door to his room with the plastic security lozenge. Inside it was clean and functional, providing the necessary minimal comforts – a double bed, dressing table unit, a television, trouser press and a tray containing an electric kettle together with a basket full of tea bags, sachets of coffee, sugar and small cartons of long-life milk noted for their resistance to being opened. The framed print above the bed was screwed to the wall, he noticed. Although an improvement on what used to pass for a modest British hotel, there was a sterile gloom about it, betraying the fact that most of those who used it were just passing through. Maybe, Hillsden thought as he unpacked, the very anonymity is a sort of refuge: you bring no memories to it and take away none.

After consulting the notes Sarah had typed for him, he sat on the edge of the bed and dialled Hyde's number, letting it ring half a dozen times before deciding that he would probably have to wait until Hyde returned from work. He spent the next hour going over the sort of questions he would be expected to answer, then switched on the television. The only channel that held his interest for a while was showing an old black and white movie – Jack Warner epitomising the British bobby and meeting his maker at the hands of Dirk Bogarde. Later, he left the room and wandered the streets, amazed by the proliferation and variety of restaurants that had sprung up since last he had been in middle England. The contrast between the present reality and the make-believe world once inhabited by gentle Jack Warner and company brought home how great the change had been. But what surprised him most was the difference in dress: with few exceptions even the middle-aged of both sexes now sported trainers and crumpled jeans – the Americanisation of England being firmly established at all levels, just as the days of Ealing films were over, obliterated by the nihilistic fantasies of Hollywood. It was as though the inhabitants were determined to ape a culture few of them had ever experienced at first-hand, but were brainwashed by the imported sit-coms and mini-series to the point that they no longer had any faith in their native identity.

He had a snack meal then rang Hyde again from a public phone. This time Hyde answered.

'Oh, good afternoon,' Hillsden said. 'My name is Robert Bartlett. Can I speak to Mr Hyde please?'

'Who are you?'

'Bartlett. From Avalon Insurance. My company wrote to you and then I believe you kindly agreed to let me pay you a visit.'

'Oh, yeah, that's right.'

'From what you've told us I think we'd be able to reduce your car insurance substantially. I'm in the area and wondered if it'd be convenient to call on you.'

'When?'

'You say.'

'Now, you mean?'

'If that suits you.'

'Well, I just got in . . . Yeah, okay, but give me a couple of hours.'

'Around seven then,' Hillsden said, consulting his watch. 'Thank you, Mr Hyde. I look forward to meeting you.'

Hyde hung up first. Returning to the hotel, Hillsden showered and, before dressing, rang Galina. Audrey answered.

'Audrey, it's me. How's Georgina?' he asked, remembering

but still finding it strange to use her new name.

'Seems fine.'

'Did you go out?'

'No, she decided against it.'

'I see. Well, let me talk to her.'

When Galina came on the line he willed tenderness into his voice. 'Had a good day, darling?'

'Not too bad.'

'Did you go to the cinema?'

'No.'

'Oh, nothing good you wanted to see? *The Jungle Book* is showing up here, that's something Lara would like.'

'Has your day gone well?'

'Lousy train journey and this hotel's not up to much. I shall be glad to be back in my own bed with you. I miss you. Listen, darling, I'm just off to keep a business appointment, but I'll ring you again. What time are you going to sleep, I don't want to wake you.'

'I don't know, but it doesn't matter if you wake me. Promise you'll ring.'

'Of course I will. Is Lara still up?'

'Yes.'

'Let me say good night.' He heard her shout for the child to come to the phone and a moment later his daughter's squeaky voice was in his ear. Why were children always out of breath when they spoke on the phone? 'Hello, precious. What have you been up to?'

'I saw a fox.'

'You did?'

'Yes, he walked through our garden.'

'Well, that was something, wasn't it?'

'And the cat that lives across the road. He was sick.'

'Was he? Oh, dear.'

'Lots of it. Bye.'

She went. Galina picked up the phone again. 'That was short and sweet,' he said.

'She's watching television.'

'Talk to you later then. Okay? Love you.'

'Love you.'

Before putting on his shirt, he wired himself, using a roll of flesh-coloured surgical tape first to attach the battery to his waist, then strapped the miniaturised recorder under his left arm. Once he had finished dressing, he carefully checked his appearance in the mirror, then left the room. It was raining when he got to the car park and the wipers on the rented car smeared the windscreen. Aiming to give himself plenty of time to find Hyde's house, he consulted his street map again before driving off. His route took him out of the city to what looked like a recently built housing estate – row upon row of neat, characterless boxes arranged back to back. He finally located Hyde's house and, as he was still early, drove on past it, noting a dozen or more 'For Sale' boards, a pointer to the long recession that was still depressing the market, Thatcher's dream of a house-owning society in ruins. Here and there, satellite dishes were stuck to the side walls, their phallic centre stamens aimed skyward to capture Murdoch's electronic Babel. Circling the estate by a different route he came upon a mosque, its dull gold minarets outlined against the turbulent clouds, and close by a wooden structure advertising itself as the local Labour Party Club – one sacred alongside one profane? Hillsden wondered. Retracing his route at a deliberately slow speed (he felt it was probably a good thing not to appear too keen), he arrived outside Hyde's house eight minutes after seven. Hyde's Honda was parked on the small forecourt. Before leaving his own car he activated the tape recorder.

Hyde opened the front door after the second ring. He was a burly man with tight, wavy hair which clung close to his scalp, clean shaven, wearing a smart denim shirt and jogging trousers, and seemed at first glance older than the age he had given on his reply form.

'Mr Hyde?'

'That's right.'

'Bartlett. Sorry I'm slightly late. These streets all look alike and I took a couple of wrong turnings.'

'Yeah, it happens. You want to come in?'

'Thank you.'

Hillsden was led into a neat, open-plan living room-cum-kitchen, furnished with a collection of matching Habitat pieces. There were no feminine touches and the only decoration was a large, framed map of the world, illuminated from behind, which showed the time zones.

'Let's sit at the table,' Hyde said. 'Can I give you a beer?'

'That's kind of you but, no, I'd better not. I'm driving.'

'Suit yourself,' Hyde replied laconically. He moved to the fridge and took out a can for himself. 'So, what have you got for me?' There was no trace of a provincial undertone in his voice. If anything, Hillsden would have placed it as a flat, London accent.

Hillsden opened his briefcase and took out the necessary papers. 'Well, now, let's see, I'll just run through your letter. You own a '92 Honda, which I take it is the one outside?'

'Yeah.'

'And under your current policy you're paying four hundred and forty for full comprehensive, with a hundred pounds excess. You have a clean licence, correct?'

'Correct.'

'Good.' Hillsden made a tick on the form. 'Anything pending I should know about?'

'Couple of parking tickets.'

'Well, we won't bother about those. I had four in the last month. They work on commission, you know, those cowboys.'

'You don't have to tell me. I hate the pigs.'

'I see you give your occupation as company director. What sort of company is it?'

'Private security. We patrol this estate, looking after the whites.'

Hillsden made no reaction to the use of the word 'whites', but said, 'It's terrible, isn't it, the way we all have to live now? And getting worse. I shouldn't complain, I suppose, because it's good for my business, but everywhere I go I see the same thing. The only growth industry in this country seems to be crime.'

'Yeah, you can say that again.'

'You're much younger than me, but I can remember when I grew up my parents never locked the front door. They kept the key on a piece of string through the letter box. Things have certainly changed since those days.'

'Yeah. So, what're you offering?'

'Sorry. Didn't mean to get on my hobby-horse. Well, now, taking into account your clean bill of health, the age of the car and the fact that you're not engaged in any of the restricted occupations – actors and jockeys are high on the list, believe it or not – I can quote you a very keen price.'

'How keen?' Hyde took another drink from the beer can.

'Give me a minute.' Hillsden took out a pocket calculator and punched in some numbers, then paused. 'I'll be frank with you, Mr Hyde. In order to compete with the big boys we have to cut our overheads down to the bone, which in turn means we can pass on the savings to our customers. Plus the fact we want your business. And since you're my first in this area, I'm going to bend over backwards.' He resumed his calculations, then paused again. 'One thing I should have asked. You have a current MOT on the car, I take it?'

'Yeah. Want to see it?'

'No, I'll accept your word . . . Now then, what comes up for full comprehensive, excess slashed from a hundred to fifty, plus free windscreen replacement for one year, is a saving to you of a hundred and eight pounds. Your premium would be three thirty-two, payable in one lump sum or, if you prefer, twenty-seven and a bit a month plus two per cent interest. If you stay with us and don't have a claim we guarantee the rate for three years.' He was enjoying himself and was secretly pleased that he had mastered the patter.

'Three thirty-two?' Hyde repeated.

'That's what I said. How does that seem to you?'

'What's the catch?'

'No catch. We want the business from reliable people like yourself.'

Hyde got up from the table and went for a second can of beer. 'Sure you won't change your mind?'

'Okay,' Hillsden said, 'you twisted my arm.'

'This is good stuff. Chum of mine goes over to France every week. Nice to get something back from the frogs for a change.'

He opened Hillsden's can before passing it to him. 'Yes, okay,' he said, 'I'll go for it.'

'You will? Wonderful. I assure you, you won't regret it. Cheers.' He drank some of the beer and relaxed for the first time since he had entered the house. 'Excuse me asking, but is that real?' He pointed to a parrot perched on top of the television set.

Hyde laughed. 'No. Fools everybody though. A girlfriend gave it to me for Christmas. Watch. Listen to this.' Projecting his voice louder in the direction of the parrot, he said: 'Pakis out.'

There was a slight pause and then the parrot repeated, 'Pakis out.'

'Cute, huh?'

'Incredible. Will it say anything else?'

'Sure. Repeats everything. Try it.'

Hillsden spoke at the bird. 'Pretty Polly.'

The parrot repeated the words.

'How the hell does it work?'

'Who knows?'

'What a novelty. I must get one of those for the office. Be a talking point with clients.' He returned to his papers. 'So, we're in business, are we? I've filled in all the necessary details, all it needs is your signature here . . . and for you to initial there and there. Did you want to pay monthly?'

'I think maybe, yeah.'

'Then you'll need to fill in a bank mandate.' He passed the papers and a pen across the table to Hyde. 'Keep the pen, by the way, it's got our telephone number on in case you need us for any emergencies.'

Hillsden watched as Hyde completed and handed back the

papers. 'I'll send you the policy later this week. You have seven days to study it before you're committed. I think that's everything, and thank you once again.' He drank some of his beer before saying casually, 'Do you get much aggro on this estate in your line of business?'

'You'd better believe it. This place is a ghetto, swarming with coloureds. What you said about your parents is true. Are they alive?'

'No, they both passed on some years ago.'

'They're well out of it. They wouldn't recognise this country. There's no Great Britain any more. Unless we're very careful we whites are going to be in a minority.'

Hillsden fingered his beer can and avoided looking at Hyde when he answered. I need to pitch my response very carefully, he thought. 'Sadly, I think you're probably right.'

'I know I'm right. Look at the birth rate, theirs and ours. We're on the decline, they're breeding like rabbits.'

Hillsden nodded. 'Nothing we can do about it, unfortunately. We've left it too late.'

'Not us – them, those useless wankers up in Whitehall. They're the ones who've sold us down the river.' Hyde crumpled his beer can and tossed it with accurate aim into the sink. 'But some of us are doing something about it,' he said loudly and the repetition came back from the parrot: 'But some of us are doing something about it.'

Hyde said, 'Where do you live?'

'Forest Gate, East London.'

'Married?'

'I was. My wife died.'

'Any kids?'

'Unfortunately no.'

'Well, maybe that's no bad thing. I've got two kids, boy and girl. So what's their life going to be? They're already outnumbered by coloureds in the classroom. Listen, my view is they're entitled to their own lives, but not here, not in our country. They should ship them all back to where they belong. Overnight you'd wipe out the drug scene, most of the crime and unemployment.'

It was the usual bigot's dialogue, Hillsden thought, belonging to the some-of-my-best-friends-are-Jews school. 'Of course, many of them are second and third generation,' he said, playing devil's advocate.

'So? Don't change their colour, does it? Listen, it isn't just us. Happening all over Europe. The Germans have got the right idea.'

'How's that?'

'I'll show you.' Hyde got up and rummaged in one of the kitchen drawers, producing a magazine. 'Take this with you. It'll open your eyes, believe me.'

Hillsden glanced at the magazine which seemed to have been crudely produced on a computer. It was headed *Action Now!*

'That tells it like it is,' Hyde said. 'The Germans are our natural allies if you study history like I have. I mean, time has shown we should never have declared war on them. If we'd have thrown our lot in with them in '39, we wouldn't be in this mess now. Together we could have taken Russia out just like that,' he snapped his fingers, 'saved ourselves the Cold War.'

'Would that have saved the Jews, do you think?'

'Well, who knows? That's something else. You ever read anything of David Irving's?'

Hillsden shook his head.

'You should. It's an education. He's got his own theories on that subject. But take that copy if you like, read it, might give you something to think about.'

'Thank you, I will.' Hillsden stood up. 'It's been a pleasure to do business with you, Mr Hyde. Enjoy cheaper motoring.'

'Enjoy cheaper motoring,' the parrot said as he left the room.

19

CONVERSATIONS

'Do you ever think about dying?' Lloyd asked. He and Pearson were eating a pizza on their knees in their unmarked car.

'What brought that up, apart from this junk?'

'I don't know, I go to sleep every night wondering whether I'll ever wake next morning. Does it take you like that?'

'No. You must have a guilty conscience about something. Been cheating on the wife?'

'What d'you think about at night then?'

Pearson put the remains of his pizza back in the box and closed the lid. He wiped his mouth on a tissue. 'God, that was revolting. I don't know how this country got hooked on pizzas. It's like the Italians slipped in a new disease when we weren't looking.'

'Mine's okay,' Lloyd said. 'So tell me.'

'Tell you what?'

'At night, what d'you think about?'

'You really want to know? Last night, I wondered whether my eldest grandson was on crack, whether the dishwasher would last out the week and whether my wife had remembered to buy a lottery ticket.'

'And had she?'

'Don't know. Slipped my mind this morning.'

'That's a reason for suicide. Imagine, you use the same numbers every week, you finally hit the jackpot, and then find it's the one time you forgot. Be worse than death, wouldn't it?'

'Cheer me up, won't you?'

'Tell you something else. You were talking about retirement the other day. That's on my mind, too. But I've worked out what I'm going to do, I've already put out feelers. I'm going to get myself a job on one of those crime-reconstruction series on the telly. They've got more police on those than there are on the beat some weeks.'

'And a better success rate,' Pearson said gloomily. 'Notice they always get their man.' He took an antacid tablet and washed it down with a diet Coke. He stared through the windscreen at the passing scene in Queensway. At that moment a traffic warden, nattily attired in one of the new uniforms, arrived by the car and took out his charge pad. Pearson wound down his window.

'You can put that away, sunshine.'

The man went on writing. 'You're on a yellow line.'

'No, what we're on is duty. Now, unless you want to be arrested for perverting the course of justice, I suggest you tear that up. We're here on official business.'

'They all try and pull that one.'

'Do they? Well, perhaps they don't all carry one of these.' Pearson produced his identity card. The warden glanced at it without a change of expression.

'You're still on a yellow line.' He tore off the parking ticket and put it behind the windscreen wipers before moving off.

'Now that has given me thoughts of death,' Pearson said. 'His death.' He put his hand around the side of the window and retrieved the ticket. He gave it to Lloyd. 'You're the driver, you pay it. I'll tell you what does occupy me at night: why did Carstairs top himself?'

'And why was he having a drink with a tycoon?'

'If he was. The owner wasn't positive.'

'Shouldn't we question Charters?'

'Gilbert already has.'

'And?'

'Strongly denies he ever met Carstairs.'

'No harm in us having a second go.'

'Swanson's adamant we don't.'

'Why?'

'Charters is very litigious, issues writs like most people tear off toilet paper. Plus Swanson doesn't want anyone smelling around our Copenhagen operation. I must admit Charters's name cropping up intrigues me though,' Pearson mused. 'I wouldn't have thought Tudor's was his scene. He's not your average disco dancer.'

'Have you seen the waitresses? All dressed like Anne Boleyn with a lot of tit showing.'

'Maybe he's like you, a keen student of history. I must admit this whole Carstairs business has me foxed. Especially since we met Mrs Carstairs. Something doesn't add up.'

'Blackmail maybe?'

'Crossed my mind. Doubt it. No money worries that we know of.'

'The autopsy didn't give us any other clues, did it?'

Pearson shook his head. 'Unless you want confirmation that his idea of a good time was anal penetration.'

'Do me a favour,' Lloyd said with a grimace. 'I don't like hearing those things. Was he HIV positive?'

Pearson shook his head. 'Clean as a whistle. One of the lucky ones.'

'What's the form with our master sleuth, Mr Gilbert then?'

'Cut and dried suicide. No further interest, over to us if we wish to pursue it. You know what they're like at the Yard, they haven't got time to solve crimes, too busy sorting out rogue coppers.'

The traffic warden passed them again. 'And if you're still here when I come back, you'll get another one,' he threw in.

Pearson checked his watch. 'May as well move off, that ponce means what he says. Drop me in Docklands before you take that meeting with the FBI at the embassy. Play it cautiously with them. Word has come down that we're to keep our cards to ourselves.'

'What's this American guy's name?' Lloyd asked as he turned the ignition key.

'Schmidt. Might be a good idea if you went over to Copenhagen on the quiet. Carstairs was getting his information from a character called Van Elst. You could lean on him, no harm done now that Carstairs is out of it.'

Just before they arrived in Docklands, Pearson remarked: 'I'm looking forward to meeting Hillsden at last. Anybody who helped torpedo Lockfield deserves our gratitude. Hillsden was a legend in his time.'

'Aren't we all?' Lloyd said.

. . .

'Hold it there,' Pearson said as he listened to Hillsden's tapes. 'Who was that, who said that?'

'A parrot.'

'A parrot?!'

'It was a mechanical parrot,' Hillsden said, enjoying Pearson's look of surprise, 'repeats everything anybody says.'

'Maybe we should subpoena it as a material witness. Switch off for a moment. Seems to me all you've got so far is fairly tame and predictable.'

'Yes, I agree. You can pick up that sort of dialogue in any pub.'

'Have you contacted him again as he suggested?'

'No, not yet,' Hillsden replied. 'Swanson thought it might look too keen. You seen this rag before?' He picked up *Action Now!*

'Seen varieties of it.'

'Any idea as to where it originates?'

Pearson shook his head. 'Could be any one of a million computers. Did Hyde have a computer?'

'Not that I saw. Didn't seem the computer type to me. Tell me, how come he's allowed to run a security outfit? He has form. Don't they vet these characters?'

'Not that you'd know of.'

'Jesus!'

'How is the rest of the operation going? Have you got any response from any of the other targets on the list?'

'Not so far. We've sent out just under a hundred brochures and so far issued seven policies to genuine customers.'

'Disappointing. Still. Want to ask you something,' Pearson said, switching subjects. 'In the old days did you ever come across one of our chaps called Carstairs?'

'Carstairs? . . . No, don't think so. What was he in?'

'D Section.'

'Doesn't ring a bell. Why?'

'He was transferred to Swanson's operation and sent to Copenhagen to plug a hole there. Weird little character. Weirder than we thought as it turns out. He tipped us off about a consignment of anti-Semitic literature coming our way, then a few days later blew his brains out.'

'What did you mean when you said "weirder than we thought"?'

'Well, as far as we knew he was a happily married man. And in the wider sense that was true. But it turns out that Mrs Carstairs is a drag queen.'

'That's a new one. Even Blunt never went that far,' Hillsden said. 'Maybe we're in for a new cycle of memoirs.'

'I read yours,' Pearson said casually. 'How did you remain sane?'

'What makes you think I did? D'you ever wonder that maybe the reason some of us go off the edge or round the bend is because the job is too awful or too ridiculous to endure?'

'Probably. I've known a few who finally can't take the loneliness and duplicity . . . That might have been Carstairs' problem. Did you ever think of ending it while you were over there?'

'There were times,' Hillsden said. 'I could have drunk myself to death at one point. I guess what saved me when I was staring into the abyss was my wife. I owe her everything. It was a bad time for her, too, until the *coup*. Having our daughter made it all possible.'

'And when this offer came, did you hesitate?'

'Yes.'

'What made you bite the bullet a second time?'

'Money. By the law of averages I'll be under the sod before my daughter's twenty-one. I wanted to leave her and my wife something I never had. Security. That sounds funny, bearing in mind our jobs.'

'And to clear your name?' Pearson asked.

'That too. Again mainly because of my daughter.'

'Are you bitter? I'd be bloody bitter if it'd been me.'

'I'm getting over it. I'd like to have the wasted years back, and lose a few memories . . . ' Anxious to get off the subject, Hillsden said: 'This man Carstairs, was he working on his own or do you have a network out there?'

'On his own. Networks are a thing of the past with the exception of the Middle East . . . ' Pearson broke off and asked: 'Do you have a glass of water?'

'Sure.'

'I need to take a tablet.'

Hillsden went into the small kitchen. 'Tap water okay?'

'Anything.'

Handed the glass, Pearson palmed two tablets into his mouth and swallowed them. 'Occupational condition. I've got one of those stomachs that produces pure prussic acid. What were you saying?'

'I was thinking if Carstairs was flying solo and his cover was blown, couldn't that be the answer?'

'Except they didn't kill him. He came home and topped himself.'

'That's confirmed, is it?'

'Yeah, I don't think there's any room for doubt.'

'How rough do these boys play? They've given me a pea-shooter, presumably with good reason?'

'I think we're looking at a future scenario that could get very rough. The signs are all there. Not that the politicians are prepared to admit it, they're more concerned with deciding where the fucking Channel Tunnel rail link ends up. The truth is governments don't work any more, they promise too much and then can't deliver. And when that happens over a long enough period, the die has been cast, and the reactionaries start moving in. There's a madman waiting in the wings in Russia, Italy's just about ready for somebody to drain the Pontine marshes again, old familiar tunes are being played in Germany . . . and we poor sods are meant to sort it all out with our hands tied behind our backs.'

Pearson's monologue had brought the blood to his cheeks and he seemed embarrassed by his own vehemence. 'Still, I expect we'll muddle through like we always do. Lose all the battles, but win the war.' He stared morosely at the tape recorder, then pressed the rewind button. 'Let me listen to this again. Did you watch television last night by any chance?'

'No, 'fraid not.'

'By coincidence, there was a documentary about Mosley. Impressive speaker. I could understand why people followed him. Odd to think that at one time he was being spoken of as a possible Prime Minister. He might have made it if he hadn't changed his colours. That's a thought, isn't it?'

20

A KILLING IN THE NIGHT

It was the first dead body PC Walters had ever seen. Now, as he stared in some disbelief at the Rt Honourable Emanuel Montague's mutilated corpse he struggled to remember correct procedures. Fumbling with his cellular phone, he twice misdialled before getting through to the station.

'728 PC Walters. Give me the duty officer.'

'What's your problem, Walters?' the station Sergeant asked.

'I'm not sure, Sergeant. Looks like a murder.'

'Hang on, son. First things first. Where are you?'

'Hamilton Terrace,' Walters stammered.

'What number?'

'What's its . . . Montague's house.'

'Shit! Who's dead?'

'Him, himself, the Minister.'

'Oh, shit!' the Sergeant repeated. 'Right, son, don't touch anything, go outside, stay there and I'll get you back-up.'

Before he had stumbled from the scene of the crime Walters had tried mentally to Polaroid his initial impressions. *If you're first on the scene be sure to register details*, had been drummed into him during training, but now he found his mind was a blank. Had he touched anything, disturbed any evidence? He couldn't remember. But he knew that for the rest of his life he would never forget Montague's dead face.

Although Montague, like the rest of the Cabinet, was entitled to police protection, it had not been thought necessary to give him round-the-clock armed protection, since the post of Minister for Social Services was not considered to be high risk. Instead, at night, his London house in this fashionable and expensive area was patrolled every hour. In addition, like his Cabinet colleagues, he had been hooked up to British Telecom's Red Care system, which ensured that if the line to his burglar alarm was ever cut, a signal would be automatically flashed to the police. It was subsequently determined that no such signal had ever been received, the control box digital print-out establishing that the installation had not been operative at the time of the murder.

During the course of his tour of duty that night Walters had twice assured himself that all was well, once at eleven p.m. and again at one a.m. It wasn't until he returned a third time, just before he was due to hand over the beat to his relief, that he noticed something different: a red swastika had been sprayed on to the front garden perimeter wall close to the entrance gate. He directed his torch to examine it more closely, then aimed the beam towards the house. The light picked out another swastika on the front door. He opened the gate to take a closer look and as he advanced up the forecourt he saw that the front door was ajar. There was a closed circuit television camera fixed above the portico, but the lens had been obliterated with black foam. He hesitated, unsure what to do next, then tentatively pushed the door wider and called, 'Sir? Mr Montague, sir?'

There was no reply. He had never met Montague, but had been told that the Minister lived alone when in London, his only staff being a housekeeper who came in on a daily basis, and a government chauffeur who picked him up every morning.

The hallway was in darkness, but he saw a faint light coming from one of the rooms leading off the hallway.

'Police, Mr Montague. Is everything all right?'

Walters took one step inside, then paused, wondering whether such a move would activate an alarm, but nothing happened. He walked slowly towards the light, careful to tread lightly on the marble floor and said, 'PC Walters, sir. Just checking. Your front door was open.' His voice sounded unreal to him, as though coming from a stranger.

He stood outside the room for fully half a minute, weighing up the options open to him. He reached behind and released his truncheon, the only weapon he carried. Listening for and hearing no sign from within, he took a deep breath and pushed the door wide open. He found himself looking into a library. The light source was an overturned lamp which lay on its side close to a leather-topped partner's desk, the crumpled shade a short distance away. He could see no sign of Montague, but he became aware of a sharp, pungent odour he could not identify but would later be told was a mixture of bodily fluids, blood and cordite. Venturing further towards the broken lamp, it was then that he saw Montague, pitched backwards in his armchair, very obviously dead even to Walters's inexperienced eyes, for his throat had been cut from ear to ear so that the head now hung at an angle. A large quantity of blood darkened the front of his torso and ran all the way down to the thick pile carpet. The Minister's red box had been placed on his chest and a notice taped to it. Walters managed not to gag and shone his torch down on the body. Even from a distance he could read the words on the notice. Wavy capitals, almost certainly sprayed from the same can that had produced the swastikas outside, spelled out: ANOTHER JEW LESS. What he failed to notice and omitted from his subsequent written account, was that Montague had also been shot twice; the pathologist later determined that two .22 bullets had been fired from less than three feet away, the first shearing off Montague's top set of dentures, the second entering his left cheek. Fired in pairs known in police jargon as 'double taps', they were the hallmark of a professional assassin.

Out of his depth, and with rising nausea, Walters backed out of the room without making any closer examination. Once in the fresh air again he had retched into a flower bed before being able to phone for assistance.

Three squad cars and an ambulance arrived in quick

succession, the lead car containing two CID officers, one he recognised as a Superintendent Goodwin, a character remote to Walters, with the reputation of being a martinet.

'Who are you?'

'PC Walters, sir.' Walters stood to attention.

'Did you originate the call?'

'Yes, sir.'

'So, show us, where is he?'

Walters led the way into the house. 'In there, sir.' He indicated the murder room. Goodwin and his team went inside. Uncertain as to what was now required of him, Walters hovered in the doorway for a few moments, but when nobody paid him any further attention, he retreated outside. Other cars arrived bringing another CID team. They brushed past him as he stood by the gate wishing he had the courage to have a cigarette. Lights went on in the houses across the street and a man appeared in a dressing-gown.

'What's going on?' the man shouted. 'Somebody hurt?'

'Nothing, sir,' Walters replied. 'Nothing to worry about,' hoping this was the correct response, 'just investigating an alarm call.'

'Pity we don't all get that sort of response,' the man said pithily. 'I waited twenty minutes the other night when mine went off. One law for them, another for us.' He stood surveying the scene for a while, then went back into his house, still muttering.

Walters's relief arrived at that moment, a taciturn older Constable named Cooper, who prided himself for never being fazed by anything.

'What's this flap about then?' Cooper asked.

'Murder, Coop.' Glad to have one of his own kind for company and beginning to recover from the shock of his discovery, Walters made the most of his moment of revelation. 'Somebody's killed the Minister.'

'Oh, yes? Was it you who found him?'

'Yes.'

'Lucky you. Glad it wasn't me. You're in for a long night,

son, writing that up.' Flashing lights from the various squad cars illuminated his smile. 'It's certainly brought out the heavy mob. Who's in charge?'

'The Super. Goodwin.'

'Oh, Christ! Well, I'll make myself scarce.'

'You're meant to relieve me.'

Cooper shook his head. 'No, son. You've got a lot to learn. First on the scene stays until the incident officer dismisses him. You can report that I arrived at the correct time, judged that the situation did not require my presence and went about my proper business, namely policing the rest of the neighbourhood as per.'

He walked away.

Mindful of what Cooper had said, Walters took out his notebook, consulted his watch and was about to begin writing up his report when Goodwin came out of the house.

'You, Constable.'

Walters straightened and turned. 'Sir?'

'What can you tell me?'

'Arriving here to make my hourly inspection, sir, I first noticed the painted signs on the wall and door.'

'What time was that?'

Walters consulted his empty notebook, hoping this would impress Goodwin. 'I have it down as 02.55, sir.'

'And?'

'Well, sir, seeing as how the front door was open, I entered the premises and called out for the occupant – the Minister, sir. Getting no response, I then proceeded further into the house where I saw a light. I then discovered the body.'

'Did you search the rest of the house?'

'No, sir, I immediately phoned the station.'

'But *after* you phoned the station?' Goodwin snapped.

'No, sir, I was told to stay outside.'

'While you were away on your beat, did you see anything suspicious, any cars cruising around?'

'No, sir, the only person I encountered during the previous two hours was a foreign lady who wanted to be directed to

Notting Hill Gate tube.'

'Uh-huh. Well, have a full report on my desk first thing tomorrow.' Goodwin gave no sign that the account had impressed him and went back into the house. Walters felt sweat trickling down from his armpits. He remained at his post for a further two hours until Montague's bagged body was removed. Goodwin and his team walked past him and drove off without a word, leaving the forensic boys to continue working. Still uncertain as to what he should do, Walters had to wait until Cooper finally returned.

'How did you make out with his nibs? Has he gone?'

'Yes. Don't know. Told him all I knew. What d'you think I should do now?'

'Piss off, if I was you, and sell your story to the papers.'

'Don't be daft. Can I go?'

'Far as I'm concerned you can.'

'Will you take over then?'

'Yeah, long as I've missed him.'

As Walters walked back to the station he went over the night's events, hoping that his luck held, that he had not committed any major gaffe. Nothing in his training or the handbooks had prepared him for finding a Minister of the Crown with his throat cut.

21

POST-MORTEMS

The story broke the following day, the first editions of *The Standard* giving it front-page headlines and devoting many column inches inside to an account of Montague's life and achievements. He was described as a devoted family man, proud of his humble origins, an astute politician and passionate supporter of the State of Israel, to which he had donated substantial funds over the years. The lunchtime television news bulletins were extended; Members of Parliament of all persuasions were united in singing his praises as well as deploring his hideous death; the Prime Minister recorded a personal tribute which was televised in all the evening news programmes. A message of sympathy from the Queen was sent to his family, and word was received that the Israeli Foreign Secretary would fly to England for the funeral. It possibly came as a surprise to many that a relatively obscure member of the Cabinet who, while alive, had never attracted undue media attention, should now be painted as a latter-day saint, whose loss immeasurably impoverished the nation's future.

Immediately after he had been informed, the Prime Minister called an emergency meeting of the Cabinet and arranged a reshuffle. Coming as it did not long after he had been deprived of Logan's predecessor, he was conscious that his original, carefully positioned team was now in disarray. When the Cabinet dispersed he had a further session with

Logan and the Commissioner of police.

'It's obvious that the security arrangements were totally inadequate. A good and valuable man is struck down in his own home simply because your people weren't capable of protecting him.'

'We do all we can, Prime Minister,' the Commissioner replied, 'but without introducing draconian measures which would restrict everybody's freedom, I think we have to accept the fact that, in a democracy, a determined terrorist, striking at random, will often succeed, whatever steps we take.'

Logan cleared his throat. 'I have to agree with the Commissioner, regrettable though it is.'

'Well, I don't accept it,' the PM said. He brandished a memo at them. 'I don't call a young, unarmed and inexperienced policeman – who's only been in the Force four months – adequate protection for a member of Cabinet. And how is it that the left hand doesn't know what the right hand is doing? A week or so ago MI5 told me that the Yanks had warned us that a hit list existed and that poor Montague's name was on it. I told them to tell you. Did either of you know that? And if not, why not?'

Logan and the Commissioner looked at each other. Neither wished to be the first to answer, but Logan was forced to. 'I wasn't aware of that particular piece of information,' he said, 'but, of course, the Home Office receives a great number of similar reports, most of which turn out to be the work of hoaxers. Every one has to be investigated and faithfully followed up, but there's a limit, as the Commissioner rightly says, to what his stretched resources can do.'

'That's always the excuse, and I don't wear it. We've poured money into the police and security services, and to be fair, so did the Tories, and yet nothing changes. We were elected on a promise to reverse the trend and something like this makes us a laughing stock. You mark my words, when the media have stopped crying crocodile tears over Manny, they'll turn on us, I've no illusions about that.'

'With all due respect, Prime Minister,' the Commissioner

began, 'the police are always used as a political football. One moment I'm being told to provide more community policing, the bobbies-on-bicycles syndrome, and the next moment asked to take a tougher line. I'm in a no-win situation. Are you saying that I should openly arm every one of my men, a Belfast scenario? Because that's the road we'd be going down. I accept that the tragic affair of last night means we must take a hard look at what went wrong and learn the lesson. However, sir, if you think it appropriate, I am prepared to let the buck stop with me and offer my resignation.' He said all this quietly, but there was no mistaking the ice in his voice.

'I don't want your resignation, Commissioner, though I applaud your integrity. But you have to shake a few rotten apples out of the tree.'

The Commissioner was dismissed, but Logan was asked to stay behind. The moment they were alone the PM turned on him. 'That advice goes for your department too. Tell everybody to pull their finger out. I gave you the bloody job, and I can just as soon take it away. I didn't drag the Party into the twenty-first century to have it brought down by a few neo-Fascists. Root them out or I'll appoint somebody who can.'

. . .

While this dialogue was taking place, a jet-lagged Marvin Schmidt woke up in his London hotel with the phone ringing. It took him several seconds to grasp which country he was in.

'Sorry? Who is this?'

'Commander Pearson. You met with my colleague, Lloyd, yesterday.'

'Oh, yeah.'

'I think you and I should meet urgently in view of what happened last night.'

'What did happen?'

'Haven't you heard?'

'No, I'm sorry, I'm still in the sack. I overslept.'

'One of our politicians, a Minister, was assassinated. He was on that hit list you brought us.'

By now Schmidt had swung his legs over the side of the bed and was coming to. 'Jesus! Right. Give me half an hour and I'll be with you. Where are you?'

'No, I'll come to you. You're at the Hilton, aren't you? I'll pick you up in the coffee shop and take you to Swanson's club.'

'Club?'

'Yes, he thinks our comings and goings will attract less attention there.'

'Okay.'

On his way to the bathroom Schmidt switched on the television. Having put his head under a cold shower he returned to the bedroom and gleaned the facts about Montague's murder while he dressed.

.   .   .

Equally unaware of the night's events, Hillsden was working at his office, going through the latest batch of replies they had received when he became aware that the light on his scrambler phone was blinking. He picked up.

Swanson wasted no time on social niceties: 'Pearson thinks we should all meet in view of this latest thing.'

'What's that?'

'Haven't you seen the papers?'

'Not yet.'

'Switch on your television then.'

'I haven't got one here. What're we talking about?'

Swanson told him.

.   .   .

'This is some place,' Schmidt said. From the moment he had walked in with Pearson, he had been impressed by the

185

polished furniture, the vast portraits of departed luminaries, the reverential atmosphere.

'Yes,' Swanson said, 'we've got some very good kit here.'

'What's it take to join a club like this?'

'A long time,' Swanson replied with a stab at humour.

He settled back into an ancient leather armchair once the drinks had been served. 'Do we look like the Five Just Men? I hope not. This place is very discreet.'

'Four,' Hillsden murmured.

'Come again?'

'The book was called *The Four Just Men*. Sorry, I get very pedantic sometimes.'

'Drank a lot of tea,' Lloyd said.

'What are we talking about now?' Swanson asked.

'Edgar Wallace, the man who wrote it. I read he had his staff put cups of tea all over the house while he dictated. So wherever he walked around he could always find a fresh cup of Rosy handy.'

'That's enough trivia, let's get down to business. Do we have any preliminary details of the autopsy?'

'Yes, basics,' Pearson said. 'He was shot twice by a point twenty-two automatic, and according to Hogg, our pathologist, the throat cutting was done afterwards.'

'Was it a Ruger?' Schmidt interjected.

'The gun? Not sure. They're still carrying out ballistic tests.'

'Freidler was killed by a Ruger, same calibre. The bullets have a low mass and velocity, seldom produce an exit wound but sure make a mess of your insides.'

'What puzzled even Hogg were a number of small foam particles he found in Montague's head.'

'The killer probably used a home-made silencer.' The other four men looked blank and he elaborated: 'An empty Pepsi can fitted over the barrel and filled with plastic is very effective with a Ruger. The smart operators prefer it to the real thing – instantly disposable.'

'New one on me,' Pearson said.

'They found the same traces when they opened up Freidler.'

'You're not suggesting it was the same man who did both jobs, are you?' Swanson said, irritated that the American was airing his superior knowledge.

'No, just that the similarity's there. In both cases it was a professional gun for hire, depend on it. But that's no great surprise, there are plenty of wet boys around when you need one.'

'What's that expression mean?' Swanson asked.

'Agency-speak for assassin.'

Pearson turned to Schmidt. 'Was Freidler on that list the Bureau supplied us with? I can't remember off-hand.'

'No. But, as you must know, he was a very prominent member of the Jewish banking community. Wall Street and Zurich felt that bullet going in.'

'Well, because of some inter-departmental fuck-up,' Pearson continued, 'the police didn't get sight of that list in time. Logan got bollocked by the PM and I got an earful from the Commissioner. Not our bloody responsibility, yet we get the blame.' He turned to Swanson. 'How come the Met were left out?'

'I've no idea. I certainly passed it on.'

'Well, we'd better tighten up all round.'

It was not to Swanson's liking that Pearson had taken over the meeting. He cleared his throat. 'I've gone through it again very carefully and as far as I can ascertain, apart from Montague, there are only two other names on the list that are our immediate concern, the first being Lord Miller, Chairman of Trans-Continental.'

Schmidt asked: 'Jewish?'

'Yes. Original name was Muller, I believe. Pillar of society. Not short of a few million. Was once a member of Maggie's think tank, serves part-time on the Race Relations Board. The other name is Paul Sheenham,' Swanson continued, 'which sounds as if it's from this part of the world, but I could be wrong.'

Schmidt shook his head. 'Yes, you are. He's an ex-basketball star. Went through the drug scene in the sixties, then became a, quote, born-again Christian, unquote. Now has his own church and a television show out of Georgia.'

'Black?' Swanson asked.

'Yes. Another one who's into the religious scam industry. You guys wait until you get some of our holy-rollers here on satellite.'

'Why would he be singled out?'

'He nightly castigates the Right, preaches that the day is dawning when the blacks will take over and has announced his intention of running for President. He's coming your way soon.'

The other four listened intently as he gave the backgrounds to the rest of the names on the list. It included two Democrat Senators noted for their liberal views, a lecturer in political science at the University of Hamburg, a New York rabbi, a prominent French sociologist, two female gay activists, several Afro-American notables, one of whom was a Supreme Court judge, and finally the Jewish head of a Hollywood studio.

'Shades of McCarthy?'

'This year's model. Hollywood is more and more the public conception of what's wrong with America.'

'I would have thought the current trend in violent films suited their purpose. Art anticipating reality.'

Schmidt said: 'Reality's the word. They're not interested in fantasy *Batman* violence. The *Godfather* syndrome is their role model.'

'Are you saying the Mob's involved?'

'Bet your life the Mob are looking to become involved somewhere along the line, ready for any rich pickings that fall by the roadside.'

'Well,' Swanson said, 'a very catholic selection from all accounts, catholic with a small c, that is. Where did the list surface?'

'It came to light during the course of an investigation into another racist murder in Arkansas. We know it originated in Germany.'

'How?'

'It was intercepted by the US mail addressed to one of the men convicted in the Arkansas case, postmarked Frankfurt.'

'What action is the Bureau taking to protect those named?'

'We've got surveillance on every American name.'

'I remember,' Pearson said, 'that when the Jackal came to London and had one of his rare failures when he attempted to assassinate a very prominent member of our Jewish community . . . he left behind a similar list which fortunately he didn't have a chance to work through.'

Swanson took over again. 'Given the steam rising over Downing Street, we can't take any chances where Miller is concerned. Are we moving on that?'

'It's done. Already in place.'

'I take it Marvin knows Robert has gone undercover?'

'Yes, I'm up to date on that,' Schmidt said. He gave a look to Hillsden. 'That's one tough assignment. I went undercover myself once. Two years. Bitched my marriage. Are wire taps allowed over here?'

'Difficult to get officially. Of course we don't always play by the rules,' Pearson answered.

'Nobody heard that,' Swanson said and switched the conversation. 'I should also tell you that a Mossad team are flying in today with the Israeli Foreign Secretary. Not something I welcome, because they're loose cannons usually.' Once again he addressed Schmidt. 'I'd like to know what your brief is. We don't want to get lines crossed.'

'This was just a stop-over to exchange information. I'm on my way to Munich, then Rome and Israel, to see if the scattered pieces of the jigsaw fit together. The murder of your man last night has moved the goal posts.'

'What d'you want from us?'

'Full details of last night's murder and any background you can give me.'

'You say you're going to Munich,' Pearson said. 'How seriously do the Germans take all this?'

'Langley's view is, not seriously enough. Despite what's been happening recently, their courts have been handing out some pretty lenient sentences. They'd like us to think it's not a big problem. Anything that reminds them of the past, they try and brush under the carpet.'

'It's difficult to read our new allies,' Swanson said, leaning back and staring at the ceiling. 'Since the reunification we've seen some ominous signs that they're beginning to flex their muscles again. And don't forget they wrote the original text book. My view is, that for all their big talk, they bit off more than they could chew when the Wall came down. Now they're having second thoughts. And they're less and less willing to admit they should feel guilt for the past. They frighten the hell out of me. Officially, of course, we have to co-operate, but I think we can interpret the rules with a certain amount of discretion. It is, after all, our show.'

Hillsden studied Swanson's bland face. He and his kind never change, he thought. Like Palace courtiers, they rebuff with studied ease any menace to the *status quo*, any threat which might reduce their influence.

22

WONDERFUL, WONDERFUL COPENHAGEN

By the time Lloyd arrived in Copenhagen it was too late for him to begin what he was there for, and in any case he felt he was owed a night off at the Firm's expense. After showering in his hotel, he strolled the pedestrian precincts, finally choosing a restaurant on the waterfront at Nyhavn to have dinner. Oddly, he was not that seasoned a traveller, having only taken occasional family holidays in Spain, and, like many of his countrymen, was disconcerted by the first sight of a foreign menu. On this occasion he studied it without comprehension until rescued by a pert young waitress who guided him to marinated salmon, followed by roast pork and red cabbage. 'And you must have a glass of *kande* with it,' she said.

'Anything you say,' Lloyd responded. When it appeared, the drink proved to be a sort of black and tan – a mixture of two beers, plus aquavit, Pernod and lemonade. After two refills, Lloyd felt no pain and required a taxi to return to his hotel.

He was hungover the following morning, and it wasn't until he had suffered a prolonged cold shower and several cups of black coffee that he felt able to face the world. While dressing he went over what Hadley had told him.

'Van Elst owns a locksmith's in an area called Stroget. You can't miss it apparently. According to Carstairs the shop window has nothing but thousands of keys in it.'

'What cover did Carstairs use?'

'Ostensibly he was on an exchange programme from our

Natural History Museum to theirs, preparing a study on the transmigration of flora for the EEC.'

'How did he feed his stuff back to us?'

'He used a book code based on a seed catalogue.'

'Jesus!' Lloyd exclaimed. 'That's out of the ark. I didn't know anybody still used that. He'd have been safer phoning it in.'

'He was old fashioned, preferred the traditional ways.'

'Not in his sex life, he didn't. What name did he go under?'

'Professor Paul Chandler.'

'Professor?'

'He felt it gave him more authority.'

'Okay, and this Van Elst was his source?'

'Yes.'

'His only source?'

'Yes. He never penetrated further.'

'Tell me about Van Elst.'

'Active member of the Danish chapter of Wiking-Jugend – Viking Youth – just a name for another neo-Nazi outfit.'

'And how did Carstairs make the connection?'

'Through a shared love of nudism.'

'What?'

'Van Elst is a fanatical health freak.'

'You telling me Carstairs went in for that?'

'Apparently, yes,' Hadley said.

'Did you ever meet Carstairs?'

'No.'

'Well, he was hardly Mr Universe. God, that's a grisly thought – Carstairs starkers with a lot of naked Viking youth. Greater love hath no agent than that he bared his all for Queen and country.'

'Well, it takes all sorts in our line of business, doesn't it?' Hadley said. 'The man's dead, so we shouldn't hold that against him. He sent back some useful stuff while he was there.'

Lloyd still carried that disquieting image of the dead Carstairs as he set out from the hotel armed with a tourist street map. On the way he stopped at a news kiosk and bought a health magazine which bordered on soft porn, thinking it might serve a useful purpose when he met Van Elst. Stroget proved to be a popular shopping centre, with the longest pedestrian zone in Europe, and he walked nearly a mile before he located the shop, its unobtrusive front tucked between two more splendid establishments. As Hadley had said, the window was inches deep in keys of all description – old and new, large, small, modern, antique, rusty, gold-plated, you name it, all heaped together.

He stood studying the display for several minutes, then moved to enter by the glass door. It was locked. He peered into the shop and could see two men. Rapping on the glass he caught their attention and mouthed 'Are you open?' One of the men came forward and unlocked the door.

'Ja? Kan jeg hjaelpe dem?'

'I'm sorry,' Lloyd said, 'I don't speak Danish. D'you understand English?'

'Yes, I understand enough.'

'Oh, good. Are you Mr Van Elst, by any chance?'

'No. Was he expecting you?'

'Not really. It's just that we have a mutual friend who asked me to come by and say hello. We share the same interests, apparently.' Lloyd allowed the health magazine to come into view.

'I see. Please step inside,' the man said.

Lloyd went past him into the shop. He smiled at the other man behind the counter but got nothing in return. He heard the shop door being locked again. He turned back and found he was looking straight down the barrel of a handgun.

'Now,' the first man said, 'what is the real purpose of your visit?'

23

PARROT TALK

Hillsden allowed six days to go by before deciding to contact Hyde again, making the excuse that he wanted to deliver the policy in person and go away with a completely satisfied client. 'It means a lot to me to get your business,' he said. 'I'll be frank with you, Mr Hyde, I've been out of work for over two years and getting this job saved my life. I'm the wrong side of the hill and not too many people were willing to give me a chance.'

Hyde readily accepted the explanation and indeed was sympathetic. 'Where are you staying?' he asked once the policy had been handed over.

'This time I'm in a motel on the other side of town.'

'Have you eaten?'

'Not yet, no.'

'Want to come out for a bite?'

'Well, I don't want to put you to any inconvenience, Mr Hyde.'

'I never eat in. Not since my wife took off.'

'You sure now? I must admit it's a bit depressing to eat on my own every evening.'

Hyde took him to one of a chain of steak houses he was obviously familiar with. 'Go for the prime rib, that's always good.'

Conditioned by years of hard drinking in Russia, Hillsden's head remained clear as they polished off a bottle of the house red wine. Facing Hyde across the patterned Formica table in the plastic-covered booth he was careful to keep the conversation away from the topic that occupied him most, and it wasn't until Hyde had finished his second helping of 'home-made' apple pie that had been microwaved into oblivion, that he casually mentioned he had read the copy of *Action Now!*

'Oh, yeah. What did you make of it?'

Acting a role, Hillsden looked round at the adjacent booth before answering in a lowered voice, 'It certainly opened my eyes.'

'I knew it would.'

'I mean, I'm no great student of politics, but in recent years I've lost all faith in governments. I didn't even vote in the last election.'

'You were out of work, right? And nobody gave a toss about you.'

Hillsden nodded. 'I don't want to give you a sob story, because I'm only one amongst many, but I lost my house – that was repossessed because I couldn't keep up with the payments – then my wife got sick, needed an operation, but of course there was a waiting list and by the time they found a bed for her it was too late. She died. Cancer.' He felt conscience-stricken at the ease with which the glib lies passed across the table, thinking, Oh God, how quickly I've slipped into my old clothes.

'That's too bad. What we stand for is not only the truth, but it's patriotic. We want to preserve the old British way of life.'

'You're actively involved, are you?'

'I play my part. Can't just lie down and let them walk all over us. Otherwise we'll end up like bleeding Rhodesia. It was all right for them to come over and fight in the Battle of Britain, wasn't it? Welcomed them with open arms then, didn't we? Then sold them down the river to that black git. Were you in the war?'

'Last two years, yes.'

'Well, then, you know. You were going to come back to a

land fit for heroes, right? You shouldn't have to work at your age. You should be enjoying the fruits of your labours. Instead you're having to graft for a living just to keep a lot of fucking jungle bunnies and druggies on welfare.'

He looked around the restaurant as though daring anybody to question his convictions, then drained his glass of wine. 'Am I right? You know I'm right. Everybody's too shit scared to come out and tell it like it is. But not us. We're going to make changes. Big changes. And those who aren't with us are going to be swept away, and when the time's right we're going to strike. You look surprised.' He beckoned Hillsden to lean closer. 'Know how many people we've already got in the movement? Twenty-eight thousand and growing every day. Not just people like you and me, but important people, people capable of taking over government when the push comes.' His speech was slightly slurred now and he leaned closer, knocking over a plastic bottle of tomato ketchup. 'Can I trust you?'

'I hope so.'

'If you're really anxious to know more . . . I'm going to do something for you. You did me a favour, I'm going to do you one. Got a pencil?'

Hillsden produced a company pen which he handed across.

'Ring this number, ask for Tony and say I suggested you call him to discuss joining the snooker club.' He scribbled the number and address on a paper napkin and handed it to Hillsden.

'Snooker club?'

'That's where our London group meets. I'll tell Tony to expect your call. Have a word with him, he can explain it more.'

'Don't have to play snooker, do I?' Hillsden said. 'Not one of my games.'

'You can always learn,' Hyde said, as he paid the bill. He had ketchup on his hand, like blood.

24

MOVING IT ALONG

It was just gone midnight when the telephone rang. It woke both Galina and Hillsden and he let it ring several times hoping that Audrey would pick up on her extension as she normally did. When nothing happened he reluctantly fumbled to switch on the bedside lamp, knocking over a glass of water in the process.

'Oh, Jesus!' he muttered, as next he dropped the instrument, the cord snaking it out of his reach. When he finally untwisted it and got the receiver to his ear a voice was saying, 'Robert?'

'Who wants him?'

'Is that seven double-nine four?' The delivery was vaguely recognisable.

'Yes,' tersely. 'Who is this?'

'It's me, the Colonel.'

It took a second or two before the name registered. 'God, Colonel, have you any idea what time it is? You've woken the whole household.'

'Yes, do forgive me, old chap, but I thought it important and this is the first chance I've had,' Rotherby said.

Galina sat up in bed. 'Who is it?' she whispered.

Hillsden put his hand over the mouthpiece. Looking at her naked, worried face, he knew her fears: in Russia midnight calls had always carried menace. 'Nothing, sweetheart, just a friend, go back to sleep.'

'Hello, you still there?'

'Yes. What's happened?'

'Reason I disturbed you is I stumbled across something I thought I should alert you to. I'll cut it short because I haven't got any more change. Your car's been bugged.'

Fully conscious now, Hillsden reached for a cigarette.

'You sure?'

'I was on my own on late shift this evening and to pass the time I was shunting around the computer, updating myself on our current wire taps. Your car phone was listed. So, watch your back, old son.'

'Why would the Firm bug me?' Hillsden said, but before Rotherby could answer, the bleeps sounded and he was abruptly cut off.

As Hillsden was untwisting the cord again there was a cry from Lara's room across the passage, and the next moment her small figure appeared in the doorway.

'What was that noise, there was a noise?' she said.

'Just the telephone, baby. Go back to bed, you'll get cold.'

'I had one of those nasty dreams.' She padded closer to the bed. 'Can I sleep with you and Mama?'

Galina roused herself again, 'Yes, come and get in here.'

The child climbed over Hillsden and settled herself between them. Hillsden felt the smallness of her as she nestled against them, twining her legs around his. He switched out the light and thought about what Rotherby had just told him. There was total trust in the little body lying beside him, but that was where trust ended, everything beyond the four walls of the bedroom carried old threats. Surprise at the news gave way to anger. Well, two can play that game, he thought, I've been there before.

When eventually he managed to get back to sleep, he dreamed he was in an unfamiliar room, playing snooker with Hadley, when two men in SS uniforms entered and Hadley denounced him. One of the SS wore dark glasses and as he was being marched away he tore the glasses from this man and found he was staring at Jock's smiling, sardonic face.

Then Jock's features peeled away revealing the skull and a maggot crawled out of one empty eye socket.

. . .

While Audrey cooked breakfast the following morning he made a casual reference to the late-night call. 'Did the phone wake you as well last night?'

'Phone? I didn't hear it.'

'It rang around midnight.'

'I'm sorry, I was listening to a concert on my Walkman,' she apologised. 'Who was it?'

'No idea. By the time I picked up whoever it was had rung off,' he lied. Now caution would have to dictate his every move.

He drove off but stopped the car in one of the lanes a mile or so from the house and, using the tool kit, searched the car, eventually finding the bug hidden behind the speaker grille in the driver's door and wired to be activated by the ignition key. He carefully replaced the grille without disturbing anything. A sliver of ice entered his mind. Was perhaps Audrey, the compliant token woman, a plant? According to her, Hadley had delivered the car prior to the family's arrival, but that in itself proved nothing. What was obvious was that somebody in the Firm still didn't trust him.

Continuing his journey to the railway station, his thoughts were more for Galina's and Lara's safety than his own. For good or bad, Russia was all they had ever known and even for prisoners there was a strange kind of comfort in the familiar. He had moved them from one prison to another, just to exact a stale revenge.

'You bloody fool,' he said aloud, as his concentration lapsed and he had to brake suddenly, his anger directed more at himself than the cyclist he had narrowly avoided.

. . .

The anger stayed with him on the slow journey into London. Staring out of the grimed windows as the train crawled past a stretch of track that was being repaired, other regrets surfaced. He remembered Abramov's offer and thought, Victor had the right idea. Don't get even, get rich. At every turn in my life, he thought, I've betrayed those closest to me: Margot, Caroline and now Galina and Lara. Abramov's unasked for confession about his brother also came back. *I loved him, but I suppose I didn't love him enough. I loved myself more* . . . Is that true of me? Is that true of me, he repeatedly thought as the train finally arrived at the terminal and he walked amongst the hurrying commuters to the barrier, then made his way to a public phone booth and dialled the number of the snooker hall that Hyde had given him.

The line rang at least half a dozen times before it was answered.

'Yes?'

'Could I speak to Tony, please?'

'Not here. He'll be in around two o'clock.'

'Can I leave a message for him?'

'We don't take messages,' the voice said and hung up.

Having left the station forecourt for the underground, Hillsden stood on the platform deciding his next move as a sudden rush of cold air signalled that somewhere in the darkness a train was approaching. Then he heard the sound of a woman crying out and seconds later two youths ran past, scattering other passengers and laughing as they took the exit stairs two at a time. The woman shouted: 'My bag! Stop them, they've stolen my bag!' but her anguished voice was blotted out by the noise of the train as it emerged from the tunnel. The waiting crowd pushed against those alighting as soon as the doors slid open, buffeting each other in their determination not to become involved. Hillsden held back, searching for the woman as the mêlée thinned. She was middle-aged, smartly dressed in a pale grey outfit, an absurd little hat perched on freshly permed hair. Not a regular, Hillsden thought, but somebody up in town for a day's shopping. As she approached he saw that the make-up on her cheeks was streaked with tears.

'They took my bag,' she said in a voice that contained no hope. 'All my credit cards, money, everything. What will I tell my husband?'

'I can give you some money to get home with,' Hillsden offered. 'If that would help.'

She recoiled from him as though such a gesture held further menace.

'Please, take this,' Hillsden said, holding out a note.

She shook her head. 'My husband wouldn't approve, I don't know you.'

As a train swooshed out of the parallel tunnel she began to walk in small circles like some clockwork toy that had malfunctioned, at one moment veering dangerously near to the edge of the platform. Hillsden put out a hand to save her and again she recoiled, raising her hand as if to ward off a blow and managing to knock her hat askew.

'I think you should go up top and report it,' he said, but she ignored him, saying as she backed away: 'Why did it have to be me? I was meeting my friend in Harvey Nichols,' as if this was the sole reason she had been singled out. She took the same exit as the youths who had ruined her day. Hillsden saw that she had a plaster on the back of one ankle where her new shoes had rubbed.

Taking the next crowded train, he stood holding on to a support bar in the swaying carriage, thinking, Should I have done more, chased the thieves, insisted she take the money? He noticed that most of the hanging straps were either broken or missing and recalled that he had been told that they were used as coshes. As a deserted station flashed into view and then was gone again, a memory of a favourite film he had seen as a child, *The Ghost Train*, came into his mind. That and *Oh, Mr Porter* – reminders of a time when travelling, like going to a Saturday matinée, had been a placid adventure. The annual family holidays in Weymouth during summers that he only remembered as hot under unblemished skies. A vision of his father, collarless shirt, braces, trousers rolled up to the knee, a handkerchief knotted at four corners and stuck on his balding head to prevent sunburn. He and his kind seldom bared more of their bodies in those pre-war days, so that when they returned home their arms and necks were burnished with russet tidemarks. Hillsden saw it all again: sepia snapshots taken with a box Brownie, faces from the past squinting into the sun, himself beside sand castles destined to be swirled away by evening and built again the next day, sad donkeys with wary infants on their backs clutching the stiffened manes, the only violence played out in Punch and Judy shows.

It came to him that what had prompted these images was the woman whose bag had been stolen. She had had the same gentle features as his mother, her make-up applied in the same inexpert way. What had his mother always worn? Yardley's face powder, that was it, and a dab of *Evening in Paris* perfume, the poor's version of Chanel No. 5. Her best clothes, too, never quite in fashion, always a few years out of date, but carefully put away after any special occasion so that a faint smell of camphor always lingered. He could see all that so clearly, but wondered what had he ever known of his parents' inner lives? Had it been good, bad, both by turns? The most he had been conscious of then was that there was always food on the table, nothing fancy, but adequate: tinned salmon for Sunday tea, followed by lardy cake that none of his women had ever been able to make since, the recipe dying with his mother. Today, looking at television talk shows, reading articles in the Sunday supplements, it seemed that anybody who had ever been famous for five minutes could be relied upon to trot out examples of their parents having failed them: naked, personal hatreds exposed for profit. *I need to find myself*, most of them said, as if anybody ever found themselves or others. We only tell what we want to tell,

Hillsden thought, we only see what we want to see, and, bringing his thoughts back to himself, he recognised that, although he knew next to nothing about his dead parents, he had never felt abandoned or disaffected because of that. Perhaps they too died knowing little of him, wishing that they could have had dialogues that went beyond a recitation of the day's events, something more than a glimpse into a life they had produced but had never understood.

Coming out of these thoughts he glanced up as the train stopped and saw that he had gone past his station. He just made it on to the platform before the doors hissed closed. Emerging irritated and disorientated into the street, he was at a loss to get his bearings. The snooker hall he had to locate was in Shepherd's Bush, an area he had once been familiar with: East Acton was an unknown country. He cursed himself for not bringing a street map. Nothing in the immediate vicinity gave him a clue as to which direction he should take. He stopped an old man pushing a stolen supermarket trolley overflowing with plastic flotsam.

'Can you help me, please? I have to get to Shepherd's Bush. Which way do I go?'

'Who did?' the old man said. His face was encrusted with dirt.

'Me. I'm trying to get to Shepherd's Bush.'

'The Lord Jesus is your only Saviour,' was the reply, delivered with the old man's eyes fixed on something in the distance that only he could see.

'Doesn't matter, sorry to bother you,' Hillsden said. He walked to a main road and was lucky enough to find a cruising taxi. He was careful not to give the exact address, just the street; people remembered taxis.

Once he had arrived, he waited until the taxi drove away, then walked to the snooker hall. It had a plain brick exterior which, inevitably, was disfigured with graffiti, and three square windows made of thick glass blocks. There was a flickering neon sign over the entrance which should have read GARRATY'S but the first three letters were dead. There was nobody on the door and he went inside to find it more spacious than the façade suggested. He guessed that at one time it had either been a car repair shop or a warehouse for it lacked any pronounced architectural features, being merely a long rectangular room, painted in a dark colour and housing a dozen full-size snooker tables under canopied lights. There was a bar down one side and a few one-armed bandits. A large notice behind the bar stated 'No Credit' and, underneath, gave a price list of the hourly rates for the tables. A trophy shield stood on a bracket in the centre of the opposite wall, surrounded by tattered photographs of past recipients. All the billiard tables were in use, the regular click of the balls being the most noticeable sound: this was a venue for serious players, not a haunt of casuals.

Some of the spectators glanced at him as he entered and went to the bar, but otherwise he attracted little attention.

'A Heineken, if you've got it,' he said to the barman.

'Budweiser or Fosters,' the barman said without looking at him, being far too engrossed by a tricky shot on the nearest table.

'Budweiser then,' Hillsden said.

Without taking his eyes off the game, the barman reached down, produced the can of beer and placed it on the counter top. 'One sixty,' he said. Only when the shot had been accomplished did he turn his attention to Hillsden. 'If you're looking for a game, you've got a long wait.'

'That's okay. I actually came in to see Tony. Is he about?'

'Table eleven,' the barman said. 'But don't put him off his stroke. He's on a break.'

Hillsden took his drink and wandered down the line of tables. Finding table eleven, he took a seat next to the player sitting it out while the man he took to be Tony made all the running. Ball after ball was dispatched into the pockets with deadly accuracy as Tony moved around the table, chalking his cue, picking his angles, then completing the execution. He was a well-built man in his thirties, wearing a checkered shirt and jeans held up by an oversized leather belt with an imposing silver buckle.

Money changed hands when the final ball found its home and the disgruntled loser drifted away. As he pocketed his winnings, Tony took in Hillsden. 'You looking for a game? Tenner a frame if you're interested. Best of three. Double or quits for the third.'

'I don't play I'm afraid. If you're Tony, a friend of yours, Les Hyde, suggested I looked you up.'

'Yeah?'

'Yes, he thought I might like to join the club.'

Tony looked him up and down. 'We don't take non-players.'

'I think he had something else in mind.'

'Such as?'

'He said you'd tell me.'

Tony stared at him and lit a cigarette American style, shaking the cigarette out of the packet. 'Oh, yeah. And who are you?'

'Robert Bartlett.'

'Where did you meet Les?'

'At his home in Wolverhampton.'

'How come?'

'In the course of business.'

'What business is that?'

'I'm an insurance agent. I sold him a policy on his car. Let me give you my card.'

Tony took the card and examined it in a way that suggested he was not impressed. 'So what did he tell you?'

'He gave me a magazine to read which explained certain things I hadn't realised before. Then we met again, had a meal together, and that's when he suggested I find out more from you.'

'Yeah, well then, he must have told you that magazine isn't available to the general public. Did he tell you that?'

'Yes, he did.'

'You appreciate anybody could come in here and say they're a friend of a friend of mine.'

'Yes, I understand,' Hillsden said.

'Given the nature of what he told you, be easy to make a mistake. I'm not saying you're not who you say you are, but I have to be careful.'

'Oh, I agree. You're quite right.'

Tony looked hard at Hillsden again. 'Pity you don't play, otherwise we could talk here. But I think it best you come back to my place. Finish your beer, I'll meet you outside.'

'Right. Thank you.'

Hillsden watched Tony walk to the bar and pick up the phone. He remained seated, watching another game until he had downed his beer, then got up and left the room, passing Tony who was still at the bar but didn't look at him.

A few minutes later, Tony joined him in the street and led him to a nearby vacant lot where half a dozen cars were parked. He went up to a battered Nissan hatchback and unlocked it.

'Want to give me a quote for this heap?'

'Sure.'

'Just kidding. Any car I drive would put you out of business.' He reversed out of the parking lot and drove through a series of back streets, eventually pulling up in front of a tower block. 'Welcome to Alcatraz,' he said, as he fixed a steel security bar to the steering wheel. 'How's your ticker?'

'My ticker? Oh, my heart, you mean? Okay, I think.'

'Needs to be because, as usual, the fucking lift isn't working. We've got to walk up seven floors.'

There was a smell of urine in the stairwell and the bare concrete walls were stained with damp and graffiti. On the third landing they were confronted with a used condom. 'Somebody had a safe knee-trembler, ha ha,' Tony said as they climbed higher. 'This dump wants blowing up, and I might just be the one to do it.'

Finally reaching the seventh floor, which was indistinguishable from the rest, Tony took him along a covered way until they reached a door at the far end. Before putting his key into the mortise lock, Tony thumped on the door: it gave back a dull, metallic sound. 'Steel,' he informed Hillsden. 'I had it specially made after three break-ins, plus the frame's reinforced. I'm just waiting for the cruds to come back with an acetylene torch.'

'Why d'you stay here? Why not move somewhere else?'

'You live on another planet or something? I'm lucky I can afford this shit-hole.'

Once inside, he locked the door again. The layout of his flat was typical of most of those in the tower blocks thrown up to relieve the post-war housing shortage: living room, kitchen, bathroom and bedroom. Made of prefabricated concrete sections of questionable durability, owned by local councils with little money to spare for regular maintenance, the flats had long since exceeded their shelf-life. Badly heated, if heated at all, many of them were now infested with cockroaches and other vermin. Only the elderly and those unable to escape out of the poverty trap endured such conditions. Drug-pushers, pimps and prostitutes who weren't bothered about *House and Garden* surroundings moved in whenever one fell vacant.

Tony's rooms had a musty smell to them and Hillsden noticed crumbling plaster on the ceilings and window surrounds. There was an unmade sofa bed in one corner of the living room, a small television set on a chest of drawers with a bra hung over the portable aerial. Seeing Hillsden's eye go to this, Tony volunteered: 'Gives it a better reception,' then said, 'just stand there.' He ran his hands over Hillsden's body in a professional search.

'Sorry about that, but I had to make sure you weren't wired.'

'Wired? What does that mean?'

'Carrying a tape recorder. You could be working for the old Bill.'

'Oh, I see. That's what you call wired, is it? I didn't know.'

'As it happens I checked your story with Les, but I was just being extra careful. Some of our people have been caught out. You want another beer?'

'If you're having one.'

'I'm having one.'

When he disappeared into the kitchen Hillsden took the opportunity to examine the rest of the room, now noticing that in contrast with the general poverty of the surroundings, there was a laptop computer on a small table, together with a stack of *Action Now!* On the wall above was a poster advertising the previous year's Notting Hill Carnival.

'So, sit yourself down and tell me more about yourself,' Tony said, tossing a can of beer to Hillsden as he returned. He cleared some clothes off the only chair while he himself sat on the sofa bed. 'You met Les . . . and what?'

'Well, we got talking about things in general . . . and like I told you, he gave me a copy of that . . .' indicating the pile of *Action Now!*, 'which I hadn't come across before. I took it home and read it and it seemed to me to spell out some home truths. Things that worry me.'

'What sort of things?'

'Crime. The way ordinary people are pushed around, made to feel they're living in a foreign country.'

'Foreign's right. Look outside. You could be anywhere. Fucking Chinese takeaways, curry parlours, Paki grocers, you name it. So go on, you got talking with Les, did you?'

'Yes.'

'He's a deep thinker is Les. I bet you found that.'

Hillsden nodded in agreement. 'He made me think. So when we met the second time I said I'd made up my mind to find out more and that's when he suggested I should contact you.'

Tony's next question took him off guard and he realised that he was not home and dry yet.

'So why do I look at you and think you don't fit?'

'How d'you mean?'

'Well, you're a bit old for a punch-up in the street.'

'Oh, I see. Is that what you do?'

'We don't look for fights, but sometimes it's necessary. If we let you in, you won't be joining the Salvation Army. And once you're in, you're in for good. We don't like people wasting our time. People who join, learn about us, then decide it's not for them . . . they cause problems, problems for us and sometimes bigger problems for them.' He crumpled his empty beer can and tossed it to one side. 'But don't get the wrong idea. You'd be joining a legit political party, but maybe some of the things we stand for might not be everybody's way of looking at things. I'm sure you gathered that from Les.'

'Yes.'

'He feels very strongly about the state this country's in.'

'Don't we all?'

'No, we don't, that's the trouble. Most people don't give a toss. We have to change all that. What I have to know is, how far d'you want to get involved?'

'All the way.'

'We have a process, see. Everybody who applies to join has to go through it. No exceptions. I have my say, but I'm not the last word. Assuming I decide you're somebody we'd like to have with us, you still have to be okayed by somebody above me. Chain of command.'

'Yes, I understand.'

Tony took Hillsden's business card out of his jeans pocket. 'This the best place to get you?'

'Yes.'

'Okay, well, if we decide to contact you again I'll send you a message just saying the snooker championship is on and tell you when and where. We don't use names over the phone. But you'll know what it means, right?'

'Yes. Snooker championship.'

He looked at his wrist-watch and for the first time Hillsden noticed a skull and crossbones tattoo on his arm. 'Listen I've got somebody else coming, so I'll have to ask you to scarper.'

'Oh, right,' Hillsden said, standing up. 'Well, I appreciate you giving me this time, Tony, and, believe me, I'm dead serious, so I hope your people take me on.'

'We'll see,' Tony said. He unlocked the door and looked out. 'Until next time, if there is a next time. Otherwise, you never met Les, you never met me.'

'Yes, I understand.'

'Make sure you do.'

On the way down, Hillsden paused to let a blade-faced girl dressed in black leather and with a Mohican hair-style go past him. She stared at him aggressively, as though, because he looked out of place, he could only be somebody she was against – a rent collector, a council official? Hillsden held his own look a fraction too long for her liking, 'What you staring at, Grandpa?' she said. 'Get lost.' She continued on her way up, her heavy, steel-tipped boots hitting each concrete step with a precise rhythm.

Hillsden continued on down. He felt as dirty as the grimed walls.

25

STRENGTH THROUGH JOY

None too pleased at being locked in a cell while the Danish authorities contacted London and satisfied themselves that he was who he said he was, Lloyd was slightly mollified when a senior officer from PET, the Danish State Police Intelligence Unit, released him and apologised for any inconvenience suffered.

Captain Mulder introduced himself and extended a large hand that gripped like a vice. He was a burly man, at least six inches taller than Lloyd, with a physique that suggested he spent his leisure hours pumping iron. 'Come and have a drink, I'm sure that would be welcome.'

He led the way to his office. 'Your colleague, Commander Pearson, thought it all highly amusing. He told me to say it would be instructive for you to see how the other half of the world lives.'

'Yes, I bet he did.'

'Is he always that cheerful?'

'Oh, he's a natural bundle of laughs.'

'Your native sense of humour.'

'Not really. He's the exception to the rule.'

Mulder took a bottle of aquavit out of the small refrigerator behind his desk and poured two generous tots. 'It's probably always a mistake, don't you agree,' Mulder said, 'to arrive unannounced?'

'Yes, being wise after the event.'

'The men who arrested you were expecting somebody else to turn up. We've had a stake-out there ever since the murder.'

'Whose murder are we talking about?'

Mulder topped up both glasses. 'I suspect the man you came to find. You were a week too late. The *Fromandskorpset* fished him out of the water,' he said, naming the combat swimmers who provide anti-terrorist capability for Danish ports. 'Tell me, what was London's interest in him?'

'We are talking about Van Elst?' Lloyd asked as the double shot of aquavit thawed his previous mood.

'Yes.'

'We had a man over here, working undercover, tracing the source of neo-Nazi literature that's currently flooding into England. Van Elst was his informant.'

'You say "had". Have you withdrawn him?'

'He's dead, like Van Elst.'

'How?'

'All the evidence so far points to suicide, which I must say has us puzzled.'

Mulder picked up the aquavit bottle again, but Lloyd put a hand over his glass. 'Not for me, it's already reached my feet.'

'Why does it puzzle you?'

'He came back to London unofficially, checked into a hotel and blew his brains out, but a short time before his death he passed on information which enabled our Customs to intercept a large consignment of a book by this man Sonntag.'

'Ah, Sonntag,' Mulder said. 'He's somebody we'd like to get our hands on if he ever surfaces here. You think there's a direct link between that incident and your man's suicide?'

'On the face of it, no. There could be a more mundane explanation. We discovered that his personal life was fairly bizarre. He was homosexual, lived with a sex-change "wife". Perhaps we're only looking at a lovers' quarrel with a tragic end.'

Mulder permitted himself a grin. 'He sounds as though he was very thoroughly vetted.'

Lloyd returned the grin. 'Well, as you know, we've made a

speciality of choosing the wrong people. Do you have any leads on Van Elst's murder? He was a member of the Wiking-Jugend, wasn't he?'

'Yes, but we don't think it was their doing. So far, they haven't shown their hand in that way. They keep a low profile. Your man, what was his name?'

'His real name was Carstairs, but he operated here under an alias . . . called himself Professor Chandler and was working on an exchange programme at your Natural History Museum.'

Mulder thought about this, then said: 'How much simpler our lives would be if we weren't so suspicious of our friends. A word in my ear and your man might be alive today.' He took out a file from a drawer in his desk. 'This was Van Elst. Mean anything to you?' He offered Lloyd two photographs. The first showed a good-looking blond in his late twenties, wearing a quasi boy scout uniform, a role model for Aryan male beauty. The death shot, taken in the autopsy room, made Lloyd grimace.

'No,' he said. 'Never seen him before.'

'As you will note,' Mulder observed, 'he wasn't drowned.'

Van Elst's neck gaped open, the bloodless flesh wound reminding Lloyd of a gutted fish on the slab.

'Shot first,' Mulder continued, 'then had his throat cut, as if they wanted to make doubly sure. Afterwards the body was stripped and dumped in the harbour. Maybe that was their little joke.'

'Joke?'

'He was a member of a nudist club. The body washed up near the beach they frequent.'

'Ah, yes. Carstairs was also a member apparently. Perhaps we should question a few of his fellow skinny-dippers.'

'First, let's pay a visit to the museum, see what they can tell us,' Mulder said. 'And then search where he lived.'

. . .

Pearson and Schmidt sat in the gardens of *The Bells of Ouzeley*, a popular pub on the outskirts of Old Windsor, killing an hour before Schmidt had to catch a plane at Heathrow. Sipping a glass of warm beer, Schmidt studied a trim cabin cruiser chugging past on the nearby Thames, its engines throttled back.

Pearson said: 'What brought you into this?'

Schmidt turned back to him. 'Sorry?'

'I wondered how you got into our line of business.'

'Oh, I joined the NYPD as soon as I was old enough. New York's finest, as they say . . . except they don't say it so often these days . . . and became a housing cop for five years.'

'A "housing cop"? You mean you handled real estate?'

Schmidt smiled. 'If only! No. Policing public housing projects. You didn't find any Joe Friday or Kojak volunteering for that shift. You were patrolling the living dead. No shortage of action. I stopped a bullet in my leg during a drug bust and figured enough was enough. So I quit, put in some time working for a government agency in Washington, found I missed the adrenalin and joined the Bureau.'

'Does the adrenalin still flow?'

'Not so often since my marriage broke up.'

'It's a wonder mine has lasted,' Pearson said. 'My wife has been on at me for ages to quit. Gives me a lot of grief. I've been hanging on for retirement and my pension.'

'How long have you got?'

'Six months.'

'It's a crock of shit, this game,' Schmidt said, sipping his beer. 'We're the fall guys led by the unqualified to do the unthinkable for the ungrateful.'

'That's good, I must remember that.'

'It's all about ass, don't you find?'

'Ass?' Pearson replied, interpreting the word as 'arse'.

'Yeah. You're either kissing it or licking it. Don't get me on the subject of politics and politicians.'

They both fell silent as a large cabin cruiser came into view. It had a flying bridge and the man at the wheel wore spotless whites and a naval cap. His passengers, three young girls waved as they passed.

'Now, that's my idea of retirement,' Schmidt said.

'Provided you win the lottery. Some joker over here collected eighteen million the other week. Eighteen million. And know what he said? "I'm not going to change my life style." He was already a millionaire, apparently.' The thought of such wealth switched Pearson to another topic. 'I don't suppose the name "Charters" means anything to you, does it?'

'Charters? No.'

'Sir Raymond Charters, to give him his full title?'

'No. Who is he?'

'A big operator on this side of the pond. Has his fingers in a lot of pies, especially publishing. Owns several newspapers.'

'And?'

'Something keeps niggling at me. When you're on a case, do you ever get the feeling that something doesn't fit and you're compelled to get to the bottom of it? The last time anybody saw Carstairs alive was in a night club and this guy Charters was also there. That much we know. Now, Charters was way out of Carstairs's league, and yet something tells me they met that night. Why? I don't like coincidences when there are corpses around. So far I've got no corroboration but, like my mother used to say, "My corns ache so it's going to rain tomorrow." Well, my corns start to bother me when I ask myself what was Carstairs doing in London when everybody, including his so-called "wife", thought he was in Copenhagen? And why would he be in that particular night club? Or Charters for that matter? There's something there that doesn't add up, if only I could discover what. If I put together a hypothetical scenario, my suspicious mind would say that Sonntag's piece of shit has to have been published somewhere on the Continent. Who owns printing works all over Europe? Our friend Charters. Two men who in the ordinary course of events would never cross paths, yet they were both in an unusual venue at the same time and later the same night our man does away with himself. It bothers me.'

'What do you have on him?'

'Charters? Nothing. He's one of the great and good. A captain of industry. The sort who got rich under Thatcher. Or richer, in his case.'

'Want me to run him through Langley's computer? Never know, we might have something you've missed.'

'Sure. You never know.'

Schmidt took out a pocket notebook and jotted down the name. 'As soon as I get to Munich, I'll make a call. Take this fax number and get your office to send the most recent photo of him you have.'

'I appreciate it.'

'I'm a Jew, remember? I hate these bastards.'

At that moment, two startlingly pretty girls seated themselves at a nearby table. Schmidt swivelled to get a better view of them. 'Think we might score there?'

'You might. I hate rejection. Come on, duty calls, you've got a plane to catch.'

'Don't know why it is,' Schmidt said as they made their way to Pearson's car, 'but whenever I see somebody I could fall for, I'm always on my way to an airport.'

.   .   .

The Copenhagen apartment Carstairs had been using was on the top floor of an old building close to the Natural History Museum. Gaining entry, Lloyd and Mulder were both immediately struck by the scent of trapped tobacco smoke in the sealed and airless rooms just below the roof. It looked as though Carstairs had left in a hurry, for the bed was unmade, the kitchen sink full of unwashed crockery and in the bathroom there was an enamel basin containing soiled underwear which had been left to soak – all the sad signs of a man unaccustomed to fending for himself. His life was laid bare in the unemptied ashtrays on the table that had served for a desk, the international editions of *The Daily Telegraph* which littered both his bedroom and living room, together with nudist magazines, the empty bottles of Scotch dotted around the kitchen, the drip-dry shirts with their crumpled collars hung over the bath. There were bottles of vitamin pills alongside a ragged toothbrush and a squeezed tube of KY jelly on the shelf above the washbasin, the bathroom itself giving off yet another stale odour which reminded Lloyd of the repellent smell of the home of a bachelor uncle he had visited as a child.

'Is this the wife you were telling me about?' Mulder asked, picking up one of three framed photographs of the same person.

'Yes, that's her, or him, as you prefer.'

'Not unattractive, if you didn't know.'

They searched the apartment thoroughly, going about it in methodical fashion. Since it was just under the roof they were soon sweating profusely from their exertions.

'Let's see if he kept any beer in his fridge,' Lloyd said.

He went to look and came back with a single bottle that they shared.

'It's funny, you can tell a lot from what a man leaves behind,' Mulder said, 'and yet the final answer is always missing. There are no text books that lead you to a man's secret thoughts, and it's those secret thoughts that determine the choice between good and evil. Had you not told me, for example, of your man's double identity, what would I have deduced from all this? A family man in love with his wife, somebody living away from home, untidy, unable to deal with domestic chores. A masturbator, perhaps, missing a regular sexual outlet, but frightened to take his pleasures elsewhere. Nothing too out of the ordinary. Just a man with average problems.'

'Perhaps we're all double-agents of a sort,' Lloyd said. He was rummaging through a chest of drawers and suddenly came across a bank deposit book tucked into a laundered shirt. He opened it and studied the contents.

'Not exactly a poor man, though. Look at this.' He handed the book to Mulder. 'I don't know the rate of exchange, but it seems he kept a healthy bank balance in Luxembourg. Regular credit entries and no withdrawals.' He showed it to Mulder.

'Interesting,' Mulder said. 'Very interesting. Van Elst maintained an account with the same bank. He also received large regular payments, and the likelihood is from the same source. We must both track them down.'

'Do Luxembourg banks divulge that sort of information?'

'Given a murder case, I imagine they would bend the rules.' He handed back Carstairs's deposit book. Lloyd examined it again before pocketing it. 'Both hoarding the spoils for the old age they never reached.'

'Tell me,' Mulder said. 'How did he communicate with London?'

'He was old-fashioned. Preferred the simplest of letter codes. Used a seed catalogue.'

'We should look for that then.'

They continued the search but found no trace of the code book. His library consisted mainly of cheap paperbacks. Tucked into one of them they found a photograph of Van Elst, nude like the bevy of youths surrounding him, taken on a beach.

'The lost leader would not have approved,' Mulder said. 'He had Roehm murdered for embracing pure Aryan youth too literally. Everything comes full circle, don't you agree? Fascism didn't die in 1945, nothing died except the dead.'

26

FURTHER DEVELOPMENTS

It subsequently emerged that Marvin Schmidt never arrived in Munich. The Lufthansa plane developed engine trouble just as it was passed to German air traffic control and the Captain judged it serious enough to divert. He was given permission to put down in Frankfurt. For some reason, Schmidt apparently decided not to resume his journey on the replacement aircraft but checked into a hotel for the night. It was confirmed that he took a taxi into the city and obtained a room in the *Neue Krame*, a moderately priced hotel in the old section. At which point the trail went cold.

. . .

Back in London, the tenuous association between Carstairs and Sir Raymond Charters continued to nag at Pearson.

'You're driving yourself against a brick wall,' moaned Lloyd, who was tired of going over the same old ground. 'You'd be better off trolling the gay bars.'

'Well, okay, but you know me, once I get a bee in my bonnet. What else do we know about Charters? Langley came up with a blank. Just humour me, look him up on our database.'

Lloyd keyed in their desk computer to the mainframe and punched in a series of codes. They waited. When the required menu came up on the monitor, he typed in a further series of commands, followed by Charters's name. Almost immediately the words *Nothing Found – Abort, Retry, Fail?* appeared.

'I thought that bloody thing was supposed to be definitive?' Pearson said.

'Tell me something in the Firm that is.'

'Try *Who's Who*. He must be in that.'

'Have we got one?'

'I've seen a copy on old Rotherby's desk. He loves anything to do with the famous.'

When Lloyd returned Pearson flicked to the requisite page. 'Here we are, Charters, Raymond . . . Quite a sizeable entry. Born 1932, London . . . now that's odd.'

'What is?'

'Doesn't give his parents.'

'Conceived on the wrong side of the blanket maybe. Or else he's ashamed of them, now that he's made it.'

Pearson read on: '*Educated Swindon Grammar School, subsequently won a scholarship to Sherborne. Married to Catherine Pitt-Saunders, no issue. Marriage dissolved 1977 . . . blah, blah blah . . . CBE 1982, knighted 1989 . . .* Then a long list of his directorships . . . *hobbies: shooting, golf and study of contemporary history.*' He snapped the book shut. 'Guess you're right, just one of my quirks. Forget it. It's just that . . .'

'What?'

'This.' Pearson picked up a file and took out the receipt from Tudor's found on Carstairs. 'Look at this again. What does it tell you?'

Lloyd peered at it. 'Various drinks and an order of scrambled eggs and smoked salmon. So?'

'The autopsy found only traces of valium and alcohol in Carstairs's stomach.'

'Well, you know what the old saying is.'

'No, what?'

'Doesn't matter what you eat, if you're sick, all you ever throw up is diced carrots and tomato skins.'

'How bloody disgusting.'

'True, though.'

'What's that got to do with Carstairs?'

'Just an interesting piece of information.'

'Keep to the subject. He must have gone to that place for a purpose. Don't forget his, quote, wife, unquote, had no idea he was in England. Nor did we for that matter. That in itself is odd enough. And I also think it's odd that a man of Charters's standing would go there on the off-chance. That's not his style. He doesn't need to ogle tits.'

'Now, there I disagree,' Lloyd said. 'He and his kind have kept the tabloids in business. The bigger they are, the more they seem to fancy a bit of rough trade. Maybe the thrill of getting caught turns them on.'

Pearson grunted. 'Well,' he replied, determined to have the last word, 'that certainly didn't apply to Carstairs. He had a bit of rough waiting for him at home. But he didn't go home, did he? He blew his bloody brains out.'

. . .

The Prime Minister had insisted on a good turn-out for Montague's funeral. With the exception of the Foreign Secretary and the Chancellor, who were both in Brussels trying to frustrate yet another Franco-German move to speed the introduction of a common Euro-currency, the rest of the Cabinet, together with the Leaders of the Opposition Parties, attended the service held in North London. The Chief Rabbi officiated and the eulogy was delivered by the Prime Minister. The occasion received respectable coverage on television, despite being overshadowed by the news that England's football manager had resigned following a humiliating defeat by the Americans.

After spending some time with Montague's widow and intimating that he had it in mind to mark her husband's distinguished career by offering her a life peerage, the PM asked Logan to accompany him back to Whitehall.

'Ever been to a Jewish funeral before?' he asked the moment they got under way.

'No, can't say I have.'

'Different.'

'Yes,' Logan said. 'Rather moving, I thought. Relief at not having to listen to those droning Church of England voices.'

'Did you get a chance to talk to the Israeli Ambassador?'

'Yes, I did.'

'And?'

'Well, naturally he's very concerned by events, but I assured him that every step is being taken to find who was responsible.'

'With a singular lack of success so far,' the PM said acidly.

'The Ambassador told me that Mossad is convinced it was the work of Al-Sharqi.'

'Who's he for God's sake?'

'Them,' Logan corrected. 'A Palestinian group calling themselves Pioneers of the Popular War of Liberation, an element of the Syrian Ba'ath Party.'

'Have they cropped up here before?'

'Who knows? There are so many bloody terrorist splinter groups, one loses track.'

'Well, when, or if I suppose I should say, they charge anybody let's make sure the thing goes through without a hitch. And let's hope he or they are from this Al-something lot, and not home grown.'

'He did ask a favour, by the way.'

'What sort of favour?'

'The Israeli Cabinet is anxious that nothing derails the current round of peace talks. They'd like to step up the Mossad presence over here, bring in some specialists.'

The Prime Minister frowned. 'We can't have foreign bods stationed here and meddling in our internal security.'

'Well, to be realistic, I dare say they already are. Or put it another way, they always have been. The Israelis are allies, after all.'

'They're also trigger-happy in my experience. What did you tell him?'

'I said we'd consider it.'

'Get back and say I've considered it and that I'm confident our security forces are able to deal with the situation. And make sure my answer's carefully minuted.'

Anxious to change the subject, Logan said, 'Absolutely. You've seen the latest poll have you? On the by-election, I mean. It's neck and neck, but we should hold the seat.'

'Yes. I'm more concerned about the selection for Montague's old seat. He only just scraped in at the General Election.'

'Has it been decided who'll stand?'

'Not yet. I let it be known that I would favour another Jewish prospect, but so far that's been resisted at local level. Just a selection of deadbeats as far as I can see. And you know how touchy the grass roots are if we try and plant somebody on them.'

'Yes. Have these early days been very different from what you expected?'

The PM frowned before answering. 'I expected having to sort out a bloody mess, if that's what you mean. And I wasn't far wrong. My main concern is to weaken the grip of the Establishment, to ensure that, beneath the surface, the same people don't continue to run the country as before. Too many of them are still in place. I need to get at their throats, and anybody else's if they don't share my views and get results.'

Logan stared straight ahead, thinking it best not to probe any further, and it wasn't until they turned into Trafalgar Square that the PM offered words of sparse comfort, as though reading his thoughts.

'Nothing personal in what I said, Ken, don't think that. I'm sure you'll eventually pull your department round.'

.   .   .

It was Sarah who took the call. She greeted Hillsden with the news the moment he walked into the office. 'He rang ten minutes ago, you just missed him.'

'Who?'

'Your friend the snooker player. The game's on.'

'When?'

'Tonight.'

'Nothing else?'

'Yes, he said the championship was being played in a different hall and you're to meet him outside Hampstead tube station at nine o'clock.'

Hillsden immediately dialled Swanson on the scrambler phone and gave him the details.

'No clue as to where he's taking you?'

'No.'

'I'll have somebody there at the tube station.'

'Is that clever?'

'Minimum presence,' Swanson said 'Have you got problems with that?'

'Yes, I have problems with that. Problems concerning my health if it goes wrong.'

'Well, we'll need corroborating evidence at a later date to identify this man Tony.' He waited. 'Wouldn't you agree? Jesus, we've got little enough to go on so far. You can't go in with a camera or a tape recorder, can you?' he asked rhetorically.

'No.'

'Well, then?'

'Okay,' Hillsden said. 'Put a man there, just one, but make sure he's good. And by good I mean invisible.'

When the conversation ended he dialled his home number. While waiting for somebody to respond he made a face at Sarah. 'Don't look so worried, I'm too old to do anything really dangerous. This is kids' stuff compared to Russia. Get me a bed somewhere for the night,' he added as Audrey came on the line.

'Audrey, it's me. Do me a favour, sleep in the house tonight.

I won't be back.'

'Understood.'

'Everything okay?'

'Everything's fine.'

'That's good. Buzz Georgina will you?' Putting a hand over the mouthpiece, he turned back to Sarah and threw her his credit card. 'Use this and get a confirmed booking. Whatever else, I don't want to spend a night on the streets.' Then he heard his wife's voice saying, 'Robert?'

'Yes, darling. How are you both?'

'We're just about to go visit the school.'

'The school?'

'Yes. I've decided she must have proper lessons. Audrey does her best, but I worry that Laura will fall behind.'

'I see. How does Laura feel about it?'

'Oh, she wants to go to school. She doesn't have anybody of her own age. This way she might make friends.'

'Well, I'm sure you're right.'

'You don't sound too sure.'

'No. I think it's a good decision. Look, darling, something's cropped up, a meeting I have to go to this evening which I can't get out of. And it means I shall almost certainly miss the last train. So, if it's okay with you I think I'll stay in town, get a hotel. I've asked Audrey if she'll sleep in the house tonight . . . Hello, you still there?'

'Yes,' Galina said.

'I'm sorry about it.'

'Yes. I was looking forward to telling you what we thought about the school.'

'Well, I'll be back tomorrow, you can tell me then.'

Again there was a silence.

'It'll only be tonight,' Hillsden said. 'And if you both like the school, I'll go and see for myself. Don't be cross, it's something I have to do.'

'I'm not cross.'

'You sound it.'

'No. I'll see you tomorrow then.'

'I love you.'

The line went dead.

'I envy you,' Sarah said as he replaced the receiver.

'What for?'

'Being able to lie so easily.'

'Necessary trick of the trade,' Hillsden said. 'If you can't lie you don't last long. Not that I enjoy lying to my wife. Make that booking will you?'

Sarah hesitated. 'Why bother with a hotel? Why don't you stay at my place? I've got a spare room.'

Hillsden glanced at her before answering, but there was nothing in her face to suggest the thought that came immediately to his mind. 'It's kind of you, Sarah, but I don't know what time I'll be through. A hotel's less complicated.'

While she rifled through the Yellow pages, he turned out the contents of his pockets, making sure that he carried nothing that might condemn him.

27

A DIFFERENT GAME OF SNOOKER

A sudden flurry of cold rain stung Hillsden's face as he emerged from the tube station entrance ten minutes before the appointed time, having decided that, if Tony was already there ahead of him, it was probably a good thing to show keenness, but he saw no sign of him and took shelter in a nearby shop doorway. Even at this hour there was plenty of traffic. One of the things he had noticed since his return was that London now seemed to have a continuous rush hour; there were very few hours in the day and night when the streets were not choked with cars.

He kept close watch, but the blur of headlights in the rain dazzled him. A young man, not dressed for the weather, joined him in the shop doorway. Hillsden saw he was selling copies of *The Big Issue*, a broadsheet by and for the homeless. More to appear normal than from any philanthropic motive, Hillsden asked the price.

'Sixty p, or what you like,' the young man said.

Hillsden gave him a pound coin. 'I don't want any change,' he said.

'Oh, thanks. Appreciated.'

'How're you doing? Have you sold many?'

'In Hampstead? You're joking. They're all Socialists up here,' he said, smiling at his own joke.

At nine o'clock, Hillsden braved the rain and paced outside the station. Now it begins again, he thought, his mind going back to the moment when Lockfield had first sprung the trap and the direction of his life had been irrevocably changed. As he stamped his feet against the cold and turned up his coat collar, he saw, as though in a bright mirror, his past self: beaten-up, a fake derelict in jail; a fake alcoholic acting out rehabilitation in the Brothers of Mercy's retreat; waiting, as now, for a messenger to arrive and lead him into an unknown country. The big issue then, he thought, was whether I'd ever come out alive. Was this to be a repetition?

The young man selling the broadsheet came to join him, the rain having eased off. 'I might pack it in soon,' he remarked as he proffered his wares to a passing couple who avoided eye-contact as though what he was offering was a contagious reminder that their turn would come. 'See what I mean?'

Hillsden nodded, but was too intent on his own mission to become involved in a dialogue. By now it was ten minutes past nine and there was still no sign of Tony. Would he come alone if he came at all, or was this just a trial run to keep him guessing – the familiar-cat-and-mouse routine that had been standard procedure for dead-letter drops in the days of the Cold War? He thought: what schoolboy games we all played then with our secret codes and miniature cameras — the toys of betrayal.

Another five minutes ticked away and he became convinced that Tony was not going to show. 'I'll have one last try,' the young man said. 'Hope your date shows up. Enjoy your snooker game.'

Before Hillsden could react the young man moved out and stood on the central traffic island in order to approach motorists halted at the traffic lights. As the signal turned green and the waiting cars cleared, Hillsden saw Tony start to cross towards him. He was forced to pause on the traffic island as a solitary motorcyclist jumped the amber. Gaining the pavement, he passed close to Hillsden. 'Follow me,' he said without stopping and disappeared around the corner. Hillsden made a show of looking at his watch again, his body language signalling a man who had been stood up. Then he made off in the same direction as Tony. Out of the corner of his eye, he saw the young man leave the traffic island.

There was no sign of Tony when he rounded the corner, but a hundred yards ahead there was a white transit van parked at a meter. As he drew level with it Tony leaned across from the driving seat and opened the passenger door.

'I'd almost given you up,' Hillsden said as he climbed in. 'I was there on time. Ahead of time, actually,' he added, trying to strike the right conversational note. 'Different car tonight.' He took a quick look in the side mirror, but the street lighting was patchy and he could not see any sign of the young man.

'Yeah. I use this one for business.'

They headed off in the direction of Swiss Cottage, but almost immediately Tony turned off and took a complicated route through a series of back streets. Hillsden concentrated on noting any prominent landmarks, such as the names of pubs, but it soon became apparent that Tony was doubling back in rather obvious fashion, unaware that his passenger was an old hand at such manœuvres. They eventually entered Regent's Park, passing London Zoo on the perimeter road.

'How is business these days?'

'Up and down.' He showed no inclination to elaborate and Hillsden did not pursue it.

They travelled for perhaps another fifteen minutes. The rain started again, coming down heavier this time and the wipers on the transit van left a smeared arc. Oncoming headlights further obscured Hillsden's view so that for the last stage of the journey he had no clear idea where they were. When they finally stopped, he saw that they were in a wide, tree-lined road, but he looked in vain for a street name. Before getting out of the van Tony said: 'From now on, do exactly as I say. Stay where you are until I give the word that it's all clear. Then follow me to the house.'

'Whose house is it?'

'Don't ask. If you're accepted, you'll find out. If not, you'd be smart to forget you ever went near it.'

Tony scouted the street, then indicated for Hillsden to get

out. They walked for some fifty yards until they reached the well-kept front garden of a three-storeyed, detached house. A flight of steps led up to an ornate front door. Like the plethora of Mercedes and Range Rovers parked along the street, it smacked of money.

They were admitted by a youth dressed in black jeans, a black shirt with epaulets, and, incongruously, a Paisley scarf around his neck, knotted cowboy-style.

He acknowledged Tony, studied Hillsden intently, but said nothing by way of greeting. He conducted them both across the large hallway where the walls were hung with abstract art of no particular distinction, the paintings crammed together so that none were shown to advantage. Opening one side of a pair of mahogany doors, the youth preceded them into the room. 'Tony's here,' he announced, but at first glance Hillsden could not see whom he was addressing. He found himself in what he took to be a library, dimly lit. Those walls that were not bookcased held another art collection, this time revealing a more eclectic taste, a mixture of styles and period: he recognised some choice examples of kitsch from the Nazi era – Aryan men in heroic poses, heavy blonde *Mädchen*, one suckling a babe at her breast. There was an elaborate stone fireplace in which a fake log fire burned and over it a large painting, this time a nude Rhine maiden embracing a wounded German soldier. Twin bookcases housing leather-bound sets flanked each side of the fireplace.

The voice which now greeted Tony came from behind a decorated screen to the left of the fire.

'Tony, come and warm yourselves.'

It was a fruity voice, bringing to mind the voice of an actor conscious that he should give equal value to all the vowel sounds.

As they went forward, the owner of the voice came into view. Although his unlined face belonged to somebody in his forties, the thick hair was snow white so that it was difficult to guess his true age. He was sitting in a metal wheelchair, his lower half covered by a tartan blanket and was smoking a cigarette in a gold holder which he waved at them both, an affectation that again seemed to Hillsden theatrical.

'So, this is the Mr Bartlett you talked about, Tony? Do sit down, Mr Bartlett. I apologise for not getting up to greet you, but this is one of my bad days. Can I offer you a drink?'

'Thank you.' Hillsden perched on the edge of a sofa on the opposite side of the fireplace.

'What will it be?'

'A Scotch, please.'

'How about you, Tony? Or are you being a good boy and don't drink and drive?'

'I could handle a beer.'

'I think we can run to that, can't we Johnny, dear,' he said, addressing the youth. 'Pour our guest a Scotch . . . I forgot to ask, what is your preference, Mr Bartlett, blended or malt?'

'Malt, I think.'

'A man after my own heart. The same for me, Johnny. So, pour ours, then get Tony a beer.' Throughout this exchange he never took his eyes off Hillsden. 'How d'you take it?'

'Oh, straight, please.'

'Very civilised. I had an American guest once,' his host said, removing the spent cigarette from the holder and immediately lighting another, 'who drank my best Isle of Islay mixed with Coca-Cola. I was somewhat stretched to be polite. They do have the most extraordinary tastes in food and drink, don't they? Some of which, unfortunately, they've exported to us. Have you ever been over there?'

'No, I never have,' Hillsden replied as the youth handed him his drink.

'You don't travel much?'

'I travel a lot in England on business. And I've been across to France on holidays.'

'You're in the insurance business Tony tells me.'

'Yes.'

'I'm a great believer in insurance.' He smiled, revealing a brace on his lower row of teeth, the sort that children wear for correction, the firelight glinting on the metal.

Johnny returned with Tony's beer already poured into a crystal brandy glass.

'A little outré for beer, Johnny dear, but we all make mistakes from time to time. Why don't you take yourself off and watch the ten o'clock news? Let me know if Arsenal won tonight. I've got money on it.'

Johnny withdrew, but not without a pout.

'Your good health, Mr Bartlett. It was kind of you to come out on a cold night, I hope you weren't inconvenienced?'

'Not at all.'

'Do relax, this isn't going to be a third degree, just a social chat to explore certain common interests. As I'm sure Tony has told you, we have to consider every new applicant with a degree of caution for the simple reason that our views on certain matters don't command universal support. That will change as we gather strength and the true facts get wider distribution.' He glanced up at the painting above the fireplace, gesturing with his cigarette holder. 'The mistake others made . . . was to identify the wrong enemy. They should never have gone to war with us. For centuries they were our allies, right up to the time of Waterloo. We have so many blood ties, as you doubtless realise . . . our royal family for instance, were related to the Kaiser. The Third Reich was a brave, much needed venture which sadly was prevented from achieving its final mission. Unless we are very diligent, our own, once great, country is in danger of making the same mistake . . . Your first name's Robert, isn't it?'

Hillsden nodded.

'Well, Robert, not wishing to preach to you, but if history teaches us anything, it shows that when the purity of a race – any race, and I could give you numerous examples, starting with the Romans and Greeks – becomes corrupted by indolence, inter-marriage with inferior, ethnic blood, then we are staring into the abyss. If we add to this a total moral collapse, such as exists today in all sections of society, which allows the degenerates amongst us openly to flaunt their vices, condoned by the churches and with those who rule us too craven to take a stand, then it's beholden on the chosen to act before it is too late. It won't be an easy task, any more than the road from Munich was easy. I have no doubt that blood will have to be spilt along the way. We must cross that rubicon without flinching. The electorate has been systematically brainwashed into believing that our Anglo-Saxon heritage will somehow be enhanced by a transition to an multi-racial society. It is one of the great lies of this century.'

Hillsden nodded, leaning forward to show his interest.

'Furthermore, it spells the end of everything we hold dear. Unless this lemming-like rush is halted, the white population of this island will become an oppressed minority. Those are the facts, Robert, and we ignore them at our peril.'

Hillsden could not bring himself to answer in kind. Instead, sipping his whisky, he said: 'It's a sobering thought.'

'But we're going to change all, aren't we, sir?' Tony said, anxious to make his presence felt.

'We are indeed, Tony. Now, Robert, I take you to be an intelligent and caring man. You care about your country, am I right?'

'Yes.'

'Certainly you care enough to come here and find out more. Am I correct?'

'Yes,' Hillsden repeated.

'That's very heartening. We need more people like you – caring, intelligent people of your age and background – so that we can dispel the false impression that we are nothing more than a bunch of yobbos and Fascists. Oh, yes, that's the word you'll hear a lot of – the usual parrot response from those who can't face the truth. That'll be thrown at you once your involvement with our movement becomes known. Are you prepared for that?'

'Well, it's not true, is it?' Hillsden responded carefully. 'I'm not a Fascist any more than you are, or Tony here.'

'Of course you're not. But let me hear your own views, Robert.'

Hillsden began a rehearsed dialogue, starting slowly. 'Well,

I suppose, like a lot of people of my generation, I've seen the changes taking place and I haven't liked what is happening. Drug pushers outside schools, perverts everywhere, old people afraid to walk the streets, our police, whom I was brought up to respect, made to look the villains while the real villains get their wrists slapped. That seems all wrong to me.'

'That's very well put, isn't it, Tony? What a lot of people think, but are too scared to say. And isn't it sad that so many have been too frightened to speak their own minds like Robert here, tyrannised by minorities.' He paused to light yet another cigarette, using the holder flamboyantly, like a character in a Noël Coward play. 'I confess to bouts of feeling useless, confined as I am to this chair. I'd like to be in the forefront, leading the way, but fate has dictated that I must sit on the sidelines. Now, Robert, I have to ask you this. By joining us, you must be aware that your life will change. It will include an actual degree of danger from now on. The police you rightly used to admire will not be on your side. They will be used against you. Heads will be broken, perhaps your own. You may end up in jail for your convictions. I want you to be aware of that.'

'No room for second thoughts, is there, sir?' Tony interjected.

'No room at all.'

'I have to give an answer now, do I?' Hillsden said, deliberately playing the novice.

'Before you leave this room. Should you have even the slightest doubts as to the commitment I hope you'll give, then now's the time to voice them. We don't take kindly to part-time followers. It's all or nothing, Robert.'

'Can I ask you one thing?'

'Please do.'

'I find what you've told me exciting, but I don't know much about politics. Does that go against me?'

'Not at all. We lead, you obey.'

'Well, I definitely would like to join,' Hillsden said.

'You're prepared to be openly identified with our aims?'

'Yes.'

'To be bound by our oath of allegiance and faithfully perform any tasks you're given?'

'Yes.'

'Regardless of the consequences?'

'Yes.'

'Then I congratulate you on your acceptance into our ranks.' Again the thin, metallic smile that had no real warmth in it. 'You have joined the élite, Robert, as the future will prove.'

The expression reminded Hillsden of somebody else who thought he knew all the answers: Philby had used the same words to proclaim his allegiance to a different cause. The spoilers always quoted from the same text, convinced that they alone were right, that any means justified their end. The man who sat opposite him, chain-smoking beneath the tacky depiction of another madman's dream, mouthing an old recipe for a new chaos, had an all-too familiar face: trust me, his smile said, I have all the answers and will lead the way to dusty death.

'You've been at a disadvantage so far, Robert, in that I haven't introduced myself. I hope you didn't take that as deliberate rudeness. Just natural caution, which I urge you to copy from now on, especially when you come in contact with those who aren't sympathetic to our cause . . . My name's Fadiman, Graham Fadiman . . . and I'm delighted you're going to be with us.'

'Likewise, Mr Fadiman.'

'I find it very gratifying that, more and more, we're able to attract people like yourself. We're gathering strength every day, Robert, and soon we're going to be on the march.' He looked at his wrist-watch. 'Oh, dear. You must excuse me, but it's time for me to take my medicine.' He leaned out of his wheelchair and pressed a bell switch at the side of the fireplace. 'I hope it doesn't disturb you, but you're in the presence of a morphine addict. A registered one, I hasten to add. One of the crosses I have to bear. Fortunately, Johnny has become very adept at administering to my needs.'

Hillsden finished the last of his drink and stood up.

'Of course, I understand. Well, it's been a very illuminating meeting for me, Mr Fadiman. I appreciate you explaining everything so clearly and I promise you I've taken it to heart. Thank you very much.'

'No, thank you, Robert. I look forward to the next time.'

As Hillsden and Tony moved towards the door, Johnny wheeled in a small hospital trolley. He was wearing surgical gloves and as they passed each other Hillsden noted an array of sealed hypodermics and vials of the drug.

'We'll see ourselves out,' Tony said.

'What an impressive man,' Hillsden remarked as they drove off. His eyes sought a street sign, but, as in the majority of London roads, the identifying plaques were placed too high on the corner buildings and were impossible for him to read without craning round and drawing attention to the action.

'Very impressive,' he repeated.

'Yeah,' Tony agreed. 'He's brilliant. Course, there are others behind him, the money men, but he's the one who decodes strategy. He's the brains.'

'That condition of his . . . being in a wheelchair, I mean . . . did he catch something like polio?'

'No. He was mugged a few years back. Two blacks jumped him one night. He was brave enough to take them on, but they stomped him, the bastards, broke both his legs with iron bars. He'll never walk again.'

'God! How terrible.'

'Don't worry, he'll get even one day. We all will. Listen, I've things to do, got another meeting to go to, so I can't take you all the way. Where d'you want to be dropped?'

'Oh, anywhere near a tube station. Where are we now?'

Tony shot him a look. 'For a Londoner you don't know your own city very well, do you?'

'I get confused sometimes at night,' Hillsden said quickly, realising the blunder. 'All these new one-way streets. I'm fine in the daytime.'

'We're in the Holloway Road. I'll put you off at King's Cross, that suit you?'

'Fine . . . When d'you think I'll hear from anybody?'

'When we've got something for you to do.'

'What'll that be?'

'Depends.' Tony fished in the glove compartment and took out a small notebook. 'Reminds me, one other thing, better we don't use your office number from now on. Write your home address and stuff.'

It was the one thing that Hillsden had not anticipated and he thought quickly. There was no question of giving the Walsham le Willows address, but what else could he put? He tried a bluff. 'D'you think that's wise, bearing in mind what Mr Fadiman drummed into me? Putting anything in writing, I mean? Why don't I ring you at the snooker place tomorrow and give you it over the phone. Will you be there?'

'Yeah, okay, good point. Try me around three o'clock.'

Hillsden's heart was still racing from the narrow escape when Tony left him at King's Cross. The moment he was inside the station he went to a public phone and dialled Rotherby.

'Colonel, it's me.' He could hear soft music in the background.

'Who is it?'

'Who else calls you Colonel?'

'Oh. Right, got it.'

'I've got a problem that needs sorting out urgently. Can you meet me?'

'Now, you mean?'

'Yes.'

Rotherby's voice dropped to a whisper. 'Bit delicate tonight, old son. I'm "entertaining".' He gave the word a special intonation. 'Been nurturing this one for a couple of months, and it's just coming to the boil. Can't it wait until tomorrow?'

'No, I need to see you now. Make some excuse and leave her with another bottle of shampoo, I'm sure she'll still be hot when you get back. I wouldn't ask if it wasn't urgent. It won't take long.'

'Where are you?'

'King's Cross. I'll wait by the bookstall.'

There was a slight pause. 'You're a shit, you know that,' Rotherby said. 'Okay. I'll be about twenty minutes though.'

Hillsden killed the wait having a cup of nameless liquid masquerading as coffee and finessing the idea he intended to put to Rotherby. It was half an hour before Rotherby came into the station forecourt.

'So, what's the panic?' he asked.

Hillsden brought him up to date. 'What I thought of was this . . . The safe house in Forest Gate. Can you get an answering machine installed there by lunchtime tomorrow? Get the type that has a remote bleeper, so I can activate it to pick up any messages. Can that be done?'

'Bit short notice, but I suppose so.'

'Get the machine first thing, then bring it to my office and I'll record a message. It'll have to be connected to a separate line, of course – will that present a problem?'

'No, there's already a spare. The whole place is wired for anything.'

'Good. You're a chum, Colonel. Here.' Hillsden felt in his pocket and took out some money.

'Don't be stupid, I don't want that. It'll be paid for out of stores.'

'No, this is for you. For your taxi fare and some condoms. I want to be sure you're going to practise safe sex.'

'Oh, very funny. I'll be lucky if I can find it after all this time.'

'Listen, I hope I didn't ruin anything. See you tomorrow, and thanks again.'

When Rotherby had gone he went to the taxi rank and gave the driver the name of the hotel Sarah had booked for him.

28

A SEARCH

Even without Lloyd pouring cold water on his suspicions, Pearson harboured his own doubts about Charters's involvement. The connection between Charters and Carstairs which had set him on the trail was tenuous, to say the least, and part of him accepted Lloyd's scepticism, but he could be pig-headed when it suited him. The time he had spent in Northern Ireland had convinced him that his instincts deserved to be trusted – on more than one occasion in that tragic country, instinct had kept him alive. Trust nobody, be pig-headed, test every doubt, follow every lead, however obscure; in his experience somewhere in every haystack a needle lay buried. He had persuaded himself that the omission about Charters's parentage in *Who's Who* was worth following up and it was the reference to Charters's early schooling that now put him on the road to Swindon. What the hell? he thought, even if I draw a blank it's a day out.

Without telling Lloyd the purpose of his trip, he made an early start, but the inevitable road works and several accidents slowed his progress and it was gone eleven before he reached the outskirts of the town. By then his empty stomach was playing up and he pulled into a roadside cafe frequented by long-distance lorry drivers and had an enjoyable, but immediately regretted, greasy breakfast.

The obvious starting point was the electoral register, and his first call was to the town council offices. He gave his name as Chalmers so that he obtained the right volume. There were two Charters listed: *John* and *Pauline*. He made a note of the address and returned the volume to the librarian. Next he went to a post office to get directions.

The house, when he located it, was unprepossessing, a stucco-fronted, post-war semi-detached that would never win any architectural awards. There was a child's plastic bike lying on its side in the front garden and a bedraggled teddy bear on the porch.

When Pearson's ring was answered, the door, held on a security chain, was opened a fraction by a young woman clutching a small boy in her arms. She was wearing yellow household gloves and had a harassed look.

'Sorry to disturb you, Mrs Charters, but I wonder if you can help me?' Pearson said.

'Mrs who?'

'Aren't you Mrs Charters?'

'No, our name's Mather.'

'Oh, I'm sorry.'

'They must have been the last lot.' The small boy slid down to the floor and tucked himself behind his mother, staring wide-eyed at Pearson. 'Can't help you I'm afraid. The house was empty when we bought it.'

'Well, I apologise for troubling you, Mrs Mather. It's just that they're distant relatives I'm trying to trace.'

'You could try the estate agent's, they might know. Chancellor's in the high street,' she said, her voice still tinged with suspicion.

'Yes, that's a good idea, thank you.' Pearson bent down to pick up the teddy bear and handed it through the crack in the door. 'Here, poor teddy got left out.'

Her gloved hand took it from him. 'Ta,' she said and closed the door.

The girl in the estate agent's was only able to tell him that the house had been repossessed by the building society three months previously, and as far as she knew the Charters had left the district.

'You wouldn't know where they went, would you? They're relatives of mine.'

'I wouldn't have a clue.' She turned to a male colleague. 'This gentleman's enquiring about that couple who lived in number forty-eight Marpleton Street. You handled that, didn't you?'

'What's the problem?'

'No, problem,' Pearson said. 'Just wondered where they moved to. I'm a cousin of theirs.'

'Well, I'll see if we kept any record.' He went to a filing cabinet and pulled out a folder. 'No, nothing here. The only thing I can remember is the wife was very upset. There's a bank reference. Barclays, you could ask there. But other than that, can't help I'm afraid.' He replaced the folder and went back to his desk.

'Is that the local Barclays?'

'Yes. Two blocks down on your left.'

'Well, thanks for your help.'

He went to the bank and after a wait was shown into the Manager's office. 'I know you can't give out confidential information, but all I'm trying to discover is whether Mr and Mrs Charters, who were customers of yours before they moved out, left any forwarding address.'

'Who are you from?' the Manager said stiffly.

'I'm not from anybody. They're family and I've only just found out they lost their home. Thought I might be able to help in some way. Did they transfer their account when they left?'

The Manager frowned and showed no disposition to be forthcoming.

'Well, I remember them, yes. They defaulted on their mortgage. Doubt if there was anything to transfer, given the circumstances.'

'No, well, I just thought I'd ask, having made the journey.'

'You understand one has to be careful in my position.' He tapped a silver pen on his blotter. 'However, I dare say I could take a look, but I doubt I have anything.' He punched something into his computer and peered at the screen. 'No, I was wrong. There was a small balance which we transferred to our branch in Yeovil. That's all I can tell you.'

'Well, that's something to go on,' Pearson said. 'I'm most grateful. Awful when you lose touch.'

'Yes. Depends, I suppose. I'd be happy to lose touch with some of my relatives.' He gave a thin smile, momentarily becoming human.

Before driving back to London Pearson decided to make one further search at the main cemetery's chapel. There he examined the Book of Remembrance and was rewarded by finding two entries. A Martha Charters had died in 1954 and alongside her name was written: *Beloved wife of William Paul Charters, who went to Jesus June 17th, may her soul rest in peace.* Leafing forward he came across a second reference: in 1962 this same William Paul Charters met his maker. Against this was written: *Much missed father of John and Pauline.*

Although disappointed that there was no mention of a Raymond Charters, Pearson noted these details. He considered travelling on to Yeovil, but then remembered that he had promised to take his wife to the theatre for a delayed birthday treat. On the return journey to London he felt the day had not been entirely wasted.

. . .

Once he had ensured that the answering machine had been installed in the safe house, Hillsden contacted Swanson to give him a blow by blow account of his meeting with Fadiman. For some reason it did not produce the reaction he had expected.

'Yes, it's progress of a sort, I suppose, but again nothing we can immediately act upon. Fanatics spouting off about the purity of the race from a wheelchair hardly justify sending in the cavalry. I'm much more concerned about a report from our man in Munich.'

'What about?' Hillsden asked.

'That Bureau chap we met, Schmidt. He's been found dead.'

'Dead?'

'Yes.'

'In Munich?'

'No, Frankfurt apparently. I'm waiting for more details, but he was discovered in an underground hotel parking lot, stabbed to death.'

'Poor bastard,' Hillsden said.

'Yes, one of the few Yanks I've ever got on with. It's a bloody pity because he could have been very useful to us,' he added with no real sympathy in his voice, just annoyance. 'I've been trying to get hold of Pearson all morning, but he seems to have gone walkabout without telling anybody. He saw Schmidt again after us, maybe he knows something more.'

'That was a nightmare I often had in Russia.'

'What was?'

'Dying in a foreign country. Why Frankfurt, I wonder? He told us he was flying direct to Munich.'

'Yes, well that's part of the mystery that has to be solved. I wish to God something would go our way for a change. I get nothing but aggro from the Home Office. One has to have balls of steel to survive in this job. I wrote my resignation the last time Logan balled me out, then thought why give the little creep the pleasure? He had the nerve to ask whether I felt I was in the right job. You had the best of it, Alec.'

'Robert,' Hillsden corrected.

'Yes, "Robert", sorry.'

'What makes you think that?'

'Well, you chaps always knew who the enemy was.'

'Did we? The enemy without perhaps, but not always the enemy within.'

Swanson ignored the veiled reference. 'Nowadays they come at us from all directions, and we're expected to operate as before but on half the budget. The last Interpol symposium

I attended in Paris, I had my hotel expenses questioned. Next thing you know with this lot they'll be asking what school I'm sending my children to.' Then he made another subject U-turn. 'D'you have any idea where you were taken last night? Although our chaps got the number of the van, they weren't quick enough off the mark and lost him.'

'Chaps?' Hillsden said. 'You promised me there'd only be one.'

'Did I? Well, I changed my mind.'

'Thanks for telling me.'

This was ignored. 'So, do you know where you were taken?'

'I looked at a street map this morning and tried to fathom the route. At a reasonable guess I'd put it somewhere in the Islington area. There's a certain amateurism about the way they operate, though I suppose we said that about the IRA in the beginning. Doesn't make them less dangerous.'

'Well, unless this Fadiman's using a phoney name, it shouldn't be difficult to trace him. We'll run him through the computer, see what comes up.'

'The character named Tony mentioned there are money men behind Lionel Barrymore in the wheelchair.'

'Lionel Barrymore?'

'Don't you remember those old films?'

'I don't even remember new films,' Swanson replied testily. 'And by the way I don't like hearing things second-hand. I'm running you, not Rotherby.'

'If you're referring to the answering machine, I had to think of something quickly.'

'Even so.'

It was the cue for Hillsden to reveal the existence of a bug in his car, but once again he said nothing.

. . .

As far as London was concerned, Schmidt's unsolved murder

was put on the back burner. It was decided that the Yanks should be left to solve their own problems. Certain disturbing incidents closer to home proved more pressing. There was a sudden spate of synagogues being firebombed; London, Bristol and Leeds were the selected targets though, miraculously, there was no loss of life in any of them despite extensive damage to property. This was followed by a number of prominent Jewish and Pakistani businessmen receiving letter bombs, posted in various parts of the country. Most of these were intercepted and defused, but one slipped through the net and a secretary in Marks and Spencer's head office had her right hand blown off. The IRA and Animal Rights were ruled out and it was the opinion of Special Branch that a new Libyan terrorist cell was responsible. Several media commentators questioned this, in view of the fact that the attacks had not been confined to Jewish targets. Others argued the diversity of the targets was a clever tactic to confuse the issue and throw the security forces off the scent. Correspondence columns in the press printed the usual quota of letters from the flog-'em-and-hang-'em school. This new campaign, coming as it did on the eve of the two by-elections, embarrassed the government, forcing it on the defensive. Logan was savaged by the Opposition in the House, the Tories having put down an emergency motion on law and order. The debate was still in progress when a serious riot broke out in Manchester as the result of a badly mismanaged drugs bust, though this was subsequently considered to have no connection with the bombing attacks. *The Times*, in a front-page leader, thundered against the increasing number of no-go areas that had become a disturbing feature of the inner-cities, saying that it was intolerable that a siege mentality had been forced on ordinary citizens who now could not walk the streets without being in fear of their lives. Various armchair pundits monopolised the television talk shows with their panaceas and the polls immediately showed diminished support for the government.

It was during this volatile period that Hillsden received the summons to meet Tony again. The message on the machine invited him to another game of snooker in two days' time, with the added emphasis that 'it was in preparation for a big match'.

Since Hillsden's first visit to the snooker hall, it had been under surveillance, with anybody entering or leaving the building being photographed by an around-the-clock team concealed in a derelict shop opposite, but, apart from Tony, nobody had been positively identified.

'He obviously passed the first test then,' Pearson said when Swanson called him to discuss this latest development and to plot a response. 'Do we have anything on Fadiman?'

'Clean as a whistle, apart from one conviction for dangerous driving ten years ago. He's a bachelor, wealthy background, only son of a man who made his pile in South Africa. The father died and the mother, who was American, appears to have returned home. The only item of possible significance is that he spent a period in Germany before his accident. While he was there, he bought a lot of Nazi art at auction, including a couple of paintings purported to have once belonged to Goering.'

'That figures – Hillsden said they were mostly crap. When is this meeting?'

'Thursday night. Tell me, are the police aware of our surveillance team?'

'No,' Pearson said. 'Tell them too much and they're likely to blow the whole thing by parking a Panda car right outside. But Lloyd and I will be around. Disguised as Stormtroopers,' he added, but Swanson did not smile.

'Let's cut the humour, shall we? I'm not in the mood.'

. . .

That evening while Galina was putting Lara to bed, Hillsden

took Audrey to one side.

'How well do you know the locals now?' he asked.

'Oh, I'm on first name terms with a lot of them. Why?'

'Are they curious about me?'

'Not especially. One or two have asked what you do. I tell them you have to be away on business a great deal of the time. And – this'll make you laugh – when they learned you were in insurance, a couple of them said they might give you a chance to quote. Do you handle bona fide customers?'

'Yes, gives me an air of legitimacy. But don't encourage them. Look out for any strangers suddenly putting in an appearance. From now on we need to be extra careful.'

'Is it hotting up?'

'Well, they've taken the bait. Whether they've swallowed it remains to be seen.'

'And how are you making out with friend Hadley?' she asked a little too casually.

Hillsden looked at her pointedly. 'Did you ever hear that story about two people who met in the street and one asked where the other was going. "To see a friend," was the reply. "Ah!" the first one commented, "You remind me of the Frenchman who received the same answer and said, 'Take me along, I never saw one.' " '

'What're you laughing at?' Galina asked as she returned.

'Oh, just some joke I heard on the radio,' Hillsden lied, not wishing to get into it.

'Will you go and read a story to Laura. Just one, I want her to go to sleep early tonight.'

'Sure. Put the coffee on, Audrey, and we'll all have a cup together. I like your brew.'

He went upstairs and read a chapter of *Charlie and the Chocolate Factory*, Lara having just discovered Roald Dahl.

'Are we always going to be here?' Lara asked when he was about to tuck her in.

'Don't you like it here? It's nice, isn't it?'

She wrinkled her nose. 'I liked it best when we were other people and you were always at home.'

247

'Daddy has to work so that he's got the money to buy food.'

'You didn't used to. Tell me again why Audrey calls Mama and me something different.'

'Just that we're in England and that's the way people speak.'

'It's not a nice name, though, is it? I think it's a silly name to call Mama,' she said as her eyes fluttered and closed with that enviable suddenness peculiar to small children. Looking at her, Hillsden felt his age and still couldn't reconcile himself to the fact that she was his; she seemed so tiny and vulnerable, especially at night.

Galina joined him in their bedroom before he went downstairs.

'Do you think she's too thin?' Hillsden asked.

'Laura? No, she eats like a horse. Why d'you say that?'

'Just asking. I'm not used to little girls, remember.'

'You get on well with big ones though.' She made it sound casual, but from the way she looked at him he sensed an undercurrent.

'What does that mean?'

'You and Audrey are always whispering together.'

'Darling, that's a total exaggeration. If you mean a few moments ago, I was just telling her a joke.' Galina's face did not change. 'What's wrong?'

'I want you to tell me jokes,' she said. 'We don't have laughs any more, you and me. Back home we shared everything, now there's somebody else.' The word 'home' hung between them and Hillsden thought, she's never thrown that at me before. It was the first step over a dangerous threshold into a room he did not want to enter. 'Audrey isn't "somebody else". She's here so that you're not alone when I have to be away. It's a difficult role for her, too, remember, thrown together with a family of strangers.'

'That's what we've become, a family of strangers.'

He saw that tears were forming and went to her. Her arms tightened around his neck. 'I'm sorry,' she said. 'But I'm so mixed up.'

'What are you mixed up about?'

'About you and everything, the way we live. I thought it would always be the same, but that was probably silly of me. It's just that I'm so frightened sometimes. In St Petersburg I always knew where you were, what you were doing. We had less there, but we had more too. I sometimes wish . . .' She didn't finish.

'What?' Hillsden said gently. 'Tell me.'

'I know you came back because you wanted me and Laura to have the things we'd missed . . . but I don't know what's meant by happiness any more. I went to church the other day, on my own, just to see if that made any difference . . . it's meant to, isn't it? You're meant to find comfort from faith . . . and I stared up at Him, on the cross, and all I could think of was . . . why do we worship suffering? Isn't there enough down here on earth without all that? Why can't we believe in a God who doesn't bleed for us? Do you ever think that?'

'I'm the last person to ask,' Hillsden said. 'I haven't been inside a church since I buried my parents.' He kissed her. 'But, darling, listen to me. This episode we're living through, it won't last for ever. I have to settle my account, but once it's finished, it'll just be the three of us again.'

'Will we have to stay here for ever?'

'No, we can go anywhere you like.'

'D'you promise?'

'I promise.'

Audrey called from the foot of the stairs: 'The coffee's ready if you still want it.'

'We'll be right down,' Hillsden answered. He kissed Galina again, wishing he could say something of real comfort to her, but his mind was filled with old thoughts, a scrapbook of memories they could not share.

29

A SECOND FRAME

This time Tony conducted Hillsden through the snooker hall to a windowless rear room where he found himself joining some twenty or more unfamiliar faces. He was regarded with a certain wariness as Tony, using only Christian names, made a few introductions. With one exception, the others present were considerably younger than Hillsden. The exception was an olive-skinned character, forty or thereabouts, introduced as Harry, whose beard-line suggested that he had forgotten to shave that day but, as Hillsden had recently discovered, the look was now dignified with the term 'designer stubble'. Some of the group wore variations of a quasi-uniform – bomber jackets, black trousers and heavy boots; his off-the-peg suit stood out in contrast. None were stereotype skinheads, though many sported hair cropped army-fashion and sat, feet sprawled, on the chairs arranged in a semi-circle, exchanging macho anecdotes which he guessed were intended both to isolate and impress him as the newcomer. A crate of beer stood on a trestle table and Hillsden was invited to help himself, which he did, drinking out of the bottle like everybody else. He took a seat next to the man called Harry.

'Your first meeting, Dad?' Harry said. There was a hint of derision in the way he addressed Hillsden.

'Yes.'

'Well, you're never too old to get wise.' It was a guttural, smoker's voice, with a polyglot accent, which, to Hillsden's ear, suggested a sandwich of Cockney and assumed American. 'And you've joined at the right time. Those who aren't with us now are going to miss out. The word is we're moving into top gear.' Harry drained his beer bottle, then volunteered in a boastful non sequitur, 'I just got back from the fatherland. You ever been over there?'

'No, I haven't.'

'Those Germans, they know what the score is, always have, we've got a lot more to learn from them, and the sooner we take a leaf outta their book the better.'

'Too bloody right,' Hillsden said, coarsening his own dialogue to suit the situation. 'That's what we're here for, isn't it?'

'You got it, Dad!'

It was then that a door at the rear of the room opened and Johnny wheeled in Fadiman. Immediately everybody stood up and shuffled to attention in a show of military discipline, Hillsden following their lead. Fadiman was wearing a green Tyrolean jacket, the collar and cuffs trimmed with leather. He lifted an arm that stopped just short of a Nazi salute.

'At ease, gentlemen. My apologies for keeping you waiting,' he said as Johnny wheeled him into the centre of the semi-circle and applied the brakes.

'A drink, sir?' Tony asked.

'Thank you, no. Cold beer doesn't sit well with me.'

'Something else then, sir?'

'No, nothing, thank you,' he said as his eyes swept around the gathering. He nodded at Harry, then fixed, momentarily, on Hillsden. 'Ah! We have our new recruit, I see. Good. I'm sure we're all pleased to welcome Robert, representing the older generation, somebody who has lived through the folly of our times.' He reached into his jacket pocket and took out a cigarette. Tony immediately struck a match, but Johnny, standing behind the wheelchair, already had a lighter poised.

Fadiman expended the first inhale. The smoke hovered in the air and, for a few seconds before it dispersed, haloed his head. 'Well, gentlemen, the purpose of calling you together was to share some good news, news I'm sure will excite you as much as it does me. We are poised to make our presence felt.' He paused for effect. 'We are to be favoured with a rare visit from a comrade in the forefront of our movement, a man who, in his writings and speeches, has consistently shown the way forward. His name will be familiar to you . . . 'He smiled, and the braces on his lower teeth glinted in the light from the bare bulb above him. 'For some inexplicable reason, our authorities have never been over-anxious to welcome him to our shores and therefore his occasional visits must, of necessity, be carefully prepared for and carefully concealed from those who misguidedly don't share our reverence . . . I refer, of course, to Herr Gottfreid Sonntag.'

His listeners leaned forward, and Fadiman smiled and nodded. 'I thought that news would excite you. Not only is he the author of several enlightened instruction manuals, he is undoubtedly a man of destiny. He sees where the mistakes of the past have landed us, and he has a vision of how to lead us out of the present morass.'

Fadiman paused again, flicking his cigarette ash on the floor, the act of a man who was accustomed to having somebody else clean up after him.

'We live in momentous times,' he continued, 'and we are the privileged few who share his vision. What I've brought you here for is to outline the purpose of his visit. In the very near future he will be recreating a flight first undertaken by the last inhabitant of Spandau . . . need I spell that out? No, I can see from your faces that you have grasped the symbolism . . . the only difference being that he will not be arriving in a Luftwaffe fighter, but, of necessity, in something more modest.' Fadiman nodded as his joke received a murmur of laughter.

'From start to finish of his visit it's imperative that we maintain the strictest security. His presence in our midst means he must take a considerable personal risk, and any breach of security would put his freedom in jeopardy. Therefore we must take every safeguard. Should anybody abuse the trust he expects from us, they will suffer swift and decisive punishment.' His eyes flicked to Harry, who nodded. 'We have our own final solution for those who betray our cause.'

'Now then, I'm sure you're anxious to know the object of his visit. Apart from wanting to reach a wider audience in this country, the intention is to make the authorities look incompetent. Plans have been prepared for him to speak at the largest rally we have yet mounted. That's all I wish to tell you at the moment. All of you present tonight have been chosen for special responsibilities. On the day, you will act as marshals for the units coming from various parts of the country. I want this to be a public relations exercise, so you will all leave your modified Doc Martens at home. And let it be written in stone, on no account is anybody to carry anything that could be described as an offensive weapon. Is that clear?' All heads nodded. 'Let's not give the police any excuse on our behalf.'

'Can I put a question, sir?' somebody asked.

'Please.'

'Is he always going to be a secret? I mean, once it's all over, aren't we going to get some publicity out of it?'

'That's a good question and I was coming to that. Once he's safely out of the country again we shall certainly maximise the publicity. His speech will be video recorded and printed copies will be given wide distribution.' He dropped his cigarette butt on the floor and Johnny stepped on it for him. 'Any other questions?'

Nobody spoke. 'We're all quite clear then. I thank you for your attention, gentlemen.' He released the two brakes on the wheelchair but before Johnny could swivel him round he issued one last instruction. 'Be sure to leave singly at odd intervals, not in groups. Good night, gentlemen.'

Fadiman's audience stood up and, led by Tony, they gave the Nazi salute as he was wheeled out. There was a rush to the beer and an excited exchange the moment Fadiman had left. Hillsden mingled with the others and let his fake enthusiasm show on his face.

'Brilliant,' Tony said. 'If he pulls this off we'll scare the shit out of them.'

'*When* we pull it off, not *if*,' Harry said.

'I meant when.'

'Then say it.' Harry turned to Hillsden. 'What did I tell you, Dad? That guy is crackerjack. Fucking brilliant dodge to fly him in like Hess. You know they murdered Hess, doncha? He was a peace-maker, but they kept the poor bastard locked up long after the others had gone, and then they murdered him.'

'Yes, it was inhuman the way he was treated.'

'Well, this'll show them. Glad you joined?'

'Definitely.'

'Want to know my motto? Some of my best friends was Jews. Neat, eh?' He laughed, beer spilling out of his mouth and staining the front of his jacket. 'You want to stay on and play pool?'

'I never learned how to play.'

'That's okay by me, I've no objection to taking money off beginners.' He laughed again, then drifted away with some of the others into the snooker hall.

'Fadiman's a bloody good speaker, isn't he?' Tony said.

'Yes, he certainly knows how to hold your attention.'

'You can see if he hadn't been done up, he could have been another Mosley. Mosley had the same gift, apparently. Too bad I never saw him. Did you?'

'I saw him on newsreels,' Hillsden said.

'You wait, we're going to have rallies like that very soon. When I get the word I'll be in touch. Make sure you're available. You're one of the chosen now.'

'Where can I get some of Sonntag's books? I'd like to read one before the day.'

'You can't buy them in a shop and the fucking Customs impounded our last shipment, but I know where there's a few. Leave it with me.'

'Les Hyde wasn't with us tonight,' Hillsden said casually.

'No, he was organising something else. We've got a lot on the boil, and Les is a key player.'

'I'm lucky to have got to know him.'

'Well, you did him a good turn and now he's done you one.

Right?'

'Yes.'

Hillsden said his goodbyes and went through the snooker hall to the front entrance, glancing up at the dark windows of the shop opposite where, he knew, hidden cameras were recording the various departures.

30

A MEAL OUT OF TOWN

That same evening another meeting was taking place in a fashionable watering hole frequented by the affluent, Le Manoir aux Quat' Saisons. Sir Raymond Charters was entertaining a reluctant guest.

'Ralph,' he said between mouthfuls, 'let's put our false teeth on the table. You know and I know this is something that's going to happen sooner or later. You can't stop it, so why don't you bow to the inevitable? Get in bed with somebody you know rather than somebody you don't know and can't trust to do the right thing.'

His guest, Lord Miller, stared down at the meal on his plate, an item of *nouvelle cuisine* colourfully arranged like an edible drawing by Matisse. Unlike the other diners he had little appetite for what was before him or what was being said. Charters, on the other hand, was enjoying both the occasion and the meal. Like many corporate predators he was never so happy as when, having identified a potential victim, he moved in for the kill.

'We've done our homework, and you're highly vulnerable, don't pretend you're not. Your company's a dinosaur and it's haemorrhaging. The banks don't give you second chances these days, and they're ready to move in. You've got big cash-flow problems, the pre-tax profits for the year end were sixty-eight per cent down, you only held the dividend by digging into the reserves. You know your mistake? You caught a cold going into too many wacky diversification schemes and you haven't helped the situation by paying yourself too much by way of salary. That wasn't politically correct in today's climate.' He forked the last of his food into his mouth.

'I've always made it clear I'd fight a hostile bid,' Miller replied.

'Fight! Who wants a fight? The only people who benefit are the lawyers. And I'm not offering you a hostile bid. How can it be hostile when I'm sitting here across the table making it easy? You go the route I'm suggesting, you walk away with a generous handshake for past services, we cosmetic it, invite you to stay on the Board for a year as an adviser, and you can enjoy the rest of your life.'

'I enjoy it now,' Miller said.

A waiter came up to the table and looked at Miller's uneaten dinner. 'Is everything to your liking, my Lord?'

'Yes, it's fine. I'm just not hungry.'

'Can I get you anything else?'

'No, thank you. Just some more mineral water.'

Charters returned to the attack the moment the waiter removed the plates and left. 'Doesn't that make sense?'

'To you, maybe.'

'Ralph, what d'you need it for? You've got all the honours. You've got your health, the best shoot in Wiltshire, nice house, grandchildren . . . and this way, the way I've laid it out, we take all the worries off you.'

Miller answered deliberately. 'I accept that, on the face of it, it's an attractive offer and I dare say a lot of people in my position would take it and run. But I built up this company from scratch, it's been my whole life, and while we might be going through a bad cycle, the banks are staying loyal, they still have confidence that, given some breathing space, I can retrieve the current situation.'

Charters shook his head. 'Don't depend on it. They'd pull the plug on their own grandmothers if it suited them. Charlie Gillard went around saying the same thing,' he added, naming a man whose business had recently collapsed in spectacular fashion, and look what they did to him. He ended up with nothing but his soiled underpants.'

Miller grimaced at the crudity of the remark as the waiter returned and poured him some mineral water.

'Can I describe the desserts we have this evening, my Lord?'

'Not for me.'

'How about you, sir?'

'Perhaps later,' Charters snapped. 'We'll tell you when we're ready.' He went back on the attack. 'Listen, Ralph, I'm sure you'll make up your own mind, no matter what I say, but I'm telling you you're running out of time. The institutions are in our camp, plus we've already got a forty-two per cent favourable response from shareholders. It's all over bar the shouting. But, as a personal gesture to you, I've come here tonight to say I'm willing to up the cash offer for the A shares to four twenty. That puts another million two in your pocket. Take it and smile.'

'Yes, that is generous, but my answer's still no.'

'How can you sit there and say that?'

'Because I'm an obstinate man who believes you're wrong.'

A note of exasperation crept into Charters's voice for the first time. 'Don't talk like an old Jew.'

'I am an old Jew,' Miller said quietly, 'and proud of it. And you just made your first mistake.'

'Oh, where's your sense of humour? It wasn't said to give offence.'

'Perhaps not, but you said it.'

'Ralph, listen to me. Believe your own Board. Both Anderson and Stanhope,' he said, naming two of Trans-Continental's executive directors, 'have come out publicly and said our bid is the only one that makes sense.'

'They can say what they like. I'm not interested in what they say.'

'You need friends at times like this. I'm your friend, Ralph. I'm thinking of you.'

'Yes, I'm sure you're acting from the very highest motives. I'm thinking of me, too. That's why I'm saying no thank you. If I lose –'

'Which you will –'

' – then it won't be for want of trying. I still have some cards I haven't played.' Miller folded his napkin. 'Now, if you'll excuse me, I'll let you enjoy your dessert. I've swallowed enough for one evening.' He stood up and made his way out.

Charters watched him go, holding a fixed smile on his face for the benefit of anybody who might be observing him. He finished his claret, wishing to give an interval before his own departure. Then he beckoned the waiter for his bill.

'Lord Miller took care of it, sir. He particularly asked us to say that he only accepts hospitality from his closest friends.'

. . .

In his tenth-storey Frankfurt office, Walter Hekelmann, a senior officer in the Bundeskriminalamt, Germany's equivalent of the FBI, studied the autopsy photographs of Marvin Schmidt on his desk, then looked up at the CIA man attached to the American Embassy. 'This violence is new violence,' he said gloomily. 'We've got used to skins killing the *Immigranten* since the renunciation, but killing tourists is something different. Well, he wasn't a tourist, I know, but to them he probably looked like one. Why was he here?'

'He wasn't meant to be,' the Agency man said. 'He was on his way to meetings in Munich, following a lead on the Freidler case amongst other things. We know he was on that Lufthansa flight that got diverted, but that's it. He made no phone calls, right?'

'Not any from his room.'

'Did he receive any?'

'He might have done. The hotel doesn't log them.'

'Was he seen with anybody else in the hotel?'

'No. Only three of the staff remember him at all. The

reception clerk, the room maid and the night manager.'

'Did he eat in the hotel?'

'He ordered room service, but when it came up he wasn't in the room.' He lifted a piece of paper. 'Here's the docket. Hamburger, French fries and a piece of Black Forest cake. The food was uneaten.'

'Something, somebody caused him to leave his room soon after he checked in. Who, why, for what reason?'

Hekelmann threw his arms wide. 'It's a blank sheet. We know nothing from the time he rang down for room service until the time he was discovered the following morning when somebody moved their car . . . He was Jewish, wasn't he?'

'Yes. Not obviously so, as you can see.'

'Well, that's another thing that puzzles me. If he was "sidewalk-cracked" by the skins, their usual targets are Turks, gypsies, Kurds, the ones who *look* different, dress differently, don't speak the language, keep to their own quarters, eat in certain restaurants and bars.'

'Can we find out who else was on his plane? Have you got a passenger indent?'

'Yes, take a look.' Hekelmann handed over a computer print-out. 'Only two other people didn't fly on to Munich. I've marked them. One was a woman, as you can see. We checked and she was sick, seen by a doctor at the airport, diagnosed as having a stomach virus. She had relatives here who collected her. The other one . . . You've got the name there . . . Thompson.'

'Thompson. Do we know anything about him?'

'Nothing much. Travelling on an EC passport. Those are the details there.'

'Has he been located since?'

'No,' Hekelmann said. 'He checked into the Savoy for one night, then left the following morning, and took a flight to Copenhagen.'

'Why do people suddenly decide to get off a plane?'

'Are you asking me?'

'I'm thinking aloud,' the agent said. 'They get off because

they've had a bad experience . . . well, that flight came in with reported engine trouble . . . or they're genuinely sick like this woman . . . But neither of those marry with Schmidt. He flew all the time, once told me he'd clocked up enough air miles to fly twice round the world by Concorde. And he sure as hell didn't have stomach trouble if he ordered a burger. But he got off that plane.'

'Perhaps,' Hekelmann suggested hesitantly, 'and I'm not trying to be smart . . . but there's one other possible explanation you didn't mention. Maybe he got friendly with somebody on the plane – one of the hostesses perhaps? – it's happened before . . . and decided to have a little fun before resuming business.'

The agent considered the idea. 'Yeah, it's happened before. But somehow it doesn't sit with Schmidt.'

'We're all tempted – away from home, foreign country, the opportunity presents itself and . . . '

'Okay, well, no harm in interviewing the crew.'

'I have that on my list. But it has to wait. That crew flew out to Los Angeles before I could get to them.'

'Could be there's no real lead to follow. Could be the poor bastard just happened to have an appointment in Samarra.'

The agent picked up a plastic bag of belongings found on Schmidt's dead body and turned the contents out on to Hekelmann's desk. 'You've been through all this I imagine?'

'Of course. They're all labelled as you can see.'

The agent picked up a small pocket diary and rifled through it. He stopped at the last reference. 'He was found on the eighteenth, wasn't he?'

'Correct.'

'There is a reference here on the eighteenth, did you notice?'

Hekelmann took the diary from him and studied the page. 'Yes, we saw that, but it meant nothing.' He handed the diary back.

'Three names: Carstairs, Chandler and Van Elst. Mind if I keep this?'

'I assumed the Bureau would take the lot and return them to his next of kin.'

Reverting to their earlier topic, the Agency man asked: 'They just kill, do they, for the fun of it? They don't rob?'

'No, they're not interested in property, only people.'

'How organised are they?'

'If you mean is there one dominant group, the answer's no, we haven't found that. They're what we call "actively connected" on occasions. Various groups will often come together at events like Oi pop concerts.'

'What's Oi, for God's sake?'

'Heavy metal rock about genocide. You never heard of it?'

'No, that's a new one on me.'

'Not to us. Want to hear one of their favourites?' He walked across the office to a radio and tape player, switched it on and inserted a cassette. 'This is "Turken Raus", played by a local outfit called Onkelz. The sound on this is lousy, but the lyric goes "Turkish cunt shaved naked, Turkish cunt shaved away".' He turned up the volume and the American listened with a stunned expression.

'How do they get away with it?'

'We try to stop them,' Hekelmann replied, turning the machine off. 'It's banned, they're banned, but there are enough pirate copies floating around.' He removed the cassette and juggled with it in his hand. 'You're looking at one cynical German agent, my friend. This isn't the cause, it's just another symptom of our problem, your problem, Britain's problem, France's, Italy's and, any moment now, Russia's. The wolves are coming out of the forest, raiding the trash cans in our backyards. How did we lose it all, can you tell me?'

'I guess we can do precision bombing or just about everything else, but we ain't found a way to destroy hate.'

'Your man's a case in point,' Hekelmann said. 'They didn't kill him for a cause, they killed because they're mindless, they were just looking for some way to pass the time between the next pizza, the next beer, the next fix. They've got shit in the head, and that's tough to destroy, too.'

. . .

Everybody was waiting for the next development.

Hillsden had reported the content of Fadiman's briefing: 'He was so careful, all he gave away was the fact that this Sonntag would be coming. No date, no time, no location.'

'Light aircraft that come in low are not always picked up on radar,' Hadley commented, and Swanson gave him a look which implied that his input was not welcome.

'If indeed he uses an aircraft. Fadiman could have invented that to throw everybody off the scent,' Pearson said. 'On the other hand, the Hess factor would be a good piece of one-upmanship if they pull it off. Are the German police keeping close tabs on Sonntag?'

'I believe so.'

'Where is he now?'

'In his home town,' Swanson answered. 'He's a window cleaner, by the way. Correction, he runs a window cleaning firm. Earning an honest living.'

'Well, Hitler was a house painter, so he's in good company.' Pearson laughed at his own joke.

Swanson frowned, 'Actually, that's a myth. He wanted to be an artist and according to some reports had a certain talent.' He changed the subject and picked up a sheaf of photographs. 'Disappointingly, only one of the men caught on camera by the surveillance team outside the snooker hall proved to have any previous form. He served three months for grievous bodily harm in a pub brawl during the height of the IRA's mainland campaign.'

'Patriotic type though,' Pearson observed, studying the report. 'He slugged an Irishman.'

This time he got a laugh from Hadley.

'But nothing on the man called Harry?' Swanson asked.

'No. Were you counting on something?'

'Yes.'

'Why?'

'Well, it's not a golden rule, but in the past I've found that

263

people who volunteer information to strangers either feel the need to boast or have something to hide. He told Hillsden he'd just come back from Germany.'

Pearson looked through the set of photographs again. 'I think we should all be aware that Hillsden is uneasy about the way it's going. He feels they accepted him too readily. The way he put it to me was he has the gut instinct that they were expecting him. Anybody share that view?' He looked around the room. Nobody spoke until Swanson broke the silence.

'Well, he's in and we can't take him out now.'

31

PEARSON GETS WARM

At the earliest opportunity and still concealing his intent from Lloyd and Swanson, Pearson drove to Yeovil, determined either to eliminate Charters from the reckoning or prove his point.

Yeovil, in Somerset, had once been a centre of the British glove industry, a town where the pungent, sour odour of the tanneries had always been present. Now, due to foreign competition, the local glove industry had all but disappeared, though the town still retained its friendly, sleepy atmosphere so characteristic of the land of Cheddar cheese and butter where, in summer, leather hit the willow on verdant village greens and ladies played bowls in blazers and soft linen hats.

On arrival, Pearson located the branch of Barclays Bank he had been given in Swindon. He saw no reason to conceal his identity on this occasion.

'It's nothing sinister,' he said, when he revealed who he wanted to trace, making up a plausible story as to why. 'The Charters are not in any sort of trouble. Just that, in the course of another investigation we came across some important information regarding a relative of theirs. It's possible they may be entitled to a sum of money.'

'Oh, I see,' the Bank Manager said. 'Well, I'm sure they'd welcome that, if it proves true.' He produced their address, writing it down for Pearson, together with directions showing how to get to the house.

The Charters lived in the lower half of a house in Woodland Grove, a hilly street close to a local landmark, the Nine Springs. He was greeted by a tall, depressed-looking man in his fifties, who peered at him through John Lennon spectacles.

'Mr Charters?'

'Who wants him?'

'Mr John Charters?'

'What's it in connection with?'

'I'm making enquiries about a relative of your family who I believe once lived in Swindon.'

'We don't have any relatives in Swindon.'

'But you are Mr John Charters?'

'Maybe. Who are you?'

'I'm sorry, I should have shown you some identification.' Pearson produced a bogus business card he carried in addition to his official pass. This merely stated: *Commander A.G. Pearson (Rtd) Loss Adjuster*, together with the name and address of a fictitious company. He handed this to Charters who examined it closely.

'This isn't some try-on, is it?'

'Try-on?'

'You from the credit company? Because if you are you're wasting your time.'

'No, I promise you.'

'Loss Adjuster's a joke where we're concerned. We've lost everything. And my wife and I have to be careful.'

'I understand.'

'I doubt it. Those people never let up. Leave you with nothing.'

'But I have got the right person? You are Mr Charters?'

'Yes.' His initial suspicions having been partly allayed, he now seemed willing to unburden himself of past grievances. 'I was off work for a few months and for the first time got behind with the payments. Next thing you know they walk in and repossess the house. Just like that. So you can understand I'm very cautious these days.'

'Yes, that sort of thing happens to a lot of people, I'm

afraid,' Pearson said. 'I sympathise.'

'So, tell me again, what're you asking?'

'Well, it's just a long shot, but since you're a Charters, and, I believe, from Swindon, I thought it worth looking you up.'

'Something to do with a will, is it?'

'Sort of, yes,' Pearson lied, feeling mean.

'Well, I could be wrong, of course, but I can't think of any close relatives still living. I had a sister, but she died . . . must be ten years ago. And there was a cousin who moved to Australia, but I've no idea whether he's still around.'

The possibility of there being some money behind the enquiry had brought about a change in Charters's attitude. 'Why don't you come in for a minute, can't talk standing on the doorstep. You'll have to excuse the place.'

Charters showed him into a room denuded of everything but essentials. A few sticks of furniture and, the only luxury, a small black and white television which Charters now switched off. 'You see what I mean, this is all they left us with.'

'Awful . . . Is your wife at home?'

'No, she does part-time at Sainsbury's. I'm still under the doctor, you see. Got a dicky heart. I'm on the waiting list for a pacemaker.'

Pearson nodded. 'Well, they do wonderful things these days . . . You mentioned a sister.'

'Janet, yes.'

'You didn't have a brother?'

'No, only the two of us.'

'Well, obviously it's just a coincidence, but I came across another Charters who was a pupil at Swindon Grammar School during the war.'

Charters frowned. 'During the war? That's going back a long way. Not me, you mean?'

'No, not you, another male member of your family.'

'Weren't any. Just me and my sister.'

'Oh, well, I'm sorry I troubled you. I must have been given the wrong information.'

'Looks like it . . . Oh, now, hold on, wait a minute. The old brain doesn't work as fast as it used to. I've an idea who you might be talking about. One of our evacuees. My late parents were Quakers, you see, wonderful people, hearts of gold. I never kept up with it after they passed away . . . life has dealt me a few duff cards and I guess I couldn't live up to my folks' standards. They turned the other cheek, but I find that difficult.' He cocked his head on one side, inviting Pearson's understanding.

'Yes, it isn't always easy to play the good Samaritan,' Pearson said. 'You were about to say?'

'Yes, what got me on that?'

'You mentioned evacuees.'

'Ah, that's right. Yes, they took in a couple of East End kids at the start of the war, real little tearaways, I might add – no manners, didn't know how to hold a knife and fork, not that I'm being critical, just a question of upbringing I'm sure . . . But after the . . . what did they call it? . . . the phoney war, when nothing happened, their parents took them back. Then, later, when the French capitulated, there was another exodus and after the Blitz started my parents took in another boy. He was an orphan we were told, his parents had been killed in the air raids I think . . . not sure about that, the old memory's a bit hazy. I seem to remember he'd been shunted all over the place until he found his way to us.'

Pearson cut in to his rambling as politely as he could: 'Your parents were obviously very good people.'

'Salt of the earth. How funny, you've brought it all back. I hadn't thought of him in ages.'

'Who are we talking about now?'

'This other boy. Carl. He went to the same school as us.'

'Carl? Not a very common name. What was his surname?'

'Ah, now you've got me. Let me think . . . What was it? Gone. I do remember my father talked about legally adopting him at one point, Carl being an orphan and that.'

'And did he?'

'Well, now, did he? No, I don't think he did in the end for

268

some reason, although Carl did use our family name. There's something called a Deed Poll, isn't there?'

'Yes.'

'Maybe that was it. Seems to strike a bell. Something to do with identity cards, ration books and that. Knowing my father, he probably didn't want the boy to feel set apart, if you get my meaning. So he went to school under our name. They used to call out the names at morning prayers, that's how I remember. Maybe you could find out whether it was done properly, I can't help you there. He was older than us two and children don't bother about those things, do they?'

'Did he stay with you all after the war?'

'No. No, he left. He was bright, clever at his lessons, cleverer than us, I suppose, because he got a scholarship and left. And that was the last we heard of him. Not that our parents wanted to lose touch, it was him, he never bothered to write or anything. Just went out of our lives. Upset my parents at the time. Not a very nice way to repay their kindness, was it? My sister and I weren't too bothered, because we didn't like him overmuch. Gave himself airs. How funny, it's all coming back now. Haven't thought about him in donkey's years.'

'Well, it was a long time ago,' Pearson said.

'Now, hang on, wait a minute. Let me see if I can put my hands on something that might help.'

He disappeared into another part of the house. Pearson heard him rummaging about, closing and opening drawers. He returned carrying a somewhat tattered album of the sort that families once treasured and hoarded mementoes in. 'Here we are,' Charters said. 'Found it.' He opened it and some loose snapshots fluttered out. 'Coming to pieces.' He retrieved them and having examined them, handed one to Pearson. 'That's the three of us.' The photograph showed three children standing by a concrete pillbox.

'There's me, that's my sister, and that's him, that's Carl. Here he is again. Bit older there. Taken at Wookey Hole caves. You ever seen them?'

'No, I haven't.'

'Well worth a visit. Now this one must have been taken on VE Day. There was a big party, bonfire, fireworks, the lot. Doesn't it seem an age ago? I suppose he could be dead by now, couldn't he?'

'That's what I'm trying to establish,' Pearson replied.

'If he is dead, I suppose you're looking to trace anybody entitled to benefit? . . . If he left anything that is. And, of course, there is a family connection, in a manner of speaking, wouldn't you say?'

'From what you've told me there's a link, certainly. Though how it would stand up in law, I don't know.'

'Don't mention the law to me. I've had enough of the law, thank you . . . By the way, I wouldn't want you to take away the wrong idea. When I say me and my sister didn't get on with him, there was no bad blood or anything, wouldn't like you to think that. Just that we were kids and he was a stranger thrown amongst us and I suppose we resented it, as kids do.'

'Understood.'

'Did you want to take any of these snapshots?'

'No, that won't be necessary. Thank you so much for letting me take up your time.'

'Hope it's been worthwhile.'

'Oh, it has. You've told me a lot I didn't know.'

'Well, feel free to come again if you want to. I could show you around the caves if you had more time.'

'Yes, that would be nice.'

Pearson hesitated, then said casually, 'You do have one rich namesake, of course.'

'Do I? Who's that?'

'Sir Raymond Charters. You've heard of him I dare say?'

'No, can't say I have. We live in a bit of a backwater here, you know.'

'You don't think he's a distant relative?'

'I'd like to think so, but I doubt it. Never heard it mentioned.'

He accompanied Pearson to the front door. 'Sorry the wife

wasn't here. She'll be very intrigued.'

They shook hands. 'Thanks once again. I hope you don't have to wait too long for your operation,' Pearson said.

'The doctor says I'll be a new man once it's done.'

Pearson had much to mull over on his way back to London. In one sense he had inched closer, but now there was a new trail to follow. He doubted whether any records of evacuees still existed after half a century; the mass exodus, first in 1939 and then again in 1940, would almost certainly have been organised at local authority level and if one was talking about a London Borough so much archive material had been destroyed in the Blitz.

Where to begin again? The name Carl, with its vaguely Germanic ring, intrigued him, but it was the original surname he needed to discover. Even so, he felt vindicated.

. . .

'I've had your favourite detective on the line,' Lloyd said the moment Pearson returned to his office.

'Who's that?'

'Gilbert the filbert.'

'Oh, yes, what's he want? I had an interesting day I have to talk to you about.'

'They pulled in Carstairs's, quote, wife, unquote, last night, looking like that actress in *Absolutely Fabulous*, apparently. Pissed out of his/her mind, and shouting his/her mouth off that her husband had been murdered because he was a spy.'

'Tell me some good news. Hey-bloody-ho! We needed that. Where're they holding him?'

'West End Central.'

'We'd better go deal with it then. We don't want Carstairs's domestic arrangements splattered all over the tabloids. By the way, you might still owe me one on Charters,' he said as they went down to the car park. 'I found out something of interest today. I don't think it's his born name.'

'Really?'

Lloyd's continued boredom with the subject irked Pearson and he did not conceal it. 'Show some enthusiasm, won't you? I don't like talking to myself. Proves I could be on the right track about him.'

'Proves nothing. A lot of people change their names.'

They argued all the way to West End Central police station with neither giving ground.

Pearson greeted the Duty Sergeant with 'I gather you've got an hysterical queen on your hands? We got the message from Inspector Gilbert.'

'Yes, he thought it best if you dealt with her.'

'Where was she picked up?'

'Legless and screaming outside a pub at World's End. She's only just quietened down. It was bloody mayhem during the night. You're welcome to her.'

'Okay, we'll sort it out. Take it from me you'll have Gilbert's okay for you to let her off with a caution.'

They were shown to the cell where 'Mrs Carstairs' was being held. Her clothes were torn and the blonde wig looked like an abandoned bird's nest. She had a bruise over the left eye and mascara had streaked her make-up. You poor old cow, Pearson thought and wondered what sort of existence lay ahead for somebody like her. He tried not to show the disdain he felt. The moment she saw him and Lloyd she began to cry.

'Oh, thank God! Thank God! Get me out of here for Chrissake! I couldn't take another night.'

'All right, all right. Don't make yourself upset again. First of all, tell us what brought this on.'

'Have you got a cigarette, please?'

Lloyd produced one and lit it for her.

'Now, we gather you've been making accusations,' Pearson said. 'What made you do that?'

'Because I want the truth to come out.'

'What truth?'

'My darling Freddie didn't commit suicide, he was

272

murdered. And I know why.'

'Calm down, take it gently. What d'you know?'

'He was a spy, wasn't he? He wasn't doing police work like you said. You were lying to me. You're all the same lying bloody devious lot.'

'Well, now, that's the saucepan calling the kettle black. You're not exactly straight, are you, if we're trading insults? We didn't lie to you, if anything we were trying to protect you.'

'Oh, some protection.' Her voice climbed higher. 'You sent one of your men to threaten me.'

'I did *what*?'

'I got a visit, didn't I? Told I'd end up the same way as my Freddie if I didn't keep my mouth shut.'

'Somebody from my department threatened you?'

'Yes.'

'Who?'

'Well, he didn't give a name, did he? But he must have come from your lot, otherwise how did he know where we lived an' all?'

Pearson and Lloyd exchanged looks. 'Now listen,' Pearson said, 'and listen carefully. Just quieten down for a moment and listen. Nobody – I repeat, nobody – from my department could have paid you a visit without my knowing. So let's put that out of the way before we go further.'

'Why should I trust you?' Mrs Carstairs sniffed.

'Because it's in your own best interest. If you say somebody came to the house, I believe you. But I want more details. Can you give us a description of this man?'

'Poncy, evil little sod, I thought.'

'Yes, fine, but what did he look like, what sort of age?'

'I don't know. Forty maybe.'

'Any distinguishing features?'

'Dark hair. Not very well dressed. About your height.'

'Would you recognise him again?'

'I bloody would. Won't forget that face in a hurry.'

'And how exactly did he threaten you?'

'He had bad breath when he got close.'

'I see, but what did he say?'

'Well, he rang first, said he had some important news to give me which he couldn't talk about over the phone. He sounded kosher, and I was taken in. He said it was urgent and would I be in if he came round right away.'

'What time was that?'

'I'd just given Monty his tea, so it'd be about, oh, six o'clock.'

'Just him? Nobody else?'

'No, just him.'

'Did he show you any identification?'

'No.'

'Didn't you ask him for some?'

'No, he was fine on the doorstep, wasn't he? Seemed what he said he was. It was only when he got inside that he changed.'

'Stop there. *Who* did he say he was?'

'Said he worked for the same people as my darling Freddie.'

'Go on.'

'Then he said . . . "Your Freddie, as you call him, was a double-crosser, did you know that?" And of course I said I knew nothing, that Freddie never discussed his work with me. Which he didn't. Then he started to slap me around, gave me this.' She fingered her bruised eye. 'Called me a lying whore. Well, you can say a lot of things about me, and fucking sticks and stones don't break my bones, but I've never been on the game, I was always faithful to my Freddie. I swore blind I didn't know anything, but he kept it up, knocked me about something savage, and all the time he was saying, "Who did he shop us to?" Then, when he couldn't get anything out of me, because I had nothing to tell him, he killed him. He killed my Monty, stepped on him and broke his little neck.' Tears streamed down her face. '"That's just a taste of what you'll get," he said. "We took care of your Freddie and we'll take care of you, so you'd better try and remember something I want to hear, because I'll be back ."'

'Here,' Pearson offered her a handkerchief. 'Look, whatever else, let me assure you of one thing. Your husband . . .' he got the word out with the barest hesitation, 'wasn't murdered. He took his own life. There is absolutely no doubt about that, so this character was lying.'

'That's no bloody comfort, is it? He's dead whichever way.'

'Yes, I agree. We can't bring him back. So now we have to think about you . . . This is what I want you to do for me. First, we'll get you out of here and take you home.'

'I couldn't, I couldn't go back there.'

'Wait, I haven't finished. You know we're genuine, don't you?'

'Suppose so.'

'Well, the police wouldn't have let us see you if we weren't. You'll be given protection and if this character pays a second visit, we'll nab him. Then, tomorrow, I'll bring you some mug shots to look at, you might be able to recognise him from a photograph. How does that sound?'

'Haven't got much choice, have I?'

'Trust me. I know you've had a terrible shock, but I promise you that man was nothing to do with us. We don't work like that. If we thought you were holding something back, either me or Mr Lloyd here would have questioned you. There's just one other thing I want to ask you before we take you home. Did your husband ever mention the name Charters to you?'

'No. Never heard of him.'

'Okay, just wait here a moment or two until I get you signed out and make a phone call. Then we'll be on our way.'

He and Lloyd went back to the desk.

'You make me laugh, you do,' Lloyd said.

'Laugh? What about.'

'When you said "husband" in there. Sounded so bloody funny.'

'Well, what else was I going to call him? She'd had a rough enough time from all accounts.'

'There you go again – "she".'

'Oh, give it a rest,' Pearson said. 'Just take care of the paperwork while I get some protection organised.'

.   .   .

Sitting across from his wife and daughter at the dinner table, Hillsden felt soiled. While he listened to Lara's chatter about what had happened on her first day at school, part of his mind kept returning to his secret life. Already, he thought, I have been trained by the Fadimans of this world, forced to speak their language, assume their hatreds, echo their prejudices. It was a heavier price for freedom than he wanted to pay. He stared into his daughter's excited face and tried to concentrate on what she was saying.

'. . . and we made clay models. I'm doing something special and secret for you, Dada.'

'Are you? I can't wait.'

'I nearly finished it and then it broke. Mummy knows what it is, but she mustn't tell you.'

'Oh, no, it's got to be a secret.'

Lara looked down at her plate for a moment, then said in the mumbled speech children use when troubled: 'We have a lot of secrets, don't we?'

'Do we?'

'Yes, tell me again why I had to change my name.'

Hillsden and Galina exchanged glances.

'Just that it's easier to spell it the English way now that we're in England,' Galina said. 'I told you that before.'

'But Dada was always English and he's changed his name too.'

'Now, not so much talking, young lady, just finish what's on your plate and then it's bedtime.'

Later, when Lara had been put to bed, Galina said: 'She's always asking me that question. It didn't matter so much before she went to school, but now I'm worried she might let something slip amongst her friends. And you couldn't blame her, because she's confused. I get confused. I nearly gave myself away the other day when I was signing for something in a shop . . . I almost wrote "Hillsden", just stopped myself in time. You're used to leading a double life, we're not.'

'I know, darling,'

'You find it easy though.'

'No,' Hillsden said.

'We've burdened her with our lives. She's fearful, too fearful about things. She shouldn't be fearful of life at her age. That'll come soon enough. The other thing she asked me today was whether it was all right for her to be in the class photograph.'

'Did you say yes?'

'Yes, but then I thought, is it safe, would you turn round and tell me I'd done the wrong thing?' She waited for him to answer. 'Should I have said, no, that's not a good idea?'

'You couldn't have said that. That would only have led to more questions.'

'I can tell from your expression though that you'd rather she didn't.'

'No. As a matter of fact I was thinking of something else you said. That we've burdened her with our lives. You could have put it another way, that I've burdened you both with my life. Isn't that the truth of the matter?'

'If only you'd tell me what the truth is.'

'Galina, my darling,' Hillsden said, 'd'you think I want to involve you any further than I have already? It's enough that I brought you both here . . . I was so anxious to give you what I thought would be a better life that I didn't think it through. Whatever else you blame me for, don't blame me for that because I did it out of love.'

'I don't blame you,' she said. 'I just didn't want you to change.'

'Have I changed?'

'Not towards us, I don't mean that. I know you love us, but I don't think you love yourself any more.'

Hillsden was jolted. It was as if, throughout dinner, she had been reading his thoughts with that startling perception women, and especially mothers, often had.

'You once said to me "I'm safe now",' she continued.

'Did I?'

'Not so long after we met. And I believed you. Should I still believe you?'

Instead of answering her, Hillsden said, 'Then do you remember that when you told me you were expecting Lara, you asked if I was pleased, and I think I said to you that I'd only been trained to recognise hatred, that love always took me by surprise. Or words to that effect. Do you remember that?'

Galina nodded.

'Well, that's still true. I often wonder why it is you still love me.'

'And you haven't answered me,' she said.

'I'm safe with you,' Hillsden replied, 'if that's what you want to hear.'

32

THE TROUBLE WITH HARRY

The first day of the following week Hillsden sat at a corner table in one of the many sandwich bars in Docklands eating a snatched lunch. From boredom he was reading somebody's discarded copy of *The News of The World*. It had been a dull Sunday: no ex-employee of the Royal family had sold the serial rights to their memoirs. He leafed through the pages wondering what gave the British press its unique facility of maximising the instantly forgettable. He turned to the financial pages and studied the advertisements for PEPs as he pondered whether he should invest some of the money he had set aside for Galina and Lara. Alongside one of the ads there was a photograph of a couple taken at a race meeting. The caption under the photograph read: *You win some and you lose some. Although his champion three-year-old 'India Rose' was ridden to victory at Kempton Park yesterday, millionaire businessman, Sir Raymond Charters, recently failed in his take-over bid for Trans-Continental.*

He looked up from the paper to find Sarah standing beside him with a worried face.

'What is it?'

She sat down opposite him. 'Somebody arrived at the office.'

'Who?'

'I don't know, he wouldn't give me his name, but he said he knew you. I told him you were out to lunch and he said he'd call back in an hour. So I locked up and came to find you.'

'Well, get your breath back. Do you want a coffee, something to eat?'

She shook her head.

'He said he knew me?'

'Yes.'

'But didn't say how or where?'

'No. I asked him if he was interested in car insurance, but he said, no, it was personal matter.'

'How long ago?'

Sarah looked at her watch. 'I'd say twenty minutes.'

'Okay, now, I'll tell you what you do. Go back to the office and I'll join you there. I want to make a phone call first. If he gets back before I do, give him brochures, chat him up with some sales talk. Off you go. I'll be there as soon as I can.'

'Right.'

They got up together and Sarah left while Hillsden paid his bill. Outside he had to walk two blocks before he found a public phone box. It was occupied and he fretted outside while two girls, jammed together inside the box, shared a lengthy conversation. The moment the box was free again he dialled Pearson's number. Hadley answered.

'He's isn't here,' Hadley said. 'What's up?'

Hillsden gave him the brief details. 'It could be nothing, but let's not take chances. How soon can you get down here?'

'I'm on my way.'

'Just come in as if you were another customer. Whoever it is, I'll try and keep him there until you arrive so you get a look.'

He hurried back to the office and the moment he got inside Sarah said: 'Oh Mr Bartlett, you're back. There's a friend of yours here to see you,' and as he turned from closing the door he saw who it was.

'Harry!' he said warmly. 'To what do I owe this honour? Don't tell me I'm going to get your business after all?'

'No, don't get excited, I was down this way and I thought I'd pay you a call. See where you hang your hat.'

'Has Sarah offered you a coffee?'

'She did, but I said no.'

'Come into my office so we can talk. I'll have one, Sarah, but no calls.'

He escorted Harry into the inner office and closed the door. 'Do you have any news?' he asked in a lowered voice.

'News?'

'The news we're waiting for?'

'No, like I said, this is just a social call. Our friend in the wheelchair thought we ought to get to know each other better.' He looked around the room, taking everything in. 'Nice set-up. How's business?'

'Not bad.'

Harry said: 'Useful little earner, insurance, I'm told.'

They were interrupted by Sarah bringing in the coffee. Putting it down on Hillsden's desk, she turned to Harry. 'Are you sure you wouldn't like one, Mr . . . ? I'm sorry, I don't know your name.'

'No, I'll pass.'

'I know you said no calls, Mr Bartlett, but there is another gentleman waiting outside.'

'Well, apologise, say I'm with a client and I'll be with him shortly.'

Sarah withdrew, closing the door after her.

'I'm surprised to see you,' Hillsden said when it was safe again. 'Tony felt I shouldn't be contacted here.'

'That so? Yeah, well, Tony has his own ideas, I go about things in a different way.' He picked up one of the brochures on the desk and looked through it while talking. 'You still got your health?'

'My health? Yes, I think so.'

'Great thing health.' He put the brochure down again and gave a thin smile. 'We all need to stay healthy. Not take chances. But, you'd know that, being in the insurance game. I don't take risks. I don't even drink coffee. Yours is getting cold, by the way.' He walked around the room. 'You landed a nice little set-up in your old age.'

'Yes, I got lucky.'

'Twice,' Harry said.

'Twice?'

'You joined us. You never know when your luck may change, though.'

'No,' Hillsden agreed. 'Not these days. What d'you do for a living, Harry?'

'Me? Nothing much. Do a bit of chauffeuring, never been one for the nine to five routine. I make a living.' He moved to the door. 'Anyway, nice to see somebody else hard at it.'

Hillsden went with him through the outer office. Hadley sat reading a brochure and looked up as they appeared. Harry gave him a passing glance.

'Be with you in a minute, sir,' Hillsden said to Hadley, following Harry into the corridor and closing the outer door.

'I'll see you on the great day then.'

'Yeah, let's hope so,' Harry said enigmatically, as he departed down the stairwell. 'I'll keep in touch, depend on it.'

Back in his office, Hillsden found Hadley using a small two-way radio. 'Leaving the building now. Medium build, brown jacket and blue jeans.'

'Are you having him followed?'

'I thought we might as well.' Hadley saw Hillsden's dubious expression. 'Don't worry. Be interesting to see what his next port of call is. Did he tell you anything new?'

'No'

'He didn't give you the date when Sonntag arrives?'

Hillsden shook his head. 'No, he just fingered my collar.'

'What's that mean?'

'You make me feel my age, Hadley. It's an expression they used to use when the police gave you a caution.'

'You think he had an ulterior motive coming here?'

'I'm sure of it. People like Harry don't make social calls. They always have a purpose. Put that in your book and learn it by heart.'

. . .

They met in one of the service stations on the M4 motorway, arriving in separate cars. Hillsden found Rotherby in the sparsely populated smoking section of the restaurant.

'You still do, don't you?' Rotherby asked, balancing a cigarette on the edge of the ashtray while he dunked a digestive biscuit in his coffee.

'Smoke? Yes, of course.'

'I was sitting here trying to think of the brand that used to have silk flags of all nations on the packets.'

'Kensitas,' Hillsden said. He opened a small plastic bucket of milk and emptied it into his tea. 'My father doted on them.'

'How brilliant of you to remember. Pity I didn't save them, a complete set goes for a fortune at auction.' A segment of his soggy biscuit fell into his coffee but he seemed not to notice. 'So what's worrying you that we had to meet in secret?'

Hillsden hesitated. He felt like a writer staring at a blank page, knowing the plot but unable to conjure up the dialogue. 'More and more,' he said finally, 'I think I've been set up. You telling me my car was bugged planted the idea and somewhat late in the day I've become convinced that I've been chosen as the patsy. I think the Fascist mob were expecting me.'

'What makes you think that?'

'Because it's all gone too smoothly. Doesn't it strike you that way?'

'Yes, to be honest. Didn't mention it to you, which was a mistake, but put that down to the general euphoria of seeing you again. What has been in my mind all along is something Masterman wrote in his last will and testament,' Rotherby replied, referring to a once banned book by a now dead member of the Firm. 'He laid down that a double-agent can't be produced out of thin air and set upon the stage ready at once to play a leading role. Which is what they did with you. He maintained that the double-agent had to be steadily "built up", as he put it, over a long period, and that in the beginning he is never an asset but always a liability. You were flung into it and it always puzzled me that you didn't protest and ask for more time.'

Hillsden took a moment before answering. 'I don't have a simple reason. Perhaps the truth is that, having been out of the game for all those years I'd become careless. Tell me, who first floated the idea of bringing me back?'

'I've never been able to track it to its source. I first heard it talked about just before Keating died. Then it didn't surface again until they started to beef up the anti-Fascist section of F Division. That was when Pearson and I got moved over.'

'What d'you make of Pearson and his Man Friday?'

'Two examples of the old school. Not too much imagination, maybe, but get there in the end. They both spent time in Northern Ireland, so they know a trick or two, but they never struck me as being plotters against their own kind.'

'So you'd rule them out?'

'I don't rule anybody out, but they seem unlikely casting.'

'How about Hadley?'

'Ah! Difficult to read our friend Hadley. Touch of La Gioconda.'

'Which comes back to Swanson. How d'you read him?'

'Sees himself as future DG. I think he'd piss on my grave if he thought it would push him another two rungs up the ladder.'

'How about my grave?' Hillsden said.

'No, you're his man. He was the one who recruited you, don't forget. You pull this off and he takes the credit for masterminding the operation.'

'So who else is there?'

'There's me, of course,' Rotherby said, draining his coffee cup.

'I trust you, Colonel.'

'Is that wise? Why trust anybody?'

'Why else would you tip me off about the car?'

'Perhaps that was a double-bluff to put you off the scent.'

Without changing his tone of voice, Hillsden said: 'If I really entertained that I'd have to get rid of you.'

'Not you, old son. You're not cut out for the rough stuff.'

'You think not?' Hillsden paused as though taking a decision, then said: 'I thought that until I had to kill Jock.'

Rotherby stared at him. 'Jock was murdered by the KGB. He was buried in Vienna, the British Council put up a headstone. I've seen the photographs.'

Hillsden shook his head. 'No, he was never buried there. That was a KGB fake. He was turned. They turned him. I killed Jock in Moscow. I smothered him with a pillow while he was drunk.'

'Are you kidding me?'

'Unfortunately, no.'

'Why?'

'Why? I had to. You see, we're all faced with having to make the ultimate choice between love and hatred sooner or later. Something Caroline said to me just before she went back into East Berlin for the last time. She said, "That's the game we're in. Not the love game, the hate game." It was the last conversation we ever had. And I had a good reason to hate Jock. He murdered Caroline.'

Rotherby's jaw dropped another inch.

'How could he have done?'

'He was sent back here for that express purpose. Caroline was the one who held the last piece in the jigsaw that could bring down Lockfield and the whole pack of cards . . . sorry about the jumbled metaphor . . . When they traded her she came back from the Lubianka a vegetable, but they still weren't taking any chances.'

Rotherby started to say, 'But you three . . . '

'Yes,' Hillsden finished for him. 'I know what you're going to say. We were the Austrian Holy Trinity until it broke up. I came back, Caroline went to Berlin, Jock was taken and like you, I grieved for him when the report of his death filtered through. But he fooled us all, and nobody more than me . . . and he was the one who betrayed Caroline in the first place.'

Rotherby was silent for an appreciable time, unable to grasp what he had just been told. 'Then you met again, obviously.'

Hillsden nodded as various ghosts flitted in and out of his memory. 'I had a GRU handler in Moscow, somebody who curiously became a friend, remains a friend as it happens. When finally they were sure of me, he thought I needed company, so he brought Jock to Moscow and put him in my apartment block. As far as Jock was concerned, he and I now were two of a kind, we'd both been turned. He was an alcoholic by then, he'd gone the way of Burgess, and with good reason, given what he'd done. And one night when he was sloshed, the whole story came out. He admitted he betrayed Caroline to save his own skin. The way he told it, he had no choice, but we always have a choice, don't we? He thought I'd forgive him, but I couldn't even forgive myself.'

'How d'you mean?'

'When they traded Caroline, when she came back and the Firm put her in that home to rot, I also betrayed her.'

'In what way?'

'I never went to see her. I was too bloody scared of what it would do to me. Oh, I pretended to myself I was the reformed adulterer, acting nobly for Margot's sake, but the truth was I couldn't face seeing what they'd done to her. Wouldn't you call that a betrayal?' Despite the passage of time, his voice cracked slightly and he reached for a cigarette which Rotherby lit for him. 'I loved her, you see.'

'Then you disappeared.'

'Yes. After that, all I had was hatred. I became so consumed with hatred I made a stupid mistake, I gave Lockfield the opening he was looking for. That devious old queen, Glanville, remember? They granted him immunity in return for his silence. He was supposed to be off limits, a burnt-out case with nothing else to offer, but I didn't give a fuck about that, I was sure I could squeeze some more out of him, and I was right. He revealed a lot more. Shortly afterwards he was found dead and suspicion fell on me since I was the last person to see him alive. Lockfield must have thought I was getting too close, and now he had the excuse he had been waiting for to silence me once and for all. He played the

Caroline card, knowing I couldn't resist it, and sent me back into the cold. Afterwards, he bolted the door by pinning a murder on me. It was neat, very neat, I'll give him that.'

'Does it ever leave you? The thought that you've killed somebody?'

'No. It's there, nudging you like an exposed nerve in a tooth. You go for a while without feeling anything, and then suddenly you bite down on it and it jolts you.'

'God, Alec, old son, rather you than me ... And what now?'

'I have to go through with it, I can't back out now, but keep your ears to the ground for me.'

'Of course. But if you've been set up, what have you been set up for?'

'That's what I haven't been able to figure out. Somebody, somewhere is playing with me.'

33

THE CLOCK STARTS TICKING

Immediately following the first intimation of Sonntag's impending arrival, a plan of action had been agreed by the combined security forces. After obtaining Cabinet approval, Logan issued a carefully worded letter, written on Ministry of National Heritage notepaper, requiring every police authority to supply details of any venue that had been booked for large public meetings over the next two months. The phoney reason given was that the Minister wished to ascertain the depth of public opinion on conservation in preparation for issuing a White Paper.

A list of some thirty-seven such meetings, widely scattered across England, and one in Scotland, had come back. All had been investigated. In the majority of cases the meetings had been organised by either charities or local councils and were established as being genuine. Three remained questionable, including the one in Glasgow, and were further scrutinised, especially the Scottish venue in view of the Hess factor. Of the two in England, both were in the Home Counties, within reasonable distance of the centre of London; one was in Amersham, and the other in Luton. In the case of Amersham, a British Legion hall had been booked by an organisation calling itself C.A.D.R.E. (Campaign Against the Destruction of Rural England), with a registered office in Harringay. The one in Luton had been booked by a similar protest group, this time under the banner Nature Comes First. Although the

Scottish venue had been booked by the SNP, it was still considered suspicious by elements of MI5, though the consensus amongst Special Branch favoured one of the two local locations nearer to London.

The offices of C.A.D.R.E. and Nature Comes First, the latter proving to be above a fish and chip shop, were covertly inspected. Both appeared to be staffed by earnest middle-aged citizens who in earlier times would have been found in the ranks of those who made the yearly pilgrimage from Aldermaston. On the surface, both organisations seemed to be outlets for legitimate protest, with no apparent connections to either the far Right or far Left.

'They both seem too good to be true,' Pearson observed.

The actual venues were carefully reconnoitred by Special Branch men, who went in under the guise of Health Inspectors. The large bingo hall in Luton which had at least six exit points was considered to be the most difficult to police, whereas the Amersham meeting in the British Legion hall was thought to be an easier prospect. The dates for all three meetings were contained within a time frame of ten days. Police leave in all three locations was cancelled during that period and extra supplies of riot gear were issued. Detachments of the Special Patrol Group were also alerted and detailed instructions issued to their senior officers. The most recent photographs of Sonntag were obtained from the German authorities and circulated to all concerned. RAF radar stations on the East coast were given phoney orders about a non-existent Nato exercise and told to be extra vigilant about tracking any unidentified aircraft. All that could be anticipated was thought to have been covered.

.   .   .

Much calmer now and, if the truth were told, mollified by the presence of a young Special Branch detective as a house guest, the man who passed himself off as Mrs Carstairs studied the collection of mug shots that Lloyd put in front of him.

'No . . . No, nothing like . . . No . . .' He paused and lingered over the next. 'That's getting warmer, except the hair was different . . . No . . .' This time he placed a hand over the eyes and nose. 'That's his mouth, he had a thin, cruel mouth, no lips to speak of.' One by one he rejected the selection. 'Sorry, don't recognise any of them.'

'Never mind,' Lloyd said. 'Have a look at this batch. They're not as clear as the others, but use this magnifying glass.'

He produced a batch of photographs taken with a telephoto lens, the work of the surveillance team keeping watch on the snooker hall. A good number of them had been taken in poor light.

'Take your time, no hurry. Study each one.'

Standing close beside him, Lloyd was conscious of a cloying perfume; not for the first time, he found himself speculating about the initial decision that led to such a life. Was it something, half-comprehended in childhood, that crept up on you? What single act forced the final realisation, and what kind of resolve was needed to make that first purchase of feminine clothes, the step that took you into make-believe land?

These thoughts were disturbed as 'Mrs Carstairs' suddenly gave a tiny, involuntary gasp, clapping a hand to his mouth. 'Him!' he said. 'That's him.'

'Which one? Show me.'

'Mrs Carstairs' pointed with a manicured finger, tipped with bright nail varnish. Lloyd took the magnifying glass. He saw that the man picked out was the one they knew as Harry.

. . .

Pearson was in gloomy mode. Lloyd found him hunched over a pile of annual reports obtained from Companies House, all concerned with companies either owned or controlled by

Charters.

'Well, our first break,' Lloyd said.

'What?'

'"Mrs Carstairs" identified Harry as the one who came to the house and duffed him up.'

'We've got to stop calling him Mrs Carstairs. He isn't Mrs Carstairs. He's a woofter in drag.'

'Okay, okay, don't get excited. Shall we get the Met to pull Harry in?'

'No, bad idea. Think what that does. It tips them off and puts Hillsden and the whole operation at risk. We can have him when the time's right for us. Meanwhile, Swanson's decided that Hillsden should move out of Suffolk and into the safe house at Forest Gate for the time being.'

'The whole family?'

'No, just use your loaf for once. Are we likely to move the whole family? For one thing, Hillsden's cover story is that his wife's dead. Swanson feels that since Harry paid a visit to Docklands there's always a chance that one of them might check out Forest Gate.'

'How did Hillsden take it?'

'He hasn't been told yet.'

'He won't like it.'

'Probably not. But it's safer than them tracking him to Suffolk.'

'What's that you're reading?' Lloyd said, anxious to get off the subject.

'Annual reports of Charters's various companies.'

'Thinking of buying shares, are you?'

Pearson looked at him with disdain. 'I sometimes wonder how you and I have survived as a team this long. For your information, I'm to establish whether any of his various enterprises trade out of Luxembourg. Carstairs's bank account, remember?'

'Oh, I see, yes. You're still flogging that dead horse, are you?'

'Do yourself a favour. Don't antagonise me.'

Ghosts reappeared in the Forest Gate house. Whether it was the confession he had made to Rotherby, or the fact that he was on his own, denied even the comfort of a telephone call to Galina except from an outside call box, more and more Hillsden found himself pulled back into the past. He frequently woke from a nightmare, unable to place himself in the strange bed, the unfamiliar room, on one occasion thinking he could hear the canary that Jock had given him as a pet, the dream so real that he reached for the bedside light switch to reassure himself that he wasn't still in that Moscow apartment where the cage had stood by the window. Another night, he awoke convinced that he had heard somebody trying the handle of the back door. He felt for the service handgun he now kept under his pillow and checked the magazine, wondering, as he slipped the safety catch, whether he would ever be able to fire it in self-defence. There was an unreality about his life; for the second time he had been divorced from everything that mattered to him. He missed Galina and Lara and feared for them, silently berating himself for his stupidity. How had Swanson described him? *You're the man who never was. We've arranged for you to die.* I feel dead, he thought, if only I could believe in something other than the past.

For the rest it was a waiting game until finally, late in the evening of the tenth day the phone rang and Tony's voice said: 'Robert?'

'Yes.'

'The party's on. Thursday, the twenty-second, five o'clock sharp, leaving from the usual place.'

'To where?'

'Don't ask. You'll find out on the day.'

The line went dead.

Thursday 22nd was in eight days' time.

34

THE ARRIVAL

Eight days later, the man who arrived at Plymouth airport on the flight from Jersey, mingled amongst returning holidaymakers and attracted no attention. Tanned, his normal flaxen hair dyed a much darker shade and wearing thin-rimmed Granny spectacles, he bore scant resemblance to the photographs that had been circulated by Interpol. The only luggage he carried was a small overnight case and a Duty Free plastic bag. Presenting a valid British passport, which gave his name as Arthur Clarke, he passed through Immigration, then took the green customs exit without being challenged. Outside, he queued for a bus into the city centre. Once there, he went into a large department store, entering by one door and leaving fifteen minutes later by another, accompanied now by a woman roughly his own age – one of those anonymous working-class British women who, pretty in their teens, had lost their early bloom: with her frizzed hair and coat of unfashionable length, she could have passed for any harassed housewife out for a shopping trip with her husband. The only item about her which caught the eye was a silk rose pinned to the lapel of her coat, by which the man had identified her at their pre-arranged rendezvous point. Threading their way along the crowded pavements they walked, arm in arm, to a multi-storey car park, avoiding the lifts and climbing two flights. There the woman led the way to a nondescript Volvo. It was only when they were both inside the car that any words were exchanged.

'No problems?' the woman asked.

'No, everything as planned,' Sonntag said. 'So far,' he added.

The woman turned the ignition key, backed out of the narrow bay, and drove out of the car park. Sonntag lit a cigarette, then, just before putting the packet away, he made a hissing sound. 'How stupid can I get?' Extinguishing the cigarette and crumpling the packet, he wound down his window and threw them both into the street.

'What's up?' the woman asked.

'I brought a packet of German cigarettes with me.'

'Well throwing them out was stupid, too,' the woman said, pleased she could score a point. 'You can get done for littering our streets.'

'Never mind that. Take a good look, is there anything about me that seems odd to you? I look British, yes?'

'Yeah, of a sort.'

'What d'you mean, "of a sort"?'

'Well, I know you're not British, but probably others wouldn't give you a second look. Have a look around – don't go by the colour of their skin – everybody's British now.'

The reply seemed to please him. He fished inside the Duty Free bag and took out some Dunhills. 'For the rest of my visit I must get used to these.'

'Or you could give up,' the woman said, winding down her window.

'Don't you smoke?'

'I quit two years ago.'

Sonntag shrugged. 'It's a mistake not to retain at least one vice.' He lit the Dunhill. 'Why give up? We all have to die sooner or later. Anything you have to tell me?'

'No. Everything's in place.'

'There have been no changes?'

'No.'

'That's good. How long will it take us to get there?'

'About two hours, the way I drive.'

'You will drive carefully, if you know what's good for you.'

The woman shrugged, changing gear and accelerating. 'I meant I shall be avoiding the motorways and taking the back roads.'

Travelling through the centre of Plymouth, they passed the shell of a church.

'They left it standing like that after the bombing raids,' the woman said.

'It's good we're still remembered.'

'Oh, you're remembered here all right. How did you manage to give your lot the slip?'

Sonntag grinned, lighting a second cigarette from the first and ignoring her grimace. 'Simple. I'm a window cleaner, remember? We have a contract to do a large office block at night. I went in with my team, but left before they finished. *Schmutz* the world over have their minds fixed in a groove.' He used the Nazi slang for 'dirt' to describe the police. 'They assumed because we entered by the service entrance we would leave the same way. I didn't.'

'And from there?'

'Why're you asking so many questions?'

'Just curious. Suit yourself. Don't tell me if you don't want to.'

'I prefer not,' he said stiffly, and for the first time she caught a hint of his true accent. 'It was the same with this trip – I was convinced they'd be looking in one direction, so I came from another. I was right, of course.'

He gave off an air of self-satisfaction, as real to her as the cigarette smoke that now made her nauseous. She was not drawn to him, having expected somebody immediately charismatic; instead he was like any other man who had entered her life. They all thought a lot of themselves, and this one, flabby and overweight, left her cold.

'I knew if we planted the Hess rumour they'd fall for it. Your authorities have always had a thing about Hess. You know why? Because too many of your countrymen would have liked him to have succeeded. Did you know that?'

'I wasn't even born during the war,' she said.

'Don't you know the history of our movement?'

'Some of it.'

'So, what makes you one of us now?'

'I hate the fucking Jews,' she said in a matter of fact way, her eyes on the road, 'they put my father out of business.' She eased her foot off the accelerator as she spotted a police car waiting in a side turning. 'Turn your head towards me.'

'What?'

'Do as I say. We're just passing a police car.'

Sonntag did as she told him. 'Do the *Schmutz* worry you?' he asked, again using the slang term.

'Why take chances? Is that your word for them?'

'Yes. Filth. What d'you call them?'

'Pigs.'

'Your pigs aren't even armed, are they? Pathetic.'

'That's changing,' she said. 'Are you worried they might arrest you tonight?' she asked, her eyes going to the rear-view mirror.

'No. I might even welcome it, for all you know. We all have to pay our dues. Going to jail for the cause is an honour. We must be willing to pay the price if necessary. Are you prepared for that?'

'I'm here, aren't I?' the woman replied with sudden vehemence. 'Driving you. Okay, you can relax now.' Her foot went on the pedal again and she pushed their speed to forty.

'Can't we go any faster?'

'Not yet. Not until we're on the dual carriageway. They've got speed cameras on this stretch.'

Sonntag pushed his seat back and stretched himself. 'Hess is my role model. He never renounced the leader. Not like that apologist Speer.' He looked at the countryside they were passing through. 'Such a small country, England. You ever been to Germany?'

'No.'

'You should. Visit our shrines, like the Luitpold Hall.'

'What's that?'

'You don't know?' he snapped with scornful emphasis.

'You don't know Nuremberg?'

'Of course I've heard of it. It's where they held the trials.'

His tone had made her lose concentration and she passed a turn-off and had to reverse back.

'What sort of person have they sent to meet me?' Sonntag said, as though addressing a third party. 'Listen, woman, it was famous before the trials. It was the place where the Führer held his great rallies. Try as they might, they couldn't destroy all of it, it was built for a thousand years. And one day we'll rebuild it exactly as it was.'

Sonntag lapsed into silence for the next few miles, only stirring himself as they passed through a belt of farmland. He suddenly pointed. 'What is that called?'

'What is what called?' the woman asked.

'That yellow.'

'Rape.'

For a reason she could not comprehend, this amused Sonntag and he repeated the word 'rape' several times, then said, 'A field of rape. That sounds very funny. Your language is absurd sometimes. Don't you think it's funny?'

'Not particularly. It's what it is. What else should they call it?'

He half-stubbed out his cigarette in the ashtray where it remained smouldering. The woman pulled a face and deliberately coughed, but Sonntag made no effort to put it out completely.

Sonntag's mood switched abruptly. 'Yes, you must come to Germany one day. Complete your education. Things are going astonishingly well for us. We are on our way, leading as always. It will take time, of course, but history is on our side, and we are not going to strew ashes over our heads for ever. We are not prepared to be humiliated any further.'

A police Range Rover going in the opposite direction passed them and the woman watched it carefully in her rear-view mirror. Sonntag followed her look. Then he said: ' Tonight we start to make history. The important thing is to leave a scar on the world.'

Once Hillsden had relayed the date, a crucial meeting had been convened, chaired by Logan. Those present were faced with a critical decision: none of the three previously suspect venues were scheduled for the twenty-second, and were thus ruled out. A further urgent search had revealed a derisory list: the few large events due to take place on the twenty-second were a meeting called to oppose blood sports in Cheltenham, an anti-abortion rally in Newcastle, a farewell concert by The Stones at Wembley and an appearance by the American evangelist, Paul Sheenham, at Earls Court. Only the latter provoked any serious discussion.

'We can't ignore the fact that Sheenham was one of the names on the CIA hit list that Schmidt gave us,' Pearson said.

'Yes, but you can't have two star performers, can you?' Swanson pointed out. 'It's absurd to think they would inject Sonntag into a mass of born-again Christians. Just doesn't add up.'

'I have to agree,' the Police Commissioner said. 'And if they were intending to assassinate Sheenham they'd hardly want Sonntag around.'

'So what do we have?' Logan interjected. 'If the information given by this man . . . remind me of his name . . .'

'His undercover name is Bartlett, Minister.'

'Well, if the date Bartlett has supplied is genuine and if their object is to obtain maximum publicity when they produce Sonntag, then it follows that at some point they have to reveal the venue. Where haven't you looked?'

The others allowed the buck to be passed to the Commissioner. 'Taking the point you've just made, Minister – namely, that we must assume they are hoping to gain publicity – we've acted on the premise they would choose a public venue. That would seem the logical course, but as you know we have uncovered no evidence that fits that scenario.'

'Are we still maintaining a strict watch on all airports and ports?'

'All immigration controls have been tightened, Minister. And that includes the Channel Tunnel, of course.'

'And?'

'Over forty suspects have been detained and questioned without success, including one individual piloting a private plane who made a landing in a field just outside Edinburgh. For a few hours we thought we had our man, but it was subsequently established that it was a genuine forced landing due to engine failure.'

'Well, this is a ludicrous situation,' Logan said. 'Here we have the entire police force, strongly supported by the security service, outguessed and out-manoeuvred by a rag-bag gang of Fascists. I gave my permission for this undercover operation to go ahead with considerable misgivings. It seemed to me at the time that it was unlikely to produce the desired results, but I was persuaded against my better judgement. I should warn you all that if it ends in humiliation, the government will not hesitate to ask for resignations.'

Again the Commissioner was the only one who found his voice. 'With all due respect, Minister, it's never an easy task to detect a crime that has not yet been committed. We still have forty-eight hours. Everybody concerned is aware of the urgency and renewed efforts will be made by the combined police forces. All Chief Constables are ready to move their forces into position the moment we get a break.'

'And if we don't get a break?'

'Well, I'm not God, Minister, I'm just a policeman.'

He met Logan's penetrating stare, but he had gone too far and he knew it. Logan rounded on Swanson. 'I don't want any further excuses, I want answers. What d'you propose to do in the forty-eight hours remaining? Can't this Bartlett man whom you have so much faith in provide the vital information?' There was no mistaking the venom in his voice.

'They have been ultra careful, Minister. All he has been able to discover is the actual date and the rendezvous point.'

Logan pounced on this. 'Rendezvous point? What

rendezvous point?'

'The London cell meets in a snooker hall, which we've been keeping under surveillance, and according to Bartlett, certain elements are to assemble there on the night to be transported to the, as yet unknown, venue.'

The impact of what he had just said took a second or two to sink in. The Commissioner turned on him. 'That's news to me. Why wasn't that brought to my attention sooner?'

Swanson looked flustered. 'Wasn't that passed on?'

'No.'

'I apologise and I shall certainly make it my business to find out who was at fault.'

'Well, this changes the whole situation,' the Commissioner said. 'They can be followed in unmarked cars in constant radio contact and the moment we know in which direction they are heading a massive police net can be drawn around them, ready to converge on the ultimate destination.' He looked at Logan, prepared to accept some appreciation.

'Yes,' Logan said. 'For the first time I've heard something that makes sense. However, I'm not prepared to tolerate or defend any subsequent charges of police provocation. I want it to succeed, obviously, but it must succeed without comebacks.'

There was further discussion and it was agreed that, unless they were fortunate enough to apprehend Sonntag prior to the meeting, he was to be taken by police snatch squads before he could address the faithful.

That was the plan. It remained to be seen whether it would work.

35

HIDE AND SEEK

A few minutes after five o'clock on the afternoon of the twenty-second, the minibus carrying Hillsden, Hyde, Harry and the other selected crowd marshals drove out of the parking area at the rear of the snooker hall. Acting on Fadiman's instructions, the occupants had modified their usual way of dressing; the majority had dispensed with their Harrington jackets and wore suits; some wore caps.

During the previous night a second police surveillance team had taken up position in a disused warehouse which overlooked the parking area. In addition an armed unit of the Special Patrol Group had been placed on the roof of the warehouse. Unmarked police cars were parked in all the exit routes from the snooker hall, each car linked by radio, communicating by code. The minibus was to be identified by the code-name 'Ambulance', while Sonntag was code-named 'Sharon' – a name suggested by Lloyd who had never recovered from seeing *Fatal Attraction*. Some thirty other unmarked cars were positioned at various points in the Greater London area, ready to tail the minibus on a relay system once it had been determined which route it was taking. Each car had one armed officer and all personnel wore civilian clothes. It had also been decided that, as an extra precaution, none of the police cars should continue the tail for more than two miles.

Before the minibus had moved out of the car park, its

description and registration number had been radioed to all units. In order to preserve his cover, none of the ordinary police taking part had been told of Hillsden's role.

The first pursuit car, a battered Volkswagen Golf, moved off, keeping the minibus in sight as it crossed Shepherd's Bush and headed north on Wood Lane, past the BBC Television Centre. At the intersection it made a left turn on to Westway. The first car followed it as far as Hanger Lane where it passed the tail to a second car. A radio message was sent to the Command room in Scotland Yard: *Ambulance heading west on Western Avenue.* Western Avenue being a dual-carriageway with an uninterrupted central crash barrier for long stretches, an immediate decision was taken to bring in cars belonging to the Thames Valley force with instructions to take over at the Northolt intersection. The pursuit continued without incident, the minibus turning left into Denham Road just before the beginning of the M40 motorway. It made a right turn shortly afterwards and headed for Fulmer Common, skirting the north perimeter of the common before going in the direction of Amersham. There another police car took over. It was still impossible to determine the ultimate destination, but the command room alerted the main back-up units, and these started to converge on Westway, following the identical route to the minibus, some twenty miles behind it. Pearson and Lloyd were in one of this group of vehicles.

. . .

Hillsden had to admit that whoever had planned the operation (and he assumed it was Fadiman) had done so with considerable skill. The moment the minibus was under way, Hyde stood up in the front of the bus and briefed them.

'First of all, I have a message from the Deputy Leader, saying he regrets he's not with us tonight, but he felt that discretion was the better part of valour. However, as he told us, the meeting will be videoed and he looks forward to the pleasure of viewing it at a later date.'

Two or three of the men applauded and Hyde held up a hand to silence them.

'Right. Now, listen carefully, and take this in, because I shall only say it once. We have it on good authority that the police, like you at this moment, don't have a clue where we're going. Because of the way this has been planned they've been looking in quite the wrong direction, expecting us to have hired some public hall for our comrade's visit. Well, we didn't. The Deputy Leader is too fly for that. Our journey tonight will take us to a large country house which until recently was operating as a health farm where rich parasites, a fair number of them flabby Jews I have no doubt, paid through the nose to lose their unwanted fat. It was purchased by one of our powerful backers who prefers to remain anonymous for the moment, and in due course it will become our national headquarters.'

He paused and consulted his watch, then turned to the driver. 'How are we for time?'

'Spot on,' the driver said.

'Keep to the speed limits and keep your eyes peeled for any sign of the fuzz.'

'Nothing so far.'

'Good. Don't want any slip-ups at this stage.' Hyde resumed his address to the troops, smug with self-importance in his role as the only one in the know. 'So, that's our destination, but before we get there we have to rendezvous with the rest of the comrades who have come from all over the country to take part.' He looked at his watch again. 'If we keep to schedule we should be meeting up in seventeen minutes time.' He glanced out of a side window as a small car overtook them. 'There will be several coachloads waiting for us. I want four of you in each coach, to act as stewards. You will make sure everybody behaves in orderly fashion. This has been planned as a military operation and it's up to you to see that everything goes off smoothly. Understood?'

He received general assent. A voice from the back asked:

'Did he fly in as promised?'

'Yeah, he flew in,' Hyde said and sat down beside the driver.

. . .

Pearson listened to the voice in his headphones: 'Ambulance now heading for Chalfont St Giles.'

'Any sign of Sharon?' he radioed back.

'Negative.'

'Nothing new,' Pearson reported to Lloyd, who was driving.

'Want to take a guess as to where we end up? My bet is somewhere in the Midlands.'

'Who knows at this stage. They're certainly taking us on a scenic tour. Funny the attraction Fascism has for so many different types. The rich are attracted because they believe it will protect their wealth, the middle-class because it feeds their prejudices and at the lower end of the scale it's a honey pot for the bully boys.'

'Taken up philosophy in your old age, have you?'

'Yes, well, some of us think about the state of the world. I've made a study of fanatics.'

'So have I,' Lloyd said. 'Many of them Chief Constables.'

'Listen. Fanatics aim their appeal towards those who are imperfectly balanced. I always remember something that John Buchan wrote. Buchan defined a fanatic as somebody who has no logical gaps in his creed. He wrote that you can't say there is any one thing abnormal about him, because he is all abnormal. Basically insane, of course, but believes his claims are brilliantly sane. Those are the ones, like Hitler, who pose the greatest threat.'

Lloyd permitted himself a nod of the head, though by now he had lost the thread of Pearson's reasoning.

'It's when he appeals to the sane and the sane respond, that's when you get revolution,' Pearson continued. 'You follow me?'

'Interesting.'

'We're facing something like that now. The time is ripe. People the world over have to have a bogey-man, somebody, something to hate. That may be a jaundiced view of human nature, but history bears it out. We had fifty years of being frightened of Russia, now the pendulum is starting to swing over to the other extreme. Communism has never been able to get more than a toehold over here, but Fascism might well.'

Lloyd just had time to say, 'Cheer me up, won't you?' when another message came through. 'Have lost Ambulance. Repeat: Have lost Ambulance. Last grid reference zero four A-for-apple seven.'

'Shit!' Pearson said. 'How the hell can those silly sods have lost them?' He consulted his map. 'Zero four A seven, that's somewhere between Chalfont and Chorleywood. Mostly woods, open countryside, a few farms.'

'Can't be holding the bloody meeting in a farm, can they?' Lloyd said.

'No, but the Ambulance could have led us on a fake run away from the main event. Oh, bollocks! Hold it here for a moment.'

He got out of the car and walked to the lead police van in the convoy to confer.

. . .

From his window seat in the Happy Eater, Tony had a clear view of the road and parking lot. He was wearing standard motorcycle gear: black leather bomber jacket and trousers. His gloves and two crash helmets with smoked-glass visors were on the chair beside him.

'Can I clear away?' the young waitress asked.

Tony spun round. 'What?'

'You finished?'

'Oh, yeah.'

'That your BMW out there?'

'Yeah.'

'Bet that moves. Don't want to give me a ride, do you? I finish in twenty minutes.'

'Another time, darling.'

The girl gave him a look as she removed the dirty plate and coffee cup. 'I see you've got a spare helmet.'

'Yeah, I'm waiting for a friend.'

At that moment the car he had been waiting for pulled into the parking lot. The woman driver flashed her headlights once. Tony got up, left a fifty pence tip on the table, paid his bill, and sauntered out. Ignoring the car, he went to his BMW motorbike, started it, and went alongside the car on the passenger side. Sonntag got out, took the spare helmet Tony offered him, donned it, and sat astride the pillion seat. No words were spoken during the change-over. Tony opened the throttle and they roared out.

The woman watched them go without expression, then took a mobile phone from the glove compartment and dialled a number she had only used once before.

. . .

The farm outbuildings, surrounded by a brick wall, were hidden from the road, and the driver of the minibus, having determined that there was nothing following him, had done an abrupt turn into the pot-holed drive and parked out of sight. As Hyde had promised, there were a number of coaches full of comrades parked behind the walls that shielded the barn from the road.

As per Hyde's instructions, Hillsden and the others divided up and immediately boarded the coaches. It was only now that Hyde revealed the final destination to the coach drivers. He travelled in the lead coach as the convoy moved out, leaving the minibus behind.

. . .

Meanwhile, Pearson and the police units were still stationary, frustrated and unable to decide on their next best move. There was still no report of any further trace of the minibus. The use of a helicopter was ruled out by the command room on the grounds that it would almost certainly be a tip-off. The existence of the convoy of coaches had been noted, and aroused no undue suspicion at first, until an alert officer in one of the unmarked cars searching for the elusive minibus spotted that all of them came from different parts of the country and reported this to the command room.

When this was radioed back, Pearson was quick to grasp the possible significance. He took a decision: 'Radio all cars to tail them and give us a map reference.' He then went over to the Chief Superintendent to share the information. 'It's a long shot, but all we've got at the moment, so leave a token force here and have the rest follow us.'

. . .

The ex-health farm had operated from a building best described as thirties nondescript, almost certainly one of those oversized country houses, with little or no architectural merit, built between the wars to satisfy the pretensions of the *nouveaux riches*. Whoever had converted it into a health farm had grafted on various additions – an indoor swimming pool, a large conservatory and, incongruously, a clock tower – the final effect guaranteed to make Betjeman turn in his grave.

Hillsden got his first view of its irregular outline as the convoy of coaches drew up in front of the closed main gates. Hyde got out and spoke into the entry-phone and shortly afterwards the gates were automatically opened and the convoy drove through.

Inside, the house had been denuded of most of its fixtures but still retained a faint, antiseptic atmosphere reminiscent of an abandoned hospital. Sonntag's audience trooped in and was directed by Hyde to what at one time had been the ballroom, and later the health farm restaurant, where the dedicated had sipped such elixirs as bottled water with a slice of lemon and nibbled the odd organic carrot. A stage had been erected at the far end with a lectern and a public address system, with Nazi flags draped on either side. Martial music was playing as the audience entered and took their seats.

Hyde mounted the platform and tested the microphone. 'I think congratulations are in order. By arriving here without mishap we have achieved a major victory over those whom we know would like to spike our guns. So be patient for a little while longer. Our distinguished guest from the fatherland will arrive shortly and I know you will join me in giving him an enthusiastic welcome.' He raised his right arm in the Nazi salute by way of illustration. 'Listen carefully to the message he brings, because it is a message we, the torch-bearers, must pass on. Tonight is a watershed in our journey towards Valhalla and in coming here we recognise the role played by another generation, those who were so shamefully betrayed. We have gathered to demonstrate to our guest that the Führer's historic struggle to establish a world order was not in vain.' He was just about to leave the stage when he returned to the microphone for an afterthought. 'At the conclusion of the meeting refreshments will be served.' This announcement was greeted with cheers.

Hillsden, seated in the body of the hall, surveyed the audience as a murmur of anticipation went through the ranks. He was conscious that the majority were considerably younger than himself. A proportion, perhaps a third, were stereotypical Fascists – chunky, with cropped hair, clean shaven, many sporting a ring in one ear; they had the cocky self-assurance of those who only find an arrogant courage when part of a gang. The rest seemed to him to have been recruited from the ranks of ordinary men willing to follow any cause that promised some excitement hitherto missing from their drab lives.

. . .

The coaches had been tailed to their destination and the information radioed back to the main police force; all units were now converging on the spot. Now, as Pearson and Lloyd, in the lead car, rounded a corner a mile or so from the final location, Lloyd was forced to brake sharply, only just stopping short of a motorbike which lay on its side in a pool of petrol and oil. There was a crash helmet a short distance away but, curiously, no skid marks on the tarmac.

Pearson reached for the hazard lights switch. Shouting, 'Go and stop the others and get them to whistle up an ambulance,' he ran to the fallen bike and found the engine was still hot. He stared around for any sign of the rider. He did not have far to look, but instead of one there were two men sprawled in the roadside ditch. Pearson's brief examination established that both were dead. Again, curiously, there were no obvious signs of injury. One man, dressed in civilian clothes, had fallen face upwards; bent stalks of foxgloves and Bishop's weed criss-crossed his chest and one of the blooms, stained with a trickle of blood rested in his gaped mouth. The second man, dressed in standard leather gear and still wearing his crash helmet, was head down in the ditch. One arm was thrust out, the hand clutching a tuft of coarse grass with stiffened fingers.

Having halted the rest of the convoy, Lloyd came back accompanied by half a dozen police officers.

'What have we got?' the Chief Superintendent asked.

'Two dead,' Pearson answered. He gestured to the ditch.

'Did they hit something?'

'No sign of anything. As you can see there are no skid marks, no obstruction, nothing. It's as if one moment they were going along normally, and then bingo. The only thing I can think of is that the brakes must have seized up, although that's rare, specially with a new job like that.'

The Superintendent told his men to remove the bike from the road and see if it started. The engine fired immediately.

'Take a closer look at the bodies,' Pearson said, 'because at first glance I couldn't see any injuries. If it wasn't so far-fetched and daft you could almost believe they both died of simultaneous heart attacks.'

'You didn't see any other vehicles?'

'No. We came round the corner and there it was. Only just missed it ourselves.'

'Right, well we can't afford to hang around here. Leave this mess for Traffic to sort out.' The Superintendent detailed two of his men to remain until the ambulance arrived.

. . .

The recorded martial music was repeated a third time. Although the audience was not openly impatient with the delay, a certain degree of restlessness had begun to manifest itself.

'Keeping us waiting long enough,' the man next to Hillsden said.

'Building up the suspense. It's an old trick,' Hillsden replied.

'Yeah, expect you're right. They always did that, didn't they? I've seen news reels of those torch-light parades.'

Hyde came from the back of the room and mounted the stage again.

'I know you're all wondering what is happening, but I can assure you that our guest is in the country and will be with us shortly. This has been a very difficult operation to mount and we couldn't afford to leave anything to chance or take any risks with the safety of our German comrade. So I do ask you to be patient, for I am sure the wait will be . . .' but he never finished, for at that moment the french windows on one side of the hall were smashed open and snatch squads from the Special Patrol Group broke in. At the same time, other squads raced in from the rear of the hall, encircling the audience and cutting off all escape routes in a text-book manœuvre that achieved complete surprise. Using a loud hailer, the Chief Superintendent issued a warning: 'Everybody will remain seated and be required to establish their identities. This is an illegal assembly and I am empowered to arrest and detain anybody who does not co-operate.'

But there was to be no co-operation. A chair was hurled at the Superintendent and this was taken as a signal for whole sections of the audience to attempt to break through the police cordon. Within minutes, the hall was the scene of a dozen or more fights with chairs being broken and used as rough and ready weapons. The initial police squads were swiftly reinforced as a hard core of the younger skinheads tried to fight their way to the stage and claim the Nazi flags. Many on both sides went down and it was some twenty minutes before any semblance of order was restored. Hillsden was struck by a flying chair early in the proceedings. Stunned and bleeding from a cut on the back of his skull, he recovered sufficiently to crawl to safety under the platform. Some time later he was dragged out by the police and put with the rest of the casualties.

Then began the long process of sorting out the mess. A few of the faithful gave their real names, but the majority, taking their lead from Hyde, gave Mickey Mouse-type pseudonyms. All were videoed by a police cameraman. Hyde was given special attention. Handcuffed, he was taken to a separate room to be interrogated by Pearson.

Pearson started on him with: 'I should formally tell you that you and others are going to be charged with having conspired to bring an illegal alien into the United Kingdom, namely one Gottfried Sonntag, a German national. It would be to your advantage if you identified him to me.'

'Get stuffed. I don't know any Gottfried Sonntag,' Hyde replied. 'This was a lawful, private meeting to debate conservation issues. I'm going to lay charges against you for unprovoked police brutality.'

Pearson stared through him. 'What were you trying to conserve, the Nazi flag ? Listen, chummy, you're out of your league, and don't make the mistake of thinking you're dealing with the local CID and can get some tricky lawyer to get you off the hook. I've got ways and means of keeping you out of circulation for a very long time. So let's try again, shall we? Herr Sonntag is a prominent neo-Nazi your mob brought over. We know that for a fact. He was going to speak here tonight, wasn't he? Tell you bedtime stories about the great Third Reich and how the Holocaust was invented Jewish propaganda. So, if you know what's good for you, you'll point him out to me. That'll go in your favour.'

'I don't need any favours. And I don't know who Sonntag is.'

'What I'm talking about, if you don't help me, chummy, is a very long stretch of porridge. You see, added to the conspiracy charge we can tack on assault on a police officer.'

'I never touched any of the pigs.'

'Wrong. I saw you myself.'

'Lying bastard.'

'But who will they believe, you or me? I rather fancy my chances. So I'll ask you for the last time, where is Sonntag?'

'Go fuck yourself.'

'No, you're the one who's fucked, chummy. We won the last war, remember?' He turned to the police escort. 'Take him out and put him with the others.'

'I'll have you one day,' Hyde said as he was led away. 'Depend on it.'

'Don't frighten me,' Pearson said. 'I'm near retirement.' He went outside just as Hillsden, handcuffed to another man, was about to board one of the charabancs, now impounded by the police. He came face to face with Hillsden, but neither of them betrayed any sign of recognition. Hillsden spat down on Pearson's feet as he passed and was cuffed by the escorting police officer.

Tipped off by a local resident intrigued by the unusual amount of police activity in what was normally a quiet backwater, the local paper rushed somebody to the scene.

'Better give him some bland story,' Pearson urged the Chief Superintendent. 'Nip it in the bud, before he starts smelling around.' The Superintendent went outside to the young reporter.

'Understand you've had some trouble here, sir?'

'Well, yes, very minor. A public meeting was disrupted by a hooligan element, but we quickly restored order.'

'A political meeting was it?'

'I don't think so. I'm told it had something to do with conservation issues.'

'Like Greenpeace?'

The Superintendent looked beyond the young reporter, affecting casualness. 'Something like that. Animal rights, I believe.'

'Yeah, that's a subject that gets people stirred up. Did you make any arrests?'

'We shall be charging some people, yes.'

'Just that it seems a very large police presence for somewhere like this. Would you say the police over-reacted?'

'No. I'm sure you agree it's much better to be safe than sorry.'

'Anybody hurt?'

'There were some minor casualties, yes.'

'How many?'

'A dozen perhaps.'

'Amongst the police?'

'Three of my officers were hit by missiles. None seriously, I'm happy to say.'

'Can I know who I'm speaking to, sir?'

'Chief Superintendent Walsham.'

'And you're the officer in charge?'

'Yes.'

'Well, thank you, you've been very helpful, sir. Just one last thing, I was told that members of the Special Patrol Group took part, the heavy mob, as it were. That's unusual, isn't it?'

'It would be if it was true. I don't know where you got that rumour. Now, if you'll excuse me . . .'

He rejoined Pearson.

'How was it?'

'Usual tricky little customer,' the Superintendent said. 'I

wouldn't be surprised if he's ringing one of the nationals right now, out to make his name. I don't think I fooled him.'

'The press are all the same. You win some and you lose some. And we lost Sonntag.'

'Definitely no trace?'

Pearson shook his head. 'No, the building's been searched from top to bottom. Might be as well to leave some men here overnight, just in case he makes a late appearance.'

'Yes, I've already taken care of that.'

'In due course I shall find out whether he ever showed from our man. But there's nothing I can do at the moment because he was taken off with the rest of them.'

'I can have him isolated.'

'No, don't do that. His cover has to be preserved at all costs. Anyway, thanks, I thought your chaps did a good job, too bad we didn't get what we came for.'

Pearson went to his car where Lloyd was waiting.

'What a pisser,' Lloyd said. 'What will you tell Swanson? He's going to go spare.'

'So, he'll have to go spare. We did what was required of us, not our fault that the target didn't show.'

'D'you think Sonntag's actually in the country?'

'Your guess. They obviously expected him to be, otherwise why bring people here? Anyway, let's go.'

Lloyd started the engine. 'Poor old Hillsden copped one. Did you see him?'

'Yes.'

'Don't envy him his lot.'

'I don't envy any of us,' Pearson said.

. . .

'Name?' a weary Sergeant asked as he booked yet another one.

'Bartlett,' Hillsden said.

'First name?'

'Robert.'

314

'Address?'

'No fixed address.'

'Employed?'

'No.'

The particulars were quickly noted. He was read his rights and told that he would be charged with taking part in an affray and would be brought before the magistrate the following morning. Then he was led to the cells.

'Can I make a phone call?' Hillsden asked.

'No,' the escorting police officer said.

'Why not?'

'Because the phones are out of order.'

'I'm entitled.'

'If I were you, Dad, I'd keep my mouth shut and thank your lucky stars you got off lightly with just a bash to the head. You should know better at your age than to get mixed up with that slag.'

'I was only there as a spectator.'

'Yeah? Well, next time stick to bingo.'

The cell door closed and Hillsden found he was sharing it with Hyde.

'You okay, Robert?'

'I caught a couple on the head.'

'Bastards.'

'What went wrong, d'you think?'

'I wish I knew. What I can't understand is why Tony didn't get any word to us. Our friend was picked up at Plymouth all right, that I do know. Listen, as soon as you get out, get word to Fadiman as to what happened. Go see him, don't phone. Here's his address. Memorise it, then destroy it, okay?'

'Right. What d'you think they'll do to us? Will it mean prison?'

'You? No. You'll get a fine and be bound over. They may have something else in mind for me.'

'Why d'you say that?'

'Because I know these things. They've already given me a going-over, not the police, some other mob, either Special

315

Branch or the spooks.'

'Spooks?'

'I forget, you're a bloody innocent, aren't you? Spooks are the MI5 boys. So just plead guilty tomorrow and play dumb. You know nothing, whatever they ask you.'

'Right, understood. Just as well he never showed. At least they didn't get him. That's something.'

'Yes,' Hyde said. 'But the question is, where is he?'

. . .

Lloyd took the same route back and as they reached the stretch of road where they had discovered the two dead bodies Pearson suddenly ordered him to stop.

'What's up?'

'That accident. Something's been preying on my mind ever since. The whole thing was bloody odd.' He reached for the radio phone on an impulse. 'Get me the Amersham police, will you?'

'What're you ringing them for?'

Pearson waved a hand for him to be quiet as he spoke into the phone. 'Give me the Duty Officer, please . . . Commander Pearson, Scotland Yard . . . Who am I talking to? Inspector Grant? I wonder if you can help me, Inspector? We were in your manor tonight on a special job and happened to come across a road accident. Two men on a motorbike. Did you lot deal with that? . . . I see. Where are the bodies now? Have they been identified? . . . Only one. Give me that name again. Arthur Clarke. I see . . . Look, there could be some connection with another case I'm working on, so I'd appreciate it if you could let me come and take a look. Not trying to poach on your territory, but I need to check out something . . . Thanks a lot. Hope I can return the favour one day.'

He replaced the phone. 'Turn round. We're going to Amersham.'

'What for?'

'To take another look at a corpse.'

36

A GAME OF DARTS

The following morning, together with fifteen others, Hillsden was fined twenty-five pounds and bound over for one year after pleading guilty to taking part in an affray. The police objected to bail in Hyde's case and he was remanded in custody for seven days.

Hillsden's first action after leaving the court was to ring Galina and to his relief Audrey answered.

'Thank God you've phoned. Your wife's been frantic with worry. I made up some excuse, said you were probably tied up in some business meeting. What happened?'

'I was involved in a minor road accident,' Hillsden said. 'Suffered some concussion and they kept me in hospital overnight.'

'Are you all right now?'

'Yes. Bit of a headache. Put her on, will you?'

Waiting in the public box, Hillsden heard Audrey shout for Galina and a few moments later he heard his wife's reproachful voice. 'Where were you last night?'

'Darling, I'm truly sorry I caused you so much worry,' Hillsden said as he began his rehearsed lie, 'but there was no way I could phone. I had to make a trip out of town and somebody else was driving, took a corner too fast and we hit another car. Nobody was seriously hurt, but I got a knock on the head and had to spend the night in hospital.'

'I thought you were dead,' Galina said.

'Why would you think that?'

'What else could I think?' A note of anger was mingled with her relief. 'You could have been dead.'

'Well, darling, I'm not, so stop worrying. Was Laura upset too?'

'No, I lied to her, made up some story that Papa had been working late and that you were still asleep when she went to school this morning.'

'That was clever.'

'No,' Galina said. 'It was just another of the lies we live with. Are you ever coming home?'

Hillsden thought quickly. 'As soon as I've given a statement to the police about the accident, I'll try and get back. Please don't upset yourself any more, I'm fine, no real damage done. I'll be back as soon as I can.'

He bought a selection of the morning's papers but only one of the tabloids carried anything about the incident and that was on the inside pages, although the headline – *Police use Sledgehammer to Crack Small Nut* – was predictably inflammatory. The accompanying story asked why it had been thought necessary to invade a small rural community in such numbers in order to disperse what their correspondent understood to be *'a peaceful meeting called to protest against the export of live animals to the EEC'*.

Hillsden walked to a nearby McDonald's for some much-needed breakfast, giving himself time to think what his next move should be. Afterwards, he made his way to Docklands. Greeted by an over-solicitous Sarah, he was uncharacteristically brusque with her. 'I'm fine, I'm fine. Get me Pearson and ask him to hold while I ring Swanson.' He did not want sympathy, he wanted solutions.

But both Pearson and Swanson were unavailable.

·   ·   ·

Pearson, like Hillsden, had had an eventful night. After viewing 'Arthur Clarke' in the mortuary and comparing his

318

features with the latest photograph of Sonntag supplied by the German authorities, he felt his hunch could prove right. The police surgeon who had carried out preliminary examinations on the two dead men and had signed the death certificates had been unable to determine the exact cause of death and listed an open verdict until such time as the autopsies were performed. 'Arthur Clarke' carried a valid British passport in that name, but the other man had nothing on his person to establish his identity.

'The bike was in perfect working order,' Inspector Grant told him, 'brakes hundred per cent, tank full of petrol, no skid marks on the road, no reports of anything untoward. In fact, the only thing we've come up with is this.' He handed over two small pieces of paper. The Star of David was stamped on both. 'We found one on each of the men, tucked into their clothing.'

Pearson feigned casualness. 'Weird,' he said. 'If I sign for these can I take them away?'

Inspector Grant hesitated. 'Yes, I suppose so. You mentioned you were in the area investigating something, Commander. Can I ask what?'

'Not for the moment,' Pearson said in a tone that precluded further discussion. 'I think, with your further co-operation, I'd like to transfer the bodies to our forensic lab for autopsies.'

'I'd need to get authorisation for that.'

'Yes, of course. If I can use your phone, I'll make sure you're in the clear.'

The Inspector still looked dubious. 'Perhaps whoever you're ringing should talk to the Chief Constable. This is all getting a bit rich for me.'

'No problem,' Pearson said. 'Just one other thing. That place down the road, used to be a health farm I believe, d'you happen to know who owns it now?'

'I think it changed hands twice after the receiver moved in. I can find out for you from the local council in the morning.'

'Would you do that and let me know personally.'

'Where will I get you?'

'Ring me at Century House.'

The name of MI6's headquarters stopped Grant in his tracks. 'Ah! Fine, yes. Will do, Commander.'

. . .

When Hillsden finally made contact with Swanson he was immediately treated to an earful of rancour. 'I've just had the mother of all meetings with Logan, wanting to know why the whole operation was bungled. What the hell went wrong?'

'What went wrong was that the man didn't show.'

'So instead, the police acted as though they were putting out a forest fire. Why did they have to be so heavy-handed? It got into one of the tabloids, which did nothing for Logan's blood pressure.'

'Well, don't shout at me, I was just a spectator. All I got out of it was a crack on the head and a night in the cells. My most urgent problem is to let Fadiman know what happened.'

'That's out of the question. I can't risk that. Much too dangerous at the present time.'

'It'll be more dangerous if I don't. Calm down and let me explain.' He related the conversation he had had with Hyde. 'So, I have to go through with it, otherwise I'm a dead man. Fadiman may tell me what we want to know about Sonntag, there's always a chance of that.'

'When do you intend to do this?'

'Today, soon as possible, assuming he's there.'

He waited for Swanson to answer. After an appreciable pause Swanson said, 'I can't say I'm happy about it.'

'Well, neither am I, but what's the alternative?'

'Have you told Pearson?'

'I couldn't get him this morning. You're the only one I've spoken to.'

'I'll deal with Pearson then. But be sure to report back to me at the first opportunity. It's vital I know every development.'

. . .

The autopsy on the man Pearson believed was Sonntag was carried out by Dr Colin Hogg, CBE, for many years the senior Home Office pathologist. A martinet in his own 'kitchen' – as he liked to call it – his many idiosyncrasies, acquired over fifty years laying bare human remains, had been elevated to heroic status amongst the small circle of his closed profession. By rights he should have retired at the statutory age, for he was now seventy, arthritic, cranky and in many ways resembled a cadaver himself. But there was a darting alertness about him whenever he operated. 'I come to life in death,' he would tell any new acquaintance, deliberately seeking to shock, for there was something of the schoolboy about him and he could not resist showing off. He might have given the appearance of age, but his faculties were unimpaired and his eyesight was keen; he boasted that he needed reading glasses only to study the obituaries in *The Times* over his usual breakfast of devilled kidneys and grilled tomatoes. An inveterate and unrepentant smoker, in his usual contentious manner he insisted that he owed the retention of his still formidable mental powers to his addiction to nicotine. It was a theory which did not commend him to the BMA, yet what could not be challenged was his uncanny skill at spotting what others missed and, despite Hogg's age and acerbic opinions, Pearson's department always requested his services whenever they wanted a definitive report.

Hogg made no apologies for scorning the regulation surgical gloves and invariably wore thick orange ones of the kitchen-sink variety, which offered greater protection against HIV infection. 'Imagine what a speculative field day the tabloids would have if the plague claimed me. I'd be bracketed with Burke and Hare in the history books. Hogg, the necrophiliac Aids victim. No thank you, I can do without that.'

Now, stooped over the corpse on the stainless steel table, watched closely by his two regular assistants, both of whom he had trained to his own meticulous standards, he dictated his findings and frequent asides into a microphone suspended over the corpse. 'Good God, he was nothing but blubber,' he said as he completed an incision and peeled back the abdomen. 'Fat, not age, shall wither a man, advice you would do well to observe, Charles.' Charles was the assistant who tended to stutter whenever Hogg asked for confirmation of an opinion. 'I notice you are still a slave to junk food and were careless enough to leave the evidence in the waste bin outside. Ah! Now that's interesting,' he continued in the same breath as his scalpel uncovered another layer. 'Take a good look both of you, you won't see a better epithelial tumour of the liver than that. Magnificent. This little beauty would have done for him in less than a year.' Charles and Graham murmured their appreciation. 'As I keep telling you, there's no such thing as natural death. Open up anybody and the horoscope is there.'

An hour later, having scrubbed up, he came out to give his findings to the waiting Pearson, lighting a cigarette before warming to the task. 'I smoke Turkish, you know. Always have, but the damn things are difficult to get. Fortunately I have an admirer in Cairo who keeps me supplied. Splendid chap, does sex-change operations. Not my idea of a career, but fascinating all the same. Now then,' he said, having expelled the first heady intake, 'eliminations first. He was not shot, he was not stabbed, he didn't die from a heart attack, nor choke to death on a surfeit of lampreys.'

Pearson waited, letting him have his moment.

Hogg went to his locker and took out his jacket. The cigarette was kept in his mouth while he put his arms in the sleeves. 'What I did discover, however, was a mark on the upper right arm made by a needle of some sort, not necessarily a hypodermic needle, more likely some form of dart fired with considerable force judging by the depth of penetration. It is my belief, which I am absolutely sure will be judged correct by further tests, that this was used to introduce a lethal toxin capable of producing death in a very short time.'

'Cyanide?'

Hogg gave him a faint, condescending smile. 'No, nothing as mundane as that, which in any case would normally be self-administered orally, a somewhat difficult feat I imagine whilst riding on a motorcycle and wearing a crash helmet.' He produced a brush and comb from the locker and arranged his sparse hair. 'I believe that, when identified, the substance will prove to belong to the family of poisons used to put down pet animals. They react extremely fast, bringing on total respiratory failure in less than half a minute. Effective little buggers. Pity the NHS is not allowed to use them on us when we're ready to fall off the perch. Sort of thing I shall give myself when the time comes. No intention of becoming a vegetable.'

'Can you do me a favour?' Pearson said.

'I thought I'd already done you one.'

'Can we take a look at the other man? Just to establish whether he died in the same way.'

Hogg gave him a long look.

'It's important.'

'Tell me what isn't with you chaps. I must be getting soft in my old age.' He turned and shouted. 'Charles!'

His assistant appeared with a worried look. 'Sir?'

'Wheel out the other one.'

As Charles disappeared Hogg said: 'Come and see for yourself. And don't worry, I'm not going to cut anything.'

A reluctant Pearson followed him into the laboratory and stood to one side as Charles and the other assistant lifted Tony's body on to the stainless steel table. Dousing his cigarette in the sink, Hogg removed his jacket, put on a new pair of gloves and started to examine the corpse. Pearson stood back.

'Tell me,' Hogg said, 'any idea what this one was wearing?'

'Some sort of leather gear.'

'Yes, that would account for it.'

'Account for what?'

'The indentation is not so deep . . . Give me a marker, Charles.'

Charles handed him one and Hogg drew a circle on Tony's flesh on the right shoulder. 'There it is, same thing. Take a look.'

Pearson stepped to the table. Hogg had circled a small discoloured area.

'That's all there is to show?'

'If I'm right, it was enough to make him shuffle off his mortal coil in a hurry.'

Before leaving the laboratory Pearson rang Inspector Grant at Amersham.

'I'd like your men to carry out another search in the area surrounding the scene of the accident. Tell them to look for two darts.'

'Darts?'

'Not the kind used in pubs, the sort that can be fired from a rifle. And tell them to be extremely careful if they find them, because they could be lethal.'

. . .

'I hope I did the right thing in coming here,' Hillsden said, 'but Mr Hyde insisted I got the news to you as soon as possible and I didn't want to trust the phone . . . in case, well, one never knows who's listening in.'

'Quite right, Robert,' Fadiman said. 'You acted very sensibly.' He manipulated the wheelchair and propelled himself round so that his back was to the light. 'We have suffered a setback, no doubt about that, but we shall recover and strike hard in return. Do sit down. Pull up that chair. Let me get you some refreshment, ring that bell for me, please. I'm sure that bruise on your head is painful. Your first wound in the cause, Robert. Think of it that way.'

'Yes.'

Johnny appeared in the doorway

'What would you like, Robert?'

'Just coffee would be fine.'

'Coffee for Robert, and I'll have a glass of champagne. That always revives my spirits. Now then,' Fadiman continued as Johnny withdrew without a word, 'tell me exactly what happened, stage by stage.'

While Hillsden was describing the events of the night before, Johnny returned and served coffee and champagne in a surly manner. When the door closed behind him, Fadiman confided: 'He's in a bad mood because I've grounded him for a week to teach him a lesson. I'm afraid his sexual tastes lean to the bizarre and I can't have this house used as a male brothel. He may have outlived his usefulness. But, go on. Hyde, you say, was remanded for seven days?'

'Yes, whereas the rest of us were let off with a fine.' Hillsden picked up his coffee cup and spoke into it. 'Do we know if Sonntag actually arrived in the country?'

'Oh, yes. We can trace his movements to the moment when he was transferred to Tony. After that, nothing.'

'And you haven't received any reports of an accident?'

'No, but then, on the other hand, I wouldn't expect any.'

'What d'you think happened to Tony?'

'For the moment I have no idea. The police were there in force, you say?'

'Yes, I've never seen so many. Had Sonntag got to the venue he would have been taken, no doubt about it.'

'On the journey there, did you notice anything untoward?'

'Untoward? No.'

Hillsden could not see Fadiman's eyes, but there was no mistaking the steel in his voice. 'We have been betrayed, Robert. There is no other answer. Somebody in our midst must be rooted out and eliminated.'

'Could it be Tony?'

'That's a good question, Robert, but only time will tell. We shall have to make many changes in the way we operate. But rest assured that this temporary setback will not go unanswered. Watch your newspapers, Robert. You'll soon be reading about the ways in which we can reply and destabilise their world. They have underestimated us, roused a sleeping tiger.'

. . .

'Let's find out whether Sonntag was ever fingerprinted by the Germans,' Pearson said the moment he returned to Century House. 'And if he was have them send us a set, together with any dental records if they have them.'

'You're still convinced it's him?' asked Lloyd, putting in his usual lugubrious two-cents worth of doubt.

'Yes, and I'll tell you my other theory, too. If it is him, and if Hogg is right, I think it's highly probable that they were both taken out by Mossad, and those bits of paper with the Star of David were their visiting cards.'

'Well, assuming you're right, if *we* couldn't trace whether Sonntag was in the country, how come they did?'

'Maybe they're smarter. If it was them, you might say they did us a good turn.'

'Or landed us in deep shit.'

'I bet you were a depressing little sod as a child. The sort that never gave anybody their ball back if it landed in your garden.'

'We never had a garden,' Lloyd said.

Pearson reached for his antacid tablets.

37

NIGHT TRUTHS

Hillsden's brief reunion with his family had not been as smooth as he had hoped, for Galina did not conceal her resentment at the way in which their lives were being manipulated. At one moment during an argument which developed after Lara had been put to bed, she said: 'And if the next call I receive is to say you're dead, what then? What happens to Lara and me?'

'It's not going to happen.'

'Oh, Alec, don't you see how it's changed us? We never argued in St Petersburg. I'm your wife, why don't you tell me what's really going on? All last night I lay awake, it was like the bad times in Russia when people you loved were never seen again.'

'And here I am, right as rain.'

'But it's in your face. I can read it in your face. You just pretend for me.'

'I'm tired, that's all. Tiredness, that's all you can see. Like you, I spent a sleepless night.'

'Stay here tonight.'

'I can't do that, sweetheart.'

'And you can't tell me why, can you?'

They were suddenly interrupted by the sound of a car approaching; a moment later the headlights beamed on to the far wall of the living room before being extinguished. Next they heard a car door slam and two voices – Audrey's and a man's. Shortly afterwards Audrey came inside and pulled a face as she spoke.

'You've got a visitor,' she said, then whispered, 'Hadley,' again with a grimace. 'Do I show him in?'

Hillsden glanced at Galina. 'I guess so. Just give us a second or two.'

Galina said: 'Why would he come here?'

'Darling, I don't know, do I?'

'I thought you told me they'd leave us alone here.'

'That's what they promised.'

'Some promise – broken like all the others. Well, I don't want to see him.'

She left the room and went upstairs just before Audrey ushered Hadley inside.

'Why, Hadley,' Hillsden said, putting on a friendly face. 'Is this a social visit or have you come to read the gas meter in case I'm fiddling the Firm's expenses? Can I offer you a drink, cup of coffee?'

'I'll take a cup of coffee,' Hadley said. 'Decaf if you have it.'

'Audrey, do we run to decaf?'

'Have to be instant,' Audrey replied, going into the kitchen, but not without some heavy body language. 'Do sit down, Hadley, make yourself at home,' Hillsden said, settling into an armchair.

Hadley sat on the sofa. 'Look, I'm sorry I turned up without warning . . .' he began, then seemed to lose confidence in how to continue. He started again. 'But I wanted to get certain things out in the open, things which have been on my mind for some time now and which I don't understand.' Again he hesitated, searching, it seemed to Hillsden, for a way to lessen some blow. 'I guess, when I was invited to join . . . I had a romantic notion of how the Firm now operated. I thought, naïvely, I'm sure, that everything would have changed.'

'Changed in what way?'

Audrey returned with the coffee before Hadley could reply. She put the cup and saucer down on a small side table and turned to Hillsden, ignoring Hadley. 'Anything else I can do?'

'I don't think so, Audrey, thank you very much.'

'I'll be next door if you want me.'

After they heard the front door close, Hillsden repeated: 'Changed in what way?'

Hadley picked up his coffee and stared at it before answering. 'I felt sure that because of the past exposures and resulting scandals the age of dirty tricks was over,' he said slowly. 'I suppose I was being naïve.'

'It's always been a dirty business that we're engaged in, Hadley . . . Sorry, what's your first name, I ought to know, but I don't and it's rude of me.'

'Christopher . . . My mother had a thing about A A Milne . . . Thank God she left out the "Robin".' For the first time his features lost their set look. 'I prefer Chris,' he finished.

'So what're you trying to tell me, Chris? I don't imagine you drove all this way for the pleasure of it or to give me a history of the Firm.'

'I think . . . and I can't be positive at the moment, but certain things have occurred to me that don't add up.'

'*What* certain things?'

'About your situation . . . The way in which you're being used. If you must know, I think you've been set up, and I thought I should warn you.'

'Why would you go out of your way to do that, assuming you're right?'

'Because I've made it my business to find out more about you, things I never knew before, such as what really happened to you in the past. See, I never had the entire picture, I was only given an edited version. When I realised the full extent of what Lockfield and others did to you, it was only then that I began to put two and two together on the present scenario . . . I became convinced it was happening again, and it didn't seem fair.'

'Fair?'

'Yes.'

Hillsden put his whisky down. 'Forgive me, Chris, I'm not mocking you, don't think that, but "fair" isn't a word I've heard too often around the Firm. "Fair game", yes. We're all fair game, as you'll discover for yourself. But I get your meaning ... Tell me one thing before you go on, was bugging my car your idea?'

Hadley coloured. 'Yes.'

'Can I ask why?'

'I thought it was a way of keeping one step ahead of them. That I might glean something that was being kept from me. But it didn't work as I planned. You don't talk much in the car.'

Hillsden gave a wry smile. 'No, for good reasons ... But "them"? Who are we talking about?'

'I wish I could answer that . . . it all seems too preposterous.' His coffee cup started to rattle and he put it down carefully. 'For instance, what first puzzled me was the ease with which you were established. They gave you a bogus set-up and supplied a list of names.'

'Who prepared the list? D'you know?'

'Well, it didn't come from Pearson, that I do know. I had to be careful about how I made enquiries, but as far as I could tell somebody in D Section put it together, that's where it first surfaced.'

'Go on,' Hillsden said, listening intently.

'Well, I wonder, weren't you surprised you got a response almost immediately? And that, without too much trouble, this character, Hyde, started the ball rolling? He arranges for you to meet Tony, and, bingo, you're taken to see Fadiman who quickly gives his blessing and shares some of their secrets. Doesn't all that seem a bit too pat to you?'

'It crossed my mind, yes.'

'And?'

'It's like quicksand,' Hillsden said. 'Once you've taken the first step into it, it's too late to turn back, you can only hope that you get out eventually.'

'And there are other things,' Hadley said, unstoppable now. 'What about Schmidt's murder? According to Pearson he was going to check on Carstairs for us, but he's dead before

330

he can do anything. Then Lloyd goes to Copenhagen and again he's too late, there's another dead body. To me that suggests somebody is one step ahead of us at every turn. Even Mossad.'

'Mossad? What have they got to do with it?'

'Pearson's convinced that Sonntag's dead and that Mossad took him out.'

'Why does he think that?'

'He and Lloyd came across a road accident a short way from the meeting place, two men dead in a ditch, but no sign that they crashed or anything. He had an autopsy carried out by that old guy he always uses if he can.'

'Not Hogg, surely?'

'Yes, that's the name.'

Hillsden gave himself a whisky, lingering over the action so that Hadley would not see his changed expression as the past returned to choke him. Why was it that everything led him back to Caroline sooner or later? 'I never thought he could still be around,' he said.

'According to this Hogg, both men were killed by poisoned darts.'

'I still don't understand why Pearson suspects Mossad.'

'They found the Star of David on both bodies.'

'I see . . . Going back to my situation, have you discussed this with anybody else?'

'Of course not, what d'you take me for?'

'Well, I guess I have to take you at face value for the time being.'

'Meaning, you don't trust me?'

'Meaning, what you've just told me says I should be on my guard. I've been out of it for a long time, I don't know you, or Pearson, or Swanson, or any of the present gang. The only link with my past is Rotherby. And Rotherby is somebody I do trust. So, since it's obviously too risky for you to make a habit of contacting me direct, assuming your suspicions are right, maybe it would be a good idea to share any future developments with Rotherby.'

Hadley hesitated, then said: 'There is something else that I have to tell you . . . I don't think it could have any connection with what we've been talking about, but you never know . . . Your Russian friend is in town.'

Hillsden reacted. 'You mean Victor Abramov?'

'Yes. The man who once controlled you. I bumped into him at a reception given at the German Embassy. He told me he was over here looking to buy a house with his new-found wealth and was anxious to see you.'

'He knew who you were?'

'He knew I worked for the Firm. It seems he still has good contacts.'

'So what did you tell him?'

'Nothing. I wanted to speak to you first. All I said was I'd try and get a message to you. He's staying at Grosvenor House.'

'Under his own name?'

'Yes, as far as I know.'

'Why the German Embassy?'

'He said he had an ongoing contract to supply them with Korean computer hardware.'

'Well, well. So old Victor finally made the big time,' Hillsden said. 'Capitalism does work.'

'Would it be safe for you to get in touch?'

'Possibly not, but friendship is worth a few risks. I'll think of a way.'

Hadley got up. 'I think I should push off now.'

'Give me a lift back to Forest Gate. We can talk some more on the way. I just want five minutes to say good-night to my wife.'

Galina had already undressed for bed; the white cotton nightgown clung to her figure, her nipples like dark stains on the fabric, and he thought, why is it that lies and guilt turn us so quickly towards lust, as though only a physical act can save us? There was so much mystery to women, whole areas that a man could never reach. They loved with their minds first, it was their minds that made the first declaration and decided when love was over.

'What did that man want?'

'He came to tell me Victor is in London.'

'He drove all this way just for that? There must have been another reason.'

Hillsden shook his head, trying to appear relaxed for her. 'I think he just wanted an excuse to give his new car a spin . . . Exciting that Victor's over here, isn't it? I just hope I can find a way of seeing him.' The words were out of his mouth before he could stop them.

'Why wouldn't you be able to see him?'

'Depends on my work.'

'Or whether you're telling the truth. Every time you tell me something different. I don't even believe you were in a car accident.' She sat on the edge of the bed. 'Are you having an affair?'

'An affair?'

'Is it the girl in your office?'

'Sarah, you mean?'

'Is that her name?'

'Of course I'm not having an affair. With Sarah or anybody else. Why on earth would you think that?'

It was the truth between them, something that for once he did not have to lie about and yet it sounded like a lie. Perhaps, he thought, adultery was preferable to deceit for a cause. Trust between them had been disconnected.

'Because you haven't made love to me in weeks.'

'That's proof of an affair?'

'It's proof of something,' she answered.

'Only of the life I'm forced to lead. And, anyway, I haven't been here.'

She looked at him defiantly. 'Give them their money back, we'll survive. I can take a job in the hours that Lara's at school. We don't have to live here, we could get somewhere smaller in a town, where there's some life. There's no life here. I pretend there's life, but there's none in this house and none outside. I have to live your lies, too, with my new name, the pretence that I'm somebody else with a husband who sells insurance policies. Why don't you tell me what's really happening to us, what you really do when you leave here? I could take the truth, but I can't go on living with a stranger.'

Hillsden knelt in front of her and took her hands. They were cold and he folded them in his own and took them to his mouth, brushing his lips across her fingertips. 'When it's over,' he began, but she pulled her hands away.

'How long are you going to go on saying that? Whenever I face you with it, that's the only thing you ever say. I'm not a child, and I was born in a country where one expected to live in fear.'

'Darling, I don't have a choice,' Hillsden said, and heard Caroline's voice saying the same thing to him by the lake at Anif. You could change names, change the country you lived in, change the woman you slept beside, but there was always a premium on happiness.

When he came downstairs, burdened with fresh guilt, he found Hadley was waiting for him in a new Nissan 400SX.

'Don't tell me the Firm runs to one of these?'

'No. Actually it was a present from my mother.' He gave a sheepish grin and Hillsden could suddenly see Hadley's whole life unfold: only son, wealth, public school, doors opening for him at every stage, always drawing the long straw of privilege. And, given all that, why this? Hillsden thought. Why, if the going was so good, choose to work for the Firm?

As Hadley let in the clutch the headlights picked out a rabbit in the middle of the road, momentarily frozen in terror. For an instant Hillsden lived with the certainty that they were going to hit it, but Hadley pulled the wheel over and they bumped up on to the grass verge. Behind them the rooks shuffled uneasily in the trees, complaining at the disturbance.

38

A DIPLOMATIC EXERCISE

'It *was* Sonntag we found by the roadside,' Pearson said. 'The prints and dental records match. The other man was a character called Tony Fuller, one of the group who screened Hillsden. We traced him easily enough because he had some past form.'

Swanson made a strange movement with his jaws and cleared his throat. 'And you're still sticking to your theory that the killings were carried out by a Mossad team?'

'Well, *we* certainly didn't take them out. It was a very sophisticated hit, they go in for that sort of thing. And let's not forget the visiting cards left on the bodies.'

'I don't attach much importance to those. They could have been planted to point us in the wrong direction.'

'Okay, who else had a motive? Not any of the Middle East boys – Sonntag was aiming to do their job for them.'

'Well, if you're right, it's quite monstrous. If it leaked out, it'd be a major embarrassment for the government, and a heap of grief for us. We'd have to admit that Israeli intelligence is superior to ours.'

'So what's new? There's nothing we can do. Let the diplomatic boys do their usual cover-up if need be. More urgently, did Hillsden get anything out of Fadiman?'

'Just vague threats of revenge. As far as Hillsden could tell, Fadiman knew even less than us.'

'And you still don't want to bring him in for questioning?'

'What would we achieve by that? He wasn't at the meeting, he'd just deny all knowledge of it, plus any interest in him on our part would almost certainly lead straight back to Hillsden.'

Pearson accepted this. 'The only other item to report is that we've traced the ownership of the former health farm. It's currently listed as belonging to a shell company registered in Luxembourg. That's some progress and I'm having a further search done. If Fadiman proved to be one of the directors, that would give us an opening.'

'Yes,' Swanson agreed, but he had the look of a man waiting to hear confirmation of a terminal illness.

. . .

When Logan put down the phone after speaking with Swanson he was in an even fouler mood than before and immediately dialled another extension.

'Logan here, give me the Foreign Secretary . . . I don't care, get him out of the meeting, this is urgent . . . No, don't have him ring me back, get him to the phone now.'

He paced to the full extent of the telephone cord, at one point getting it twisted which added to his frustrations. 'Reggie . . . Kenith . . . Yes, I'm sorry, but you'll appreciate why in a minute. We've got a very tricky situation staring us in the face and I need your help. Our security chaps are convinced that a Mossad squad, operating here illegally, carried out a political assassination a couple of nights ago . . . some neo-Nazi. What? . . . Yes, bloody unbelievable on our doorstep . . . so we'd better get on top of it as soon as possible. Can you have an off-the-record talk with the Israeli Ambassador . . . you're on good terms, aren't you? . . . I thought so, yes . . . Oh, that's a good idea, use the Security Council Vote next week as a quid pro quo . . . Look, I'm sorry to push it on to your plate, but I thought you'd be our best bet. I'll send over such details as we have, so that you go into the meeting briefed. Thanks,

Reggie, I shan't forget the favour.'

He hung up.

Like Logan, Telford, the Foreign Secretary, had not had an easy ride in his new office since the Labour government had taken power, and many of his preconceived notions of the changes he would bring about had proved non-starters. He had quickly found that shuffling the pack of faces that constituted the British government did not alter the state of play; other world leaders continued to further their own nationalistic aims regardless of Britain. It had come as a shock to Telford to realise that H.M. Principal Secretary for Foreign Affairs was often reduced to the role of spectator around the international poker table – allowed to sit in on the game but frequently unable to match the high stakes.

That morning, when Logan dragged him out of a meeting, he had been attempting to formulate a strategy for his forthcoming summit in Peking on human rights, and the death of a neo-Nazi demagogue did not figure high on his list of priorities. However, he was a great champion of Cabinet loyalty and requested the Israeli Ambassador to pay a call as soon as possible. He gave no details to the Embassy, but said the matter was one of urgency. The request was acted upon later that same day.

'I do apologise for summoning you at short notice, Yoram, but it seems you and I could have a shared problem of some delicacy.'

'Tell me a problem that isn't delicate these days,' the Ambassador said.

'Perhaps you'd be good enough to read this report from MI6. Can I get you a drink?'

The Ambassador looked at his watch. 'Why not, the sun's nearly over the yard-arm. I'll have a gin and tonic, if I may. Plenty of ice.' While Telford prepared the drinks, the Israeli Ambassador studied the papers he had been given. 'Interesting,' he said, as he finished and waited for Telford to make the first move in the chess game they were about to play.

'As you've just read,' Telford said, 'our security boys have come up with the theory – possibility, rather – that Mossad could have carried out the assassination. D'you think such a possibility is credible?'

'Well, of course it's unthinkable that my government would sanction such an action by any of our agents within the boundaries of another sovereign state.'

'Of course,' Telford readily agreed.

'Therefore, on behalf of my government, I must formally register a strong protest regarding such an implication and refute it.'

'Yoram, I understand your position totally, and it's noted.'

'However,' the Ambassador continued, and his features relaxed slightly, 'having said that, it's not beyond the bounds of possibility that certain individuals – who may or may not have a connection with our security forces, I'm certainly not in a position to confirm that – could have taken it upon themselves, without my government's authority or knowledge, to act unilaterally. Such things have happened before and doubtless will happen again, given the legitimate feelings still harboured by those whose families suffered in the Holocaust.'

'Always on the cards, I suppose. And for our part we haven't admitted that this Nazi was ever in the country. Nor will we.'

'That's helpful. And, naturally, it would be quite wrong for my government to interfere or influence your judicial processes, nor would we attempt to do so, but I can't help thinking that it would serve no great purpose – if we accept the hypothesis in these papers – to create a situation whereby both our governments were unnecessarily embarrassed. Don't you agree?'

'Absolutely.'

'Much cleaner if the whole thing could be discreetly buried. One could imagine that in certain quarters the death of this man, however achieved, might actually be welcome news.'

'I'm sure you're right,' Telford said, thinking quickly as he saw the door the Ambassador was opening. 'It's delicate, of course.'

'These things always are at the time, but they tend to get papered over by more important issues.'

'Yes, yes,' Telford answered gravely. 'So, how best to handle it, d'you think?'

'All this on the understanding that I am not admitting that any member of Mossad was involved . . . '

'Take that as read.'

'However, I shall make the necessary enquiries and if it transpires that two of our operatives entered the UK illegally we will deal with them in our own way. And, in the unlikely event you were ever called upon to make a statement, you could say quite openly that the Israeli Embassy denied all knowledge and you were content to accept our assurances that we were in no way involved.' He smiled. 'Which of course we weren't.'

Telford returned the Ambassador's smile. 'Absolutely. No good purpose would be served by raising dead issues. Much the cleanest solution from both our standpoints.'

'As to the man himself,' the Ambassador said, 'he's your concern. And since you tell me there's no documented evidence that he ever entered the country, and since we didn't kill him, I don't imagine his disposal will present any insuperable problems.'

'I'm sure you're right. Let me top up that gin. And while we're here together, Yoram, Shelagh keeps reminding me that it's about time we returned your hospitality. How about you and Rachel coming to dinner on the eighteenth? What's your diary like?'

. . .

The following day, two Israeli citizens were taken in a closed car straight on to the tarmac at Heathrow and put on an El Al aircraft prior to the rest of the passengers boarding. All previous references to their presence in England were destroyed following a regrettable administrative error.

That problem out of the way, the question of how to dispose of Sonntag's body remained. It was Rotherby who came up with the answer. 'Sonntag never entered the country, did he? "Arthur Clarke" was the one who set foot on this sceptred isle. Let Mr Clarke be the one who departs. Who are we to take away a man's name?'

So, with the full co-operation of the Bundeskriminalamt, the remains of the erstwhile 'Arthur Clarke' were put aboard a night cargo flight to Frankfurt. Rather than risk having any paperwork that could be traced back to Hogg, a second death certificate was prepared by MI6 and presented to Customs at Heathrow. It was judged to be sufficiently accurate in that it gave the cause of death as cardiac arrest and aroused no suspicion. The coffin was collected in Frankfurt by plain-clothed members of the German police posing as undertakers acting on the instructions of 'Clarke's' relatives. Instead of being removed to a mortuary to await burial, the coffin was taken to a remote country area. There the body was removed from it, placed behind the driving wheel of a previously wrecked car and doused in petrol. The vehicle was then set on fire. The burnt-out shell and charred remains of the occupant were discovered the following morning by a farmer. After a suitable interval, the authorities issued a press release stating that, with the help of dental records, their investigations had identified the victim as Sonntag, and that tests on the vehicle had established that the probable cause of the accident was a faulty brake cable. No witnesses had come forward and they had been unable to establish why Sonntag had been travelling on that particular stretch of road, which was a notorious black spot.

A funeral took place shortly afterwards in Sonntag's home town, attended by over two hundred sympathisers, many of them wearing swastikas. Although the police kept a low profile, skirmishes broke out when an attempt was made to drape the coffin with the Nazi flag, and several arrests were made.

The paperwork in England and Germany relating to a man named 'Arthur Clarke' vanished from the files. Only Hogg's original post-mortem report was deemed protected under the Official Secrets Act and locked away marked 'never to be revealed'.

Tony Fuller's nearest and dearest were informed that he skidded and died in a road accident whilst travelling at excessive speed.

39

FOREIGN BODIES.

Following his usual routine, Pearson lay soaking in the bath, listening to the early morning news bulletin on a portable radio, wondering why it was that he felt scarcely human these days. The news seemed to be confined to social minutiae: a well-known soap opera performer had been outed, a pit-bull terrier on death row had been granted a seven-day stay of execution, and the Bishop of somewhere had questioned the validity of the Virgin birth.

Pearson lifted a soapy hand to switch the radio off when the bulletin continued with, 'The death was announced this morning of Lord Miller, the Chairman of one of Britain's largest companies, Trans-Continental. His body was found by his chauffeur and it appears that he died as a result of gunshot wounds. Foul play is not suspected. Lord Miller was seventy-three, and was created a Life Peer in 1987. Trans-Continental was recently the target of a take-over bid, following the collapse of its share price.'

Pearson heaved himself out of the bath, grabbed a towel and went downstairs to his study and dialled Lloyd's home number.

'Did you hear the news just now?'

'No, I didn't have it on.'

'Old Lord Miller has copped it.'

'Christ! He was on Schmidt's list, wasn't he?'

'Yes. How many does that make?'

'Three.'

'Did they give any details?'

'Just that he died of gunshot wounds. Foul play not suspected, but that's just the local CID. I'll find out more.'

The obituaries were respectful, recording the passing of one of the old school of entrepreneurs who, in recent years, had failed to move with the times and diversify. Comment in the financial columns concentrated on the most likely outcome being a management buy-out, funded by a yet undisclosed white knight. The shares rose by twenty-seven pence in expectation.

Later that same week there was a small story tucked away on the inside pages of two papers stating that the body of a middle-aged woman had been washed up on the Devon coast and identified as Miriam Cohen, a resident of Plymouth. Even if Pearson had noticed the item, which he did not, he could have been excused for not making any connection.

. . .

Still harbouring thoughts of Galina's unhappiness and the wounding exchanges of the previous night, Hillsden walked up South Audley Street, heading for Grosvenor House. He had decided that, come what may, he had to see Abramov again, the magnet of the years they had shared in Russia powerful enough for him to put the possible risks to one side.

It was one of those rare, perfect days when parts of the centre of London make an attempt to take on the characteristics of a Mediterranean resort. Chairs and tables appear outside pubs and sandwich bars, swiftly occupied by coatless businessmen braving lethal concentrations of carbon monoxide to sip warm beer. Policemen shed their jackets, workmen on building sites strip to the waist, St James's Park is transformed into a grassy beach for mating rituals, bewildered tourists wrongly dressed for the expected Arctic conditions adjust their light meters, young girls stream out from the offices and shops at lunchtime to perambulate in the sunshine of Regent Street with figures alarmingly revealed, strangers exchange smirks as they pass on the hot pavements and while it lasts a sort of unnatural gaiety persists as though a performance of *King Lear* having been announced, the curtain goes up to reveal *A Midsummer-Night's Dream*.

As he turned into the hotel forecourt he came face to face with a devastatingly pretty girl, obviously bra-less, and in all probability American for she had that clean, long-limbed, shamefully healthy look seemingly made for magazine covers. Momentarily stunned, Hillsden stepped off the pavement to let her pass and caught the scent of her perfume. The chance encounter stayed with him as he entered the hotel foyer. As he made his way to the reception desk, he suddenly caught sight of Fadiman in his wheelchair, attended by Johnny. Fadiman was engaged in earnest conversation with a man Hillsden did not recognise: stocky, with the florid complexion that possibly indicated a heavy drinker, wearing an impeccably cut suit. Rather than risk drawing attention to himself by suddenly turning about, Hillsden proceeded at a leisurely pace to the concierge's desk. There he changed his intended enquiry about Abramov and instead asked for a Mr and Mrs Pearson. The concierge consulted the list of guests.

'We don't appear to have a Mr and Mrs Pearson, sir. Did they have a reservation?'

'I thought they did.'

'I'll check the forward bookings.' The concierge tapped an instruction into the computer. 'No, sir, nothing in the future either.'

'How odd. I must have misunderstood them. Sorry to have troubled you.'

'No trouble, sir.'

Hillsden lingered by the desk, picked up a free tourist brochure, and while making the pretence of studying it, shot a glance to where he had last seen Fadiman. The other man had disappeared and Johnny was releasing the brakes on the wheelchair preparatory to conducting his employer to the exit. Hillsden let them go out of sight before crossing the foyer to one of the house phones.

'Mr Victor Abramov's room, please,' he requested when the switchboard answered. After the room phone had rung at least half a dozen times the operator came back on the line.

'Mr Abramov is not answering, sir. Would you care to leave a message?'

'No, it doesn't matter. I'll try him again later.'

As he recrossed the foyer he saw the man that Fadiman had been talking to. He was now sitting in the middle of an all-male group taking coffee. From their uniformly smart suits he took them to be business executives. He continued on through the foyer and out into the hot street, pausing in front of a shop selling all manner of surveillance devices – briefcases with miniature cameras built in, night sights, phones that could not be tapped – and was still staring in the window when somebody called out 'Robert'. Momentarily he paid no attention, then when the name was repeated he turned to find a taxicab by the kerbside. The passenger window was open and Fadiman beckoned him.

'I thought I recognised you,' Fadiman said as Hillsden approached. 'Can we give you a lift?'

It was then that Hillsden saw that it was not a taxi for hire and that Johnny was driving.

'That's very kind.'

Johnny got out and opened the door and Hillsden climbed inside.

'Can you ease yourself past my chair?' Fadiman asked. Hillsden took the jump seat and sat facing him.

'Where're you making for?'

'I've got a call to make in Pimlico,' he said, choosing a location at random. 'Ebury Street.'

'A famous address,' Fadiman said. 'Did you know Mozart once resided there, as did Noël Coward, George Moore and, more importantly, Sir Oswald Mosley.'

'Really?'

'Oh, yes. Well, I can drop you at Victoria, it's on my way, no problem.'

'Is this your personal taxi?'

'Rather smart, eh? No, a friend lends it to me. It's one of the few vehicles able to take my chair.'

'That's the sort of friend to have.'

The traffic was halted around Hyde Park Corner as a troop of mounted Life Guards, escorted by police, clopped their usual diagonal path across the island towards Buckingham Palace.

'Tourist fodder celebrating a dying dynasty,' Fadiman remarked, then added, 'Toytown stuff.'

By the time the mounted troop had disappeared, the traffic was backed up as far as Knightsbridge and Piccadilly and it took another five minutes before it was unsnarled.

'Have you found out anything more?' Hillsden ventured.

Fadiman nodded. 'Some of it, yes. But as I promised you, we've already struck back.' He took out a packet of cigarettes and his holder, then clicked his fingers. 'Decisively, in the only way they understand,' Fadiman said. Johnny pressed the cigarette lighter on the dashboard and a few seconds later passed it back over his shoulder. Hillsden handed it on. Fadiman lit his cigarette and gave back the lighter before continuing, 'We eliminated the informer.'

'Who was it?'

'Nobody you would know, Robert. A dirty little Jewess, who played a double game, but she wasn't a very clever little Jewess . . . I'm sorry, I'm blowing smoke in your face . . . You're new to it all, Robert, but you've had your baptism, and the price you paid was to be beaten over the head and thrown in jail. I did warn you, however, that the road ahead was not going to be easy for any of us.'

'How did you discover this . . . this Jewish woman was the one?'

'How? That wasn't difficult once Harry had a talk with her. He's rather single-minded, our Harry. Doesn't make friends easily, but he was fond of Tony. He took Tony's death very personally.'

'Tony's dead?'

'Regrettably, yes. Both he and Comrade Sonntag were killed by an Israeli murder squad, doubtless in collusion with MI6. They'd be only too happy for somebody else to do their squalid work.'

Still presenting himself as a man unable to take in such revelations, Hillsden stared at Fadiman open-mouthed. 'But there was nothing in the papers.'

Fadiman flicked his ash towards the ashtray in the door and missed. 'Doesn't that make my point? There was no mention of it. To me that proves they were hand in hand. It was a blow, Robert, I don't conceal that from you. We shall have to be more ruthless in future, and rest assured we're already planning to widen the scope of our operations. There'll be a role for you to play when we get even. I'm sure you'd welcome that.'

'Yes, I would,' Hillsden said. 'I never knew such things went on.'

Fadiman patted him on the knee. 'But now you do. You've been given your first experience of the sort of people we're up against.' He looked out of the window as the taxi pulled into the kerb. 'This is as far as I can take you . . .'

'Well, thank you again for the lift.'

'My pleasure.'

Hillsden closed the taxi door and watched as Johnny pulled out into the traffic, then he took the precaution of walking in the direction of Ebury Street for a hundred yards or so before doubling back and going into Victoria Station to ring Swanson.

· · ·

'It's the Kell files I'm particularly interested in,' Pearson said. 'Can you dig those out?'

Harrison, the keeper of the Firm's archives, whose bald and pointed head gave him the appearance of a garden gnome, fixed him with a pained expression.

'You sure you mean Kell?'

'Yes.'

'Are you serious? You do know what you're asking for, do you? You couldn't live long enough to get through all of those. There was a moment when those upstairs thought it would be useful to put the whole lot on our database, but we did a time and motion study and calculated it would take somebody working seven days a week the best part of five years. The man was barking, a human squirrel. I pointed out that of the four million plus names he collected, ninety per cent were dead.'

'Do squirrels bark?'

Harrison, not noted for his sense of humour, glided past this and pursued his own line of thought. 'Unless you've got time to waste, I suggest you think again.'

'I don't want all of them. Just the war years will do if you can put your hands on them without too much trouble.'

'I can put my hands on anything,' Harrison said archly, immediately offended that anybody would question his system. He led the way between the parallel rows of shelving housing his dusty charges. 'The man was obsessed, of course. Saw subversives everywhere, made McCarthy look like Pollyanna. The early years are written in copperplate. Works of art in their way, I suppose . . . Now then . . . they should be around this section as I recall . . . Yes, here we are. My system seldom fails me. Nineteen thirty-eight, thirty-nine . . . Haven't been touched in ages, hence the dust. They were restricted until a few years ago, God knows why.' He extracted a series of box files, and plonked them on a table. 'Help yourself. I think you'll find them dull reading. Anything else you require?'

'I wouldn't mind a cup of instant coffee.'

'Don't insult me. I grind my own beans,' Harrison said. 'And only best Colombian,' as he walked away trailing the reproach like a cloak.

Harry had a strong feeling that he would soon be asked to kill again. It didn't occupy him overmuch either way. One did it, one got paid and moved on. He had always failed to understand why others got so het up. He never selected the targets so there was no personal involvement, it was just a shopping list he worked through. The phone call came, a name was given, it was left to him to work out the details, which was how he preferred to work. He never wanted to know the reason, and he never exceeded his instructions. Others might be tempted, but then others weren't as careful as he was, maybe they got some extra pleasure out of it. Harry wasn't in it for pleasure, he was a professional doing a job for money. Once the phone call was received he went into training: no alcohol, no sex, no new acquaintances; everything concentrated on the detailed when and how of the event until it was over. Afterwards there was plenty of time for extra stimuli.

He waited to see if his hunch was right and hoped that the next one would give him more of a challenge: the last two had hardly tested him.

. . .

Pearson couldn't help being impressed by the opulence of Sir Raymond Charters's office and lifestyle, especially since reading that Charters had received a £1.4 million bonus in addition to his monster salary as Chief Executive of the company. He had calculated that in the highly unlikely event that Charters's tax lawyers didn't shelter any of it and the Revenue took forty per cent, he would still be left with well over a million. Sitting on the deep leather couch sipping the cup of excellent coffee provided by the receptionist, he passed the time working out that it would take him a good forty years to earn that amount.

Making a show of consulting his wrist-watch, he deliberately caught the receptionist's eye. She smiled sympathetically.

'I'm so sorry about this', she said. 'We try our best to keep Sir Raymond's diary straight, but it doesn't always work out.'

'Happens to us all.'

Pearson had observed that keeping underlings waiting was one of the prerogatives of power, and Charters was certainly exercising that power in his case. He had arrived a few minutes before the appointed time and had been made to cool his heels for the best part of thirty minutes. Maybe, he thought, men like Charters had a graduated scale for these things. Equals were admitted immediately, others according to their social status or usefulness.

'Can I get you another coffee?'

'No, thank you.'

'Would you care to see today's *Financial Times*?'

Testing her sense of humour, Pearson said: 'I'm not playing the market at the moment', and saw that she was uncertain how to interpret this.

'Oh, right.'

The door to Charters's office finally opened and his secretary came out. 'I do apologise, Commander. Sir Raymond will see you now.'

'Thank you.'

She held the door open and closed it behind him. Charters's office was furnished in matching rosewood: his desk with its array of telephones, fax machine and personal computer, the fitted bookshelves with their sets of leather-bound volumes, the coffee table and side chairs, all were fashioned in the same rich wood, presumably as a symbol of their owner's taste and wealth. He was making a statement, as the Americans put it. There were several oil paintings on the walls, and Pearson trod an elaborately patterned Oriental carpet as he went forward to greet Charters.

'Commander, please forgive me for making you hang about. I hope my people took care of you?'

'Yes, I was well looked after, thank you.'

Charters took a seat by the coffee table and Pearson did likewise.

'Some days are sheer hell.'

'I know the feeling,' Pearson said.

'Do you smoke?' Charters pushed a silver cigarette box towards Pearson. 'Feel free if you do.'

'I won't at the moment, thank you.'

'So, to what do I owe this honour from somebody of your eminence?'

'I can't say I'm conscious of having any eminence.'

'Well, it's not every day that one has a visit from a senior officer of MI6. How can I help you?'

'Well, it's just a general enquiry really, to ask if you could throw any light on the death of Lord Miller.'

Charters nodded. 'Oh dear, yes, that. A very sad business from all accounts. I always think it must be quite terrible for the families of a suicide. Death should always have some dignity.'

'You knew him, of course?'

'Yes. I won't say he was a close friend, but we certainly socialised. Birds of a feather, you know, we tend to frequent the same watering holes and talk the same shop. I mean, in one sense I suppose, we were antagonists.'

'In what sense is that?'

'As business rivals. We overlapped in certain areas. I'm sure I don't have to tell you it's very cut-throat these days, especially since Black Monday. The stock market has never been the same. Then we've had the Maxwell scandal, all those unfortunate Names at Lloyds, Barings going under . . . things which were unthinkable a few years back.'

'Yes, I understand . . . Am I right in saying that you dined with him not long before his death?'

If Charters was surprised by this question, he concealed it. 'I believe I did, yes.'

'Did you notice any change in him on that occasion?'

'Not that I can recall. Old Ralph was very much a one-man

band. Kept his thoughts to himself.'

'And at the time, if the papers are to be believed, you were in the process of making a bid for his company?'

'We were looking at his company, certainly.'

'It was described at the time as a "hostile bid". I'm not quite sure what that means.'

'It's just City jargon. Roughly, it means that the bid is not entirely welcome.'

'So do I take it that he wasn't keen?'

'No, and I understood why. He'd built up the company from scratch, it was very much his baby. He knew he was vulnerable, but he wanted to hang on as long as possible.'

'And it didn't go through?'

'No, we analysed the numbers and decided they didn't add up from our point of view. Happens all the time, we're always looking for companies that could be useful. Diversify or die is the word today.'

'That could have been a factor then?'

Charters took a surreptitious glance at his watch. 'Factor?' he queried.

'The state of his business. Being aware that predators were stalking him.'

'I don't think I'd describe myself as a predator,' Charters said with a ghost of a smile.

'No, nor would I. That's just a word I've picked up from the tabloids.'

'Ah, the tabloids! They're the bane of everybody's life. But to answer you, I dare say that he did have concerns about whether he would have to bow to the inevitable. There's no doubt his business was going through a rough patch. That was obvious to anybody from the share price.'

'But apart from that you didn't get the impression of anything out of the ordinary the last time you saw him?'

'Forgive me, Commander,' Charters said, 'but what is the purpose of these questions?'

'Just to find out as much as we can about the state of his mind prior to his death.'

'Who knows what goes through a man's mind before he decides to commit suicide?'

Pearson did not answer immediately. Instead he reached for the cigarette box on the coffee table. 'D'you mind if I change my mind?'

'Please. I'm a cigar man myself, but I try to hold out until after lunch. Here, let me get you a lighter.' Charters got up and went to his desk, picking up a lighter in the shape of a pistol.

Once his cigarette was alight, Pearson said: 'What if he didn't commit suicide, Sir Raymond? What if he was murdered?'

Charters stared at him. 'Am I to take that remark seriously?'

'I certainly meant it seriously, sir.'

'Good God. That's shocking news, if it's true. Is there any evidence to that effect?'

'Certain things about his death aren't crystal-clear.'

'But that's a matter for the police, surely, not your department?'

'You're absolutely right, sir, and the police are handling that end. The reason we were called in to assist is that matters of security could be involved.'

'Security? What're we talking about? Industrial espionage?'

'I wouldn't like to speculate at this point,' Pearson said.

'It would surprise me if his company had anything worth stealing in this day and age. He didn't have any defence contracts as far as I know. Are you implying that he was mixed up in something else?'

'I wouldn't imply anything, sir, until we've got much further.'

'You've really shocked me, you know. I take it that what you've told me is not common knowledge?'

'I'd appreciate you treating it in confidence for the time being, yes. For the sake of his family as much as anything else.'

'Are they in the picture?'

'Not entirely.'

'I must write to his widow. Meant to do it before.' Charters went to his desk and scribbled a reminder. 'Only wish I could be more helpful. God, we live in strange times, don't we?'

'We certainly do, sir.' Pearson extinguished his cigarette and got to his feet. 'Thank you for your time and I'm sorry I gave you a shock.'

He paused in front of one of the paintings depicting small boats in a fishing harbour as he went towards the door. 'You've got some very nice paintings. I particularly like this. Who's it by?'

'Kit Wood,' Charters said. 'He died young unfortunately. Yes, it's very pleasant. Bought it years ago.'

'I wish I knew more about painting. This reminds me of Devon where I was evacuated during the war. That all seems another world now. Life was a lot simpler in many ways. Were you an evacuee yourself?' he added, still studying the painting.

'Yes, I was. Didn't end up anywhere as nice as Devon though. I got shunted down to Swindon.'

'They pushed us all over the place, didn't they? The war changed a lot of lives, mine included. I lost both my parents in the Blitz.'

'Likewise,' Charters said.

'In London?'

'Yes.'

'We're both orphans of the storm then. Well, thank you once again, Sir Raymond.'

They shook hands and Pearson was halfway out of the door when he paused. 'There was just one other thing. Does the name Carstairs mean anything to you?'

Charters's face did not alter. 'Carstairs? Carstairs?' he repeated. 'Can't say it does. Should it?'

'Only that his name cropped up in connection with this affair. I thought possibly it might ring a bell. As you said, you businessmen of a feather tend to frequent the same watering holes. It was just a thought.'

The moment Pearson had left the room Charters dialled a number.

'What're you playing at?' he said angrily when the line was answered. He listened for a few seconds, then interrupted with, 'I couldn't care less about your problems. Just get these people off my back.'

. . .

'Did you ever stop to consider that we're not the romantic heroes of fiction?' Hillsden said. 'I'll tell you what our fiction is: it's tales told to idiots about little men serving little causes, just expendable pawns out in a no-man's land between two sets of barbarians, minor players in a game we didn't start, half the time don't understand and which most of us will never live to finish. If I had my time over again, I wouldn't waste my life on it.'

'You realise that sort of dialogue could condemn you as a bad risk,' Swanson replied.

'Then do me a favour, have me reclassified. I was condemned long ago.'

'Yes, I keep forgetting that . . . But right now you're an invaluable member of the team. Tell me about this man you saw with Fadiman in Grosvenor House – that interests me. Had you ever seen him before?'

'Not that I can recall.'

'Would you recognise him again?'

'I think so.'

'Why were you in Grosvenor House?'

Caution determined Hillsden's answer. 'I'm an insurance agent, remember? One of the enquiries we got was from a character who runs a car-hire business in Manchester who wanted us to quote for a fleet of Rovers.'

'Somebody connected with Fadiman?'

'Could have been. But he didn't keep the appointment.

What I don't understand is why we haven't pulled in this Harry character.'

'I prefer the waiting game,' Swanson said with no change of expression. 'There's more to be gained by letting them think we're still in the dark.'

'Think? I thought we were,' Hillsden said.

. . .

'Back again?' Harrison said.

'Let me see the Kell files for 1939 and '40 again.'

'You writing the old bugger's biography, or something?' Harrison asked. 'You're the second one who's asked for them in the space of a week. The bloody things gather dust for fifty years, suddenly they're on the best-seller list.'

Pearson kept the surprise out of his face and voice. 'Who was that?'

'No idea. I was off sick. Our Ethel would know. I'll ask her.'

'Well, it's not important. I only wanted those two particular years, if you'd be kind enough to get them for me. And I wouldn't say no to another cup of your freshly ground Colombian. That went down a treat last time. Gave me a kick-start.'

'Oh, good, I've made a convert, have I?' Harrison looked gratified that his expert knowledge of the bean had been recognised. 'The secret is to keep them in the fridge until you need them. It brings out the flavour. To my mind the aroma of fresh coffee is intensely erotic. You don't take sugar, do you?'

'No, haven't you noticed, I'm sweet enough?' Pearson said and was ashamed of having said it, but the news had rattled him.

It was too much of a coincidence, he thought, as Harrison shuffled away. Even without being told, it had been obvious from his first visit that the files had remained untouched for half a century, lying dormant there like some Dead Sea Scrolls. Why the sudden interest immediately following his own enquiry? Giving himself time to think before Harrison returned, he reached for his cigarettes, then remembered smoking was no longer permitted in Archives. Authority was needed by anybody outside the Firm before they were allowed to examine classified information, and for some pointless reason the Kell material had always been regarded as ultra-sensitive. Probably, he thought, because in the wrong hands they could confirm the utter uselessness of most of the collected information – from Sarajevo to the Somme, to Munich, many of the guesses had been disastrous, setting the pattern for disasters to come.

Harrison returned empty-handed. 'Well, I'm sorry, but you're out of luck, Commander,' he said. 'The two years you wanted are out. Any others interest you?'

'Not at the moment,' Pearson said, getting up. 'I'll come back on another day.'

'Oh, aren't you going to wait for your coffee?' Harrison said, aggrieved.

'No, just been called on my bleeper,' Pearson said. 'Thanks all the same.'

'Oh, what a pity, I've got the kettle on.' But Pearson had already gone. On his way out, he stopped in at Ethel's cubbyhole. With her immaculate starched blouses and severely neat hair, Ethel brought to mind the days when hospital matrons ruled the roost, and indeed there was a sterilised air to her office: nothing was ever out of place. Although forced reluctantly to accept the electronic age, she still considered her own filing system, compiled over the thirty years or more she had been a fixture in Archives, to be superior. The computer, like the absence of men in her life, was merely another cross she bore with fortitude.

'Ethel, my darling,' Pearson said, 'if you'll forgive my blatant sexual harassment so early in the day . . . those Kell files. How long are they likely to be out?'

'I've no idea, Commander. They didn't say.'

'Well, it's not that vital. Who took them, by the way?'

'Somebody from your lot,' Ethel said. She flicked a large Rotadex. 'Young Mr Hadley.'

'Ah! Hadley,' Pearson said. 'That explains it. I'll get them from him. May I say, you're looking radiant this morning, Ethel. You must have a new lover.'

'Really, Commander, whatever next? The things you come out with.' Her hand fluttered to the small locket around her neck, but as she watched him go she thought, always such a gentleman, unlike some. She reached down below her desk and took a small compact out of her handbag and powdered her nose, her morning made.

40

LINKS IN THE CHAIN

'Rotherby, you belong to the London Library, don't you?'
Pearson said.

'I certainly do. Best library in existence.'

'Well, in that case, could you do me a small favour? I'm
trying to trace something and our records are very sparse on a
certain subject.'

'What subject's that?'

'The history of 18b. Well, actually, anything to do with the
emergence of the British Union.'

'Battle of Cable Street and so forth?'

'Yes, but with particular reference to 18b.'

'I'll go today.'

Pearson lingered a moment longer. 'That a picture of your
cat?' he said, pointing to a photograph on Rotherby's desk of
a grossly overweight Persian that resembled a furry Buddha.

'Yes, that's Mr Pooter. The wife was maniacally doggie, but
I was never keen myself, much prefer the pussies. Fastidious,
fascinating creatures, altogether superior to dogs. Cleaner
habits all round. I read somewhere that two thousand tons of
dog poo is left on London streets every day.'

'I've stepped in half of it,' Pearson said as he departed
again.

· · ·

The call Harry expected came after midnight and h
recognised the voice immediately. He listened, smiling, as h
was told a name.

'When?' he asked.

'I leave that to you. The sooner the better,' the voice saic
'But vary it this time. Your trademark is becoming to
familiar.'

'Understood.'

The line went dead.

. . .

'Run an errand for me,' Pearson said. 'Go ask Hadley if he'
finished with the Kell files.'

'Why don't you just ring him?' Lloyd said. 'He was at hi
desk when I went past just now.'

'I have my reasons.'

Lloyd went into his Watson impersonation. 'What a man o
mystery you've become, Holmes.'

'Just tell me what he says.'

When Lloyd left the room, Pearson stared down at the fou
volumes Rotherby had obtained from the London Library
They had not provided the information he was looking fo
Reaching for the phone, he dialled Scotland Yard and askec
for Gilbert.

'Archie, you thought I'd forgotten, right?'

'Forgotten what?'

'That I owe you a dinner. How about tonight?'

'What's the catch?'

'No catch. God, life has really soured you. You did us ̀
good turn over Carstairs's suicide, remember? I like to pay
my debts.'

'I can't tonight.'

'Okay, then pick another day.'

'Is it just you and me, stag?'

'No, doesn't have to be. My treat, let's include the wives.

Amaze them.'

'We could do Saturday.'

'Saturday it is. I'll make the booking and let you know.'

'Well, thanks, sorry I jumped to the wrong conclusion.'

'Story of your life, Archie, that's why so many crimes go unsolved. By the way, how good are the Yard's wartime files?'

'I knew it, I knew it,' Gilbert said. 'You didn't ring just to invite me out to dinner, you crafty sod.'

'What d'you mean, we've just made a date.'

'Come on, don't give me that. What d'you want?'

'I may be on a false trail, but you know me, if I'm chasing a fox, I've got to run it to earth. I need to find out details of 18b detainees. From the little I've been able to discover, we didn't handle the arrests, that was left to Special Branch. D'you have any idea whether those files still exist?'

'Come over and take an unofficial look.'

'Archie, you're a prince.'

'That dinner had better be good.'

'You can order *à la carte*, not the set menu, how's that?'

'Drop dead, George.'

.   .   .

Examining the Yard's files, Pearson was astounded by many of the names and cases documented. It was no surprise to find all the prominent members of the British Union, but the inclusion of others such as a masseuse from Elizabeth Arden smacked more of hysteria than any considered effort to safeguard national security; it seemed highly improbable that such a motley collection, unarmed, unorganised and having no discernible relationship with each other, could have presented any real threat.

Pearson knew what he *had* to find if his supposition was to prove correct, but after two fruitless hours he began to feel that once again he would go away empty-handed. Rather than admit defeat, he concentrated on that week in May 1940 when the new powers had first been used, looking for cross-references of detainees sharing the same name. It was during this second search that he singled out a family named Hain who had been arrested in Albemarle Street, London, on May 23rd. A footnote indicated that Hain and his wife had both died within a month of each other. Against Hain's name the word 'suicide' was appended in red ink. The fate of their child was not given, there was merely a notation that he had been taken into care by an official of the Westminster Council on May 27th 1940. Pearson took copies of all the relevant entries, then left the Yard and returned to his office.

'So, what happened to you?' Lloyd questioned him. 'You ask me to run an errand, then disappear.'

Pearson brandished the Xerox copies. 'I'm getting close to Charters at last,' he said.

'Oh, God!' Lloyd said. 'Here we go again.'

'Just read these,' Pearson pushed the Xerox copies at him.

When he'd finished, Lloyd looked up, unimpressed. 'So? A family called Hain. Where does Charters come into the reckoning?'

'I think he was the son, that Hain was his given name. I traced a connection that led me first to Swindon and then to Yeovil down in Somerset. If I'm right, Charters was born Hain, the only son of Carl Hain, described there as an art dealer and listed as a Nazi supporter. The parents were both arrested under 18b shortly after the fall of France, then both died within a very short space of time afterwards, Hain committing suicide as you can see from the footnote.'

'Yeah, okay, well?'

'Well, you remember that, significantly, Charters's entry in *Who's Who* omits his parentage.'

'So what? Most people doctor their entries. Women always omit their real ages if they can get away with it.'

'Wait, hear me out. I traced a surviving member of the

genuine Charters clan to Yeovil and this guy told me his parents had taken in various evacuees during the war, including an orphan boy he only remembered as Carl. They lived in Swindon at the time. Subsequently, this Carl took their name, left his foster home at the end of the war and they never heard from him again. When I went to see Charters ostensibly enquiring about Lord Miller's death, I got him to admit that he was an evacuee . . . And guess where? Swindon! You have to admit the facts start to slot together. Tell me you're impressed for once.'

'Yeah,' Lloyd said reluctantly, 'you're beginning to make a case.'

'You perverse bastard, is that all you can say?'

'It still contains a strong element of the coincidental.'

'Well, think back, how did Charters come into our reckoning? Carstairs's suicide, yes? And, okay, coincidence, but men have been hanged for less. Then ask yourself what was Carstairs doing in Copenhagen. Tracking down the source of all that Fascist literature flooding into the country, right? Who owns printing presses on the Continent? Friend Charters. Who's well-heeled enough to be payrolling Fadiman and company? Charters again. And we know that both Carstairs and Van Elst were on somebody's payroll, getting regular sums from Luxembourg. I checked with the CAA, Charters's private jet logged eleven flights to Luxembourg in the past eight months.'

'My, you have been a busy little beaver. The big question mark is how d'you prove Charters was once an evacuee named Carl? So he changed his name. Big deal. So did Cary Grant. It's not a criminal offence. Give me a motive.'

'It's staring you in the face. Revenge. Parents arrested under notorious wartime legislation, imprisoned without trial, and both died in prison. Years later orphaned son decides to get even.'

Lloyd grimaced. 'Is that why you were so keen to see the Kell files?'

'God! I'd forgotten them. What did Hadley say? Why did he want them?'

'He didn't', Lloyd said. 'Swanson asked for them.'

They looked at each other.

41

A DEATH IN THE FAMILY

'What do you think?' Abramov said as he gunned the new Lexus from the slip road on to the motorway, the needle moving effortlessly to seventy-five as they headed for Suffolk.

'I don't have your thing about cars, Victor. All I care about is whether they start when I turn the key,' Hillsden replied.

'When I ship this home, it'll sell in a flash.'

'If it's so good why would you sell it?'

'Because I'll treble my money. You're no businessman like me.'

'Is that what brought you over here, to buy a car?'

'No, I'm looking at property. You've no idea how much Russian money is pouring into your impoverished country. A lot of it being washed, of course, but I'm clean, a legitimate capitalist at last. We always said we'd take you with our bare hands.'

'Don't tell me you're going to buy a grouse moor and wear tweeds? I somehow don't see you playing the lord of the manor.'

'Why not?'

'Because you'd be bored stiff.'

'How's Galina? Is she bored stiff?'

The question touched a raw nerve and Hillsden edged around it. 'I think she hasn't found it easy.'

'And how about your little daughter?'

'She's settled in better than I expected. In fact, she's staying with a little friend tonight.'

'And you? How does it feel to be back in harness? Is it like the old days?'

'Same chessboard, different players. I hope you've still got my insurance policy in a safe place.'

'Of course. Listen. I know you turned me down before, but once you've fulfilled your part of the bargain here, let me cut you in on my operation. I'm making so much money it scares me. I can't spend it fast enough. And I want to widen my operations, because I don't intend to be trapped in Russia when the next *coup* comes. And believe me, it will come. Think about it.'

After a pause, Hillsden said: 'Maybe I'm not that ambitious. If I survive this one, we've got enough to live the way I want.'

The Lexus made little sound as it drove down Walsham le Willows's deserted main street and turned off into the long lane leading to the house. As they approached they could see lights burning in Audrey's annexe but curiously the house itself was in darkness.

Victor got out and stood savouring the clean air. 'It's so quiet out here,' he said.

'Yes, took some getting used to at first.'

But as Abramov collected the gifts he had brought for Galina and Lara, Hillsden became conscious that the stillness had a different quality from usual. Normally he would have expected to hear Audrey's radio – she seldom switched it off, saying that although she didn't listen all the time, she liked the background sound for company – but that night it was missing, although he noticed that the door to her annexe was ajar. He led the way towards the house and called out to let Galina know they had arrived. There was no response. The fact that there were no lights on anywhere puzzled him.

'Where is everybody?' he said. Above him in the chestnut tree the rooks answered him with a rustling of wings. He turned the handle on the front door but it was locked, and he found he didn't have his key.

'Darling?' he shouted. 'Hello . . . We're here.'

They waited, but again there was no response.

'Sorry about this,' he said to Victor. 'Not much of a welcome. Let me go find out where they are.'

He went towards the half-open doorway of the annexe. 'Audrey, you there?' It was at that moment that he knew with absolute certainty that something was horribly wrong. He pushed the door wide open and saw that the room had been trashed, the furniture overturned, lamps and Audrey's collection of china ornaments smashed. He went no further, but called Victor, at the same time giving him a cautionary gesture.

Victor put the parcels on the bonnet of the Lexus and joined him.

'Something wrong?'

'Take a look.'

'Jesus!' Victor said in the open doorway. 'Have you got a gun?'

Hillsden nodded and produced it. He motioned for Victor to accompany him and together they walked to the rear of the cottage. There they found the kitchen door open and could smell burning. Reaching inside, Hillsden felt for the light switch. As the light came on the first thing they both saw was Audrey's dead body. She was lying face upwards at a right-angle to the Aga cooker. There was an acrid smell originating from a saucepan on the Aga which had burnt dry and close to her body another, smaller saucepan that had contained a sauce; the contents had spilled in a pool close to Audrey's head and at first they mistook it for blood. Hillsden knelt to examine her and could find no wounds, but from the bruising circling her neck there appeared little doubt that she had been strangled. From her position, Hillsden's immediate thought was that she must have been taken from behind.

Taking a torch from one of the kitchen shelves, Hillsden led the way as they cautiously approached the living room. Switching on another light they saw that apparently nothing had been disturbed here. Continuing to the stairwell they climbed to the first floor, pausing on the landing to listen for any sounds that somebody was still in the house. All was quiet, too quiet. The door to his and Galina's bedroom was wide open, the room beyond in darkness. Hillsden edged to one side of the door, silently indicating to Victor to move to the other side. He shone his torch around the room but could see nothing untoward.

'Galina?' he said softly. 'Darling? It's okay, it's only me and Victor.'

Getting no answer, he steeled himself to go inside the room. Everything was undisturbed, the bed made, nothing out of place. He handed his gun to Victor. 'You have it,' he said. 'You're more useful with them than I am.'

They checked the bathroom, all the closets and Lara's room, but found nothing, eventually going downstairs again and conducting a more thorough search there, including the garage where they found both cars but still no sign of Galina.

'Let's look around the garden,' Victor said.

Using the torch, they first scanned the area around the house before moving to the large patch of lawn and shrubbery at the rear. There was a lean-to greenhouse at the end of the garden, with a number of panes of glass missing. Hillsden had intended to repair it but had never found the time. The previous owner had given the glass a wash of paint to reduce the heat during the hot summer months. A grapevine had once flourished inside, but now only a few dead tentacles poked through the holes. One of the hinges on the door had rusted and the door hung at an angle.

Hillsden and Victor approached the greenhouse from opposite ends, and while Hillsden shone his torch through a broken pane, Victor, gun in hand, pulled the door open so that he could enter. The torchlight beam swept across the dusty wooden staging, taking in a galvanised watering can and a collection of earthenware pots containing withered plants. Hillsden angled the beam downwards and it was then that he saw part of Galina's body under the staging at the blind end.

Hillsden thought: 'Oh, God, don't let her be dead, not that.'

He said as calmly as he could, 'Darling, it's me, don't be afraid, you're safe now.' And as he spoke he saw a movement and a moment later her face came into view, streaked with dirt, her hair cobwebbed. Victor went forward to help her up and bring her to Hillsden at the door. She clung to her husband without being able to speak.

'It's okay, it's okay,' he soothed. 'All over.' He carried her up the garden and round to the front of the house to Victor's car. Once there, he put her into the back seat and got in beside her, cradling her in his arms. Her whole body shook against him, attacked by a sudden ague. Victor opened one of the parcels he had left on the bonnet and took out a bottle of malt whisky.

'Let her have a sip of this.'

Hillsden held the bottle to Galina's lips. 'Just take a little, sweetheart, it'll warm you.' Then to Victor, 'See if you can find a rug or a blanket inside.' While Victor went to search, Hillsden massaged her cold hands, all the time murmuring words of comfort, but it was some time before she stopped shuddering. The first thing she said as she came out of shock was, 'Audrey, where's Audrey?'

'Don't worry about Audrey, she's fine,' he lied. 'When you're able, tell me something of what happened. But take your time, there's no hurry, everything's all right now.' He offered the bottle of whisky again, but she waved it away.

'I was outside,' she began, 'getting some herbs for the dinner, when I heard a car. I thought it was you . . . and . . . and I was just about . . . just about to come back to the house . . . when I heard Audrey cry out . . .' She stopped and the tears came, damming her breath.

'Take your time,' Hillsden repeated. He wiped some of the dirt from her cheeks with a handkerchief. Victor returned with a blanket and between them they tucked it around her.

'I stopped halfway,' Galina said when she was able to get her breath again. 'Then there were lots of crashes, things breaking . . . and the radio, Audrey's radio, that suddenly stopped. And after that it went quiet . . . something warned me not to call out . . . I just crouched down on the path . . . and in the light from Audrey's window, I saw a man come round the corner of the house and I lay flat and didn't move . . . When he disappeared again, I crawled to the greenhouse and hid myself in there. I was so frightened.'

Hillsden said, 'How long ago was this?'

'I don't know. An hour maybe. It seemed for ever.'

'Then did he drive away?'

'I don't know.'

Hillsden and Victor looked at each other across her.

'Where's Audrey, what happened to her?'

'She's okay, just resting like you,' Hillsden lied again.

'She's dead, isn't she? I know she's dead, you're just saying that.' For the first time she became aware of Victor, turning to stare at him, not making the connection.

'Hello, Galina,' Victor said, smiling.

'It's Victor, darling. Remember?'

'Oh, Victor . . . yes,' Galina said, then returned to the thought uppermost in her mind: 'The man did something to Audrey, didn't he?' Galina said, more insistent now that she was recovering.

'No. He just trashed the place. Burglars always do that if they can't find anything worth stealing. I think the best thing is to get you away from here. Victor will drive you to London, won't you Victor?'

'Sure.'

'I don't want to go to London.'

'Listen. Listen. I'll stay here and take care of Audrey, then I'll collect Lara from her friend's and we'll all spend the night in Victor's hotel. I can pack some clothes and overnight things for you both and bring them up with me.'

He hoped he had persuaded her, but she wasn't having it.

'What d'you mean, you'll take care of Audrey? Tell me the truth.'

'I am telling you the truth. Audrey's like you, she had a shock.'

'Then why isn't she with us?'

'Darling, just do as I suggest, be a good girl. The important thing right now is to get you away and into bed somewhere you'll feel safe. You know Victor, and you know he'll look after you until I get there. Right, Victor?'

'Absolutely.'

He seemed to have persuaded her at last.

'You promise you'll bring Lara?'

'Of course I will. I'll join you as soon as I can.' He kissed her, then eased himself out of the back seat. As he and Victor met by the driver's door, Victor slipped him the gun which he quickly slid into a pocket. 'Can you remember the way back?'

'Yes, I think so.'

'Just keep straight on out of the village. About two miles and you'll hit a main road. Make a left and you'll pick up the signs to the motorway. Go south.'

'South.'

Hillsden gave Galina a last look; her eyes were closed, but her face was still taut. He watched the Lexus until it was out of sight, then went into the house to do all the things that needed to be done quickly. The first thing was to call Rotherby. The line was busy when he dialled it, but he had the operator interrupt for an emergency. A concerned Rotherby finally answered.

'Don't ask questions, Colonel, just listen. We've had some bad news here in Suffolk. Poor Audrey's met with a fatal accident and I'm going to need help. Get Pearson down here and tell him that it's something Hogg will have to deal with. Got that?'

'Right. You want me, too?'

'Yes, because you know the way.'

'Anybody else hurt?'

'No, thank God. Don't waste time talking, just get here.'

When he put down the phone he steeled himself to go back into the kitchen. Avoiding the pool of sauce, he knelt beside Audrey again and gently closed her staring eyes. Then he made a careful search of the surroundings in the hope that he might find some clue, but whoever had killed her had left nothing that was obvious. After securing all the downstairs doors and windows and drawing the curtains, he went up to the bedrooms to pack toiletries and clothes for Galina and Lara. He had a last look around their own bedroom, wondering if he would ever see it again. Afterwards he went down into the living room, poured himself a stiff whisky, turned out the lights and with the gun close to hand, settled down to wait for help to arrive.

The house was still, but, from across the fields, he heard a vixen scream.

. . .

Three hours later, he was still sitting in the darkness going over all the possible permutations of what lay ahead, when the headlights of two cars briefly pierced the drawn curtains. Opening the front door he saw Pearson coming towards him, followed by Lloyd and Rotherby.

'You did well, made good time,' he said.

'The roads are deserted at this time of night. What've we got?' Pearson asked as Hillsden led them inside the house to the kitchen. The three arrivals stared down at Audrey's body.

'She didn't deserve that,' Pearson said. 'She was a trooper, our Audrey. One of a kind.'

'The best,' Rotherby agreed softly.

Lloyd and Pearson went closer to the body. 'Looks as though they used rope,' Lloyd said. 'Wire would have cut into the neck.'

'He,' Hillsden corrected. 'According to Galina there was only one.'

'The wife's okay, though?'

'She hid herself in the garden, thank God, and fortunately our daughter is away, staying with a friend. I had Galina taken to London.' He became conscious that he had stopped using their phoney names.

'What's that mean?' Pearson asked.

'A friend took her.' Then seeing the blank looks: 'I drove down here with a friend we'd invited to dinner.'

'Don't scare me,' Pearson said. 'What sort of friend?'

'Somebody I got to know in Russia.'

'A Russian?'

'Yes.'

'Oh, great, that's all we need with this mess. How could you bring a Russian down here?'

'Don't panic. If you must know, he ran me there, but he's out of the game now, and I'd trust him with anything. We both know each other's secrets.'

Pearson looked very dubious.

'George, I promise you, he's okay.'

'He'd better be. We're in deep enough shit as it is. You didn't ring the police?'

'No. The only call I made was to the Colonel here. What do we do about the police?'

'Nothing. We deal with this ourselves.'

I've been away so long, Hillsden thought, I'd almost forgotten that the Firm is a law unto itself when it comes to protecting its own interests.

'The urgent thing is to get things cleaned up and get out of here,' Pearson continued. 'Apart from this room, where else did he go?'

'He turned over Audrey's annexe, presumably to make it look like a burglary.'

'Nowhere else?'

'No. I've checked. The rest of the house wasn't disturbed.'

'Right, well you and Rotherby take care of her place while we do what's needed in here.' He turned to Lloyd. 'Back your car up as close as you can to the door, and fetch in the necessary.'

By the time Hillsden and Rotherby came back Audrey's corpse had been put into a body bag and the kitchen made tidy. 'Lucky we didn't have any blood to deal with,' Lloyd said. 'We don't want any DNA tests coming back to haunt us.'

Between them they carried the bagged body and put it on the back seat of Pearson's car, then covered it with a blanket.

'Let's make one last check,' Pearson said, 'because you and the family are not coming back.' He registered Hillsden's quick look of concern. 'This place is history.'

'I agree,' Hillsden said, 'but I'm wondering how best to deal with that. We'll have to have some story for the village. The neighbours are not unduly nosey, but they're bound to wonder why we did a moonlight flit.'

'No problem. Tomorrow you ring a couple of the local stores and tell them your firm's relocated you suddenly and you're having to put the house up for sale. Cancel the newspapers and milk. Happens all the time. We'll make sure the furniture and the rest of your belongings are removed.'

Hillsden still looked dubious. 'Somebody will have to notify Laura's school as well.'

'Fine, whatever's necessary will be done,' Pearson said, a note of irritation creeping into his voice.

'It's not just me, remember. I have a wife and child to think about. Where they're going to be dumped next.'

'We'll decide that in the morning, just get out of here. You and Rothers make a last check before you go.'

He drove off, with Lloyd following in Audrey's car.

'Never seen him edgy like that,' Rotherby said.

'No. Easy for him. I've still got to concoct some story for Laura when I collect her . . . How do you explain any of this to a child?'

They went back into the house and made sure nothing had been overlooked. Hillsden collected a few more personal belongings, including the doll Rotherby had given Lara the night they had arrived in England. Then he switched off everything and locked up.

'You get off,' Hillsden said. He stood and watched Rotherby drive away, then turned and had a last look at the house, trying to collect his thoughts and frame the right words to say to Lara before he, too, left for the last time.

When the disturbed rooks had settled, the night was still again.

42

SHADOW BOXING

Hillsden woke after a few hours' fitful sleep. It was some moments before he could relate to where he was, taking in the unfamiliar wallpaper, a different lamp and telephone on the bedside table, furniture that he did not recognise. The bed he found himself in, that was strange too, larger, softer, with white linen sheets. He turned his head, for a moment totally disorientated, then, as he saw Galina curled and sleeping beside him, his fogged mind began to clear. There was also a single bed in the room with Lara asleep in it and he remembered that Victor had arranged for this knowing that the child would not want to wake in an alien hotel room and find herself alone. Victor, he now recalled, had taken care of everything, somehow achieving what Hillsden had been dreading – breaking the news of the murder to Galina.

He became aware of a faint rumble of traffic, again odd after the silence of the house in Walsham le Willows. He looked at his watch and found that it had gone ten o'clock. Not wanting to wake Galina and the child, he padded to the bathroom and closed the door. The marble floor struck cold on his bare feet as he stood and urinated. There was a telephone on the wall adjacent to the toilet and when he had sluiced his hands and face in cold water, he rang the operator and asked to be connected to Victor's room.

'Oh, good, I was afraid you might have gone out,' he said when Victor answered.

'No, I deliberately stayed in my room until you called.'

'Thanks so much for all you did last night.'

'Listen, what are friends for? Are they both okay?'

'They're still asleep. The other thing I have to thank you for is telling Galina about Audrey. I wasn't looking forward to that.'

'Well, she kept asking me. I guess in her heart she knew the truth, so in the end I told her. She cried at first, but we sat talking – in Russian as a matter of fact, we slipped back into that – and I gradually calmed her.'

'Victor, I can't thank you enough. You must let me know what I owe you for the room.'

'Forget it, all taken care of. I love any excuse to use my new American Express card. I feel like the man in the TV ads.'

'Well, I have to ask you another favour. Can you look after them today until I've sorted things out?'

'Sure, no problem. Tell Galina to ring me when she's ready, I'll be here.'

Hillsden hung up and went back into the bedroom. Galina was now awake, although Lara hadn't stirred.

She whispered: 'Oh, darling, I thought you'd gone without saying anything.'

'As if I'd do that.' He sat on the side of the bed and she clung to him.

'I imagined I'd dreamed it all until I woke up in this room.'

'I know.'

'Poor Audrey,' Galina said, and cried silently. Hillsden held her close and let her cry. 'What's going to happen to us?'

'I'll deal with everything as soon as I can. You're quite safe here and Victor's waiting in his room for you to call him. How will you explain it to Lara when she wakes up?'

'I'll tell her you've decided to give us all a treat. Children don't question those things.'

Hillsden gently eased himself out of her embrace. 'Here,' he picked up the room service menu and gave it to her. 'Order the works, spoil yourself for once.'

'We won't have to go back there, will we?'

'No,' Hillsden said and kissed her. 'That's over.' He left the room, closing the door quietly.

. . .

Pearson said: 'Are we agreed then that Alec's cover is blown?'

'No. Why d'you say that?' Swanson sounded edgy. He frequently sounded edgy these days and was quick to take offence. He went to the window and made a show of examining his bonsai tree, prodding the soil around the small trunk.

'Audrey was murdered last night. You don't imagine they were just after Audrey, do you?'

'I'm keeping an open mind.' He poured a small amount of water around the base of the tree from a bottle he kept for this purpose. 'Unlike some, I don't jump to immediate conclusions, and I'd remind you I'm running Hillsden, not you.' Now, he fiddled with his wrist-watch strap and Pearson noticed the watch was one he hadn't seen before, an expensive chronometer, the type that showed the date, phases of the moon and God knows what else. 'It's always possible the unfortunate woman surprised a burglar and was killed as a result. That's a familiar occurrence these days, they've got nothing to lose since the death penalty was abolished. Violence isn't confined to the inner cities, in fact research shows people are just as likely to be attacked in out of the way villages.'

'If it was just a burglar, how come nothing was stolen?'

'Was there anything *worth* stealing? You say her room was trashed, which rather proves my point. It's another well-known fact that thieves smash up everything if they discover they're going to go away empty-handed. I'm told they often defecate in beds, like dogs marking their territory.'

Pearson and Lloyd exchanged looks.

'I think it would be fatal to make a hasty decision on Hillsden,' Swanson continued. 'Wait and see what their next move is.'

'We're playing with his life,' Pearson said, the image of Audrey's sprawled body in front of the Aga still vivid in his mind.

'He knew the risks when he took the job. It's what he's getting paid for.'

'And what happens about poor Audrey?'

'Already taken care of. Cremation, tomorrow, before questions are asked. Fortunately, she didn't have family. It was thought best to deal with it as though she died of natural causes.'

'How does that fit in with your other theory?'

'Meaning?'

'Meaning, if she was murdered by some casual intruder, shouldn't the police be looking for her killer?'

'The police won't be looking for anybody,' Swanson said at his blandest, fingering a small shaving nick on the side of his usually immaculate face. 'You played a part in that, by acting as you did and removing all traces. What you don't seem to appreciate is that there is a great deal more at stake than the regrettable murder of one minor operative.'

'Oh, I do appreciate that,' Pearson answered, the sarcasm unconcealed. 'It's always good to know that the Firm hasn't lost its touch in dealing with embarrassments. It's something we can all look forward to, should we meet with an accident.'

Before Swanson could frame a reply, the light on his scrambler phone started to blink. He picked up and immediately said: 'Ah, Alec, I'm glad you contacted me. We were just talking about you . . . Yes, awful, she'll be sadly missed.' His eyes flicked to Pearson as he said this. 'Everything's been taken care of, have no worries on that score, there'll be no comebacks where you're concerned, that episode is finished . . . They have? When? . . . That's very interesting. It bears out what I believe. I'm firmly of the opinion that last night's events had no connection. I think it's important you make the meeting . . . No, I disagree . . . I share your concern for your family's safety . . . but not to go to the meeting would leave us in the dark as to their future intentions. If they're planning a reply to Sonntag's death, it's vital we find out what . . . We need all the help we can get at this stage and you're the only one we have on the inside track . . . You have my word, the family will be taken care of . . .' Now he listened again. 'I'm sorry, no, we can't abort the operation on what I consider is speculation and not proven . . . I have to insist . . . What condition?' He listened, frowning. 'Well, that may be difficult, but I'll try. I can't promise, of course, you know how sticky the Yanks are . . . But I'll keep my side of the bargain if you do likewise. Good. I'll wait to hear from you.'

He replaced the receiver. 'Fadiman has contacted him and wants a meeting. I consider that a good sign.'

'A good sign?' Pearson said.

'Yes.'

'Unless they intend to make sure of him this time. Having failed last night.'

'Are you saying he shouldn't go to the meeting?'

'Well, we can't let him go in unprotected. Where is the meeting?'

'At Fadiman's place.'

'When?'

'Tomorrow night.'

'Then we'd better make arrangements to be around.'

Swanson's face clouded again. 'What d'you mean by "around"?'

'Close by. Let him go in wired with a panic button.'

'That's a risk.'

'The whole bloody thing's a risk. We should have moved in on them long ago. Leaving Fadiman aside, we've got enough circumstantial evidence on Charters for me to have another go at him.'

'I didn't take kindly to you seeing him the first time without my knowledge,' Swanson said airily.

'I thought we were a team working for the same end.'

'A team with me at the head.'

'Okay, I chalked up a black, but that doesn't alter the fact that I believe I can make a case against him.'

'And if you're wrong,' Swanson said with real venom, 'he'll have a case against us. I would remind you that I'm answerable to the PM himself if this operation self-destructs. You may be near retirement, but I'm not.'

Lloyd stepped in before the dialogue became more heated. 'Can I ask what else Hillsden was saying about his family?'

'He wants them out of harm's way, otherwise he won't go along.'

'And you agreed to that?'

'I agreed to think about it.'

It was Pearson's turn to harden his voice. 'No, you agreed to it, I heard you.'

'Then you also heard me say it would be difficult to implement his request.'

'And what was his request?'

'He wants them to be sent out of the country, to the States, under the witness protection scheme.'

'Why not?'

'Again, it may be against policy.' Swanson fingered the tiny scab on his face and it started to bleed again. He went to his desk and took out a tissue, dabbed it and examined the stain.

'I don't see why the Yanks wouldn't agree to that. They owe us a couple of favours.'

'Cost,' Swanson said. 'Who pays? One can't expect the American taxpayer to take in our lodgers.'

'Oh, bull! You think the American taxpayer gets a monthly audit of everything Langley spends?' He turned away motioning Lloyd to follow him as he moved to the door. 'You concentrate on policy. I'll concentrate on protecting Hillsden.'

Once outside the office he slammed his fist into his palm. 'What is it with Swanson?'

'You questioned his judgement.'

'What judgement? He hasn't made any. You know his game-plan? He's desperate for the old blade on his shoulder, so he's going to kiss arse all the way to Downing

Street and back.'

    'So, what's new?' Lloyd said.

43

ARRIVALS AND DEPARTURES

It was unusual for a London taxi to be seen in the small Oxfordshire village of North Stoke, which was more accustomed to Land Rovers and Mercedes estates, but late that evening one drew up outside the closed gates of Sir Raymond Charters's listed Grade II Queen Anne mansion. Harry got out and spoke into the entry-phone. A moment later, the gates swung open and he drove inside and parked alongside a number of other cars. Helped by Harry, Johnny manhandled Fadiman's chair up the flight of porch steps. The impressive front door had already been opened for them by a manservant who then took over and wheeled Fadiman inside.

He was trundled across a marble hallway past busts of Wagner and Nietzsche and conducted into one of the rooms at the rear of the house where a group of a dozen men were already assembled.

'Ah, Graham,' Charters said, coming forward to greet him. 'Sorry to drag you out at night, but I thought it was important for us all to meet. You know most of our comrades, of course, but we also have two new faces.' He singled out the newcomers. 'Charles Doyle from Belfast, and I'm particularly pleased to welcome Colin Adamson from Combat 18.' The introductions made, Fadiman nodded at Hyde and others he knew by sight.

Charters took the centre of the room and stared around. His eyes were clear to the point of blankness. In his own residence, surrounded by his own possessions, he had the assurance of a man who knows that money buys most things, especially people. 'I called this meeting,' he began, 'in order to update our strategy and regain the initiative. As you're all too aware, we recently suffered the loss of our distinguished German comrade, Gottfried Sonntag. Gottfried is dead, but his spirit and writings live on.' He paused to acknowledge the murmur of approval. 'He was murdered because we had an informer in our ranks. That informer was speedily detected and eliminated. Because we have a mole in position, our intelligence usually keeps us one step ahead, but we had not reckoned on the Jews, on Mossad. They were ruthless and clever, I give them that. Clever in the way the killing was carried out and clever, too, in the way they acted in collusion with the security forces to conceal the true facts. In the future, we must match that ruthlessness and cleverness.' He let this sink in before continuing.

'I am not somebody prepared endlessly to finance a lost cause. I have funded this organisation for the past three years and now I want a return on my money. Isolated acts, such as disposing of the odd Jew, killing a few ethnics and instigating riots in the ghettos have achieved very little. At best they have merely caused the authorities temporary concern. I want to explode their smug complacency, make them tremble in their beds. The example of the IRA struggle is before us. Violence pays. Violence makes the headlines. Violence means you are taken seriously. So, the time has come to put that example to work. That is the primary reason for bringing you here tonight. We have the money, and we have the brains . . .' Charters waved a hand towards Fadiman. 'Our chair-bound comrade has ample reason, as I have, to get even. Tonight, he will outline a brilliant plan which I am confident will change our destiny. He has studied the tactics by allied organisations in America, Germany and Japan, and adapted them for our uses. We cannot establish a new political order with speeches. Like the Führer before me, I consider democratic politics a historical irrelevance. If the hour demands it, we must build a new order on corpses.'

He spoke in a terse, but modulated voice, making eye contact with his audience. If any of those present found his words melodramatic they showed no sign.

'No more pinpricks. We need to bring off something as big as Oklahoma and Tokyo, something that cannot be concealed and commands the attention of the world media. I shall not elaborate further, but hand over to the architect of the plan, Comrade Fadiman.'

He relinquished his position as Fadiman wheeled himself in front of the ornate fireplace.

'I don't know that I deserve full credit,' he began. 'As our leader has intimated, I have merely borrowed something old, something new from abroad. My real contribution was to zero in on a particular event that is due to take place very shortly. It is an event ideally suited to the purpose we have in mind and if we bring it off, as I am confident we will, it could change the course of history. Every year, the character of London, our capital city, is traduced and transformed by a celebration so repulsive that words fail me. It is that celebration that we intend to finish once and for all, and regain our national sovereignty . . .'

Outside, in the illuminated grounds, Harry and Johnny leaned against the bonnet of the taxi, enjoying a joint.

'Something big in the offing, right?' Johnny said.

'You said it.'

''Bout time.'

'Yeah. Look forward to a bit of real action for a change.'

. . .

When the briefing finished, Fadiman remained behind for a private meeting with Charters.

'You intend to use this man . . . remind me again of his name,' Charters said.

'Hillsden. But he goes under the name of Bartlett,

Robert Bartlett.'

'Is that a wise move? I thought he'd outlived his usefulness.'

'Not quite. By involving him directly one last time we achieve two things. First, we ensure that he becomes the prime culprit should – God forbid – anything go wrong.'

'You say "God forbid", but what are the risks?'

'Negligible. Second, we need a courier, but once the things are safely delivered back here, he's expendable. He'll have served his purpose, as we always intended, and can then be eliminated. As you will recall, when I first came up with the idea, we needed somebody inside their network who would report to our mole, and at the same time protect our mole . . It's worked very well so far.'

'Except they're smelling around, getting too close for my comfort. This man, Pearson, for example, hasn't been idle.'

'Well, Carstairs caused a problem, I admit. I was never happy about Carstairs, but you overruled me.'

'I wasn't to know he'd commit suicide. That started the whole investigation,' Charters said. 'You promised me Harry would take care of him.'

'And he would have done. It was just that Carstairs took matters into his own hands before Harry could get to him. Nobody could have foreseen that.'

'How far has this man Pearson gone?'

'We know that he's been down to the West country and questioned one member of your wartime foster family, but that produced very little.'

'But you reported he'd also been tracing back through the Kell files. That's the danger area.'

'Raymond, my dear, relax,' Fadiman said, lighting a fresh cigarette. 'That's a dead issue. The pertinent files, the ones concerning you, met with an unfortunate mishap and were inadvertently shredded. We have a safe pair of hands in the right place when they're needed. Where, if you will allow me to say so, I think you should be more careful is in some of your business pursuits. Forget going after Miller's old company.'

This was not to Charters's liking. 'It represents a very quick profit.'

'But what shall it profit a man if he gains Miller and loses the main prize?' Fadiman said unctuously.

'Perhaps you're right,' was the grudging response.

'I know I'm right in this instance. Always distance yourself. We are on the brink of a breakthrough.' His cigarette ash was just about to fall and Charters reached for an ashtray. 'Thank you. Tell me one thing, because I've never been quite certain. Is it just revenge that drives you on, or is it something more? I was taken by something you said tonight.'

'What was that?'

'About politics being an irrelevance. Surely, you don't really believe that? After all, when we come to power, won't you be seeking the ultimate office? I know I would, if I was in your place.'

Charters did not answer immediately. 'If there was no alternative, I would have to consider it seriously,' he said.

. . .

From the rear windows of the unmarked surveillance van, Pearson had an unrestricted view of Fadiman's house. He and Lloyd were in position early on the evening of the following day, equipped with cameras and state-of-the-art listening devices. Deliberately flouting Swanson's orders, Pearson had ensured that this time Hillsden went in wired: a minute, but highly efficient microphone and micro-transmitter had been built into the arms of Hillsden's spectacles.

Hillsden arrived outside the house by taxi shortly after nine o'clock and was admitted by Johnny. The watchers in the van had no idea whether there were others inside. They heard Hillsden say, 'I'm sorry I'm a little late. I had trouble getting a taxi,' and Johnny's uninterested response, 'Too bad,' as he conducted Hillsden into Fadiman's presence.

'Reception's good,' Pearson said as Fadiman greeted his

visitor with, 'You've recovered, I hope?'

'Recovered, sir?' Hillsden's voice sounded cautious.

'From that blow on the head you suffered for the cause.'

'Oh, that, yes. It wasn't anything too serious. The only after-effect was that my eyesight blurs from time to time. I shall have to get stronger glasses.'

'Good man,' Pearson muttered.

'Your first wound stripe, Robert,' Fadiman replied. 'You proved your worth. I flatter myself that I'm a good judge of character, and I was immediately taken by your positive attitude the first time we met. Did you know that?'

'Well, I hoped you were, yes.'

'Some of our flock are none too bright. We've made mistakes in the past . . . early on, when we were feeling our way. But you weren't one of them. I saw at once that you have a brain, Robert. That's what I was looking for. There is a time and place for brawn, and a time for guile.'

The expression struck a chord in Hillsden's memory and while he listened to Fadiman he strove to remember who had first said that to him.

'That's why,' Fadiman continued, 'I've brought you here tonight, to discuss a special mission. You're not married, are you, Robert?'

'Not any longer. My wife died.' He almost stumbled over the three words, wondering when, if ever, he would be free of the Judas factor.

'Perhaps it's not a bad thing to be unencumbered. I never married either. I've always felt it simplifies one's life not to have human emotional entanglements. That was Hitler's great strength, you know. It enabled him to see his destiny with crystal clarity. I know he married in the final hours, but the bunker ceremony was simply a symbolic act. Wagnerian in its beauty. He wished to show those who had abandoned him – that gross Goering especially, who revealed his true colours when the end was in sight – that there was still one person who would follow him to the grave. Do you appreciate that?'

'No,' Hillsden momentarily lost concentration, then recovered. 'Now you've explained it, I can see what you mean.'

Earphones on, Pearson grimaced. He gesticulated to Lloyd to put on his headset.

'Have you ever stopped to think, Robert, what our world would be like today if this country had been led by somebody of our vision? Instead of whole cities being polluted by the dregs of Africa and the Caribbean and television corrupting our minds with Hollywood's Jewish filth and Communist propaganda, we would have been cleansed of all that. You fought in the war, I believe?'

'Yes, towards the end.'

'I'm sure you were brainwashed to believe that it was a righteous war, like we all were. That we would triumphantly emerge into a brighter, more glorious future. But what did we get for our sacrifices? Fifty years of living under the threat of Stalinism, ourselves governed by crypto-Communists, the wealth of the Empire given away to black illiterates while we lived on handouts from the Americans. Do you wonder why I and others like me strive to keep the flame alight? You and I may not live to see the final solution, but at least we shall have played our part.'

There was a pause and then the listeners in the van heard Fadiman say, 'Can you hand me that lighter. Thank you.' His intake of breath as he dragged cigarette smoke into his lungs was clearly audible. 'You must forgive me. I have so much time, confined as I am, to think of what might have been. It obsesses me, Robert. I have these two wasted limbs but I am determined not to allow my grey matter to go the same way. The years are not on my side, that is why I have devoted myself to the furtherance of the cause . . . Forgive me, I'm forgetting my manners. Please pour yourself a drink.'

Pearson and Lloyd heard the sound of Hillsden's chair being scraped back and then the chink of a glass.

'How about you, sir?'

'Thank you, no. Alcohol doesn't sit well with the new

drugs I'm taking. Now, I'm sure you're wondering why I asked you here alone. I have a purpose, Robert.'

Pearson checked the recording machine and adjusted the volume.

'For some time now, I and others have been seeking a way of destabilising the present government. Our aim has always been to foment the sort of social unrest that would pave the way for our alternative. It's the classic route, Robert, as I'm sure you know, and I have studied the lessons of the masters. We've had our successes, but nothing that truly achieved the desired results. However, at long last I believe I have found the answer, but there is still some way to go before it can be put into effect. There is a role for you to play, Robert. An important . . . no, a vital role if you're prepared to accept it.'

'What does it involve?'

'I'm coming to that. Tony's death was a great loss to us, he was a key member of the planning committee. I have chosen you to take his place. You're going on a journey, Robert. To Copenhagen. There you will be met by our friend Harry and told the second part of the operation.'

'What exactly do I have to do?'

'Harry will tell you. It's a question of security, you appreciate.'

'Press him, press him,' Pearson muttered in the van.

'When do I go?'

'Tomorrow. We are working to a very tight schedule. I hope that doesn't present any problems?'

'No, I can report sick. How long will I be away?'

'Not long. If all goes well, you'll be back in two days. Your air ticket and a generous sum of money are on that table . . . You look worried, Robert.'

'No,' Hillsden said. 'Just taking it in. I'm just amazed, stunned that I've been chosen.'

'Yes, I thought you might be. But then, you see, you have special qualities for the return journey . . . An honest face, Robert.'

. . .

Hillsden thought: One can go for months without mishap – never breaking even a fingernail, never nicking the sleep-swollen flesh when shaving, living a placid, uneventful life – and then the razor slips, a hammer strikes a glancing blow, one trips on a loose paving stone, or there is a sudden stab of pain, and life changes.

Now, as he watched Galina and Lara drive away from the hotel in the American Embassy limousine, he asked himself: Am I for ever to carry an image of the faces of those I love disfigured by the agony of separation? I believed I was buying peace for all of us, but always there are deceptions to be practised, goodbyes to be said: peace was taking a late flight to Washington.

'You say you love us,' Galina had said, hunched on the hotel bed, 'and yet you do this to us.'

'Not me, them. They gave me no choices.'

'Them, it's always them. Couldn't you tell them that you've had enough, that you've done your bit?'

'My dear, it's not like that, not as simple as that,' he had said, and her pain travelled through him as though they were both touching the same electric wire. 'Don't let's quarrel in the little time we have left. I did what I thought was best for you. I wanted you both to be safe. And it won't be for ever, this agony will finish one day and then we'll be free.' The banality of his words, words that he had used too often to give comfort, sickened him; it seemed as though all he could ever give them both was not love but his own despair.

'If you're ever free,' Galina said.

Having watched the limousine pull out into the traffic, its darkened windows denying him a last glimpse of his wife and child, he carried the loss of them back into the hotel like excess luggage. He waited by the lifts in the crowded lobby, oblivious to those intent on the evening's pleasures, thinking back to what Galina had once said: *I don't know what's meant by happiness any more.* The lift doors slid open noiselessly.

391

Entering, he pressed the button that would take him to ar empty room.

A few minutes later, he stood staring at reminders of thei hurried departure – one of Lara's dolls lying on the floor in a position that reminded him of Audrey.

He began to pack a small overnight bag when there was a knock on the door and he admitted Victor.

'Did they get off?' Victor asked.

'Yes, they've gone.'

'I'm sure it was the best and wisest thing.'

'Yes.'

Victor looked at the half-packed bag. 'You don't have to go. Stay. You can stay here as long as you like. You need company at a time like this.'

Hillsden looked at him. 'No, I can't stay. Funny, isn't it, that you and I should end up friends, seeing as how we began?'

'Has something else happened?'

'Yes, but don't ask me what. You're a free man now, and you've done enough, don't get involved any further.'

Abramov embraced him. 'Alec, we're two of a kind, don't forget that. When we meet again, as we will, I'll make sure you get smart like me.'

. . .

For the umpteenth time Harry stared up at the arrivals board in Copenhagen's airport, searching for the latest information on the delayed British Airways flight. As he watched, the details were scrambled then rearranged, and to his relief he saw that it had finally landed. He took up a position by the barrier but it was still some twenty minutes before Hillsden came out of the customs hall.

'Christ! You gave me a bleedin' heart attack,' Harry said as they met. 'Come on, we've got to make up for lost time. Do you have luggage to collect?'

'No, only this.' Hillsden indicated his hand baggage.

'Good. You're learning. Luggage can be traced back to you.'
They threaded their way through the crowds and walked to a parking lot.

With Harry at the wheel of a British licensed Ford estate they took the scenic coast road, heading for Gilleleje, the small fishing port on the northern tip of Sealand.

During the journey Hillsden several times attempted to find out details of the next stage but Harry was deliberately vague. 'How long have you been over here then?'

'Enough to do the necessary.'

'And this place, what're we going there for?'

'We're meeting somebody who'll hand over a package which you'll be taking back to London.'

'Just me? You're not coming with me?'

'No. You'll be on your tod. Driving this.'

'Why's that then?'

'Because that's the way it's been planned.'

'What happens to you?'

'I make my own way back. Just follow the map, make sure we don't lose the way.'

They drove on into the gathering gloom and it was dark by the time they reached the outskirts of Gilleleje. 'We're meeting at a restaurant. I can't pronounce it, but it's marked in that guide, so keep your eyes peeled.'

'Hos Karen og Marie,' Hillsden read out an approximation of the name. 'It's got a good write-up, let's hope it lives up to it. I couldn't eat any of that plastic airline muck.'

'Eating's the least of our worries. Keep looking.'

They drove around until Hillsden spotted a sign giving the name of the restaurant on a two-storey, unpretentious wooden building facing the harbour. After parking the Ford on the quay, they went inside.

'What're you going to have?' Hillsden asked when they were seated. He studied the menu which featured a variety of fish dishes. 'Want to go for the house speciality?'

'What is it?'

'Fish.'

'Don't they have a burger?'

'Doesn't look like it.'

'Well, order that whatever it is then.'

'Want a beer with it?'

'I don't drink when I'm on a job. Nor do you.'

'Oh, right.'

When the meal came, Harry stared at the unfamiliar fish on his plate with deep suspicion. 'What is this?'

'No idea, smells good, though.' Hillsden tucked in. 'Any special reason why you chose this place?'

'I didn't choose it, dummy. Fadiman did. According to him it's got symbolic associations.'

'Really, how's that then?'

'During the war the Jews used it as an escape route to Sweden. That appealed to him.'

'He's clever, isn't he?' Hillsden said, wiping his mouth. 'Generous, too. You should see the money he gave me, just for a couple of days.'

'Not his dosh, is it? He just hands it on.' All the time Harry's eyes were on the entrance. He looked at his watch. 'He should have been here by now.'

'D'you know what he looks like?'

'No idea.'

'How will you recognise him then?'

'How d'you think? He'll make himself known with a password.'

Always careful to portray himself as a novice in such matters, yet at the same time wanting to gain Harry's approval by flattering him, Hillsden nodded sagely. 'I see. Of course, I should have known you'd have thought of everything.'

The flattery worked and for the first time since they had set out from Copenhagen, Harry dropped his bombastic pose. 'Well, some of us have done this sort of thing before, you know.'

After a pause and while wiping his plate with a piece of bread, Hillsden tried to capitalise on this opening. 'Whose money is it then, any idea? Stands to reason, running an organisation like this must cost a bomb.'

'Yeah, you can say that again. Know how much I've got on me?'

'No. Tell me.'

'Fifty grand.'

'Get away!'

Harry nodded and patted his waist.

'And you got it through? You were lucky not to be searched when you left.'

'I didn't have it when I left, did I? Picked it up in Luxembourg.'

'Fifty grand!' Hillsden said. 'God, they must trust you.'

'Yeah, well, I'm part of the inner-circle, aren't I?'

'Who keeps that sort of money in his bank account?'

'Somebody who isn't short of a few. Ever heard of a man called Charters?' Harry asked, now unable to resist airing his superior knowledge.

'No.'

'Very big and out of your league. Goes everywhere by private jet.'

'And is he the one who bankrolls us?'

'He's our principal backer, yeah. But that's not for everybody to know.'

'No, of course not. It's safe with me.'

Suddenly Harry's expression changed. 'Hold it, this could be our man. Don't look round, just act normal.'

A man roughly the same age as Harry, blond, Nordic, tanned, approached their table and then seemed inadvertently to knock against it as he passed. He stopped and apologised, first in Swedish and then in sing-song English. 'Please, excuse my clumsiness.'

Harry replied: 'You're welcome,' and the man continued on to the bar. As soon as he had gone Harry motioned for Hillsden to get up and leave. They paid the bill and went outside to the van to wait. Some ten minutes later the man joined them and climbed inside.

'Any problems?' Harry asked him.

'No problems, but I must explain,' he said. He took two four-packs of lager from his plastic bag, handling them with care. Upturning the packs he displayed them to Harry and Hillsden. All eight cans were marked with a black cross. 'Important precaution. They've been primed then resealed under high pressure, but they're completely safe until opened. Even so, always treat them with respect.'

Harry took the packs from him and examined them gingerly, studying the authentic Tuborg logo. 'Neat. Very neat,' he said. 'Your people do a good job.' He put the packs beside him on the seat, unzipped his security belt and took out a wad of notes. 'Fifty thousand, as agreed.'

The man checked them slowly. 'Yes,' he said finally. 'Correct. Thank you. Have a safe journey home.'

He opened the passenger door and was gone.

'What exactly did he mean when he said, "primed"?' Hillsden asked. 'Are they bombs?'

'Of a kind.' Harry placed both packs inside a cardboard box filled with wood shavings and made sure they were secure. 'A very special kind, so treat them with respect.'

'Semtex?'

'You don't know much, do you? That's plastic, you don't need to put that in tins under pressure.'

'I thought perhaps it had been done like that so that we could smuggle it in.'

'No, Semtex is yesterday's news. This is canned gas. You've heard of Sarin, haven't you?'

'The stuff they used on the Tokyo underground?'

'Ten out of ten.'

'Christ! For us to use?'

'That's the idea. So, let's get going.' He checked the box once more. 'And you can drive the first leg, but take it easy.'

On the return journey to Copenhagen, Hillsden kept his questions down to the minimum, anxious not to press too hard, but wanting to find out as much as he could while Harry was in his current expansive mode. 'They must want this stuff for something special if they've paid fifty thousand for it,' he said at one point.

'Yeah, they haven't told me the exact details yet, but it's big, I know that. Fadiman dreamed it up, apparently, or so Johnny told me.'

'He seems a bit out of place, that Johnny. I mean, he's not like the rest of us.'

'He's an iron, if you ask me.'

'Iron?'

'Iron hoof – poof. Haven't you heard that before?'

'I see. D'you think Fadiman is, too, then?'

'Doubt it. I don't think he does anything except sit there and dream up ideas.'

'Like this one. Wonder what he's got in mind?'

'We'll find out soon enough,' Harry said.

They parted company at Copenhagen airport where, for the second time, Harry went over the details for the rest of Hillsden's journey. 'So, have you got it straight? Here's your ticket and the booking for the hovercraft. Be sure you make that particular time. That's important, because you'll be met at Dover.'

'By you?'

'Maybe, maybe not. Here's the money, some Deutschmarks, most of it in Francs to buy the rest of the beer. You know how to pack it?'

'Yes,' Hillsden said. 'I take out two packs and replace them with the phoney ones, then reseal the case.'

'You got it.'

'If I'm asked in Customs, I came over to buy stuff for my granddaughter's wedding.'

'Good. If you stop anywhere for a bite, make sure the car's locked and parked where you can see it all the time.'

'Will do.'

'Good luck.'

Harry disappeared into the airport terminal.

. . .

Hillsden drove at a steady speed until he crossed the border into Germany and took the autobahn. He kept careful watch in his mirrors all the time in case Harry was having him tailed, but saw nothing to arouse his suspicions. He stopped at the first service station he came to, locked the van, purchased coffee and food, then made a telephone call from a public booth.

Swanson answered. As briefly as he could, Hillsden gave him details of his return trip to Dover, together with a description and registration number of the car. 'The cargo is volatile, so needs careful handling at your end.'

'Understood,' Swanson said. 'Are you on your own?'

'At the moment, yes. My companion flew back earlier. But he or somebody else will meet me on arrival.'

'Nothing else?'

'Yes, tell Pearson I finally found out who paid for my trip. Tell him his hunch was right.'

'You've done well. Good man, congratulations. Travel safely.'

It was only after he had resumed his journey that it occurred to Hillsden that praise coming from Swanson was out of character.

44

A GAS LEAK

'I think it would be dangerous to take them in the actual terminal, in view of what Hillsden said.' Swanson looked around the assembled company. 'He described the cargo as "volatile" and my reading of that is they're bringing in some type of explosive. I would have thought – and, of course, I defer to you, Commissioner – that our best bet would be to set up road blocks a mile or so out on all roads leading from Dover, and intercept them there. Less danger to the public. I think it's a fair assumption they'll be heading for London.'

The Commissioner of Police considered this. 'Yes, I think that's probably a wise move. D'you agree, Commander?'

Pearson nodded. 'Yes. Yes, I do.' He looked to Lloyd, seeking his approval too. For once, he thought, Swanson has had a good idea.

'I'll put Robertson in the picture immediately,' the Commissioner added, naming the Chief Constable of the Kent constabulary, 'and ask him to put a maximum force at your disposal, including armed units.' He went to the map. 'They'll need to cover the A2, the A20 and the A256. Is he coming across by ferry or hovercraft?'

'Hovercraft.'

'They'd better post somebody in Customs who can confirm he's arrived.'

'You should also inform the Kent lot that it's our man driving the car. If it comes to a shooting match, we don't want

Hillsden taken out,' Pearson warned.

'No, that's a very good point,' Swanson said. 'But let's hope it won't turn into a shooting match.'

'Since our team are the only ones who can identify Hillsden,' Pearson added, 'one of us should be at every road block.'

'And at Customs,' Lloyd interjected.

Swanson said, 'I'll take Customs.'

'How long have we got?'

'Just over fourteen hours. Hillsden's booking is for the last departure of the day from Calais.'

'Then I suggest we get cracking,' the Commissioner said. 'Commander, if you'd like to come with me, we'll start to put this thing together.'

Pearson paused at the door. 'That's all Hillsden told you, is it?'

'Yes, just the bare details. He obviously didn't want to elaborate over the phone,' Swanson said evenly.

'Right,' Pearson said after a pause, then followed the Commissioner out.

'It seems we're near the end,' Swanson said.

'Let's hope so,' Lloyd answered but, like Pearson, there was a note of uncertainty in his reply.

. . .

Hillsden arrived at Calais with nearly two hours to spare before his hovercraft departure. As instructed, he visited one of the numerous warehouses selling discounted beer and wine to eager day-trippers out for a bargain. There he purchased a quantity of Tuborg four-packs, together with two crates of sparkling wine, before joining the line of cars and trucks awaiting to board the *Princess Margaret*.

As luck would have it, the Channel was like a mill pond and the crossing remarkably smooth. Spot checks were being carried out by Customs at Dover and he was one of those stopped. The Preventive Officer had the look of a man who had heard and seen it all before. Opening the tailgate, he examined the crates of beer and wine.

'These for personal use?'

'Yes. Not that I'm going to drink the lot,' Hillsden said, 'though I dare say I'll have my fair share. Got my granddaughter's wedding coming off next week and this is my contribution. Grandads always have to cough up, don't they?'

'I wouldn't know,' the Preventive Officer said, 'I'm not even a father. Anything else?'

'No.'

He walked around the vehicle and peered inside. 'Okay, good luck next week.' He moved to the next vehicle.

As Hillsden climbed back behind the driving wheel he thought he saw Swanson standing in the window of the Customs shed, but with other cars behind him anxious to get going, he couldn't be certain. Just outside the Customs area he spotted Harry waiting for him and pulled alongside.

'You made it then?'

'Yes. That was a good tip of yours about the wedding.'

'Trust me and you won't go far wrong.' Harry got into the passenger seat. 'I'm full of good ideas,' he said. 'Come on, don't let's hang about.' He looked into the back of the car as they moved off. 'Where did you put the stuff?'

'The crate next to the wine.'

'Right, do just as I say and keep alert.'

'Where are we heading for?'

'Just do as I say,' Harry repeated in a flat voice, 'take a left here.'

Hillsden did as instructed. His eyes flicked to the rear-view mirror. A motorcycle seemed to be hanging on their tail some hundred yards behind.

'Now take another left,' Harry commanded. Hillsden noted that Harry's eyes never left the side mirror.

When they reached a large intersection, instead of taking one of the main roads out of Dover, Harry ordered him to turn

left on to the secondary B2011, heading in the direction o
Folkestone. Checking his mirror again, Hillsden saw that the
motorcycle was still following them.

They proceeded through the suburbs with Hillsder
keeping to the reduced speed limits. He sensed that Harry
was tensed, waiting for something to happen. They wen
another half a mile, entering a stretch of road where the speec
limit was increased to forty mph.

'Put your foot down,' Harry commanded. 'Go!'

The car lurched forward as Hillsden did as he was told.

'Be ready to make a fast turn to the right in about a hundred
yards, after the next set of lights.'

Hillsden checked his mirror again: the motorcyclist was
still behind them in the stream of traffic. The traffic lights
changed to amber as they approached.

'Keep going, jump the lights,' Harry said, and Hillsder
obeyed, crossing the intersection on red. He noted that the
traffic behind them was stationary.

'Now!' Harry shouted, 'and flash your headlights twice.'

Hillsden made an acute right turn and found they were in a
cul-de-sac. Straight ahead were two large wooden gates
Seconds after he gave the signal with his headlights, the gates
were opened.

'Drive straight in and up the ramp into the truck.'

Now they were inside the forecourt of what appeared to be
a factory where several men stood waiting beside a large
furniture pantechnicon, with its rear doors open. Two
wooden planks formed a ramp leading up into the belly of the
pantechnicon. Hillsden gunned the car up and drove inside
The doors were immediately closed behind them.

'Out you get,' Harry said. He dived into the back of the car
to lift the crate containing the doctored beer cans.

Climbing out of the estate and exiting through the cabin of
the pantechnicon, Hillsden now saw that a Bentley turbo with
darkened windows was parked nearby. It faced the exit, had
its engine running and the boot open. The ramp was already
being removed as Harry joined him and placed the crate in

the boot.

'Get behind the wheel, and put that chauffeur's cap on,' Harry said, as he got into the rear of the Bentley.

Somebody shouted, 'All clear.'

'Let's go.'

Unaccustomed to the power of the Bentley, Hillsden shot forward and only just missed hitting one of the main gates. He righted it with a touch of the power steering and they surged clear.

'Turn right,' Harry instructed. 'And head for Folkestone, but ease off, keep to the limits. Act like a fucking chauffeur.'

'Jesus,' Hillsden said, 'this thing has a mind of its own.'

'Bet you never thought you'd be driving something like this.'

'No.'

'He's got two.'

'Who has?'

'Charters. Know what they cost? With the extras he's got on his, you don't get any change out of a hundred and eighty. So make sure you don't bang it.'

'That was neat back there,' Hillsden said.

'Yeah. Worked a treat. And the last thing they'll be looking for is a Bentley.'

. . .

'What d'you mean, you've lost them?' Swanson shouted into the phone. 'It's pathetic.'

The Kent Superintendent at the other end of the line did his best to remain polite. 'All I can say is, sir, they didn't pass any of our road blocks. The car was tailed but contact was lost on the Folkestone Road, which we were not instructed to cover. Immediately we were informed we cordoned off the entire area, and are still carrying out searches. But so far nothing.'

'Well, you'd better come up with something, that's all I can say.' Swanson slammed down the phone.

. . .

Once on the M20 motorway, Hillsden was urged to put his foot down, and despite the situation he found himself in he derived some pleasure from the joy of driving the Bentley. He was forced to slacken speed again when they joined the heavier traffic on the M25 and headed north.

'Where are we aiming for?' he questioned.

'You'll see soon enough. Pull into the next service station, I have to make a phone call.'

'Why stop? Use the car phone.'

'They can be tapped. Don't you know anything?'

If Hillsden thought he would have a chance to make use of the car phone himself, he was immediately denied this when they pulled into the service area.

'Give me the key,' Harry said when they both got out. He locked the car and pocketed the key. 'Stay with it.' He walked inside. Hillsden thought quickly. Taking a discarded wrapper from a rubbish bin he wrote Pearson's telephone number and in capitals underneath, POLICE EMERGENCY. RING THIS NUMBER AND GIVE MESSAGE: 'GET CHARTERS, YOU WERE RIGHT'. He stuck this on the windscreen of a nearby saloon car, securing it under the wiper blade. It was a forlorn hope, but the best he could do.

Harry returned a few minutes later and they resumed their journey.

'There's been a change of plan. We're not going into town, it's considered too risky. Seems somebody tipped them off. Keep going until you hit the M4, then head for Reading to begin with.'

'Who could have tipped them off?'

'That's a good question which needs to be answered,' Harry said flatly. 'Keep your eyes peeled for any sign of the fuzz.'

'I've been doing that already,' Hillsden said.

. . .

'Don't take it out on me,' Pearson said. 'None of us fucked up. You say you definitely saw him come off the hovercraft.'

'Yes,' Swanson said.

'Was he on his own?'

'At that point, yes.'

'Nobody met him?'

'I didn't see anybody.'

'It seems likely somebody did. Otherwise Hillsden would have acted on his own initiative.'

'You think so?'

'Don't you?'

'I'm not sure. I've had doubts about Hillsden in recent weeks. What if they've got to him?'

'If they've got to him why would he contact you to arrange a reception committee? That doesn't add up.'

'Nothing adds up at the moment except I shall be carrying the can back for a total cock-up. It just seems too fortuitous that they elected to take the one route we didn't have covered, and apparently the Kent police only put one unmarked motorcycle cop on his tail. The bloody fool lost him.'

'Perhaps the idea of road blocks wasn't so good after all.'

'We can all be wise after the event. I acted as I thought the situation demanded.'

'Absolutely. But as you've often remarked, you're running the show and the buck stops with you,' Pearson said, finally sticking his own knife in. 'So, is it back to the old drawing board? What's your next move?'

'The priority is to find Hillsden, I should have thought that was obvious.'

'Yes,' Pearson replied, 'but it's the obvious we often overlook, isn't it?'

. . .

The Bentley eased its way past the electric gates of Charters's mansion and parked next to a London taxi.

'Some pad,' Hillsden said admiringly as he switched off the engine and applied the brake.

'Yeah. Don't forget when you meet him, he's a fucking Knight, so be respectful. Open the boot.'

Harry went to the rear of the car and removed the carton containing the cans of Sarin, treating it with respect. To Hillsden's surprise the front door was opened by Hyde.

'Oh, good, you're out,' Hillsden said.

'Yes, been out some time. They dropped all charges in the end. Course, I was provided with a good lawyer.' He admitted them into the hallway. 'How are you after your travels?'

'Fine.'

'Mission accomplished, we understand. Is that the cargo?'

'Yeah, eight of the little beauties,' Harry replied. 'They should put a few to sleep come the day.'

Hyde escorted them across the hallway to Charters's study, allowing Harry to precede him into the room. As Hillsden followed the other two he saw Fadiman swing round in his wheelchair and beyond him another man he took to be Charters.

'Raymond, I don't think you've met Harry and Robert before,' Fadiman said, making the introductions.

'No. But I understand congratulations are in order.'

'Thank you, Sir Raymond,' Harry spoke for both of them. 'Where would you like me to put these, sir?'

'Oh, on that table. Let me make room.'

Harry put the carton down on a round Georgian gaming table which held several piles of leatherbound books. He took out one of the beer cans as Charters, Fadiman and Hyde gathered round.

'They look harmless enough,' Charters said. 'And very authentic.'

'I thought they'd do a good job,' Fadiman leaned in and picked up the can. 'Our German comrades said the Swedish chapter could be relied upon. I think we're going to make history with these.'

'Don't shake it,' Charters admonished, and took a step backwards.

'Oh, they're quite safe until opened, sir.'

'Even so, let's not press our luck.'

'Any problems on the way here?' Hyde asked.

'No. It all worked a treat.'

'And, you Robert . . . ' Fadiman turned to Hillsden, 'did you enjoy the trip?'

'Yes. Especially driving the Bentley.'

'Ah, yes, that was an extra perk, I'm sure. You performed admirably . . . except in one respect.'

He was still smiling, but Hillsden became conscious that the other three men in the room were staring at him.

'What was that, Mr Fadiman?'

'I think you know, Robert.'

Hillsden felt somebody else come into the room behind him.

'A certain phone call you made, Robert, which had it not been received by the right person would have damned all our plans.'

'Phone call? I didn't make a phone call, that was Harry, wasn't it, Harry?'

But Harry just stared at him without answering. Harry knew his place.

'It's somewhat too late for bluffing, Alec,' Fadiman continued, and the first use of his real name hung in the air between them. 'You see, we know who you are, we've always known. But we thought it a pity not to make some use of you before we discarded you. This seemed an appropriate occasion, an extra precaution on our side should anything go wrong . . . Being in the insurance business, Alec, you should have anticipated that.'

Hillsden took a step backwards and turned, only to find the ubiquitous Johhny in the doorway with a gun in his hand.

'Good try, dear,' Johhny said.

. . .

Pearson and Lloyd had not been back in the office long when the phone rang. Pearson picked up the receiver.

'I'm sorry, who d'you want? . . . Yes, you have the right number, but who d'you want to speak to, Madam? . . . I can't say until you tell me what this call is about . . .' He gesticulated at Lloyd and put the call on the speaker phone.

'I see . . . and where was this you say?'

The woman's voice answered: 'At a service station on the M25. I found it stuck on my windscreen when I came out. I thought it was a joke, but when I got home my husband said I should ring, seeing as how it said police.'

'No, you did quite right. Tell me again what was written.'

Pearson reached for a pen.

'Police emergency. Ring this number and give message: "Get Charters, you were right." '

'Charters?'

'Yes.'

'Spelt C-h-a-r-t-e-r-s?'

'Yes.'

'Nothing else?'

'No, that's all there was.'

'And how long ago was this?'

'About three hours ago.' They heard her saying something to her husband. 'Yes, that would be about it.'

'Well, I'm most grateful. You did the right thing.'

'*Are* you the police?'

'Yes, we are. My name is Commander Pearson. Could I have your name, Madam?'

'Thomas. Mrs Thomas.'

'And your number, should we wish to contact you again?' He wrote it down. 'I more than appreciate your co-operation, Mrs Thomas, very public-spirited of you. Thank you so much, you did the right thing.'

He hung up.

'It has to have been Hillsden.'

'Yes,' Lloyd said. 'The timing fits.'

'So what about an apology?'

'Okay, so your hunch about Charters was correct.'

'Don't overwhelm me with congratulations, will you?'

'Okay,' Lloyd repeated. 'I admit you're a genius, Holmes, I'm just slow on the uptake.'

'The fact that Alec resorted to such a chancy, desperate tactic means he wasn't alone. By a piece of good luck he stuck the message on the right windshield and our Mrs Thomas came through . . . But where is the poor sod now? And what were they bringing over?' Pearson asked, thinking aloud.

45

SOLUTIONS

Rendered secure and immobile, bound and gagged with nearly an entire roll of wide-gauge industrial tape, Hillsden was locked in a wooden gazebo that stood at the end of a herbaceous border in Charters's extensive grounds.

'However you dispose of him, I want no knowledge of it,' Charters said. 'There can be no question of any connection with me or this house, is that clearly understood?'

'Totally,' Fadiman said. 'I think you know me better than that, Raymond.'

'I'll leave you to it, then. I've got other business to attend to. Help yourselves to drinks, but make it quick. The sooner he's off the premises, the better. Whatever you decide, I want it done tonight.'

About to leave the room, he paused, looking at the cans on his Georgian table. 'Those too. I want those removed.'

'Of course, Raymond.'

'The first question we have to ask,' Fadiman began when Charters had gone, 'is whether Hillsden is worth more to us alive or dead?'

'Dead,' Harry said.

'Yes, just curb your natural instincts, Harry, and think it through. Swanson's original plan, which we all went along with, and which had a certain logic to it, was cunning in the extreme. Give me a light, Harry, I think better with a cigarette in my mouth.'

Harry obliged.

'In order to service us, he needed a go-between. That protected him and also was intended to provide a scapegoat if necessary. This Hillsden fitted the bill perfectly. A man with a history of defection. A man at one time wanted for murder. A man, it could easily be believed, intent on revenge against an establishment that had deprived him of his freedom. Swanson parlayed that through with his superiors employing his usual skill, and it certainly worked as intended. We were always kept fully informed of any progress they made. Admittedly, there was a blip.'

'Remind me, what was that?' Hyde asked.

'Carstairs committing suicide.'

'Oh, yeah, that's right.'

'Had Harry taken care of him we would have been spared Pearson's enquiries. Sir Raymond ordered him to return to Copenhagen, and Harry would have taken him out there, as he did Van Elst. That way it would have looked like just another homosexual murder, no big deal. Dying here led the danger man, Pearson, to instigate a line of enquiries which could well have led back to our host. He got very close. Only quick thinking on Swanson's part prevented him finding the last pieces of the puzzle.'

'Let's get back to Hillsden,' Harry said. 'You heard what Sir said, he wants him out of here.'

'All right, Harry, all right, don't tell me what to do. A hasty decision now could ruin everything.'

'Top him, that's the best thing.'

'You could be right, but where and how?'

'I know what I'd do.'

'So tell us.'

'Test one of these cans on him. We've got eight, more than enough, let's see if they work. Better find out now rather than later.'

Fadiman waved his cigarette holder and Hyde was immediately there with an ashtray. 'You've got such an evil mind, Harry. That must be why I'm fond of you, despite your obvious shortcomings. Well, now, let's consider that. Where?'

'That's no problem. I know places.'

'Such as?'

'Disused lock-up garage. Plenty of those around. Or better still, a condemned tower block. Put him in one of those, they wouldn't find him for months. Probably blow it up before they found him.'

Fadiman nodded. 'And you'd take care of it?'

'Be a pleasure.'

'Let me be devil's advocate. Bear with me, I'm not pouring cold water on your solution, I think it has considerable merit But let me go back to my original question: is he worth more to us alive?'

He looked from Harry to Hyde, but neither ventured an opinion. 'You're not sure. Neither am I. On balance, I think he's better dead. My only concern is a worst scenario, where Swanson is exposed. The contingency in his plan was always that, in such a scenario, he could hide behind Hillsden, reveal him as the mole.'

'If Hillsden's dead that could still work,' Hyde said.

'Yes, you're right. Well, now, do we vote on it?' Fadiman extinguished his cigarette. 'Harry?'

'Well, you know my vote. Whichever way you look at it, alive, he's a liability. Just leave it to me.'

'Very well, I'll go along with that. We do, after all, have other pressing matters. And I agree it would be highly sensible to test the material before the day.'

'What is the day?' Hyde asked. 'Am I entitled to know now?'

'It's a special day,' Fadiman said. 'The start of the Notting Hill Carnival. Where better to make our statement?'

'Oh, boner!' Hyde said. 'Brilliant!'

'Thank you. Now, before you deal with our friend Hillsden, let's remove those. Hyde, you'd better take charge of them and arrange distribution.'

'Except two,' Harry put in. 'One for him outside and one for me.'

'Yes, fine. One last thing, Harry. As an extra precaution, I don't want you to go back to your own place until this is over.' He produced some keys from a pocket. 'I keep a small cubbyhole in Greek Street, which I want you to use. Stay out of sight until the day. We'll get all the final details to you there.' He held out the keys. 'The number's on the tag; one key for the front door, the other for my flat on the top floor. You'll find everything you need there, Johnny keeps it well stocked.'

He watched as both men carefully removed the cans. 'Oh, and Harry,' he said as they reached the door, 'don't forget, I shall be anxiously awaiting your call about the result of the test. A lot hangs on it.'

. . .

'Now what?' Lloyd asked. 'Why're you undecided? Let's go.'

'Just had a thought. Why did he give my number, not Swanson's?'

'First one he thought of probably.'

'I wonder,' Pearson mused. 'Something Swanson said keeps coming back to me. That he was having doubts about Hillsden. Yet he was happy for Hillsden to go back into the lion's den. The two things don't add up. Unless . . . '

'What?'

'Let me think. What if he knows more than we do?'

'Who're we talking about now?'

'Hillsden. Keep up with me. What if he deliberately contacted me, instead of Swanson? What does that tell you?'

'I don't know what you're getting at.'

'It makes me think he had a good reason. Who has consistently kept us from moving on Fadiman and Charters?' He looked straight at Lloyd. 'Swanson, right? Who thought of the road block scheme and then put himself at the point of entry? Swanson again.'

'But the whole scheme was Swanson's baby from the start. Like you said, he's an arse-licker out for number one. Why would he sabotage it when we're in sight of the end? Much more likely he wants to grab all the kudos for himself.'

Pearson took two of his stomach tablets, always a sign, Lloyd recognised, that he was agitated. 'I know what first sent the warning lights flashing, but stupidly I put it out of my mind.'

'What?'

'The missing Kell files. Who had them last? Swanson again.' Pearson strode across the room and hit his forehead with one open palm somewhat melodramatically. 'I'm so bloody dense, no wonder I'm near retirement . . . Of course, of course . . . Get the DG on the blower.'

'The DG?'

'Never mind, I'll do it myself.' He picked up the phone and dialled an unlisted number.

'What're you ringing him for?'

'If I can convince him I'm right I'll need his authority to obtain the warrants.'

'Convince him about what?'

'That we've been leaking like a sieve,' Pearson said as he fretted for his call to be answered.

. . .

Trussed like a chicken, Hillsden lay face downwards on the warehouse floor, painfully inching his way towards the sheet of corrugated iron. At the back of his mind was the hope that he could find a jagged edge against which he could scrape away at his bonds. The effort cost him dear and he had to rest and recover after every heave. He persisted until he was only a foot or so away from the door, his clothes soaked in what, from the smell, he took to be diesel oil. It was now that he felt something cold fall on the back of his head; the sensation was repeated a few seconds later, then at closer intervals. He managed to roll over on to his back after three attempts and stared up at the corrugated iron roof. There were gaps in it

414

and he could see a glow in the night sky. It was raining and water dripped down, now splattering his face.

At that moment the door was unlocked; it struck him a glancing blow as it was pushed inwards.

'Oh, trying to make a run for it, were you, Dad?' Harry said. 'Bit late for that. You're not going anywhere.' He bent down and carefully placed a beer can containing the Sarin on the floor, then dragged Hillsden to the far end of the warehouse, turning him over on to his stomach again.

'I've brought you your Horlicks, to make sure you get a good night.'

He laughed at his own joke and, grabbing Hillsden by the hair, twisted his head round so that he could see the can.

'There it is. I thought we'd test whether it's past its sell-by date. Want to be sure that the carnival goes with a swing, don't we? Put all those nig-nogs to sleep. Pity you won't be there to see it.'

Harry retrieved the can, then produced a dampened teacloth with which he covered his mouth and nose. Taking a deep breath and holding it, he knelt down, gripped the can with one hand and pulled the catch open. There was a hiss as the pressure was released. Harry quickly got to his feet and backed out.

. . .

After a stall of nearly two hours, during which time there were a series of urgent debates between the DG and an extremely dubious Home Secretary who refused to take a decision until the matter had been agreed by Downing Street, authority was finally given and warrants issued for Pearson and his teams to go into action. Backed by armed units from the Met and three county police forces, the raids were to be carried out simultaneously once Pearson, who had claimed the right to arrest Charters, had his unit in position in North Stoke. Rotherby headed those going after Fadiman, while

415

Lloyd and Hadley accompanied the units seeking to take Hyde and Harry. At top level it had been agreed that, to thwart any possible tip-off, no move would be taken against Swanson until the first swoops had netted the other players. Swanson's apartment block in Pimlico was cordoned off by a force from Special Branch who were poised to go in once the signal had been given. It was emphasised to all concerned that the number two priority was to locate Hillsden. In every case, the warrants had been issued on conspiracy charges under The Defence of the Realm Act.

It was raining steadily when Pearson's group, numbering twenty men, arrived in North Stoke. All but one of their vehicles were parked at a discreet distance from Charters's house, and half the force dispersed to cover the walled perimeter of the grounds. Pearson, together with four armed policemen, including a Chief Inspector, was poised outside the main gates in a Range Rover. To achieve maximum surprise the wall was scaled and the automatic gate mechanism activated from the inside. As the gates began to swing open, security lights illuminated the entire area and alarm sirens sounded. The Range Rover accelerated through and surged towards the house, followed by the remainder of the police.

Pearson was first out as the Range Rover scattered the gravel drive by the entrance to the house. A startled manservant was brushed aside the moment he opened the front door, and as Pearson and the Inspector entered the hallway Charters, in a dressing gown, appeared at the top of the staircase. He stopped, staring at the armed police confronting him and his manservant spreadeagled on the hall floor.

'What's this all about? How dare you come bursting in like this.'

The Chief Inspector stepped forward. 'Sir Raymond Charters?'

'Yes, what of it?'

'I hold a warrant for your arrest, sir, and must duly caution

ou that you have the right to remain silent, but that anything
ou do say can be . . . '

Charters cut him short. 'Don't spout that garbage at me.
This is an outrage. You'll be chopped for this, all of you.'

Unimpressed, the Chief Inspector went back over the same
ground. 'Anything you do say can be used in evidence
against you. Do you understand your rights?'

'I bloody well do and I demand the right to ring my
solicitor.'

'You'll be granted facilities at the station, sir, once you've
been formally charged.'

'Charged with what?'

'Conspiracy under The Defence of the Realm Act, sir. Now,
if you'd like to get dressed and accompany us . . . '

'And what if I refuse?'

'Then I'll have no alternative but to handcuff you, sir, and
take you as you are.' He nodded to two of his men who
moved to the staircase. It was only now that Charters
appeared to recognise Pearson.

'I know you, you're that bloody MI6 type who came to my
office.'

'How good of you to remember a face on such short
acquaintance, Carl,' Pearson said evenly. 'Perhaps you'd
prefer to be charged under your born name of Hain?' He
turned and spoke into his mobile phone, 'North Stoke
achieved, all units go.'

As Charters went back up the stairway followed by the two
armed officers, Pearson addressed him again.

'There is one thing that would stand in your favour. We're
anxious to know the present whereabouts of one of my
officers, Alec Hillsden. You know him as Robert Bartlett.'

Charters paused halfway up the staircase. 'You're wasting
your time. I have no knowledge of the man under either
name.'

'Just as you have no knowledge of making payments to the
late Mr Carstairs,' Pearson answered, getting in the last word.

Hadley and his team were not so lucky: they found Harry's flat bare and despite being relentlessly turned over it offered up no clues as to the whereabouts of its absent owner. Apart from a few soiled articles of clothing discarded on the bathroom floor, there was little to indicate human habitation. The small refrigerator encrusted with ice in the sordid kitchen contained only a stiffened portion of pizza and a carton of stale milk. There wasn't even a torn piece of paper in the waste bin.

Deflated by the lack of success, Hadley ordered the broken door to be secured and returned to base.

Rotherby, on the other hand, encountered no problems when arresting Fadiman and Johnny. In view of his disability, once charged Fadiman was remanded to the hospital wing at Brixton. After being allowed to consult his lawyers, he declined to answer any questions. Bail was refused.

Once confirmation had been relayed to the Yard that both Fadiman and Charters were in custody, two senior officers from MI5 detained Swanson. He offered no resistance and was taken to a house in the Home Counties to begin prolonged sessions of interrogation.

. . .

Meanwhile it was Lloyd and his team who came away with the most valuable piece of the puzzle.

Arriving outside Hyde's house, they were relieved to find the area deserted save for two stray dogs circling each other around a broken street lamp, bent over the road like a wilted sunflower.

Drawing their guns, the team went past Hyde's parked car to the front door, treading carefully. Lloyd had already detailed two of his men to cover the rear of the house. Two more took up positions on either side of the front door before he hammered on it. After a pause a light came on and they heard the sound of somebody descending the stairs.

A voice said: 'Who is it?'

'Me, Harry,' Lloyd answered in a passable Cockney accent. 'Let me in, I'm in trouble.'

A bolt was shot back, then a key turned in the lock. As the door opened a fraction the two armed policemen lunged forward, knocking Hyde backwards. Before he could recover, they and Lloyd were inside and had slammed the door shut.

'What the fuck?' Hyde exclaimed. He was wearing only a pair of striped boxer shorts.

'Check the upstairs,' Lloyd ordered, and one of the men went in search.

'Now then, sunshine,' Lloyd pushed Hyde against the wall. 'We want to know what happened to Bartlett.'

'I don't know any fucking Bartlett.'

'I have a warrant here which says you do, that you're part of a conspiracy aimed at threatening Her Majesty's realm. Shall I read you your rights?'

'Get lost!'

'No, let's do it by the book.' Lloyd recited the statutory caution, then they backed Hyde at gunpoint into the living room. 'Sit down. Now if you tell us what we want to know I might be persuaded to give you a character reference.'

'I don't have to tell you pricks anything.'

'It's all over, sunshine. Nobody's going to help you but me. So start thinking of yourself, use what little grey matter you possess and do yourself a favour.'

'Go fuck yourself.'

'You're becoming monotonous.'

The policeman returned from searching the upstairs area. 'No sign of him up there.'

'Right, well, tear the rest of the place apart and have your chums outside go over the garden.'

'I'll have you lot for this,' Hyde snarled.

'Don't bank on it. You won't be out in time to get me. I'll be dead before you breathe fresh air again. You're looking at life and no remissions.'

'That meant to frighten me?'

'Where's Bartlett?'

'I've told you, I've never heard of him.'

'But you've heard of Gauleiter Fadiman, haven't you? And Reich Chancellor Sir Raymond.'

'No, nor them neither.'

'That's funny, they know you.'

'You can bluff all night, you won't get anything out of me,' Hyde said, but a hint of uncertainty had crept into his voice.

'Well, I'm in no hurry. You keep a pet parrot I see. Bartlet told us about that. Looks as though its battery's dead. Shal we try again? Where's Bartlett? The sooner you tell me the sooner we can get you tucked up in a nice warm cell.'

'Get fucked.'

'You know, sooner or later we're going to have to teach you some manners. I'm starting to be offended. But I'm a patient man and I've got nowhere else to go. Matter of fact I could do with a drink while I'm waiting. D'you mind if I help myself to something?' He went to the fridge. 'Oh, dear, proper old Mother Hubbard, aren't you? Just one can of beer, so I can't ask you to join me.'

Lloyd took the can out of the fridge and curled a finger inside the ring on the lid. Hyde jumped up, gabbling. 'Don't touch that! Please, for fuck's sake don't open that thing . . . I'l tell you everything, just put that down! Put it down!' The startling change in him and the sheer panic in his voice as he backed away into a corner took Lloyd by surprise. Puzzled by the hysterical reaction, he studied the can more closely.

'What have we here then?'

'Don't mess with it, please. Do as I say, for God's sake . . . I will talk, but first put it down.' All his previous bravado had disappeared and his shout suddenly activated the mechanical parrot: the beak opened and closed and it repeated 'put it down'

Lloyd placed the can on the coffee table between them. It was only now that Hyde visibly relaxed.

'Okay, sunshine, how's that? Now, start talking.'

. . .

Events moved quickly.

Following Hyde's confession, the suspect beer can was rushed to the Ministry of Defence's laboratories, Porton Down, where it was confirmed as containing Sarin.

In the early hours of the following morning a further number of arrests were made by armed teams drawn from the Thames Valley, West Midland and Hampshire police forces. Quantities of neo-Nazi literature were recovered from the premises raided and specialist personnel wearing full protective clothing and respirators removed five other cans of Sarin. They were subsequently rendered harmless. D Notices had been issued to the media and no mention of these operations reached the public.

. . .

Playing hide and seek in a condemned warehouse close to St Pancras Station, Charlie Bostock, aged eight, desperately sought a place to conceal himself before his friend finished counting to twenty. Clambering over some old packing cases, he hid behind some sheets of corrugated iron and ducked low. He heard his friend shouting 'I'm coming,' and lay as flat as he could. It was then that he saw the man's body a few feet away, and it wasn't just an ordinary man, but somebody lying at a curious angle, tied like a parcel, with black tape wound around his face. There was a puddle of oily water close to the man's head and the man did not move. His eyes seemed to be staring right at Charlie. Panicked, Charlie scrambled to his feet and cried out for his friend. 'Pax!' he shouted. 'Come here quick!'

His friend came into view. 'What's up?'

'Look! This bloke.'

Both children stared at the body as their small world

changed for ever.

'Why's he like that?'

'Don't know.'

'Is he dead?'

Charlie took a small step nearer.

'Don't touch him.'

'Not going to.'

'We'd better go fetch yer Mum.'

Not taking their eyes away from the silent body, they backed away, then turned and ran.

.   .   .

Pearson kept vigil outside the intensive care unit where frantic efforts were being made to keep Hillsden alive, but as the hours passed without any discernible change in his condition it became obvious that the battle was being lost.

Shortly before dawn the Staff Nurse in charge of the unit called Pearson to the bedside. 'I think it's any moment,' she said.

'Can it do any harm now if I talk to him?'

'No.'

Pearson lifted the plastic sheeting enveloping the bed and put his face close to Hillsden's. 'Alec, it's me, Pearson. Can you hear me?'

Hillsden's eyelids fluttered briefly.

'Did-you-find-out-anything-else?'

Again there was the slightest of reactions.

'Alec-try-and-remember,' Pearson said, louder this time.

Hillsden's lips moved and Pearson bent closer still.

'What? Say again . . . !'

Hillsden made a sound, but whether it was a last, dying breath or a partly formed word, Pearson could not be sure. It sounded to him like 'calm' or perhaps 'carn'.

A second later the screen for the machine monitoring Hillsden's heart went blank. The Staff Nurse tapped Pearson on the shoulder.

'You're too late,' she said. 'He's gone.'

46

REVELATIONS

There was little time for grief. The consensus was that the eighth, and, as far as anybody knew, last can of Sarin, must be in Harry's possession, though none of those arrested was prepared to grass on him. After Hyde's initial willingness to save his skin, once in safe custody, he had clamped up. All Harry's known haunts were being kept under close observation, and computer enhanced close-ups of the photos identified by Carstairs's companion were displayed in all police stations and post offices. But Harry had gone to earth. A further and more extensive search of his flat revealed a Ruger automatic concealed behind a panel in the bathroom, together with a home-made silencer fashioned, as Schmidt had once described, from a Pepsi Cola can. The crime of murder was now added to the warrant for his arrest.

'You're good at crosswords, Rotherby,' Pearson said as he once again tried to read a meaning into Hillsden's dying word. They were gathered together with Sarah in Hillsden's Docklands office, going through the files for a third time in the hope that they could turn up a clue to the mystery.

'He either said "calm" or "carn" but it was so faint that I can't be certain. Can you think what he might have been trying to tell me?'

'Could it have been Calne, the place?'

'I don't know.'

'Maybe it was just "calm",' Hadley offered. 'You know, he

was saying that he felt calm dying.' He looked at the others. 'No?'

'Yes, I suppose that's possible,' Pearson said.

Rotherby was jotting words down on a notepad: 'Cairn, Carmine, Carnage, Carnation, Carnal . . . any of those suggest anything?'

They pondered, but nobody could think of anything.

'What about "Carnival"?' Sarah said suddenly.

The four men looked at her.

'Just a thought, but the annual Notting Hill do begins at the end of next week,' she said.

'"Carnival",' Pearson repeated. 'You could be right. You could indeed. Why didn't we think of that?'

'Because men are not as bright as women,' Sarah said perkily.

Pearson rounded on Lloyd. 'That meeting Alec had with Fadiman which we bugged – did Fadiman ever mention Notting Hill?'

'Not that I remember, no.'

'Jesus! If Sarah's right, it figures, though, doesn't it? If they're planning to revenge Sonntag's death, what better opportunity? Oh, Christ! You don't need much imagination to visualise what would be the result if any of that bloody stuff was released in the middle of that crowd. Carnage and panic on a frightening scale. The police are anticipating well over a million people. All those bastards would have to do is plonk the cans down in the crowd and walk away. Dear God, dear God.'

The thought that he might, at last, be close to the truth, made him almost incoherent. 'When it was used in Tokyo it was in a confined space and therefore more hideously effective, but according to reports, even released in the open air it's lethal to those in the immediate vicinity.'

'How effective would just one can be?' Lloyd asked.

'One killed Alec, didn't it? And until we find Harry, we don't know there is only one. We've only got Hyde's word for it. We'd better move fast.' He rounded on Rotherby. 'Get on to

Control straightaway, tell them we have good reason to believe the carnival's the target and that it's vital to track down Harry. Tell them we want every available man they can give us. And, Sarah, you alert the bods at Porton Down that we're going to need their expertise. Find out what precautions, if any, we can take. Do it now, both of you.'

After they had left the room, Hadley said: 'That cold, calculating bastard.'

'Who?'

'Swanson. I had my suspicions from the start. If only I'd acted on them earlier, but I was the new boy, I didn't have any real proof and I didn't want to speak out of turn. I did talk to Hillsden once, but only in a roundabout way, warning him to be on his guard. Now I wish to God I'd gone further, I wish I'd had the courage of my convictions; if I had Alec might still be alive. That'll be on my conscience for ever. When I think of the way Swanson snared poor old Alec – to promise a man freedom, knowing you are taking him to his death. That's the action of a man steeped in shit.' His vehemence brought a flush to his face. 'The prick wanted revenge, I suppose. It all falls into place now.'

'What's that mean? Revenge for what? He didn't know Alec before this.'

'Oh, it goes back a long way. I never had any real proof until I stumbled on something. But even then it was only hearsay, I needed to dig deeper . . . It was at a party of my mother's. She's something of a fag hag I suppose . . . Since my father died she collects gays, finds them amusing and no threat . . . About two weeks ago she persuaded me to host one of her soirées. There was a character there I hadn't seen before, titled, the sort of prat you see in those arse-paralysing features in *Tatler*, not obviously gay, but his mask slipped after two or three of my mother's Martinis. He got me on my own at one point and made a pass . . .' Hadley's face went a darker shade of red. 'Nothing I couldn't cope with . . . Mother and I had a major row about it afterwards . . . Turned out this queen had been in the Firm during Lockfield's time . . . Mother knew all about him, she loves dishing the dirt . . . Anyway, during the course of the row, she let slip that Lockfield was gay. "I don't know why you're so stuffy about my friends," she said. "That place where you work has always been a hot-bed, as you must know." I couldn't argue about that, but then she said: "And that man who's your boss, well he's no wallflower. Timmy told me . . ." that was the name of the character who made the pass at me . . . "he was Lockfield's toy-boy as a teenager. Lockfield left him all his money."'

'You're sure she meant Swanson?'

'Definitely. I questioned her at length. Then I made it my business to check Lockfield's will. My mother was right. Swanson was the sole beneficiary.'

'But where does revenge come in? I'm still not with you.'

'Think about it. It was Alec who fingered Lockfield and as a result Lockfield topped himself. What better motive than a lover's grief?'

'Dear God,' Pearson said finally. 'Now I've heard it all. I thank my lucky stars I'm getting out.'

'Well, I don't have your experience,' Hadley replied, 'but I've already come to the conclusion that in this game we've never heard it all.'

47

A CALYPSO FOR THE DEPARTED

Just before six a.m. on the first day of the carnival, Pearson and a group of senior officers from Special Branch stood outside the Elgin Arms on the deserted corner of Elgin Crescent and Ladbroke Grove in the Notting Hill Gate area. They were being briefed by the police Commander with overall operational responsibility for the event. While their discussion took place, squads of uniformed police started putting crash barriers into position. Other teams, wearing protective clothing, rubber gloves and boots, lifted manhole covers and descended into the sewers, sealing the manholes with heavy tape once they had been declared clean. There were fewer parked cars than usual in the surrounding streets, since many of the local inhabitants had followed their custom of giving the celebrations a wide berth.

'If what we are prepared for does happen,' the Operational Commander said, 'and the device or devices are activated, then our task will be to saturate and contain the immediate areas and attempt to minimise the number of casualties. I've studied the lessons learned from Tokyo. There they had three separate incidents resulting in eight dead and nearly five thousand injured. I'm not making comparisons because here the gas will not be released in a confined space. That having been said, nobody can predict for sure how this substance will perform, or for how long it constitutes a lethal threat. In the opinion of the Army experts much depends on the prevailing weather conditions. It's one of those times when we might welcome thunderstorms, since one body of opinion is that heavy rain reduces the penetration, but storms are not predicted. In fact we are expecting a long day of fine, humid weather with temperatures above the average. We shall be getting hourly reports on the air quality from the Met Office. I'm no expert, gentlemen, I'm a fatalist who believes in planning for the worst scenario.'

He addressed Pearson. 'How many of your people have ever come face to face with this man?'

'Only two, I'm afraid.'

'Hmm. So the majority will have to rely on the photograph.'

'I'm sure you've thought of it,' Pearson said, 'but the likelihood is he'll be wearing some disguise . . . even a carnival mask.'

'Yes. Don't depress me any further.' He looked around at the sombre group. 'That being so, gentlemen, what we could be facing before this day is over, is wholesale panic. It will be our task to prevent that panic turning into a full scale riot. The history of this carnival in recent years has been a happy one. Excellent relations with the organisers and crime kept within containable limits. But it only takes a spark. The use of poisonous gas has always carried a particular dread for most people, understandably so. It's happily been an unknown country up until now. Let's hope it remains so. I suggest that we use the time still at our disposal to check and check again that every possible or probable risk has been anticipated. I want all divisional officers to assemble again at the command post at twelve noon. Thank you and good luck.'

He walked away to his car.

. . .

By ten a.m. the green coaches of emergency police were in position all over the area, the occupants equipped with gas masks in addition to riot gear. The number of spotter video cameras had been trebled from the previous year's event, two-man teams of police marksmen armed with high-velocity rifles occupied rooftop vantage points overlooking the carnival route. In addition to the regular police presence, three Army Disposal Squads and units trained in chemical warfare had been brought in. Plain-clothed officers were stationed at Latimer Road, Notting Hill Gate, Royal Oak and Westbourne Park underground stations and on all main bus routes. In all, over twelve hundred officers were deployed.

By noon, upwards of a million revellers were converging on the area and the numerous steel bands were already vying to be heard above each other. The first of the elaborately decorated floats began its stately progress to the assembly areas escorted by bedecked, plumed and altogether magnificent dancers. Food vendors had fired up their jerk chicken stalls and the carnival was under way, gaining in momentum every minute and conducted in an atmosphere of good humour. There were few incidents other than the arrests of half-a-dozen pickpockets, a few lost children and one heart attack. The sun shone, the floats amazed, the street dancing was frenzied and the general mood of the vast and ever-swelling crowd had never been better.

.   .   .

It was shortly after seven p.m. when Harry left Fadiman's hideout and cut through the back streets to Tottenham Court Road. He took a bus as far as Queensway, alighting there and walking to Westbourne Grove, losing himself in the crowds as he proceeded to Chepstow Road. Because of the news embargo he was still unaware that Hyde and the others were to play no further part, and, despite Pearson's fear, he had not bothered with any disguise, relying on the dense crowds to conceal him. By the time he arrived, the police had estimated there were still in excess of one million people on the carnival streets.

Harry stopped and purchased a leg of barbecued chicken. The can of gas was secured in a pouch attached to his trouser belt and concealed under his jacket. While eating the chicken, he threaded his way through the unsuspecting crowds, looking for the ideal spot to use his device. It had been decided that the can would be activated shortly after nine o'clock, when the tired police would be fully occupied with shepherding the revellers home. He finally chose a location at the junction of St Luke's Road and Tavistock Road, where six or seven of the huge sound systems were in close competition. The cacophony of sound, he felt, would add to the panic he hoped to produce and at the same time hinder the police. Having made his choice, he next carefully studied which escape route he would use. His usual confidence never deserted him.

. . .

As the day progressed without alarm, Pearson's apprehension mounted rather than diminished. The only two members of his own team who had ever come face to face with Harry were Hadley and Hillsden's erstwhile assistant, Sarah, and he knew the odds were stacked against them. Both had been circulating in the crowds all day, Hadley with an armed plain-clothes man, and Sarah with her police boyfriend. At intervals they had reported back to him, always in the negative. With the memory of Hillsden's last moments still vivid, Pearson could not bring himself to believe that their luck would hold. The effort of concentration as he made slow progress through the raucous and increasingly ragged, but seemingly inexhaustible revellers, studying every face he passed, caused his stomach to spasm. He was forced to rest, leaning up against the railings of a house until the pain subsided. A grotesquely masked dancer offered him a drink from a bottle of rum, but he declined with a forced smile. The dancer consumed the rest of the contents in front of him, then suddenly fell, insensible, to the pavement, a happy look on his face, out to the world.

Pearson waited until the spasm eased and looked at his watch. It was just before nine o'clock.

. . .

Half a mile away from where Pearson was resting, Sarah and her boyfriend approached the junction of Tavistock Road and St Luke's Road. The crowds were still thick here, but good natured, and several times Sarah had to refuse an offer to join in the dancing. The steel bands were still going full blast. I was at this moment that further back in the crowd three teenagers, petty thieves from the Brixton area, started to ram raid through the crowd, bag-snatching as they went, relying on speed and brute force to achieve their getaway. A precisely this moment Sarah and Harry were separated by less than ten yards. A few minutes earlier Harry had removed the can from the pouch. He now held it firmly in his right hand, pressed closely to his body at thigh height, and was edging his way to the spot he had pre-selected.

At the end of their run the three bag-snatchers scattered in different directions, cannoning off anybody unfortunate enough to obstruct their flight. One of them ran straight into Harry, sending him crashing to the ground. Then this same youth changed direction and this time hit Sarah, knocking her over as he made his escape.

It was while she was lying, semi-stunned, on the ground that Sarah glimpsed a prone Harry through a sea of legs. He was a few feet away from her and the hand that still clutched the can was momentarily in her eyeline. She saw him start to clamber upright and screamed, 'There! That's him! Get him!' but her voice was lost in the hip-hop, jungle sounds bursting from the mammoth speakers.

She crawled towards Harry and managed to hook an arm around one of his legs. Harry hit down at her with his free hand, but she hung on. He chopped another blow on her forearm, forcing her to release her grip, then pushed his way into the crowd. It was only then that Sarah's boyfriend grasped what was happening and dived for him, bringing him down in a clumsy tackle. Both men engaged in a frenzied, confined struggle, now egged on by the crowd who believed that one of the thieves had been apprehended. With his free hand Harry landed a karate chop to the throat and as her boyfriend doubled in pain, Sarah saw Harry go for the release catch on the can. She screamed, 'Stop him!' and a burly onlooker wrenched Harry's head back causing him to relinquish his grip on the can. It flew out of his hands and rolled beneath one of the steel drums. Sarah scrambled to reach it, wrapping her bloodied knuckles around it and hanging on for dear life. When police reinforcements arrived it was with some difficulty that they prised her fingers loose.

POSTSCRIPT

Galina never remarried. She and Lara now have American citizenship and live in Phoenix, Arizona, where she manages a computer warehouse owned and financed by Victor Abramov.

Hadley left the Firm without regret and joined a merchant bank where he is very successful.

'Mrs Carstairs' sold her story to the *Sun* and is now co-habiting with a plastic surgeon in Miami.

Pearson retired and bought a house on Gozo. In the last Birthday Honours he was awarded a CBE in the Civil List.

Lloyd took early retirement and found he had a talent for writing detective stories, several of which have been sold to television.

Rotherby died of a heart attack and left all his money to a feline charity.

Even with remission, Swanson was not expected to be released until the year 2010.

Fadiman served two years of a seven-year sentence in an open prison and was then paroled on compassionate grounds. He is working on his memoirs.

Sir Raymond Charters was acquitted on appeal, but stripped of his knighthood. He sold all his companies in England and emigrated to Chile.

Hyde was killed in a prison brawl, while Harry was given two concurrent life sentences for the murders of Montague and Lord Miller.

Victor Abramov purchased an estate in the Cotswolds having made a killing in the currency market. He enjoyed the English way of life, even to the extent of learning to play cricket.

NEWS ITEMS

Adolf Hitler's legacy is proving hard to kill in Austria, the country of his birth. For the second time in a year the country is being terrorised by a wave of neo-Nazi letter bombs. The Mayor of Vienna, Helmet Zilk, lost half his left hand and almost died of loss of blood after opening a letter bomb sent to his home. The current campaign coincides with the retrial of the man seen as the leader of neo-Nazis in Austria, Gottfried Kussel, thirty-six, currently appealing against a ten-year sentence for his Fascist activities.
– Sunday Express, 1994

Israeli agents are mounting a major undercover operation to 'contain' the threat to London's Jewish community posed by Sunday's rally of Muslim fundamentalists at Wembley. The team from Mossad will work with the full approval of MI5 and MI6.
– The Standard, 1994

German police raided fifty homes across the country after an attempt to hold a neo-Nazi rally in Triptis, in the eastern state of Thuringia. Arms, ammunition, chemicals and propaganda were seized.
– Independent on Sunday, 1995

Two brothers, aged sixteen and seventeen, neo-Nazis from Salisbury Township, Pa., are accused of beating their parents and brother, eleven, to death. Victims were beaten until their faces were unrecognisable.
– Arizona Republic, 1995

British Jews Suffer 'World Tide Of Hatred'.
– Headline, 1995